Mine to Love

Quicksilver Garou:
Lost & Found Mates
Book 1

FIOLA FAELAN

Dedication

I have a wealth of support, from my amazing son and equally amazing daughter-in-law to actual blood-sisters and sisters-from-other-mothers, and even an informally adopted brother, not to mention amazing girlfriends. You ladies and gents know who you are.
I appreciate and love you all.

Don't be left out!

For updates about new releases, occasional contests, and all things paranormal romance, sign up for my VIP mailing list and be rewarded with an adult coloring & puzzle book!

Go here to sign up:
https://BookHip.com/NTFASXP

To all the lupus warriors out there....

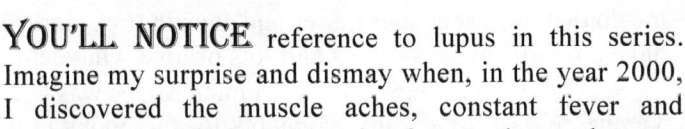

YOU'LL NOTICE reference to lupus in this series. Imagine my surprise and dismay when, in the year 2000, I discovered the muscle aches, constant fever and exhaustion I'd been experiencing for months was because I had lupus.

This disease is insidious and strikes some down way before their time should have been up. It manifests in your body attacking major organs—including your skin—and connective tissue, thinking they're the enemy needing to be vanquished.

I actually count myself lucky because, although I frequently feel like crap and have no energy, after nine years on the typical medication prescribed for this disease, in 2009 I weaned myself off—and thank goodness, because it can eventually cause blindness. I'm 'usually' able to control it through adherence to a strict diet regimen, shunning the sun—*completely*—and taking certain supplements to help my body battle this disease.

One day, when I was particularly annoyed and upset with my symptoms, my writer brain came up with the premise for this new series. What if there were a subset of women with lupus who also had ancient DNA which matched them to men with human and wolven souls? What if the women—Cinnabar Twins—had somehow lost their ability to be detectable by the men—Quicksilver Garou—and they were the veritable two ships in the night, never to meet their mates.

The Garou, although long-lived, would eventually die out, lonely and unmated. The women would battle their disease, alone, and never know they had a mate out there dying to meet them, and that mating would provide longer lives, greater strength and a way for them to beat back their disease.

Because, face it, folks with this ridiculously evil disease want it to go the hell away. I wouldn't mind having a sexy, uber-alpha man with a wolven-half help me do that. Mix sensuous kisses and amazing sex, and you have a recipe for sexy-times and lots of love. Oh yeah!

So, Quicksilver Garou: Lost & Found Mates was born! Ten percent of the royalty payments for the books in the series will be donated to the Lupus Research Alliance.

To my lupus consociates out there, I send you warmth and a sincere hope for health and healing.

Slàinte Mhaith,

If you're new to the series…

FOR HUNDREDS OF YEARS deep desire, *deep need*, drove generations of Garou man and wolf combined into a powerful package replete with extra senses and amazing strength—to find their mates. They were unsuccessful—and desolate. A virus had ravaged the women who would be their mates, effectively damaging them and their offspring, rendering both undetectable by the Garou.

The chance of finding love, of recognizing their mate when paths crossed, was slim to less than none. This didn't bode well for the continuation of their kind—or their happiness—since Garou must mate with their one and only in order to produce offspring.

They longed for what the older generation had— the emotional and physical bond, that psychical thread that bound them together—but they weren't holding their breath they'd ever find their one.

Turns out the human man who'd discovered the Garou's secrets—the constant threat hanging over their heads like a guillotine—has been working feverously to reverse engineer Garou DNA in order to gain the longevity, the enhanced strength and senses, along with the ability to shift the ancient race had that only occurs after mating—and has somehow also discovered the history of their mates, known as Cinnabar Twins.

Little do the Garou know the madman's experiments were successful in flipping back on what the virus had damaged and turned off in the women—

once again making their mates detectable. Discoverable.

When a Garou and his mate meet in the first spine-tingling book in the series—Mine to Love—the recognition is instantaneous and incendiary. The woman struggles to believe, but both Garou and mate soon switch from disbelief and suspicion to fighting for their lives, before falling in love and tearing up the sheets.

It's a race against time and evil intentions to rescue the women still in captivity—the Cinnabar Twins—and protect the Garou and their mates across the globe.

This series contains explicit sexual content & graphic language. Not intended for those under the age of 18.

He's finally found his fated mate ...

And she doesn't want him.

Carrick's always known that he'd never find his mate. Never fall in love. Never have a family. After a disease wiped out the Garou's ability to detect their mates before he was born, it's a fact he's been resigned to his whole life.

Until Nia fell into his life.

His attraction to her is immediate and powerful, and he doesn't fully understand why until one of his brothers clues him in—

She's his mate.

But Nia's still reeling from her kidnapping and subsequent escape from a crazed lunatic who's running experiments on people. This striking, powerful man telling her she's his fated mate? It doesn't compute.

Even if she is attracted to him ...

She needs time. Time to process. Time to heal. Time to grieve the loss of her sister.

Time for revenge on the bastard who did this to her.

Carrick and his brothers are determined to liberate the other captives of the lab. And Nia's determined to go with them, except she's still too weak from her time there to be of any help.

Unless ...

If she mates with Carrick, she'll be rewarded with super strength and speed.

Will she mate with him, bind herself to him forever, for the chance to avenge her sister? And will he let her, knowing she's only using him?

Mine to Love is a steamy fated mates paranormal romance featuring a dominant, protective hero and a heroine who's not afraid to go after what she wants. Grab your copy today!

Chapter One

NIA'S FINGERS whitened around the steering wheel as she wondered what she'd been thinking, taking backroads to get home from Morgan Hill.

The wiser choice would have been along main arteries, on a well-lit freeway through South San Jose. Even if it took longer. These winding, narrow backroads? Dark as Hades, and way too isolated for her peace of mind.

Cabin fever had hit hard that morning, and she'd been desperate to be outdoors, to shed that trapped feeling. The one she'd lived with for six interminable months in a small, concrete cell. She stuffed those memories back down where they couldn't hurt and concentrated on the road.

Driving all the way to Morgan Hill with her furry bodyguard riding shotgun, and indulging in a much-needed hike around the Coyote Valley Open Space Preserve, went a long way in restoring a semblance of normal, of freedom, in her. She rarely strayed from the tiny community of New Almaden, but sometimes the trapped feeling sent her scurrying away from the small enclave.

Having escaped captivity and Denton's painful experiments almost a year ago didn't mean she was safe, though, and she really shouldn't take chances like this, driving on a seldom traveled road after dark. She'd turned onto McKean five minutes ago, her headlights piercing the inky darkness a measly hundred feet ahead of her rusted bumper. It was as if it sucked every bit of ambient light past that point into a huge, black hole.

Learning to embrace the night because of her disease didn't mean she wanted to be out traversing inky roads after dark. If not for Max, her big Belgian Malinois sitting next to her, she'd be a quivering mass of nerves, instead of merely scared shitless and ready to jump at every damned shadow.

What if Denton had found her and was simply biding his time until she was foolish enough to be out like this? Alone and vulnerable, where he and his guards could scoop her up with no one the wiser.

She suppressed a shudder and felt a bead of sweat snake down her spine at the thought of being back in that small cell, or the stark, sterile laboratory strapped to a cold, hard table awaiting another needle and painful infusion.

Every crossroad became a possible ambush. Every light in the distance threatened to be headlights of a car containing his bullyboys, ready to drag her back to his facility in the middle of the Umpqua National Forest in southern Oregon.

She shook her head, pushed back the impending panic attack and concentrated on her surroundings, searching out and noticing the occasional pinprick of porch or barn lights gleaming in the hills.

A shaky sigh of relief and a soft whine of commiseration from Max broke the silence as she sped past the gently lapping water of Calero Reservoir, signifying she was finally close to home. A glance to her left revealed the stingy reflection of an almost full moon in the water, although the stygian morass surrounding her continued to suck all light from the night.

Her all-terrain tires hummed as she sped down the lonely road, rolling through the foothills like a tumbleweed trying to outrun a dust storm. She rotated her aching shoulders and fervently thanked every god and goddess she could think of for guiding her safely down this two-lane road with no nasty surprises.

She was almost home and couldn't wait until she was safely behind her security system and sturdy locks. A glance at Max, tongue hanging out in a goofy grin, had her quirking her lips in a fond smile as she came to a stop where McKean t-boned Almaden Road. His dark eyes gleamed with intelligence as the streetlight bounced off his handsome, classic Malinois face.

She injected a lighthearted tone in her voice and reached over to scratch behind one ear, eliciting a groan of pleasure from him. "How about a juicy bone when we get home?" Her mouth quirked even higher at the low whine she got for an answer, the human translation of 'yes, faster' easy to discern.

His whines, grunts, and growls were all she needed to know exactly what he meant. Didn't need words. Which was a good thing, considering Max couldn't use words as much as he seemed to exhibit human intelligence.

After suffering through Denton's experiments, her innate ability to communicate with animals was even more refined and attuned to not only dogs, but wolves, too. She could practically have conversations with them, both verbally and psychically.

At least she could trust what they said, even if it was only growls and grunts. They didn't deceive with their every word, every breath. Didn't kiss you one day and betray you the next. Like the asshole who'd played on her emotions, sucked her into trusting him and then betrayed her, landing her in that 5 x 5 cell in Denton's converted metal barn turned torture facility.

As terrifying as the thought was, she wanted nothing more than to go back to that facility, free any other captives still locked up, and avenge her sister's death. But she needed to get well first. Get her strength back. Not practically collapse after any adrenaline rush or outlay of energy. She was already feeling depleted just from her hike at the park today. She couldn't afford to wind up a prisoner. Never. Again.

She turned left on Almaden Road, heading deep into the heart of New Almaden, and glanced at the occasional house as it passed by, wondering what was going on behind the walls. Wondering what it would be like to be part of a family. To have a partner waiting for her, watching her back. Worried about her. Loving her. Protecting her as she would protect him. Missing her if she went missing; someone who would turn the world upside down to find her. Rescue her.

Quit dreaming, girl. Wish in one hand and spit in the other, the grandpa in one of her foster homes used to say. See which gets filled up first.

Annoyed with herself for even going there, she slowed to a crawl as a tidy, yellow bungalow set back from the two-lane country road came into view on the right. Its verdant green, immaculately manicured, postage-stamp-size yard had every blade of grass standing at attention in military precision, like a Marine's haircut. High and tight, not a blade out of place. Vibrant flowers rioted color where they rimmed the yard.

She shuddered as she remembered, just yesterday, the child who'd toddled unsteadily from that front yard right into the road. Directly in the path of her big nubby tires. The young mother had been hot on the tike's heels, screaming hysterically. Too far away to save the little girl.

Sharp reflexes on Nia's part were the only thing that averted disaster. Her yank on the wheel as she'd stomped on the brake pedal and veered onto the shoulder had nearly tipped the vehicle, and would have sent Max to the floor if not for the harness snugged around his chest, firmly anchored to the seat.

When she'd flung herself out the door and swept the child from the road into her arms, the mother had surprised the hell out of her by wrapping them both in a fierce embrace, her head barely reaching Nia's shoulder. She'd frozen, the toddler clutched in her arms. It had been so long since anyone had hugged her. So long since she'd felt a kind touch. She'd just wanted to stand there and soak it in.

Her initial shock aside, she'd led the woman out of the harmful sun and into the shade of a tree and learned, within the space of five minutes, that her name was Simone.

She was single, new in town, didn't know a soul, and hadn't realized the lock on the screen door was faulty or that her daughter would pick today to discover she could walk.

And the child's name was Rachel. One-year-old, apparently already walking, as of today, adventurous and cute as a button.

Simone had cried buckets of happy tears that Nia had stopped on a dime. She remembered wanting so badly to accept Simone's invitation to step inside for a glass of iced tea.

How she wished she'd been free to accept that invitation, but knew in her heart there was no way. She couldn't make friends. Couldn't expose people to danger. It was imperative she stay invisible. Alone. Lonely.

Shouldn't be too hard in New Almaden. The unincorporated community about twenty-one miles south of downtown San Jose was like an isolated town unto itself.

She *was* practically invisible. As long as she stayed under the radar.

And that, unfortunately, meant no new friends. No friends at all. Period.

Shrugging off the memories and her melancholy, she slowed as she rolled closer to Simone's place. Her eyes narrowed at the old beater parked cockeyed in front of that tidy bungalow, its front tires crushing the pretty peonies at the corner of the drive, its grill buried in the huge oleander bush close to the street.

It wasn't Simone's vehicle, which was a vintage Jeep Cherokee. She'd seen it parked in the driveway yesterday. And there was no house across the street or next door anyone would be visiting.

No way Simone would let some stranger in her house. She'd gleaned that much about the woman in their brief conversation yesterday, nervousness practically broadcasting its own frequency from the petite woman.

Nia pulled to a stop in the middle of the empty road twenty yards from the house to scrutinize the car and around the cottage.

No way in hell did that car belong there. Nope. Not as protective as that mama was of her daughter. Not with the fear she'd seen swirling in Simone's pretty hazel eyes. Fear that had nothing to do with the toddler's near miss.

She'd recognized a kindred soul. Recognized the wariness and caution beneath the surface. Recognized the same stark terror mirrored in her own eyes.

Simone had mentioned not knowing anyone in town. Nia had known deep in her bones the young woman was hiding something.

Something bad if she'd read those deep shadows in her eyes accurately.

Nia's need for anonymity immediately went out the window as fear shot through her at what that sweet young mother and her daughter could be suffering.

Her career as a security expert BA, before abduction, gave her the expertise to make split-second decisions and defend herself, honed even sharper in the last year.

It was the only reason she was still alive. And free. She sped up, pulled behind, and barely nudged the crooked bumper of the beater with her ancient Land Cruiser.

After she flipped the dome light off, she eased the door open, giving silent thanks to the WD40 she'd liberally applied to the hinges just yesterday, and motioned Max out her door to follow.

As she rounded the rear of her vehicle, Max bounded in front of her and stopped with four paws planted, ears flat to his head, sharp teeth silently bared in a snarl, halting her progress.

She blessed her incredible night vision when she saw a man slip out a side window, a small bundle tucked under one arm.

Her eyes widened in shock, then narrowed in rage when she realized the bundle was the little girl who'd been in her arms just yesterday. Her dagger was out of her boot, sunk into the rear tire of his car, and back into her boot before he had both feet on the ground.

No way in hell was she risking him getting away with that precious bundle. His car disabled, she crouched and sprinted soundlessly across the grass to the front corner of the house, Max a lethal shadow keeping pace.

With her back pressed against the clapboard wall next to the small porch, a hand signal from her sent Max under the hedge across from her.

She figured she had one chance, and only one chance, to get that little girl out of his arms without injury.

Her almost telepathic connection with Max had them moving in tandem as the man crept to the front corner of the house, the still girl tucked under one arm. Max followed her silent command and shot from under the bush, growling fiercely.

The bastard's eyes widened in fear and he bobbled the toddler like a doll, just as she'd hoped. Her hands snaked out and snatched the little girl away from him while Max went for the guy's leg, but the gun he whipped out and pointed at her snarling protector made her heart stutter.

She tucked the little girl tightly but carefully under one arm like a football and felt a shaft of fear as she hung there, lifeless like a rag doll. Enraged and scared to death for the little one tucked up against her, and for Max with that damned gun pointed at him, she pivoted and kicked sideways, her Brazilian Jiu-Jitsu training bursting forth. Her boot hit his hand with a crunch and his gun went flying under the hedgerow, bisecting this lot from the next.

"Fucking bitch! Gimme the kid."

"Hell no, asshole!"

Instead of running, he whirled and swung, catching her with a hard fist to her temple. Unable to duck the blow and keep hold of Rachel, she stumbled and grabbed the porch rail while tightening her hold around Rachel's little torso, wishing to hell the house wasn't so damned isolated, and Simone would burst out of the door with a bat or something.

Where were neighbors when she needed them? Her heart skipped a beat to think the reason their fight hadn't woken Simone and brought her outside was because this bastard had done something to her.

He snatched at Rachel, and she dodged back toward the front door. Knowing she couldn't fight him off and protect the unconscious child too, she slipped her hand into her pocket and palmed her car fob, pressing hard on the panic button, the blare of the alarm and flashing lights accomplishing what she couldn't.

"You fucking bitch!"

With one last punch connecting painfully with her collarbone and a hard kick to Max's head when he went in for another snarling bite, he dove for the hedge where his gun lay. He scooped it from beneath a bush and ran to his car, only to realize her SUV blocked him in at the ass end and the large oleander at the front.

He swiveled and aimed the gun at her but must have thought better of it since she was holding Rachel, turned and sprinted across the street through the sparse orchard and was soon out of sight.

Nia stumbled to the door and sank to the porch, her collarbone throbbing, head pounding and dizzy from the punch to her temple. If she thought the hike had depleted her, this was going to cause a major crash, and soon.

She pressed the button on her fob again to silence the alarm, the sudden quiet jarring after the fight, and gave a careless swipe at the warm trickle of blood tickling her temple.

Scared to death at the stillness of the child, afraid whatever he'd given the little girl could be fatal, she scooted back and held her finger on the doorbell. Max whined and wobbled his way to the porch, the kick to his head having knocked her poor pup for a loop.

Seconds later, she heard light footsteps on the hardwood floor and a curtain at the window above her head fluttered in her peripheral vision just before the door flew open.

Simone peered out, eyes snapping down to connect with hers before widening in shocked recognition. Nia grabbed her hand and tugged, knowing there was no time to waste.

"Get us inside, quick."

The woman's eyes widened even more when she saw her baby nestled against Nia's chest. "Rachel? What are you doing with Rachel?"

Simone's eyes narrowed as she focused on what Nia knew was a rapidly rising lump on her temple and the blood now trickling down her cheek to her neck, then quickly tracked the yard. Her eyes swept to Max, wobbling at Nia's feet, then to Rachel again.

Nia gasped in pain as the young woman grabbed her arm and dragged them into the house as if they weighed nothing, Max padding through the door behind them.

Simone was a hell of a lot stronger than her size indicated. Nia stayed just inside the door, watching in relief as Simone slammed and locked the door, then sat down right there with her on the warped hardwood floor and reached out her arms for her daughter.

Nia handed the unresponsive child to her mother and pulled her phone from her pocket, swiping to unlock before hitting the phone icon and tapping out nine-one-one.

While she waited impatiently for an answer, she turned to Simone to see her check Rachel's pulse and respiration. Open her mouth. Lift her eyelids and check her pupils with a calmness that belied the terror shining in her eyes.

Everything a doctor or nurse would do. It was glaringly apparent Simone was scared to death and worried about her daughter, but she'd pushed all that aside and was performing a medical triage of a patient. Medical training or common sense? Doctor, nurse, paramedic?

Nia spoke up to clue her in while waiting for emergency services to answer the phone. "Was driving home and caught a guy climbing out your side window with Rachel in his arms. Fought, got smacked a coupla times, he got away. Had a gun."

The dispatcher's gritty voice in her ear interrupted, asking her the nature of her emergency. "I need an ambulance at… what's your address?"

"Nine thirty-seven Almaden Road."

"Nine thirty-seven Almaden Road, about three quarters of a mile south of McKean, on the right. Attempted child abduction. The child's about one, pulse strong, but she's non-responsive. He must have drugged her."

She watched as Simone's eyes snapped to hers at her words, widening in terror before narrowing and flashing back to her daughter. "No, the man's gone. We're inside, doors locked. Yes, okay. We'll be fine until they get here."

Ignoring the operator's reassurance help would be on the way and instructions to stay on the line, she disconnected the call, opened the back and ejected the sim card, then tucked the burner phone back in her pocket and the sim in the small change pocket, making a mental note to run it through her crosscut paper shredder when she got home.

Her smart phone was safely in her purse, and she would never use it for something like this, where they could track her.

She turned to the distressed mother and hoped Rachel would be okay until emergency responders arrived. "There may be a delay because of a crash snarling the intersection at Blossom Hill and Almaden."

She pressed one hand on the floor and braced the other against the front door, trying to stand, only to fall smack onto her butt again. "Ohhh, man."

Choking down a wave of nausea and dizziness, she dropped her head between her hands; her elbows propped on her knees. Dammit all to hell! She had to get away before the cops showed. Needed to stay off the grid.

At the feel of a small, strong hand gripping her bicep, Nia raised her head cautiously, hands braced on her quads and tried to temper the nausea.

She marveled at how Simone battened back fear and questions, admiration for the young mother when determination filled her eyes.

With the smaller woman's hand cupping her elbow, she stood and stumbled to the couch, then laid a trembling hand on Simone's shoulder. "Rachel's pulse still strong?"

"Yes. What happened? Thank God you were here!"

She watched a crack break open in Simone's emotional armor when she realized if not for Nia, she'd have woken in the morning to an empty crib. Nia's eyes lowered to the precious child in her mama's arms and reached out a finger to brush soft, curly red bangs from the little girl's forehead.

"I was driving home from a hike in Morgan Hill and saw an old beater-car parked half on your lawn; it's still there, by the way. I flattened a tire." She met Simone's shimmering hazel eyes.

"I just knew, after meeting you yesterday, there was no way you'd let a stranger in the house at night with your baby here." On another wave of dizziness, she leaned back against the soft cushion, arm shielding her eyes, and swallowed hard against the rising sickness in her throat.

"I need to tell you this, then get out of here. I can't be here when the cops show and can't tell you why. Just say you aren't sure who helped. That you don't know where I live. Which you don't."

Simone's eyes sharpened. "Why? Are you in trouble? Do you need help?"

"It'll buy me some time. The fewer people who see me, the less chance of me being recog…" Nia caught herself. The knock to her head must have knocked her good sense right out.

She didn't know this woman from Adam. Even if she felt deep in her bones she could trust her to keep secrets, it wouldn't be safe for Simone to know anything about her.

A knowing light flitted through Simone's eyes, and she saw them widen when they locked on the small scar high on her right cheekbone, courtesy of Denton.

Nia watched in shocked fascination as Simone held her gaze and nudged her colorful hairband up to reveal a matching scar on her right temple at her hairline.

A unique pattern that would be too much of a coincidence they hadn't gotten the scars from the same man, especially since the ring he wore was a one-of-a-kind antique. Or so he'd bragged on more than one occasion. Too damned much of a stretch.

But how were they free, and here in the same small town deep in south San Jose, California? If in fact Simone had also been a guest in Denton's prison, no way would he have voluntarily let her go. She'd escaped, too.

Nia didn't believe in coincidences, and she'd never seen that pattern before—the scientific symbol for mercury set above a howling wolf's head—until she'd watched the ring on that ham of a fist just before it connected with her face. How did she miss seeing the scar yesterday on Simone?

Her bangs must have hidden it, which were currently pulled back from her forehead, the scar covered by the hairband.

When their eyes locked again, a bond of pain, of recognition, of sisterhood, flashed between them. Two souls, bound by abduction, agony and more than likely a shared illness—lupus, but with a twist. Running. Hiding. Terrified of being found. Of going back to the torture and confinement they'd both suffered.

A sisterhood based on fucked-up genetics, mysterious DNA and hidden family history. She saw fierce determination settle in Simone's eyes and the bond strengthened.

Simone grasped Nia's hand tightly. "Tell me quick what happened. I'll keep descriptions vague, say that I was in shock and remember little about you. That it was dark, and you didn't come into the house. Hurry!"

Nia knew they would need to talk. To share how Simone and she had escaped from the same fringe group, as crazy as that sounded, they were both hiding from. She knew Simone understood, at a primal level, the danger associated with being recognized. That safety was in staying under the radar. All the way under. And maybe in finding an ally, someone who would know if they disappeared again. Someone who would give a damn and do something about it.

"We'll talk, later. I'll contact you. What's your phone number? Will it blow your cover, to have the paramedics and cops show up?"

Simone gave a quick shake of her head. "No, it's okay. I've changed my features—my hair, and even my body—are different enough. And I won't let them take her to the hospital. My ID will hold up under scrutiny, too. Give me some info I can share to keep them appeased, and then get going." She recited her number, Nia putting it to memory. She sagged in relief and filled her in.

"As I mentioned, when I exited the truck, I saw a man climbing out of the window at the right side of the house. I'm guessing Rachel's room?" At Simone's nod, she continued, "Max and I confronted him. I grabbed Rachel, but he was quick and got in a couple of hits before Max scared him off. You need to up your security. If this isn't random, then they've found you. If so, I'm betting kidnapping Rachel was a way for Denton to lure you back into captivity. He'll stop at nothing to get us back."

SWEAT BURNED CARRICK'S eyes as he launched another kick at one of the Muay Thai heavy bags suspended from the barn rafters. He dropped to his feet and shook his head in disgust as it ripped free and crashed against the thick, timbered wall.

"Hey, what's that," his annoying brother called out, "number four, just this week? I thought for sure that new cable was strong enough to hold."

Carrick glared across the room at Reese, currently on a flat bench powering through a barbell press, then switched his glare to their buddy Dak when he snickered. The thought of wiping the smirks off their faces was tempting, but he knew if they started grappling, they'd never get back to working out.

He looked around the converted barn in satisfaction, taking in the alternations they'd made in the past six months. The Quicksilver Council, formed over a thousand years ago, had tasked him, Reese and Dak with protecting the Garou who lived in the area, and to look into the recent disappearance of two long-time residents. In order to provide that protection, they needed to stay in top shape and be able to work out at their full potential, hence the barn converted into a gym on his property.

The Garou thrived here, close to what was buried in the Capitancillo Hills, near enough to reap the physical and mental rewards. This ranch was perfect, set two-thirds of the way back from the road on one hundred acres, at the edge of Quicksilver Park. Isolated. Just what they needed to establish a base of operations as local Garou law enforcement, while masquerading as volunteers for local emergency personnel and the forestry service.

Sweat dripping, breath sawing in and out, hands on lean hips, he sauntered to the fallen bag, squatted and grasped it on each side, then hefted it onto one shoulder as he rose. He strode over to Dak, fifteen minutes into a plank, and dropped it with a thud next to the man's head.

"Wasn't the chain that broke. The damned leather isn't strong enough."

Dak gave another quirk of his lips without breaking form as Reese settled the barbell on the bar catchers, rose from the bench and squatted next to the bag. "Need to order some bags those big-ass MMA fighters use. Maybe last a coupla weeks, instead of a coupla days."

Carrick strode to the old-fashioned round-top fridge to grab water, spinning before he opened it at his brother's shout of, "Catch!" He turned just in time to wrap both arms around the bag as it winged across the room and crashed against his chest. Rocked back a step, he narrowed his eyes and considered winging it right back, then grinned. "You're still a brat, little brother, just like when you were a snot-nosed kid."

He tossed it into the corner of the kitchen area, then turned and pulled open the fridge door to grab three icy bottles of water. One he launched at his brother's head, the other at Dak, now upside-down in a handstand, heels against the wall while he powered through push-ups.

The man was stronger than an ox. Had better balance and dexterity than a ballet dancer. Carrick grinned to see the big man catch the bottle with one hand without wobbling, then push up one handed, flip, and land right-side up in a crouch.

He relished having these guys close at hand, living in their own cabins on the property. Also relished having this gym. Somewhere they could train out of the public eye. No way in hell could they work out in a regular gym for any length of time. Before they'd finished converting the barn to a custom gym, the fitness club down the street had been the only game in town.

They'd toned down their workouts; hadn't been able to lift at their full capacity. Hadn't been getting a good, strong workout and the need to hold back, to ensure they didn't draw untoward attention to themselves, frustrated them all. After all, exhibiting superhuman strength didn't help them stay under the radar.

He toasted his brother and Dak with the water bottle. "Damn, it feels good to lift and work the bag again without holding back."

Reese nodded. "We kicked ass getting the reno done. Who'd of thought a drafty old barn could turn into something rivaling Pump and Press?"

Dak gave another quirk of his lips that passed for his smile. "I can just see sending one of their bags through a window."

"Yeah, wouldn't go over too well, would it, Dak?" Carrick guzzled half the water. "You hungry? I'll spring for a couple of meat lover's pizzas when we're done here." He turned to Reese with a frown. "Did Hale get back to you with the information he'd found on Denton and the Garou history?"

His brother's scowl said it all. "Got some Garou history, but still waiting to hear if he found info on Denton. I hope to hell he finds out who's been sniffing around and gets a lead on where the two missing men are."

Carrick's money was on Denton, the sadistic ass. There were rumors he'd gone from just suspecting the Garou existed to somehow getting hold of actual proof. They didn't know what form that proof was, unfortunately, or where he'd obtained it.

They'd long suspected traitors in the Garou community, but had ferreted no one out yet. The Council feared Denton had resorted to kidnapping Garou to conduct experiments or, god forbid, dissecting them like lab animals to reverse engineer their DNA.

Carrick jerked around as *Sea Wolf* blasted from his phone on the kitchen counter, crooning a snippet of the lyrics. Dak's phone chimed in right behind with *Wolf at the Door*, and Reese's simply howled. It would have been funny had it not been going on midnight and no reason for any of their phones to ring. Much less all three. At the same time. It was either the council calling about another abduction or a local emergency. Neither was good news.

They turned and ran to the counter, Carrick's quick glance at the phone screen before he swiped his thumb to answer it showed the local Almaden fire station was calling. "Canavar!" Dak and Reese grabbed their phones but didn't answer, knowing Carrick would get the info and fill them in.

Twenty seconds later, his eyes snapped to Dak's, then Reese's. "We're on it. Be there in five, tops." He disconnected and pivoted. "Attempted child abduction. Asshole took off, the kid's unconscious, mother's home alone with her."

They ran for the big double doors, not bothering to change or dress, covered in nothing but gym shorts, workout shoes and sweat. Carrick snapped out orders. "Nine thirty-seven Almaden is just over the hill, same side of the road. We'll take the Ducatis."

It was damn lucky they lived so close to the attempted abduction, about a mile down on the same side of the road, accessible via a trail that ran behind the properties fronting Almaden Road, and they'd left the bikes outside after a tour of the property before working out.

They'd all gotten the same call because Reese and Dak were sister-city volunteer Forest Rangers with EMT and emergency services training, and Carrick volunteered with the local Search & Rescue.

As volunteers, they were ready to pitch in when local emergency response couldn't get to a scene on time, allowing Carrick and his buddies to be first responders and suss out the situation, providing medical care, and even protection when needed, until Fire or deputy sheriffs could arrive. He hoped to hell the child was unhurt, and the mother was holding it together.

They weren't formally on call this weekend, but as volunteers were never really off duty. Carrick knew emergency dispatch had tagged them because of the multi-car, multi-injury accident currently blocking the intersection of Blossom Hill Road and Almaden Expressway.

It was apparently tying up the bulk of South San Jose emergency crews and had called out their local Almaden area Fire folks, too. A paramedic engine was heading back in their direction, but no way in hell were they going to wait and chance fifteen or twenty minutes, not when it could mean life or death. And what if the son-of-a-bitch was still in the vicinity? Dispatch said the mother and kid were alone. Unprotected.

They'd get there in time. There was no way he was going to fail. Not like he did in New Idria years ago, when the faction they were fighting had blind-sided them, succeeding in almost mortally injuring his aunt and uncle because he hadn't been fast enough, or clever enough, to thwart the bastards. Guilt still battered him over that.

Their phenomenal speed and night vision had them on the Ducati Multistrada 950/950 dirt bikes and up to forty miles an hour in two seconds, across his field in a flash. All three knew every pothole, bush and rock on Carrick's land and cranked up to motocross speed on the barely there trail from his house to the gate on the south side of the property.

As they crested the small hill an eighth of a mile from the boundary of his land, the light on the back porch of their destination shone like a beacon, being the only house on his side of the street in that direction. He remembered it being a desolate looking little cottage from the rear, with a surprisingly manicured, immaculate front yard rimmed in color with a compact porch at the front door.

He'd checked out all properties within a two-klick perimeter of his before he'd bought the ranch, and no one had been living in the house. That had changed just a couple of months ago, though.

He'd seen glimpses of a petite dark-haired woman and red-headed child as they'd moved in but had paid little attention, and hadn't seen them since. If they weren't a threat or didn't need help, or weren't part of the Garou community, they weren't on his radar.

As they approached the narrow gate in the fence bordering his property and public land, he reached into the small pouch hanging from the handlebars and pressed the security fob to open it. With inches to spare, he shot through the opening, Reese and Dak hot on his tail, pressing the button when they cleared the opening to close it behind them.

He was thankful for the dirt trail that stretched for a few miles running between his property and Quicksilver Park, dipping closer to the road near his gate, continuing between the back of their target's house and Quicksilver Park, before continuing on for another couple of miles.

"This is it!" Carrick gunned around the house to the front and stopped just short of running his front tire into the bumper of an older SUV slowly rolling away from the gravel bordering the small lawn and pulling onto Almaden Road, lights off, the license plate smudged with just enough grime he couldn't make it out.

He jumped off his bike and knocked the kickstand down. "Hey! Wait!" He stared after the Land Cruiser and wondered if he should give chase. Was that the bastard who'd tried to take the kid?

His inner debate ended when he looked at the driver's reflection in the SUV's side mirror and locked onto moss-green eyes set above high cheekbones and a strong nose, currently illuminated by an oncoming truck. Not their perp, but a woman. An extremely beautiful woman with a fall of mahogany curls framing her bewitching face.

He stood frozen, couldn't look away as a wave of heat flashed and burned just under his skin, dizziness assaulting him, almost dropping him to the ground. *What the hell?* Their personal Garou doc had recently given him a clean bill of health. If not for that, he'd think he was having a seizure.

"Woah. Damn." He wavered on his feet and stumbled back, grabbing the seat of his bike to keep from falling on his ass, unable to look away from those mesmerizing eyes in the rearview mirror. He narrowed his eyes to keep her in focus as shadows claimed the SUV and his glimpse of the mystery woman.

His skin prickled and his senses sharpened as an alluring scent tickled his nose, making his cock twitch and his skin feel even tighter, the fire to flash hotter. *What the ever-loving fuck?* Notes of cinnamon and nutmeg danced through the air, and he clenched the muscles in his abs and ass when he realized he was suddenly one stroke away from coming in his pants.

He was at a fucking emergency call, for god's-sake! Nothing like this had ever happened to him before. He stood there dazed and tried to catch hold of an elusive memory as it tickled his subconscious, something he'd heard as a kid, but for the life of him he couldn't grasp it. Fuck, he could barely stay on his feet!

Chapter Two

NIA EYED her rear-view mirror as she backed away from the kidnapper's car, praying she made her getaway before emergency personnel showed. Her hands jerked the wheel when a big dirt bike skidded to a stop behind her, almost kissing her bumper.

She shoved the gearshift into first, wrenched the wheel to get around the piece of shit car crunching Simone's flowers and pressed the gas, Max giving a woof of complaint as he scrambled for balance on the passenger seat.

Her eyes widened at the sheer size of the shirtless guy who leapt from the bike and took an aggressive step toward her Land Cruiser, his chiseled body and hard-planed face like a modern-day Samson or Hercules. His broad, ripped shoulders, outstanding pecs and enormous biceps and triceps enraptured her, causing a delicious throbbing between her legs. Impressive lats veed to trim hips and quads the size of small tree trunks sprouted from workout shorts hitting mid-thigh ramped her up even higher.

Her eyes snapped up to meet his in the side-mirror, and she was astounded to see them glow an otherworldly silver, appearing almost molten. Transfixed, her foot eased off the gas as the sensation of a silken web formed between them, seeming to irrevocably bind them together.

She caught herself, dragged her eyes away from the mirror and pressed harder on the gas pedal, her hand automatically manipulating the gearshift into second, then third, eyeing the mirror again as she accelerated down the road, her gaze inexorably drawn back to the giant of a man who'd jumped off and yelled at her. With the wind through the open window whipping loose curls around her face, the sound of his deep voice echoing after her sent chills skittering up and down her spine.

The effort it took to pull her eyes away and watch the road was shocking. As she gained distance from Simone's house, she alternated between glancing at the road before her and the Adonis in her rear-view. She was astonished the musculature and stature of the guy was still obvious at this distance, and wondered why just that quick glimpse was etched in her brain. Why on earth she had the wild urge to turn her SUV around, drive back to Simone's house and ask that man to wrap her up in his massive arms.

Holy shit! What was up with that? She'd never in her life had such a visceral reaction to a man! Max gave a low whine, sensing her turmoil and she glanced over at her big protector, surprised to see him facing the back window, staring at the big guy currently growing smaller in her rearview, muscular legs spread, biceps bulging, fisted hands on his lean hips.

As she sped down the road, she was glad she'd gotten into the habit of keeping just enough dirt smudging her license plate to make it difficult to read, but not enough to draw attention from the deputies as a brazen attempt to obliterate the numbers and letters.

She'd also checked out the New Almaden area when she'd first arrived to determine what a common vehicle was, then purchased an older Land Cruiser that was almost a clone of about ten others in the area, a faded black that blended into the night. Who'd have guessed they were so popular? She'd paid cash for it to a retired woman who was moving out of the area and registered it in the name of her new persona, created by her sister and found in the stash of documents and money she'd left for her.

Regardless of how hard it was to read her license or how vanilla her vehicle, she needed to get home before that behemoth who'd shouted at her, or one of the emergency responders rushing to Simone's, decided they wanted to track her down. She trusted her new friend to keep her identity secret, since the woman shared a horrific secret with her. A madman had held them both against their will. And they'd both escaped.

Nia was dying to know Simone's story. She snorted at her terrible choice of words. The truth was, they'd both been on a death track if they'd stayed captive. The experiments the sadistic ass ran on them would no doubt have killed them, eventually.

Either outright, or they'd have died from the damned, insidious disease lupus, since some of his experiments exposed them to anything and everything bad for someone suffering from the disease, so he could then see how they fared, after his infusions, without the typical meds.

Apparently she and Simone, and who knew how many others, shared an anomaly in their blood, not typically found in most lupus patients, and he'd muttered over and over something about her being perfect for the garoe. Whatever the heck that meant.

How on earth she and Simone had both landed in New Almaden after escaping was beyond her. After getting away from Denton she'd chosen San Jose, thinking it would be easy to stay hidden in one of the many suburbs, and maybe he'd think she'd want to be as far away from the West Coast as possible, when in fact she'd just moved one state below where his facility was, in the middle of an Oregon national forest.

As she'd been driving around the outskirts of San Jose looking for a likely spot to hunker down, the closer to the small enclave of New Almaden she'd approached, the more she'd felt an almost physical pull.

The farther she'd driven down Almaden Road into the heart of the small community, she'd felt physically and emotionally stronger, her exhaustion not as acute, a sense of safety blanketing over her. It was such a dramatic and noticeable difference, she'd stopped at the small New Almaden post office, grabbed a newspaper and looked for a house to buy, right then and there.

She'd lucked out and found a fixer-upper that had been vacant for over a year, far from the road nestled amidst trees, and bought it on the spot for cash, then turned it into a small fortress with plenty of security on the house and surrounding acreage.

She needed to talk to Simone, to find out how long they held her in that asshat's laboratory, how long since she'd escaped—before or after Nia? She also wanted to know why Simone had chosen New

Almaden. Did she also feel safe, feel stronger here? Why did this area call to her, and why did she feel stronger and more centered since arriving? It was this small community, near the old quicksilver mines, that called to her.

Nia wondered if she'd have ever realized that madman had imprisoned Simone if not for the kidnapping attempt tonight, and both of them recognizing the wicked scar marring their faces, courtesy of that bastard's signet ring.

Before she'd driven away, she'd promised to call Simone on a burner phone later that night to see how Rachel was doing, and so they could meet, or at least to trade stories over the phone and come up with a better plan to stay hidden. God knew they could both use each other for emotional support and for protection. Safety in numbers.

It had been hell the past ten months, not having anyone she could talk to, no one to share the horror stories of being captured, of being experimented on. And of course, since escaping, she'd stayed hidden and under the radar.

She'd dared not go to the authorities. Who would have believed such an outlandish story? Besides, how could she know who Denton had in his pockets, or who was working with him? She did not know who she could trust, and trusting the wrong person could get her locked in an asylum or some government facility being experimented on.

Now that she knew Simone had suffered the same pain, danger and indignities she had, and was also in hiding, Nia would damn well do whatever it took to help keep her and little Rachel safe.

Nia had failed her sister in that regard, hadn't been able to protect Aleesha after her capture, and her dear sister had died because of her inadequacies. Her breath caught on a sob and she willed it back, refusing to succumb to tears. She would be strong. And she would not fail Simone or her daughter.

When Max laid his big black and tan head on her lap, she gave him pets for being so brave. "You're such a tough guy, yes you are. Thank you for helping save Rachel tonight. I'm sorry he hurt you, but we'll take care of that when we get home. How about some extra treats tonight?"

His low woof of agreement had her thanking whatever deity was watching over her the night she escaped the lab. She shuddered, remembering the feel of the scalpel she'd stolen slicing through the guard's neck when he'd tried to rape her. He was an asshole who had wandering hands whenever he brought her to and from the lab, and was sadistic to both her and her furry buddy.

Max had been one of their new guard dogs, but that guard's way of treating both humans and dogs was with violence and intimidation. Took after Denton in that regard. Max apparently didn't appreciate being whaled on or yelled at any more than Nia did.

After she'd done the deed, Max had jumped up and licked her across the face instead of chomping a piece out of her, then taken her hand gently between his sharp canines and led her deeper into the facility to a secret back exit opposite where the lab was located, accomplishing in just minutes what would have taken Nia much longer to do. And all without being caught.

She shoved the memories back down and locked them in a tiny corner of her mind where they couldn't consume her, took a left off Almaden Road onto Bertram, then another left onto Cinnabar Hills Road and traveled about half a mile before pulling onto a skinny trail and up to a rusted chain-link fence you couldn't tell was actually a gate, stretched between two battered railroad ties set deep into the ground. Past the fence, the trail disappeared through dense trees, looking unused and overgrown, then wound through the forest to where her house nestled in a small glade.

Just as she pulled off the main road, she pressed the button on a retrofitted garage door opener and the chain-link fence dropped neatly, flat to the ground from the right-hand post. The clever design had a strong steel cable attached and inserted into a device of her own making, hidden in the post. She rolled over the links, then pressed the button again, and the cable, which rolled smoothly, pulled the fence back up into place in its hiding place in the hollowed-out part of the post.

She glanced back at the road, a part of her wishing the big guy who'd almost kissed her bumper with his bike would show up. Her body was hot and bothered, and the thought of being safely wrapped in his arms and then naked, getting busy with that mammoth muscled body, was an erotic picture in her mind.

She knew better than to fantasize, but also knew exactly why she felt this way. She'd been running and hiding for ten long months and had been a captive for almost six months before that. Who wouldn't want someone to help fight off that madman? To help her stay safe? And who wouldn't want to get busy with someone built like Hercules?

Not that she wasn't capable. She'd been ace at self-defense and several martial arts, but she was fucking exhausted from being hypervigilant, afraid if they found her and snatched her up again, no one would be the wiser. When half a dozen men with tasers and handguns had jumped her, even her training hadn't saved her. No way she could have come out on top of that shit-show.

She gave herself a mental head-smack and stiffened her spine against any desire to have that big man at her side. Or under her. On top of her. Inside her. Sheesh!

Okay, she was lonely and horny as hell. She'd not been with a man, much less in any kind of relationship, since just before they'd snatched her, and that had turned out to be one of the biggest mistakes of her life. To think she'd gone to bed with that asshole.

The sex had been okay, but not stellar. Heck, not even particularly good. She'd gone out with him for a couple of months, and he'd sold her out to Denton for a measly five grand. She'd wondered if he was a lure Denton used to suck women like her into a false sense of security before betraying them for a pocket full of cash.

Her mind veered back to that guy on the motorcycle and her panties dampened even more, her pulse pounded and all kinds of fantasies bounced around in her head. What would it feel like to slide her hands over that massive masculine body and have his big hands run across hers? His cock inside her? She'd never in her life felt this over-the-top sexual heat and desire.

Not to mention, now that she thought of it, there'd been that odd tug, a pull toward him, like a thread connecting them and locking tight—so similar to what she'd felt when New Almaden had enticed her to venture deep into its hills. Only this had a sexual element to it, was much stronger, more enticing. And a ghost of it was still there.

Enough, she told herself firmly as she drove around a sharp bend, hidden from the main road in seconds, and finally able to breathe a sigh of relief at being tucked away in her own private forest. She couldn't wait to be locked in her fortress, as safe and sound as she could make it.

"Okay, my brave fella. Bet you're hungry, huh? I know I am. Boy, that adrenaline dump kicks my butt every time. So much worse since Dr. Asshat injected me with who knows what. Knew it was going to be bad just from our hike, but after fighting that dude? Shew! You want turkey and rice as a treat for being such a hero tonight?"

She grinned at Max's woofs and growls as he answered, letting her know he was indeed hungry and that they should also snuggle on the couch so she would feel better. Oh, he didn't say exactly that in so many words, but she knew those particular sounds meant he would eat and then nudge her to the couch or bed, where he would then lay against her, protect her, until she relaxed enough to sleep.

Or at least lose the anxious, sick feeling in her tummy. As Nia approached a gnarled oak tree split years ago by lightning, marking the halfway point to her home, she slowed to a crawl and tapped her tablet to wake it, glancing down to scan the map and ensure all anchors on her land showed green.

She'd spent her first few days in New Almaden wiring her land and home, so she'd be aware of any incursions. The app she was using was an invention of her sister's, and if any unwanted guests infiltrated her property, it ensured she would get an early warning, allowing her to get inside the false basement she'd hidden and rigged with more weapons and food stores, which conveniently had an old, reinforced tunnel leading under Cinnabar Hills Road to a small cottage about half a mile behind Hacienda Cemetery, which she also owned.

The only reason she had the money to rig the place, and to lie low without having to work, was because of her sweet sister. Aleesha had been a hacker extraordinaire and electrical engineer, had tracked and found Nia in Denton's makeshift prison, breached his computer firewall, transferred a shit-ton of his money into a secret joint account she and Nia had, then shown up at the facility—alone—to rescue her from his clutches.

What a tragedy that had become. Aleesha had underestimated the bastard and his goons. They'd captured her, allowed her just seconds with Nia, then dragged her into a cell right just down the hall and killed her within minutes after she'd attacked the guard. Pain speared through Nia's heart to remember the night she'd heard her sister die in that fucking cell.

They'd carried her past Nia's cell as if taking out the trash, and Denton had taunted her with her sister's death for days. She'd sworn she would take him and his crew down hard, no matter how long it took—and free any other captives.

She'd just have to figure out a way to get her strength back and stay alive while she did it.

She breathed a sigh of relief as she rounded another sharp turn and pulled up to the attached garage. Another press of the small electronic device rolled the door up and she did a quick visual survey before pulling in, then pressed the button to roll it back down, keeping an eye on the rear-view mirror to ensure no one ducked into the garage behind her. She trusted her security system, but you could never be too careful. She had the scars—emotional and physical—to prove it.

With a quick pat to Max's shoulder, she opened her door and swung her leg out, then stepped to the ground, only to sway and clutch the oh-shit bar as a wave of dizziness swept through her. She'd expended a ton of energy rescuing Rachel and had been running on adrenaline since then, not to mention the energy spent in their jaunt to the park in Morgan Hill. Now that she was home and safe, every bruise, scrape and ache from the fight roared to the front. She needed one of her energy drinks, but even that seemed like an impossible task right now.

She clutched her pounding head, realizing being popped by that asshole's fist did more harm than she'd thought. Dizzy spells and extreme fatigue had plagued her off and on since her escape and she'd chalked it up to stress, along with whatever experiments Denton had performed on her. When he was infusing her and running those experiments, she'd known they were going to come back to bite her on the ass, and sure enough, they had.

With the way her head was spinning, she figured a concussion on top of the energy she'd used was going to cause this episode to be much worse than usual. As the swirling spots before her eyes faded and blinked out, she realized Max had slipped behind her and jumped to the ground, tucking his wide head under her hand to provide support.

She scratched the fave spot behind one ear and he gave a doggy groan, leaning against her and wagging his tail. "Okay, my man, let's see if I can get into the house without face-planting, hmm? I'll replenish the carbs and electrolytes before I feed you, then sit my butt on the couch."

With one hand on his head, she reached back into the cab to grab her backpack, sliding it across the seat, then up onto her shoulder. She took a cautious step toward the kitchen door, nudging the SUV door shut with her elbow. The minute she got in the house, she would feed Max, pop a couple ibuprofen, gulp at least one if not two energy drinks, take a quick shower or at least clean her injury, and then relax in her love-seat recliner, her furry buddy snuggled next to her.

If she set her alarm for every couple of hours, she'd wake to ensure the concussion didn't do her in. Max's extensive training included knowing to nudge her and bark if she didn't wake after the alarm played three times. She would call Simone in sixty minutes or so. That would give plenty of time for the emergency responders to come and go, and she and Simone could come up with a plan to keep them all safe. And give her the opportunity to convince Simone to let her install a security system in her house ASAP, pro bono.

Darned if the mystery man didn't pop into her head again when she thought of safety. What was it about him that obsessed her? That made her think of hot bodies on cool sheets, of him standing beside her to help ward off the evil stalking her? Why him, when in all her years she'd never felt this kind of reaction to a man, much less one she'd not even met in the flesh yet? Just that enticing glimpse of the big guy in her rear-view was now burned into her memory.

It was depressing as hell she'd have to make do with her fantasy of the man. No way could she date, much less consider a relationship, with evil incarnate after her. She impatiently swiped tears away from her cheeks.

She was just tired and in pain. No way was she crying because of a lost chance at—what, some kind of relationship? With some guy she'd caught a glimpse of and didn't even know? Dream on, girl.

With one hand still on Max's head for support, her head spinning and spots again dancing in front of her eyes, Nia staggered toward the door leading into the mudroom. If she could just make it into the house, she'd be able to gulp down one or two energy drinks, then sit and get her bearings while they kicked in.

Have they cleared out of Simone's house? Can I call her for help? A drawback to being on the run from bad dudes was you couldn't call nine-one-one unless you were on death's door.

Not wanting to be so stubborn that she died on her garage floor, and knowing from her conversation with Simone she was an RN, Nia pulled her android phone from her backpack, unlocked it and keyed in Simone's phone number.

She'd rather use a burner to call her, but realized she hadn't replenished her stash of them in her backpack, and she wasn't sticking the sim card in her pocket back in the burner she'd called 911 with. She also needed to remember to shred that sim card.

To heck with waiting to be sure Simone was alone with her daughter. If nothing else, Nia could at least ask for help, and Simone could come as soon as everyone had left.

She stumbled and would have face planted if not for the steadying presence of her four-legged bodyguard. She made it a foot away from the kitchen door before she tumbled, and threw her free hand out just before she hit the cold floor, Max giving a deep woof while attempting to steady her.

As she collapsed to her knees, then slid sideways, she thought how tragic it would be if she died in her garage before meeting her mystery man.

Chapter Three

CARRICK SHOOK his head as he clutched his Ducati's handlebar, relieved his symptoms had ebbed enough he no longer felt he was going to land on his ass. He glanced toward the house to see Dak and Reese dwarfing a short, curvy, dark-haired woman as they led her through the front door, a sleepy-looking red-headed toddler cradled on her shoulder watching him with solemn brown eyes as they walked into the house.

The woman turned her head to look his way and wavered a moment, then called out, "That's not the guy. The car nosed into my oleander is his, and he's long gone. I hope. Ran across the street into the orchard."

Carrick watched her look around cautiously before allowing Dak to nudge her into the house ahead of him.

Reese stood eyeing him with concern, aware something was wrong. "Hey, man, you okay?"

Carrick nodded and lied through his teeth. "Yeah, sure, be right there."

He glanced down the road and watched the Land Cruiser's taillights disappear around the bend, torn between wanting to chase after the woman or do the right thing and help Simone.

He shook his head and strode toward the house, willing his hard-on to subside and the tingles zinging up and down his spine to stop.

He took the porch steps two at a time and entered the house, that spicy scent slapping him in the face again, ramping him back up and setting him on edge.

He closed and locked the door behind him, not wanting them to be caught unawares if the asshole came back, then stood behind Reese, glad to take a backseat while his brother questioned the woman and Dak examined her daughter.

He was never shaky or distracted during a crisis, but damned if he could pay attention while wrapped in that fragrance and fighting off this unwelcome, bizarre reaction. He had no fucking clue what was going on.

While Dak checked out the little girl, more alert as the minutes passed, Reese sat on a low coffee table in front of the woman. "Were you hurt too?"

"No." It was clear she was fighting residual fear and an adrenaline crash, her voice wobbling as tears trailed down her wan cheeks, her hand trembling when she brushed the moisture off her face. "I was asleep and didn't see him; I woke a little to what I thought were animals outside, then woke fully when I heard a car alarm and the doorbell ringing."

Carrick spoke up, trying not to fidget as the damned tingling under his skin continued to distract him. "While Dak checks out your daughter, can you tell us what happened? The three of us are emergency services volunteers with EMT and paramedic training. We were working out on my ranch, just over the hill, which is why we're not in uniform. A multi-car accident is holding up Santa Clara County Sheriff's Department and fire services, so they alerted us and asked that we respond."

He watched as tears continued to spill over, a slim hand covering her mouth to hold back a sob. She visibly gathered herself, keeping one arm wrapped securely around her little girl. "I was sleeping, and Rachel was asleep in her room. At least I thought she was! I always lock and check all the windows and doors before going to bed."

Reese held up a hand to calm her. "We're not placing blame, ma'am. Folks up to no good want to get inside, they'll get through locks. Please continue."

"Like I said, I thought I heard animals fighting on the porch, but was so tired, I didn't get out of bed. Racoons and coyotes are always in the area at night, and I've learned to ignore them. Then I heard a car alarm go off and right afterwards, the doorbell rang constantly. When I opened the door, I saw Ni—a woman sitting on the porch against the wall, and she was holding Rachel."

She choked back another sob, and Carrick could see the reality hit of what could have happened if someone hadn't intervened. She'd have woken in the morning and her daughter would have been long gone.

She glanced down at the little girl, then turned to Dak. "How is Rachel? Is she going to be okay?" She turned back to Carrick and Reese. "I'm an RN, and she seemed fine, just a little groggy when I examined her, but I'm so upset, I want you to look her over too, in case I missed something."

Dak met her eyes and then turned his attention back to Rachel. "Her vitals and breathing are good. She's more aware, coming out of it now. Probably given light sedation, enough to make her drowsy. When the paramedics arrive, they may want to transport her to hospital, to monitor her and do blood tests."

If Carrick hadn't been watching closely, he would have missed the sudden tensing of Simone's shoulders at the mention of the hospital. Or was it blood tests? Did she have an awful experience in the past?

He knew why he and the guys didn't let anyone at a 'normal' hospital take their blood—too dangerous since they had anomalies not found in regular humans. But why would that worry Simone?

"I'm not sure about going to the hospital. What if he comes for her there? We don't know why he targeted her. No, it would be too dangerous. I can just monitor her at home for the rest of the night and then take her to her pediatrician in the morning."

Carrick shared glances with Dak and Reese, knowing her reticence in going to the hospital didn't go unnoticed by them, either. Maybe she didn't have medical insurance? Although it was the law now that people carry insurance, he knew there were those who just couldn't afford it. And they couldn't force her to let them take her daughter, especially since she wasn't exhibiting any adverse symptoms.

He gave a noncommittal nod. "We'll see how she's doing after the paramedics get here."

He struggled for calm, that buzzing up and down his spine lessening a little, but that elusive spicy scent was still teasing his senses and every erogenous zone on his over-sensitized body. Sweat continued to gather on the back of his neck and slip down his spine like a lover's tongue.

Annnd, he didn't need to be thinking shit like that! He thought he'd done a good job of hiding his turmoil and discomfort, but Reese stood suddenly and jerked his head toward the small kitchen just off the living room.

"Hey, man, let's look around while Dak's doing his thing." Reese turned to the Simone and gestured toward the kitchen. "We'll be back, ma'am. We're going to check out the back door and windows. Dak will stay here with you and your little one while we wait for emergency responders."

Simone nodded distractedly, while Dak continued to monitor Rachel. "Oh, of course." She looked around warily, as if she'd find the asshat lurking in the corner of her living room. "Do you think he'll come back tonight?"

Reese shook his head. "No, nothing like that. Just want to see where he entered and double check your doors and windows. We'll stay out of your daughter's bedroom, though, until the forensics folks investigate."

Carrick rose and followed his brother across the room and into the kitchen, surprised to see the back door locked with two deadbolts, a regular doorknob lock, and topped off with a knob jammer. Overkill, unless maybe all the locks were already there when she moved in? Looked shiny new, though, and that knob jammer had to be hers. He turned to his brother with a head-jerk toward the door.

"This woman wants to make sure no one gets in. What's in her past to make her ramp security up to this level? And be nervous about going to the hospital? If she's this careful, how'd someone break into her daughter's room without waking her?"

He turned to see Reese watching him closely and scrubbed a hand across his face before motioning him closer. "Before you ask, I have no fucking clue what's wrong with me. It hit me when I got off my bike, just as that Land Cruiser took off. After I stood there a moment, I felt a little better, then in the house it got worse again. I've never felt this way before, man."

Reese's concerned gaze sharpened at Carrick's words. "What're your symptoms?"

"Jesus, if it were anyone but you and Dak, I'd be embarrassed as hell. Okay, first symptoms were dizziness, feeling heat bloom under my skin, making it feel prickly—not itchy exactly, just way too sensitive." He clasped his hands behind his neck and leaned over, then righted himself and propped them on his hips. "I can't concentrate for shit, and it's all I can do to calm my dick down, cause it won't quit trying to salute my abs, my spine tingles like I'm gonna orgasm, and there's this damn enticing smell of cinnamon, nutmeg and something else I can't identify that's driving me bat-shit."

Reese's eyes kept widening as Carrick described his symptoms, his harsh whisper full of awe when he spoke. "Fuck me, Carrick. I know exactly what those symptoms are! I've been reading up on the Garou history Hale shared the other night—haven't finished it—but what you're feeling happens when you're near your mate, or where your mate has been recently. Especially if their emotions are ramped up."

Carrick stumbled to the small pine dining table, jerked out a chair, and sat down heavily. "The fuck you say?"

"I'm serious, bro. In the old text they're called Cinnabar Twins, named after 'penetration twinning' of the actual ore, and because Garou and their mates only thrive near quicksilver deposits and mines. If you'd actually met her, the symptoms woulda been even more exaggerated, if you can believe it, but what you just described is exactly what I read last night. Was gonna share with you and Dak tonight, after I'd finished reviewing what he'd sent. We need to find out who Rachel's mystery savior was. I'd bet the bank she's your mate, and that she's the woman in the Land Cruiser!"

Carrick stared at his brother in disbelief. "There haven't been mates for Garou in over three hundred years. I need to find her, get together with her, convince her to be with me."

He stumbled to his feet and started for the living room, determined to find out who the little girl's protector was. Not two steps away from the chair, Reese grabbed his arm and scolded him in a low voice. "Stop! You go in there looking like that and making demands, you'll scare the shit out of Simone. Sit down and get a handle on this, bro. I'll go see what I can find out."

Carrick stumbled back to sit on the chair again and watched his brother exit the room, stunned and not sure he believed what his brother told him about Cinnabar Twins. He dropped his head into his hands, elbows on knees, and concentrated on steadying his pounding pulse and erratic breathing.

He could hear the low drone of Reese's voice in the living room, no doubt comforting Simone and her little girl while trying to pull information about the mystery woman at the same time.

He wanted to be in there questioning Simone about the woman who'd come to her daughter's rescue, but knew Reese had made the right call. No way could he calmly ask Simone questions when what he really wanted to do was demand she give them the information so he could jump on his bike and track down his mate. His mate!

Never in a million years had he or any of his friends thought they would ever find their mates. In his family, his papa and uncles were the last Garou who'd found mates, and that was over three hundred years ago. They'd all resigned themselves to Garou eventually dying out, although that would take hundreds and hundreds of years, considering their longevity.

There were Garou, like Dak's adopted father, Mateo, who lived in Sonoma near Hale and was close to his dad's age; the poor guy had been waiting hundreds of years for his mate, and they'd recently seen signs he'd about given up. Carrick had been working on him, attempting to convince him to make the move to New Almaden so they could keep him busy, make sure he didn't lose all hope.

They could use his expertise as ex-military in protecting their kind in the area and be part of any rescue should it be necessary. It was time for him to leave Sonoma, anyway. He'd been there long enough that regular folks—regular *humans*—would start questioning why it appeared he never aged.

Carrick's parents still looked like they were in their fifties and were both four hundred-plus years old, which was the reason they and other Garou traveled from country to country, place to place, so neighbors didn't get suspicious when they didn't visibly age.

It was a damn shame so many Garou were without their mates. There were theories about why the females seemed to disappear from the face of the earth. A few scientists within the Garou community believed a virus or disease had swept through the population and had killed a good many of them. Cinnabar Twins who hadn't died from the virus were no longer detectible by their Garou mates. He'd bet their offspring were undetectable as well.

When the virus ravaged that generation's population, the orphaned female children—Cinnabar Twins, as Reese called them—wouldn't know about the anomalies running through their blood that made them special. They would have no oral history, typically passed down through the generations and with no community to be raised in, were clueless they had Garou mates longing to find them, cherish them, protect them—and love them unconditionally.

The veritable two-ships-in-the-night analogy, able to pass each other on the streets with neither feeling that inexorable link, the need to touch, to be together. The link that clearly shouted MINE, my mate!

The female also didn't have the longevity of the male Garou, not until they mated, and the Garou shared the little something extra they had in their semen, along with the unique serum injected into the woman from their fangs. This posed another problem in that, until they mated, the women would die after a typical human lifespan, having never met their Garou mate.

Not that all Garou males had female mates. There were male to male pairings who met, felt the mating bond just as strongly, fell in love and bonded just like the male to female pairings. Unfortunately, that didn't do a thing to make babies and continue the line of the Garou, since they were only fertile with their true female mates.

No wonder I didn't know what was wrong with me. Enough time had passed that his generation, and the generation before, had all but forgotten the stories told when they were youngsters.

Hell, there'd been an entire generation of Garou growing up, not finding their mates. Not experiencing the disorientation, the overwhelming sexual desire and pure focus on the other person that just about struck a man down upon initial contact. There would be no first-hand knowledge, and since it had been hundreds of years, who would remember what amounted to a fairy tale from when they were kids?

The older generation had stopped having children. Even if they had amazingly long lifespans, there reached a time when, like humans, the sperm just wasn't producing kids, and no one felt like raising kids when they were several hundred years old. Especially if they'd already had several when they were younger.

Carrick was a heartbeat away from heading back into the living room to see what was taking so damn long when he heard knocking on the door, followed by Reese's low voice and a deputy announcing himself. Feeling he finally had a handle on his emotions, and not wanting anyone to question why he was hiding out in the kitchen, he strode into the room to see paramedics from Almaden Fire, along with county deputies, entering the small living room.

The emergency response community called on Carrick, his brother, and DAK to find lost hikers regularly, so they were on a first-name basis with many of the first responders.

"Hey, Brad." Carrick reached out a hand to Bradley Gifford, the tall, lanky lieutenant from Fire Station 28, and shook the man's hand. He nodded toward Dak and Simone. "Dak can give you the rundown on the child. Reese and I have checked out the house, except the child's bedroom, which we're assuming is the point of ingress and the crime scene. Witness says the perp left through the side bedroom window."

Reese stepped forward, nodding at Sergeant Drumford from the sheriff's office, a guy built like a tank who they frequently met for a beer or two at the local watering hole. He gave the sergeant a recap to bring him up to speed.

Sergeant Drumford nodded toward Simone after Reese filled him in and asked quietly, "How's the little girl? Was she injured?"

Dak came forward and shook his head. "Seems to be fine. The perp may have used light sedation. She was out for a about five minutes, then just groggy. She's come fully around now and doesn't seem to suffer any ill effects. The mother doesn't want her taken to the hospital, though."

The sergeant narrowed his eyes. "Why not? They should examine her."

Dak gave an affirmative grunt. "Yeah, not sure why. Simone, the mother, got scared and tense when I mentioned the hospital. Reminds me of women at a shelter running and hiding from an abuser. Simone's an RN, says she knows what to look for and will take her daughter to the hospital later if needed."

Sergeant Drumford glanced at Simone and shot a frown at Gifford. "Hmmm. Okay, let me chat with Simone while Rissa examines the child. Appreciate you guys getting here so fast." He motioned for the paramedic who'd just jogged into the house, then followed her over to Simone and her daughter.

Dak, Reese and Carrick all moved to the side to let Drumford and Gifford, along with Rissa, approach Simone and Rachel. They wanted to be close enough to overhear in case Simone shared additional information she'd been reticent to share with them, or to see if her story deviated from what she'd told them.

As Rissa examined the little girl, Drumford sat across from Simone and gently took her through the night's events. "Sounds like your Good Sam and her dog have some type of training in protection. Maybe military," Drumford said, then waited a beat. "Have you seen her around the area? Have a first name?"

Simone shrugged. "Oh, I don't—I didn't ask her name and haven't seen her before." Her eyes darted to the left just before she covered her mouth with her fingers, then fiddled nervously with the edge of Rachel's sleeper. "I don't remember seeing her in the area before tonight. Maybe she was just visiting someone?"

Carrick glanced at Dak, then Reese, and got a chin lift in silent agreement before looking back at the nervous woman. She was exhibiting classic signs of lying, or at the very least, holding back important details. Disappointment set in when they heard nothing new that would help lead them to the mystery woman or shed light on why Simone refused to take Rachel to the hospital.

Simone glanced toward Carrick, quickly averting her eyes to watch Rissa examine her daughter, who was currently playing with the stethoscope and apparently not bothered in the least by a group of strangers invading her home. "With my focus on

Rachel, when the woman said she needed to leave, I didn't ask her to stay. She'd already done so much and had to get home to cope with her injury."

Simone looked up again at Carrick, then Reese, and Dak, and motioned toward them. "She waited in her vehicle until they showed up to make sure the guy didn't come back, and then she left."

Drumford turned to Carrick. "Did you see her leave? Make and model of her vehicle and license?"

Carrick didn't want anyone else to find his woman, so kept his answer vague and lied through his teeth about the type and color of the SUV. "Older model Bronco, faded tan, with the license partially obscured by grime, no plate light, and no streetlight in front of Simone's house, so couldn't make out any details."

Drumford continued circling back around, asking Simone about the woman's description, and Carrick gave silent thanks when she just shrugged and shook her head at the sergeant, then turned to fuss over her daughter, clearly unable or unwilling to share more details with them. He'd bet his ranch on the latter.

She was clearly protecting the woman, for what reason he couldn't fathom, but it was in his favor. It would give him a chance to track her down without interference from the sheriff's department. He nudged Reese with his elbow and gave a subtle jerk of his head toward the door, watching as his brother repeated the action with Dak.

Drumford glanced up as they strode toward the door, but Carrick didn't want to be delayed any further. "We'll email our report to you both tonight. Nothing else for us to do here."

At the sergeant's nod, they strode out onto the porch and to their Ducatis, by silent mutual agreement not saying a word until they were safely behind the walls of his home.

The further Carrick sped away from Simone's, the more he felt like himself again. Though he still felt edgy, the hot buzz under his skin had finally faded to almost nothing, and his cock no longer throbbed to the beat of his heart. Was no longer ready to spring to action. He was almost back to normal, except for the craving settling deep in his soul for his mate's enticing scent. And to gaze into her bewitching gem-green eyes again.

He had to figure out who she was or go slowly crazy knowing she was in the vicinity but lost to him. Hell, he didn't even know if she lived in the San Jose area, much less New Almaden. Maybe she was a tourist, interested in the old quicksilver mines in the hills, and only in the area for a short time. That thought was even more horrifying.

No! No fucking way! He refused to believe fate would be that callous, to give him a taste of what it was like to be near his mate, but never actually meet her, never claim her. Besides, there weren't any hotels in the direction she drove off in. Although he guessed she could be renting someone's house via one of those air-whatever apps. Hopefully, she was a reclusive resident. He just needed to be patient a little longer.

With what he'd put in Simone's kitchen, they'd have answers soon. Or he'd go out of his ever-loving mind.

Chapter Four

CARRICK WORKED hard to calm his thoughts as they bounced over the same route they'd taken to get to Simone's, his fob opening and closing the gate leading back onto his property and home.

He shook his head when Dak shot a concerned look his way and nodded toward the ranch, revving his bike to high speed. No way was he discussing what had happened until they were safely behind the walls of his home or gym.

There was enough security surrounding and on the property that the second someone set foot on his land, or messed with one of the buildings, they would know. And when inside any of the buildings, they could shout to the heavens and no one could overhear them or record them, regardless of what spy-tech they had.

It went without saying it was imperative no one overhear what he was going to share with Dak. The Garou had been a well-kept secret for hundreds, hell thousands of years, with only a few outside their kind trusted enough for them to confide in and enlist their help when needed.

That is, until a year ago when they discovered Denton had somehow found out about them, and was dangerous to their very existence if left unchecked.

They made quick work of parking the bikes in the oversize garage attached to back of the ranch house, then strode to the door leading into the mudroom. Carrick pressed a thumb to the biometric reader, then checked the authenticator app on his phone for the onetime code and entered it into the keypad. Some would call his security measures overkill. He called it a basic necessity.

After the door closed behind them, Carrick held up a hand to curtail the questions. "Don't know about you, but I need a drink while we talk." He eyed Dak and Reese. "Beer or whiskey?"

They strode through the kitchen and down the hall into his office, floor to ceiling bookcases filling two walls, a large desk along another with a sidebar and tall gun safe behind it. He strode around the desk and grabbed the bottle of Wolven's Howl Bourbon Whiskey off the sidebar, founded by his grandpa in Slovenia, and now run by his cousin, strategically located near the cinnabar mines in that country.

Reese nodded yes to the whiskey, while Dak waved him off as he headed to the fridge in the corner. "I'll grab a beer."

Carrick gave a chin lift and poured a healthy splash in both tumblers, handing one to his brother.

He took a sip of his whiskey, welcoming the burn on its way down. He hoped to God he could get his body and mind to calm the fuck down enough to come up with a solid plan to find his mate. She had to be a resident here in New Almaden. He refused to accept any other outcome.

He'd go stone-cold crazy if she wasn't.

Taking the next step to discovering the mystery woman's identity, he pulled his phone from his pocket, pressed a thumb on the screen to unlock it, hit the special app on the home screen, then pressed the pulsing icon representing the bug he'd placed on the small ledge of the doorframe in Simone's kitchen, after he'd realized she was his only link to his mate. They always kept a couple of the mini-bugs in their wallets, never knowing when it might come in handy to snoop.

He'd stoop to invading her privacy if it meant learning the identity of his mate, and more importantly, so as not to leave the woman defenseless in case the bastard came back for a second try at her daughter.

He strode to the oversize couch and sat on the edge, laid his phone on the coffee table and pressed the play icon. Dak crossed the room and raised a brow at the voices coming from Carrick's phone.

"Where'd you put the bug?"

"Top of the kitchen doorframe. She's short enough she won't see it unless she climbs on a chair right next to the door."

Dak continued to the recliner and dropped to sit, shooting a chin-lift at Carrick to spill the beans on his behavior at Simone's and why he'd bugged her home. Knowing Dak lacked patience, he launched into his story, the voices of the deputies and EMT droning in the background as they finished up their interview and tried to convince Simone to let them transport Rachel to the hospital.

Carrick took another bracing sip of whiskey and recapped for Dak, then took another long sip to calm his anxiety.

Dak eyed Carrick for a few seconds, obviously working the problem in his mind. "What'd you come in contact with when you got off the bike? How is it I didn't notice anything when you came in the house? Granted, I was examining Rachel and getting the scoop from Simone, but still."

"Didn't come in contact with anything. I was about ten feet away from the driver of the Land Cruiser—my bike almost knocked her bumper—and her window was down. The symptoms ebbed after the vehicle continued down the road but ramped up again on the porch and when I entered the house, where the scent was stronger. I'm still edgy, but the ramped-up feeling is muffled now."

Carrick paused as a thought rushed through his mind, and he speared a hand through his hair in frustration. ""You know what? Now that I think of it, the way I feel right now I've felt a few times over the past couple of months; once when I was down at the post office, and a few times when we were at the fence line setting up security. Not as acutely, but still."

Carrick turned and lifted his glass to Reese. "Tell Dak about Cinnabar Twins."

He tuned them out as Reese brought Dak up to speed on the Cinnabar Twin info he'd shared earlier at Simone's, then tuned back in when Dak nudged him with his boot.

"You say you've had the same symptoms, only to a much lesser degree? I'm betting it's because she'd just been at the post office or had driven by or stopped at the side of the road near where you'd been working."

Carrick shook his head at hearing that. "Man, I didn't know what to think those other times. It was that feeling you get when you're sure someone's looking at you, along with a jolt of arousal, only not even half as intense as what I felt earlier."

Dak nodded. "You probably got hit with a bunch of pheromones and stress hormones at Simone's. The woman had fought off the attacker, had been on the porch and in Simone's house. Maybe she fell or stopped at the back of her SUV, so it was more condensed there."

Reese looked thoughtful. "Here's more of the information I haven't shared. After the pair complete the mating, they're still able to sense each other. If they're in close proximity to each other, they can sense emotions, almost thoughts, and when they're farther apart, it's more a ghost of a sensation. But still there. And apparently, this feeling of arousal will abate somewhat; but they stay hot for each other, and only each other, the rest of their lives."

Dak shook his head and leaned back in his chair, muscular legs stretched out and ankles crossed. "Man, after all this time, Carrick can sense his mate? How the hell, after hundreds of years, and in an out-of-the-way place like New Almaden, could his mate suddenly appear? Or if she's been here a while, why can he sense her now and not before?"

Carrick eyed Dak and his brother. "It's either a fuckin' miracle, or she'll disappear, and I'll go crazy with not having her."

"Let's go with the miracle and track her down." Reese was ever the optimist. "If we can get some info from Simo…"

Carrick tensed and held up a hand, pointing at his phone.

By the lack of conversation and bustling activity in her house, and sudden ringing of her phone, they could tell everyone had vacated the place.

Reese shot a concerned look at his brother and Dak. "You think they left anyone behind to monitor her house, in case the guy comes back?"

Carrick shook his head. "Bet they didn't. I know they're short-staffed. They'll probably just have a deputy do a drive by two or three times tonight, if they're in the area and not out on calls elsewhere. Wouldn't hurt for us to take shifts for the next couple of nights, just to monitor things."

Dak gave a sharp nod. "Yeah, don't want anything to happen to that little girl, or her mama."

At the continued ringing of the phone, Carrick started to rise. "She doesn't answer that phone, and I'm heading back over there to see what's wrong."

"Nia?" Simone answered the phone cautiously.

He settled back on the couch and looked from Dak to Reese, then leaned forward when he heard the feminine voice of the caller, muffled and weak but audible.

"Simone, yeah, sorry. Everyone gone?"

"Yes, they're all cleared out. What's wrong? You don't sound well at all."

"Yeah, I hate to ask. You think you can safely come to my house? I…" The caller groaned, and there was a canine whine and growl in the background.

Carrick jumped to his feet. "What the hell? Is she hurt worse than Simone thought? We need to get back to Simone's so we can follow her." Carrick grabbed his phone off the table, ran into the hall, down to the laundry room and kicked off his shoes, stripped off his shorts, then jerked on his BDUs.

He donned his combat boots, lacing them quickly, then grabbed a black t-shirt from the stack on the dryer and pulled it over his head. He dropped his phone, still broadcasting, into a front pocket, fastened his pants and sprinted back to his study.

Reese and Dak mimicked his actions, switching into the clothes and boots they'd left earlier when they'd dressed for the gym. Carrick ran to the tall gun safe behind his desk, twirled the combination back and forth until it clicked, then swung open the door and grabbed his Smith & Wesson M&P nine mil.

Simone's voice came through full of alarm, loud and clear, while they geared up. "Nia, what's wrong? Let me get Rachel ready, grab my medical bag, pack a backpack in case I stay the night, and I'll be on my way. My jeep's in the garage, so I can leave safely. Tell me your symptoms and share your location on Google maps, right now. Before you pass out."

Nia had to be the woman who'd saved Rachel. His mate! What was wrong, though? How severely injured was she? Simone had told them the guy she'd fought had gotten a solid punch to her temple. Jesus, they needed to get there and check her out.

No way they could risk the hospital, not with her blood anomalies as a Cinnabar Twin. It was also dangerous for the Garou's blood to be scrutinized in a mainstream lab, the major difference being the extra prostaglandins in their bloodstream and seminal fluid that normal humans didn't have.

His heart rate ramped as he grabbed his shoulder holster, slid the gun in, secured it, and slipped his arms into the straps, shrugging his shoulders to settle it. He then reached in and grabbed his ka-bar tactical knife, already in its sheath, and secured it to the belt on his pants.

He backed up and motioned for Dak and Reese, now also in BDUs and t-shirts, to grab their weapons. They mimicked Carrick's actions, shrugging into their holsters, then grabbing knives and tactical flashlights.

"I'm dizzy and nauseous. Collapsed in the garage. Can't get into the house. Probably from that asshole punching me in the head. Ever since those damned infusions, I burn energy like crazy. Need my energy drinks. Can't get them. Did Denton experiment on you too?"

They all froze at the mystery woman's mention of Denton.

"I've been different since I got away, but when I got out of my 'cruiser, I—shit, my head hurts—I collapsed before I could get in the house. I can't get back up. Text me when you get to the chain fence. I'll turn off security until you get to my house. Follow the drive and be careful. Make sure you're not followed."

Nia's last words were a mere whisper of sound, but the bug in Simone's kitchen was the best their Garou geek had invented, and with Simone no doubt back in her kitchen, they could hear her clear as a bell.

Carrick pinned his friends with an incredulous look. "Denton? What the fuck? What's that bastard done to her? This just gets more bizarre."

Simone's calm voice came across again. "Okay, I just pulled up Google maps. I head toward the post office, turn left on Bertram and another left on Cinnabar Hills. You're less than ten minutes away. I'm packed and getting in the Jeep. No worries, I'll be careful. I've dodged Denton for a year, I'm not getting caught now."

Carrick turned shocked eyes to his brother and friend. "Holy shit. Denton had them both, and they escaped? They're lucky to be alive. I can't believe they're both running from that motherfucker. This just got a lot more complicated. We need security on both of them, as of tonight. Dak, you have your med kit?"

Dak sprinted to grab his kit from the laundry room, and Carrick felt fire licking at his self-control. "If that bastard was experimenting on both of them, that must mean Simone is a Cinnabar Twin, too. As far as we know, Denton is only targeting Garou with his fucking studies and trying to infuse humans with our strength and abilities, but this proves he somehow found out about Cinnabar Twins and has something up his sleeve with them, too. But were they Twins to begin with, or human? And if they were Twins, how the hell did he determine that and find them? Either way, he's fucked with their DNA or something, and we need to figure out what he did. That must be the reason I can sense Nia. He altered her in some way. We need to get Bah up here with his equipment so he can run tests and monitor both of them."

Dak was right on their heels. "It'll take Bah at least three hours to get here from Sonoma. I'll text him from the vehicle, tell him to get his ass down here; maybe Hale, too."

Reese called shotgun and jumped into the front passenger seat of Carrick's FJ Cruiser, while Dak settled with his medic bag on the seat behind him. Carrick dove into the driver's seat and fired up the engine, hit the button to open the big garage door and impatiently waited for it to rise, then gunned it, barely clearing the bottom of the rolling door.

He followed the gravel driveway across his property, between the trees and shrubs, rocks pinging against the undercarriage. The gate swung open well before they reached it; the FJ fitted with a security device the gate recognized.

He drove through, then stopped about twenty feet from Almaden Road, lights out, engine idling and waited for Simone to pass, figuring hers would be the only vintage Jeep out this late at night, and knowing this was the only road she could take to get to Nia's.

Reese leaned forward and peered out at the dark road, a hand on the dash. "She should pass soon."

No sooner were the words out of his mouth than they saw a beige, original model Jeep Cherokee pass under a streetlight, Simone briefly illuminated at the wheel, before being claimed by shadows as she headed deeper into the heart of New Almaden toward the Quicksilver Museum.

Carrick depressed the clutch and took his foot off the brake to roll the FJ forward, pausing where his drive met macadam to wait for her to get further ahead so they could follow undetected, then pulled onto the road.

Dak rumbled from the back seat. "No telling how savvy Simone is. She mentioned being able to spot a tail. Better hang back, no lights."

"No worries, running lights-out and hanging back." Carrick was thankful their enhanced vision allowed him to navigate through the dark without headlights.

"Bertram's coming up. Hit it when she turns so we don't lose her in the hills. There are a shit-ton of driveways and dirt lanes off that road."

Carrick didn't need his brother to remind him, as they'd all scoped out the area to become familiar with

New Almaden when they'd first moved here, but he nodded in acknowledgement anyway and sped up, turning sharply onto Bertram to keep her in sight.

She rounded the first bend, and he accelerated again, her taillights like red eyes in the night. He put a fist to his chest when that invisible thread binding him to his mate suddenly tightened, and fought to concentrate as the electricity zipping down his spine increased.

He tossed a glance at Reese, met Dak's eyes in the rearview, then looked forward again to keep an eye on the jeep. "That connected feeling, like being pulled toward something, just ramped up again along with some of the other symptoms."

Reese glanced at Carrick, then over his shoulder at Dak. "Must be getting close. She's turning onto Cinnabar Hills. Better catch up. No clue what the woman meant by 'text me when you get to the chain fence', but we don't want to lose her if Simone turns off into the trees."

Carrick stepped on the gas and rounded a bend in the road just in time to see brake lights flash before Simone turned left onto a barely-there lane flanked by dense oak, towering redwood trees and overgrown bushes.

He rolled to a stop a hundred feet before the lane, then backed onto a skinny trail deep amidst the trees and brush to the right of the road they were on. He tucked the FJ behind a copse of redwood trees in a spot just wide enough that anyone passing from either direction couldn't see it.

They quickly exited the vehicle and Carrick hit a button on the fob to lock it, no beep sounding or lights flashing since he'd long ago disabled both, the dome light dark as well.

They jogged silently across the street and onto the lane, ducking behind tree cover to watch as Simone sat in her vehicle, oblivious to being watched and no doubt texting or calling Nia as instructed.

Their eyes widened when the rusty chain-link fence in front of her vehicle, hanging between two old railroad ties, suddenly dropped flat to the ground.

They hung back as she rolled over it and drove slowly down the tree-shrouded lane until she turned a corner and disappeared from view, then sprinted forward and darted through the railroad ties, barely clearing the makeshift gate before the fence jerked back into position.

Reese eyed the setup over his shoulder—being their resident tech geek he appreciated clever inventions—then sped up to keep pace with Carrick and Dak. "Pretty cool."

They continued their steady jog in the wake of the Jeep, keeping to shadows so a glance in her rear-view mirror wouldn't reveal them to Simone. She was driving slowly enough they could, with their enhanced endurance and speed, keep her taillights in view.

As they rounded another bend and spied a sprawling ranch-style home with an attached garage to the right, they ducked back into the trees on the edge of the clearing where it sat.

Carrick vibrated with impatience, his worry for his mate and buzzing sexual desire rising within him like hot magma as Simone came to a stop a couple of feet from the garage but remained in her Jeep.

"Jesus, if this is how I'm going to feel whenever I'm near this woman, I'm in big trouble. Damn, I feel possessive and protective as hell, distracted, and my cock has a fucking mind of its own. Gonna drive me batshit."

Right when he was about to break cover, Simone climbed warily from the Jeep, looked all around, then opened the back-passenger door and unbuckled Rachel from her car seat, pulling the sleeping child out and onto her shoulder, then grabbed a medical bag to sling over the other shoulder.

She approached the garage door and knocked, calling softly, "Nia. Nia!" She looked around again, mumbling to herself while apparently trying to decide what to do. They watched as she pulled her phone out of her hip pocket, swiped to unlock, and pressed on the screen, cocking her head at the ring echoing in the garage.

"If that door doesn't open, we need to break into the garage," Dak said tonelessly.

When the ringing stopped and Nia hadn't answered, Simone huffed and hit a button to disconnect and then call again. This time a soft voice answered as the first ring ended, clearly audible to Carrick and the guys.

"Hel—hello? Who's this?" the voice slurred.

"Nia! It's Simone. You called me, remember? I'm outside your garage. Can you open it?"

"Simone? Oh! Yes, I don't feel good. I'll push the button. Damn, if I can find it."

Carrick turned to Reese and Dak, worry almost sending him over the edge. "She sounds worse than before. When she gets the garage open, we're going in to help."

They both nodded and waited, ready to follow his lead.

When the door didn't open and another groan came through the phone, his patience snapped and he sprinted past Simone, ignoring her small shriek of alarm as she jerked to the side. He was counting on Dak and Reese to explain their presence and keep her calm.

Carrick squatted, wedged his fingers under the edge of the roll-up door and pulled, his quads bunching with the strain, his groan turning into a roar as metal screeched and the abnormally heavy door finally shot upward.

He strode into the garage, his eyes snapping to the woman sprawled on the floor near the door to the house, a large black and tan dog laying protectively at her side, ears and eyes alert but not aggressive.

The sight of his mate, of being this close to her, of seeing her with his own eyes, almost brought him to his knees. A primal voice he'd never heard before shocked him with a growled 'Mine!' in the back of his mind, and all the symptoms he'd experienced at Simone's rushed through him again with the force of a wildfire, quickly suppressed this time by concern for this woman.

In two strides he was next to her, crouching down while eyeing the larger than usual Belgian Malinois. He lay his hand on her shoulder, the zing up his arm at first contact almost knocking him on his ass.

It took every ounce of self-control he possessed not to pull her protectively into his arms where she belonged. He heard Dak attempt to reassure Simone, fibbing as he told her they'd been on their way to her house to check on her and Rachel, saw her leave, and followed her.

Carrick turned at the sound of Simone hyperventilating and knew they needed to calm her down. "Looks like your friend needs some help. Dak has his medical kit with him, and we'd like nothing more than to see if we can provide aid. I know you're a nurse, and Dak was a medic in the Army, as we explained before. Between the two of you, I'm sure we'll be able to help her."

They didn't have time to wait for Simone to wrap her head around the fact they'd followed her here, but he also didn't want to scare the hell out of her. He couldn't confess they had a mutual enemy, since she'd immediately know they'd been listening in on her conversation. He'd protect them and get both of them to open up.

"I know you have no reason to trust us…"

The feel of Nia's hand clutching his made that invisible connection snap to attention and set all his nerve endings on fire. She attempted to rise, oblivious to the fact it was a stranger she was grabbing, only to collapse to one knee, barely supporting herself with one long-fingered hand spread flat on the concrete floor.

"To hell with this." He dropped to one knee next to her, but not in time to catch her before she slid sideways and landed on her butt again. She grabbed her head and moaned as Carrick gripped her shoulders to keep her upright, then wrapped his arms around her when she slumped forward.

"What was *that*?" She jolted, then shivered at the contact, raising her head to peer through her unruly mass of curls, her eyes immediately snapping shut as she moaned and pushed ineffectually against him. "Who're you?"

"I'm Carrick." He glanced at Simone and fudged the truth, worry eating him up inside. "We know Simone, and we're here to help. Where are you hurt?"

He motioned a still-nervous Simone forward so she could reassure Nia, and made room for Dak as the big man dropped to his haunches on the other side of her. That other 'self' in his mind howled and demanded he take care of his mate, that he claim her and make her well.

Damn, if he didn't get his new primal-self under control and learn to tamp down that growly voice, no way would he be able to concentrate.

Was Nia as affected, physically and mentally, as he was? If so, did she feel the over-the-top sexual pull and sensations, the desire to hold on and never let go? That invisible connection linking them together? Probably not, considering her injury, pain and exhaustion.

Although, what with her jolt, her gasp at his touch and resulting confusion, she must have felt something too, and probably wondered what the heck was happening to her.

He watched as Nia pushed her hair out of the way, her eyes still tightly shut as she wrapped surprisingly strong fingers around his bicep, and a deeper protective urge hit him. That other voice growled in the back of his mind. Protect! Mine—ours. Mate!

Holy shit, that had to be the Garou side of him finally coming forth. His dad had mentioned it over a hundred years ago, that their wolven-side didn't make itself known until a man met his mate, but hell. He didn't realize it was like having another living being inside him. Even more fierce, possessive, primal and protective than his already admittedly alpha human-side.

Nia gasped and tightened her hold on him. "You need to help Rachel! She's in the house with her mother." Her eyes slit open, her gaze fixed on his pecs. "The dude is gone. I'm fine. Just go!"

It was apparent that, in her mind, she was back at Simone's, having just fought off Rachel's abductor. Still confused, she gave a weak shove to his shoulder and ordered him again to check on Rachel. Then, instead of pulling her hand away, she gripped his forearm and didn't let go.

She'd yet to look past his chest, her head cradled in one hand, her waterfall of chestnut corkscrew curls again hiding her face from him. A face he was dying to see.

"Dammit, what's wrong with me? Why won't you listen to me? Go! Rachel needs you more than I do."

He stroked a hand up and down her sinewy back in an attempt to cease her anxious ramblings. "She's being taken care of, Nia. Where are you hurt? Look, right over there, Simone and her daughter are here and she's worried about you. You're home, in your garage, remember?"

"Not hurt. Not bad, at least. I have to go. Can't let Denton find me. Not going back to that cell. Can't go to the hospital. Don't call anyone. Promise me!"

She struggled to rise again, clearly on the verge of panic at the thought of being recaptured, or being taken to the hospital, unaware she was safe, only to crumple against him again, still wrapped in his arms.

Carrick supported her head and back, laying her onto the ground on her side so Dak could examine her, his palm continuing to cradle her head, her curls covering all but her plump, sensuous lips. It was all he could do not to pull her back into his arms.

He slid his hand off her shoulder to grasp her bicep, muscle flexing under his hand. He gritted his teeth against the urge to snatch her up and take her home to the safety of his ranch.

A zing shot up his arm, straight to the core of his soul. Their connection inexorably tightened every time they touched, and that primal part of him growled another command to make her his, to protect her.

He ruthlessly tamped down the almost out-of-control surge of emotion and brushed away silky curls, finally revealing her stunning face, silently cursing his trembling fingers.

It mesmerized him when his fingertips grazed her cheek and her eyes popped open, making him captive to her gaze. He rocked back on his heels when their eyes locked, the brilliant green he'd seen reflected in her side mirror suddenly flecked with silver and red. Her whispered words revealed she indeed felt their connection.

"Holy shit, are you real? What is it about you? Do I know you? Do you feel that? Whoa, we're—linked somehow. Can I keep you?" She looked a little shocked at her words. "Oh god, did I say that out loud?"

His lips quirked to see her beautiful, otherworldly eyes widen when she realized she'd spoken her thoughts aloud. He was dimly aware of Reese murmuring for his ears only.

"That nails it, Carrick. Cinnabar Twin's eyes change just like that when their mate touches them, when they meet for the first time. Flecks of silver and red, just like cinnabar ore. It becomes permanent after they seal the mating."

Not only were they now positive she was a Garou's mate, a rare Cinnabar Twin, he was absofuckinglutely sure she was his. He welcomed this, hell, embraced it and didn't want to let her go. Had to convince her they belonged together.

Was she suffering because of the fight earlier? Or was she ill because of something Denton did when she was in his clutches? He'd kill the man if so. Hell, they planned to capture or kill him anyway, but if he'd fucked her up, Carrick would ensure he suffered before dying.

They needed to figure this shit out. He couldn't lose her now that he'd found her. And they needed Bah here, now. Dak could handle basic medical triage and treatment, but Bah specialized in Garou DNA, and more complex blood tests and treatments.

He turned to Dak, remembering he'd texted the doc earlier. "What did Bah say? Is he on his way? We need to know what Denton has done to both of them, and possibly Rachel, too. No wonder Simone wouldn't let them take her daughter to the hospital."

If he couldn't convince the ladies to move to his ranch, he was moving in with Nia. He couldn't risk losing her now.

He wouldn't survive finding and losing his mate.

Chapter Five

NIA GAVE a huff at the stubborn man when he refused to leave her side. Didn't he realize Rachel was more important? Frustration shot through her at being found before she could make her escape from Simone's house.

The strength and fortitude that had enabled her to stay one step ahead of Denton this past year had failed her tonight when instead of making it to her vehicle and safety, she'd instead fallen and lay breathless with dizziness and pain. The cool, hard floor soothed her battered temple, but did nothing to ease the pounding in her skull.

Wait. Cool floor? Should be grass. Wasn't she on Simone's lawn?

When she clutched an impressive bicep, she flinched in shock at the physical and psychical zing that shot through her body, hitting every erogenous zone she had, and even some she'd not known about. Her headache was muted instantly, and all but forgotten.

What was it about this guy? She could count her sexual experience with men on one hand—to be honest, on two fingers—and they'd been lukewarm at best. One had been over a year before her run-in with Denton and his minions, and the other just before. That asshole was the reason Denton's crew had captured her. Not a strong endorsement for interactions with the opposite sex, that's for sure.

With this big guy, though, not only couldn't she bring herself to remove her hand from his boulder of a bicep, that weird thread or connection was growing stronger by the second, and it was all she could do not to lean into him and beg him to sweep her away.

When he wrapped strong, blunt-tipped fingers around her bicep just above her elbow, she was sure somehow the sensation was tattooed on her skin. Damn, a double jolt of possessiveness about swallowed her whole.

What was *that* all about? She'd never had a possessive bone in her body and wasn't sure she liked the feeling. This connection was interesting, though, considering the only other connection she'd ever had with anyone was with her sister, who was more like a twin to her than a sibling born two years apart.

When he brushed the hair from her face, she cracked her eyes open and leaned into the caress, suddenly eager to get a clear look at him. The spectacle of pure male perfection crouching over her captivated her.

He wasn't traditionally handsome; no, this big guy had a hard-planed, angular face. Extremely masculine. Meet him in a dark alley and she'd be booking it out the other end. Regardless, she drank him in and couldn't take her eyes off him. "Wow."

The answering molten heat that flashed through his eyes, the flush streaking across his hard cheekbones and the slight clench of that big hand clearly told her he was just as affected by her as she was him.

It's a good thing I'm already down, 'cause I'd have fallen right at his feet at his first touch. Hell, at her first eyeful of this guy, and begged him to never let go. She wanted that chiseled body up against hers. Preferably sans clothing. Damn, she didn't want to look away from those captivating, otherworldly silver eyes.

His voice was a deep rumble, and she could swear she felt the vibration emanate from his diaphragm, down his arm to hers, directly into her soul. "Just stay there and try to relax, you're not at Simone's, you're home and Rachel is safe. See?"

The jerk of his head to the area behind him unlocked her gaze, and she glanced around until Simone and her little girl swam into focus. She gasped and reached out a shaking hand. "Simone? What's…?"

She groaned and swallowed convulsively as another wave of nausea hit, willing the sickness down to a manageable level. She did not want to lose the contents of her stomach in front of this Adonis.

She needed answers—needed an energy drink even more—but also wanted to know what the heck was going on. "What happened? Why are you here, with Simone? Who are you guys?"

Her confusion was almost as painful as the rockets shooting off in her skull, and her second attempt at sitting up went the way of the first when she made it upright, only to pitch forward and land again in his arms.

The feel of bulging biceps and muscular forearms sent another jolt through her already overwhelmed system as they circled her waist and he went from propped on one knee to sitting right there on her garage floor, pulling her onto his lap and settling her onto his tree-trunk quads.

But wait—the big man said she wasn't at Simone's. Gah! This confusion was killing her. She tore her gaze away from Simone and Rachel, braced a hand on his broad shoulder and leaned back in the loose circle of his arms to look around.

At the sight of her Land Cruiser across the garage, memories of making it home safely and then collapsing rushed forward and coalesced, finally in the correct sequence of events, with the memories of the attack and attempted abduction of that sweet little girl slotted where they belonged.

Still dizzy, but caught up with where she was and why, Nia brought her eyes around again to the man holding her almost possessively on his mammoth, muscled quads. The stubborn man held her securely, and she realized she was right where she wanted to be.

She sighed and tucked her head into the warm cleft between his shoulder and bristly jaw, breathing in his enticing scent and succumbing to the pain, fear and exhaustion. He tightened those magnificent arms around her, and as her fingers clenched on his bicep, she could swear he growled 'mine'.

His growl sounded just like Max. Max! Where was he? Her furry bodyguard had been woozy, just like her, as they'd stumbled across the lawn at Simone's. She reminded herself once again she was home, though, and would never have left without Max, so he must be here somewhere. Then why wasn't he growling to keep these strangers at bay?

"Max. Where's Max?" She pulled her head back a bit, this time not attempting to remove herself from the safety of his arms. Her focus fractured, and she jolted as she felt that silken web solidifying between them. She would swear it irrevocably weaved them together. What the ever-loving hell?

"Who's Max?" The muscled giant sounded pissed and suspicious. Almost—jealous?

"My dog." She couldn't keep the snap from her voice. She knew he was just trying to help, but she had to make sure Max was here and safe. With one hand clutching her aching head and the other braced on his broad shoulder, she eased around to see Max lying a half a foot away, head on paws, the picture of healthy, unconcerned canine.

Locking his watchful eyes on the stubborn man, Max then tracked to her before giving a slight thump of his tail as if in approval. The fact her furry buddy hadn't taken a bite out of him shocked her.

Her canine protector let no man get close to her. That wag and relaxed look in his intelligent eyes told her right there he approved of not only this big guy, but everyone in her garage.

Unbearably weary, and trusting Max to know enemy from friend, Nia leaned back into the big guy's comforting embrace, closed her eyes and tucked her head back under his chin, marveling he was big enough she actually felt petite in his arms.

She attempted to banish the next thought that slipped and settled into her mind. That she felt like she was finally home, wrapped in those muscular arms. That she belonged to him. Just as he belonged to her.

Where the heck did that thought come from? She belonged to no one. No longer trusted men. Couldn't risk letting down her defenses.

Her eyes popped open again at the feel of cool fingertips on her wrist, competently taking her pulse. Not her savior's, though. One of the other giants. She felt no response to his touch, other than someone caring for her.

She glanced sideways to see a stern-looking man even larger than Carrick looking at a big-faced, complicated watch on a sinewy wrist before glancing up to pin her with eyes the color of the darkest chocolate set into a striking face with skin of the richest mahogany.

When he spoke, he used words as if he had to pay a fee for each one. "Check your eyes, yeah? Look here." He pointed to his nose, penlight in hand.

Nia turned her head obediently to face him, looking at his bold nose as instructed, and quelled a flinch when the penlight in his hand flicked on and he moved the bright light from eye to eye.

He grunted and looked at Carrick. "Pupils are fine. Gotta nasty bruise and cut there. Need a butterfly on it."

She closed her eyes again, weary all the way to her bones. "I'll be fine. I didn't eat or hydrate enough today, and the adrenaline during the fight depleted me. Not to mention that lucky pop to my head. Ever since Dent... uh, when my blood sugar and electrolytes deplete, I get this way. Just need my energy drink, then some food. And a couple ibuprofen for this damn headache."

The stubborn man continued as if she hadn't even spoken.

"Should hook her up to a glucose & electrolyte IV, get her hydrated."

Nia flinched at the thought of a needle in her arm and cracked open one eye to shoot the medic a stern look. "No needle. No way. Just need to replenish. I've got something in my backpack that'll help."

She let out a sigh of pleasure to feel Carrick's callused fingers trail along her jawline before gently tugging just enough to turn her face toward him.

"An IV will do the job faster. I promise there's nothing harmful in it."

She groaned and closed her eyes as another wave of dizziness and pain rolled through her head, dampening but certainly not obliterating the connection she felt for this big stranger.

"Please." She hated the pleading tone in her voice but was almost at the end of what little strength she had left and just wanted to swig an energy drink, maybe two, and get inside to rest. "Just grab a bottle out of my bag and get me into the house. I'll feel better about ten minutes after drinking it. Can't stand needles."

She'd learned soon after escaping that whatever experiments Denton had run on her caused her to burn through her reserves at an almost unmanageable rate. She'd started carrying bottles, whenever she left the house, filled with her own concoction of glucose, protein, creatine, BCAAs, betaine and beet juice, along with fifty milligrams of caffeine.

When she raised her eyes to his, she once again felt like she'd finally come home. Absolutely ridiculous. Must be the injury messing with her emotions.

His eyes drew her in, never having seen eyes such a light gray, appearing almost silver, rimmed with a skinny ring of darkest blue. Eyes that light against his cinnamon skin tone were beautiful. She idly wondered what mix of races he was, then gave a mental shrug. Family trees had fascinated her for years—probably because half of hers was a mystery—she and her sister were clearly a mix of races. It didn't matter, other than the results on this man were *wowza*.

She shivered to see another flash of lust and heat darken his eyes to molten mercury, causing her girl-bits to pulse and heat blast to through her, her body burning just for him. *How is this even possible?*

She felt a small, gentle hand on her shoulder just before Simone handed her the bottle she'd requested. "Rachel's fine, Nia. Let's worry about you and get into the house. Dak is a medic, so between him and me, we'll get you back on your feet. These are the guys emergency response sent when you called nine-one-one. First, though, did you turn the alarm on your property back on?"

"Yes, but please close the garage door. My phone will unlock the kitchen door."

"Roger that."

She turned her head at the deep voice and noticed the guy behind Carrick rivaled him in size, and had similar features, and had her phone in his hand, his face lit up like a kid at Christmas. *Brothers, cousins?*

He glanced at her, then back at her phone. "Did you set up your own security? This shit rocks. I've never seen an app like this before." He must have found the app her sister had created, and with a tap of his finger, the garage door lowered. The snick of the locks on the kitchen door showed he had no trouble navigating her app. Smart dude.

"Yes, did personal protection and my sis was the tech geek, covered electronic security; we had our own company. This is her design. Learned from her. Sensors on the gate, property and house, with AI recognition of anything detected. No false alarms when animals are on the property. Facial recognition, too."

Before she had a chance to ask him to crack open the bottle Simone had handed her, Carrick rose effortlessly, with her held securely in his arms. At her height and weight—she was five-ten and a muscular 165—the man must be strong as an ox to rise using only his quads and glutes.

What was her fascination with this guy, anyway? Shouldn't strangers in her house concern her, even if Simone vouched for them? Instead of terror at Denton possibly reacquiring her, though, all she wanted was to stay in this man's arms. And maybe sometime soon, get naked and busy with him.

If only she weren't so shaky and didn't feel like puking her guts up, she'd fantasize about that. Better to concentrate on keeping the contents of her stomach firmly where they belonged. Deciding to go with the flow and trust Simone's judgement, and her pup's, she kept her eyes closed and head firmly nestled in the crook of his neck, letting the conversation wash around her as she breathed in the intoxicating musk of his warm skin.

She didn't even have the strength to open her eyes when they stopped just inside the kitchen door, the big guy's rumbly voice vibrating against her breast. "Wait Simone. Reese clear the house. Dak will follow, and we'll get Nia settled so he can do a more thorough exam. Then you both need to fill us in on what's going on. Nia mentioned Denton. It seems we all have a mutual enemy, folks, and I can tell you right now, he won't give up. You're vulnerable alone. Let's get a plan together to protect the three of you. Especially since we think he or his enforcers are in the area."

Nia jerked at the mention of her tormentor's name, a groan erupting when the pounding in her head ramped up at the spike of fear and sudden movement. "Denton!" she hissed. "Just who are you people?"

"I want an answer to that, too." Tension laced Simone's voice again.

Nia wondered if she and her newfound friend had just stepped into the fire, or if these guys were truly allies. Trusting her gut and her dog, she tamped down her urge to interrogate them when Reese spoke up and ushered them inside.

"All clear. Couch okay, Dak?"

"Yeah, get her settled. Simone? How 'bout you and Rachel over on that love seat. Reese, you're on guard. Carrick? Yeah, you're on her other side, man."

When Carrick leaned down to place Nia on the couch, she inadvertently tightened her grip on his big bicep, subconsciously not wanting to leave the haven of his arms.

Her actions had an immediate and wonderful consequence when, instead of setting her on the couch, he pivoted and sat with her on those muscly quads again. Her sigh of relief garnered a gentle squeeze and reassurance.

"I've got you, baby."

Chapter Six

CARRICK HAD every intention of setting Nia on the couch so Dak could do his thing, but when the grip on his bicep clearly signified, at least to him, she wanted to stay in his arms, he turned and sat, her heart-shaped butt a sensuous weight on his quads.

He eyed her big furry shadow as the Malinois sniffed around the living room, giving Dak and Reese a once-over before stopping in front of Carrick, paws up on the couch next to his legs to stare into his eyes, as if judging whether he was worthy of protecting his mistress. Carrick held the canine's gaze and tried to reassure him with a calm, confident alpha look that conveyed *I've got your six, and your pack member's, too.*

It must have done the job, because with a swipe of Max's tongue across the hand cupping Nia's hip, the dog dropped to the ground to lay a foot or so away, head on paws, eyes tracking from one person to another, relaxed but clearly on guard.

Carrick let out a breath he hadn't realized he'd been holding, knowing Max's opinion would inform Nia's, and needing the big canine to accept him.

Especially since, if he had anything to say about it, he would be around them both from here on out.

He released the tight rein he had on his emotions and thoughts, allowing them to riot and hope that, unless he was way off the mark, she was aware of him on a cellular level, felt the invisible web that was weaving them together, and was slowly accepting it, even if she didn't understand it. He'd bet his ranch she felt the same intrinsic belonging, the same soul searing longing—not to mention the out-of-this-world sexual pull—he did.

His mate. It was astounding, and the thought he'd awaken and this would all have been a dream terrified him. A tap on the back of his head had him jerking out of his thoughts and turning to see Reese shoot him a chin lift, along with a look that clearly said 'get your head out of your ass' before his brother headed into the kitchen.

Yeah, he needed to get his head on straight if they were going to ensure Nia was on the road to recovery and get her secured at his ranch, regardless how much convincing it took, along with Simone and Rachel. He would make damn sure Denton didn't get his blood-stained hands on them again and went down for his crimes and cruelty. No matter what, or how long, it took.

Considering Nia was a Cinnabar Twin, and no doubt Simone was too, it wasn't at all odd they ended up in New Almaden near the ore in the old cinnabar mines, even if they were oblivious to the draw. The mines were within a mile of where they all lived, which is why he and other Garou also lived in this area.

He considered it a fucking miracle she'd ended up here, just down the road from him, considering there were so many other locations with cinnabar ore deposits not only in the United States, but across the world. It was a known fact among their people; being near the ore strengthened them, lengthened their lives, and sharpened their senses.

Throughout time, you could find Garou settlements near cinnabar mines all over the world. The Quicksilver Garou were hard-wired by their DNA to gravitate to and live near the ore.

The discovery of Cinnabar Twins was astounding, though, and he wondered at Denton's role in triggering, in both Nia and Simone, whatever it was in Cinnabar Twins that once upon a time allowed the male Garou to identify their mates when nearby. To experience the very symptoms that had almost knocked him on his ass earlier. That he was *still* experiencing. It was a miracle Garou could once again find their mates because of Denton's machinations. *How many women had Denton altered and experimented on? A few? Several. Hell, hundreds?*

He felt horrified and hopeful at the same time, with his thoughts continually looping back to two things—he couldn't believe he'd found his mate, and there had to be more women out there. More in captivity they needed to find and free, by God.

This wasn't just a case of keeping these women and the child safe. It would turn into a war—was in reality already a war—for survival, where they had to plan their strategy and, with Garou forces, rescue prisoners and keep them safe and housed as well. But they had to up their game and timelines. It was earth-shattering, and although horrifying, had a silver lining that bode well for the longevity of the Garou—

the ability for mates to find each other, have children and prevent them from dying out.

He glanced at Simone, wondering who her mate was, if it was someone he knew, as slim a possibility as that was. There were still hundreds, possibly thousands, of Garou spread across the globe.

Maybe more since there was no formal census or records tracking them, other than the database Ramil had started recently, locked tight on a server with no internet access in the bowels of their Sonoma site.

They had to take care in releasing this information, or every single Garou male in the world would show up in New Almaden in the hopes Simone, or any captives they rescued, was their mate.

Dak's voice brought him out of his head. "Share your story, Nia."

Carrick suppressed a sigh at Dak's customary stinginess with words.

"Open this first, please." Nia handed Carrick the energy drink she'd been clutching in her trembling hand all this time.

Dak reached for it instead, removed the cap and handed both back. They waited while she chugged half the liquid, replaced the lid, then stirred in his lap to get more comfortable. Carrick tenderly brushed a lock of hair from her face, trailed his hand down her muscled arm, and linked his fingers with hers to provide comfort and solidarity.

She gave two pats to his pec. "I'll feel better soon, don't worry."

The foreign, anxious and possessive emotions currently making him want to climb the walls and howl settled when she relaxed more fully against him and, instead of pulling her hand from his, tightened her hold on his fingers.

Carrick explained what they needed to know, narrowing her narrative. "What Dak means is how do you know Denton, Nia? What experiments did he run? If he gave you drugs, any chance you know what they were? How long since you escaped? We'll get Simone's story after yours."

He ran a hand down her toned back, stopping short at the swell of her pert ass and back up again to her shoulder, careful not to take liberties that would make her uncomfortable.

As much as he craved getting his hands on her body, he understood and believed firmly in consent and would never step over that line. Didn't mean he wouldn't take advantage of their Garou to Cinnabar Twin bond, though, and encourage her to reciprocate his affection.

He wanted more than her body, though. He wanted her trust. Eventually, he wanted her love.

"You said you've been wondering if you've been unwell because of what he'd done to you. Dak, or the doctor heading to New Almaden from Sonoma, may need this info to help you."

When she hesitated before speaking, he looked down to see her glance at Simone, who gave a slight nod in silent agreement or permission. He felt her tense slightly before she relaxed again and began talking, her first words a warning to him and his buddies.

"For two women who've had friends, and a boyfriend, betray them," Nia said, a touch of bitterness coloring her husky voice, "we're banking on you all being as trustworthy as you seem. Max isn't alerting and seems to trust you, too. I'm counting on having a mutual enemy gives us a common cause."

He gave a gentle, reassuring squeeze of the fingers twined with his. "You bet your ass we're trustworthy, and you, Simone and Rachel can now consider yourselves under our protection. Denton has been after us for years and has gotten a few of us alone. We've had three disappearances over the last two years I'm attributing to the bastard. Which is why we moved to New Almaden. A couple of men disappeared from this area about seven months ago."

"You said 'us'. Do you mean your family, or friends?" All eyes leveled on Simone when she gave them a hard-eyed look, daring them to prevaricate or outright lie.

Reese jumped in. "We'll get into that after we hear your story, promise. It'll tie in with why Denton abducted and experimented on you both."

When Nia shifted and groaned in pain, Carrick tucked her closer, moving his hand resting on her shoulder to massage the back of her neck, her groan turning from one of pain to relief.

"Ohhh, that feels so good. The caffeine in my drink should help soon, too."

Carrick turned to Simone. "Go ahead and fill us in while Dak gets Nia's vitals, and I see if I can get her neck to relax and the headache to back off. Then Nia can continue, if she's up to it. Dak can decide on other tests needed, or if we should wait for Bah."

Simone gave Carrick a considering look before launching into her story. "I have lupus." She turned to Nia. "You too?"

At Nia's slight nod, Simone continued her story. "About eighteen months ago, I had an odd flare, with symptoms worse than usual, the sensitivity to UV light much worse than before. It had been years since I'd seen a doctor for this disease; had been in remission, managing it myself without medication through nutrition and supplements, and completely shunning UV."

She turned and pressed a gentle kiss to Rachel's freckled temple, then continued. "I made an appointment with a new rheumatologist, who ordered blood tests to check the usual ANA/DNA levels, antibodies to histone, ANA Screen Reflex to Cascade, along with skin biopsies, because the lesions didn't resemble the usual lupus rash. The results differed vastly from a typical lupus patient. Apparently, they differed from a typical human, however I didn't find that out until later. After they'd grabbed me."

Dak turned from Nia to glance at Simone. "Where was this?"

"Bend, Oregon. I'd been living there for about four years, was an RN at a small practice near downtown. The rheumatologist ordered the tests redone; thought the lab had screwed up. He sent me to a new lab, and they took me into a room at the back of the building. The technician had no sooner shut the door than I smelled something sweet and blacked out. I woke at the facility in the middle of the Umpqua National Forest, on a large ranch that was converted into Denton's compound. They'd converted a huge metal outbuilding, probably was a barn, into their lab and cells.

Reese looked like he wanted to kill someone. He turned to Nia. "Is that where you were, too?"

"Yes." Nia's voice quivered on that one word.

Carrick broke in, noticing Simone was flagging, her arms trembling from holding her daughter for so long. Even small, the weight would become unbearable after a while, especially with Simone so petite and her daughter on the big-side. Must take after the dad. Rachel was out for the count and not liable to wake anytime soon. "Simone, why don't you relax on the love seat and lay Rachel down? You look like you're about to collapse."

As if she'd only just noticed how exhausted she was, Simone swayed and plunked herself down on the small couch. She gently laid her daughter next to her, outstretching one leg in front of the child to keep her from rolling off, then pulled a fleece throw from the back to drape it across the sleeping child. She leaned back on the couch and ran a finger across her daughter's curly red hair, so unlike her own straight, ebony locks.

"As I mentioned, the second lab I went to was different than the one I'd gone to before. They supposedly specialized in drawing blood for and analyzing autoimmune diseases there on site with a quick turnaround. I woke in a soundproof, concrete cell. Denton came in and explained rather cryptically that I had DNA of an ancient race, and that the odd strain of Lupus was a result. He wouldn't expound on it, though. The most he would tell me was he suspected some virus years ago had ravaged people who carried this DNA, and had altered the survivors somehow; they weren't detectable, whatever that means. His mission, as he called it, was to turn back on whatever had been switched off. Only he wouldn't tell me what 'detectable' meant, nor what the consequences would be."

She hesitated, and then continued. "My skin is more sensitive to the sun now and my eyesight is more acute, with the benefit that I no longer need to wear glasses. I'm also stronger than I used to be, although I become exhausted faster, and my endurance isn't what it used to be. Not as wiped out as Nia gets, but I still need to be careful how much energy I use, or I wind up in bed. With a toddler, that's hard to manage."

Nia stirred and spoke up, her husky voice going straight to Carrick's heart and libido.

"The consequences for me are intermittent exhaustion, more so than is typical for Lupus. If I expend a great deal of energy, or have an adrenaline spike, I'm incapacitated. That's why I carry my energy drinks with me wherever I go."

She gave Max a fond look before continuing. "As strange as it sounds, I can also sense when Max wants me to do something. Any canine, actually, domestic or wild. It's like we communicate without speaking. I know, that sounds absurd, but it's true. My hearing is better, and my sense of smell more acute. The fucker told me that the experiments were to alter my DNA so that what he called our 'male counterparts' could detect us within a certain range, and definitely when we touch."

At Simone's gasp, Nia turned to her with a commiserating look. "I'm betting he didn't share that bit of info with you."

"No, he didn't, the ass." Simone looked mad enough to chew nails.

Nia gave a nod in agreement, her eyes sparking with ire. "He was using stem cell therapy, said he had cells from before the virus hit from mummified remains he'd found thawing in permafrost, somewhere in the Northwest Territories in Canada. He used stem cell IV therapy, and also the much more painful intrathecal method—one of the nurses was sympathetic and shared technical details with me."

Carrick tightened the arm draped around Nia's shoulders when she shuddered from the wicked memories. She needed comfort, and he could no more ignore her needs than breathe under water.

Dak looked up with a scowl from monitoring Nia's blood pressure. "Oh, man. Intrathecal means lumbar injections. In the spine. Hurts like hell."

Carrick couldn't suppress a growl at that news. The thought of Nia suffering through the injections, and whatever else Denton had done, infuriated him. "Fucker will know what pain is when I'm done with him."

Simone sighed and nodded. "Hurt like the devil, and he seemed to get off on our pain."

Nia grimaced and nodded. "Denton wasn't aware narcotics don't work on me as well as other people, takes way more to knock me out, so I faked being unconscious while he held discussions with the doctor. Sometimes I'd be completely out during the infusions, and other times not. He said there was a group called the garoe or something, and they were the ones he was targeting. That he wanted to breed us so the offspring would be like the ancient race, not the lesser hybrid out there now. Although I have no idea what the differences between the two are. He didn't expound on that."

Dak jerked up at her words. "Motherfucker. Could that be where our guys disappeared to? Could Denton have them, and they aren't dead? And what's this about an ancient race?"

Simone and Nia focused wide eyes on Dak and asked practically in unison, "You're garoe, or however you pronounce it, aren't you?"

When they didn't answer right away, Nia sat up straight on his quads, turned her head and looked up at Carrick.

"Just who the hell are you? And what are garoe?"

Chapter Seven

NIA WATCHED as Carrick turned to Dak, then Reese, before answering. "Yeah, we're Garou. You're pronouncing it correctly, and it's spelled G A R O U. The virus Denton mentioned affected females with your DNA, known as Cinnabar Twins. They weren't Garou, but they had that special DNA and odd lupus strain too, and these women are, for want of a better word, our mates. There's one person out there who matches to one Garou male. Mates aren't always hetero, but for mates that are male/female, the male can only have offspring with their mate. Also, they feel connected, their bond is physical, mental and psychical, and after they complete the mating, each wants nothing more than to be with the other, to protect them and make them happy. Not subservient, but a soul deep empathy, compassion, and passion for their mate. We can share more history and details later. Let Dak run his tests first, okay? Do you need another of your drinks?"

She glanced down at the empty bottle, her hand still trembling a little, and nodded. "Yes, I could use another one. The first isn't working as well as usual.

And we'll wait for additional information, but I'd like to hear it tonight or tomorrow at the latest."

Carrick gave her hand a squeeze. "Absolutely, Nia. Full disclosure. We don't have any reason to hide anything or keep secrets from either of you."

Dak gave her a nod and agreed. "Yes, tonight. Reese, just water. Nia, I need a urine sample to run the tests; should have done it before you had your first drink. Afterwards, you can drink or eat whatever you want. Need to check your urine calcium-to-creatinine level. That'll tell me if you're deficient in calcium. If so, that could mean a Vitamin D deficiency. Common in people with Lupus. Your energy drink is a good start, but there's a history of deficiencies in women with your DNA, with symptoms similar to yours. It could be you feel like crap not only from adrenaline overload and energetic activity, but from these deficiencies, too. If your tests turn out the way I expect they will, we need to get you started on a special supplement I have."

Nia didn't know what to think. These men seemed above board, and what they were telling her wasn't all that outlandish, considering a mad scientist had kidnapped her and Simone, and had experimented on them. Told them they had weird ancient DNA and had mentioned the garoe himself. Although Denton had mentioned nothing about Cinnabar Twins.

She pushed away from Carrick's chest, her hands wanting to linger as if they had a mind of their own, and slipped from his lap to sit on the couch next to him.

Noting Carrick's reluctance to release her didn't help; it made her want to settle back on those hard quads and let someone else have her back, let this weird link she felt with him solidify and continue to strengthen as it had since he'd first touched her in the garage.

As trite and cliché as it sounded, it was like she'd been an incomplete puzzle, with myriad pieces missing, and when they'd touched, all those missing pieces had fallen from the sky and locked into place, making her whole again.

And revved up her libido and desire to never let this man go.

Nia wanted nothing more than to stay in Carrick's arms, but being needy and meek was never her schtick. She felt better after downing most of her homemade energy drink, along with that amazing neck massage, and the chance to just sit still, catch her breath, and replenish her reserves.

Sure, she needed another energy drink, and felt like she could sleep for a week, but thankfully didn't feel like she was going to face plant anymore. And thank god, she no longer felt she was going to lose her stomach.

She gave herself a mental slap and welcomed the nudge to her hand from Max. She hadn't noticed him getting up from the floor, but knew he'd sensed her rising tension and was reassuring her he was there and ready to protect her.

Her sweet boy had been watchful but calm during their discussion so far, which was unlike him. He was normally a fierce protector, but Max must feel an affinity for these men and understood they would help him keep her safe.

As ridiculous as it seemed, Max seemed to consider them now part of his pack and was sharing his alpha role with the big man next to her, which was unheard of.

At the feel of Carrick's thick fingers squeezing hers, she glanced at his starkly masculine face, captivated once again by the heat flashing through those molten silver eyes.

"Thank you." Nia took the glass of water from Reese, took a couple of long sips, then passed the bottle to Carrick when Dak handed her a specimen container.

Dak spoke up again. "Before you head to the bathroom, what other symptoms have you had, if any?"

Nia answered first. "I used to be energetic and in pretty good shape, even with Lupus."

"You're still in good shape." Carrick raised an eyebrow at her sidelong glance.

"I trained in a variety of martial arts, was successful in my personal protection gig, and aside from the typical annoying Lupus symptoms and occasional flares, since I escaped Denton I've been feeling even greater fatigue, have bone pain, muscle weakness and cramps, and tingling in my face and hands off and on. And I'm frequently dizzy. I also have no reserves left. Absolutely none. As I mentioned, if I have an adrenaline rush or exert myself too much and don't compensate by staying hydrated and eating frequently, or downing a couple of my drinks, I collapse like I did this evening. Although not quite as bad. I think the pop to the head, and terror at seeing that guy crawl out the window with Rachel, exacerbated it."

She hesitated, embarrassed to admit this symptom. "And I'm depressed, where I've never really had that issue before."

She looked at Simone. "Any other symptoms you haven't shared?"

Simone frowned. "Pretty much the same, though as I mentioned, my exhaustion isn't as extreme as yours. I was wondering if it was something Denton had done, but no way could I go to a hospital."

Nia nodded in agreement, then added with a bite to her voice. "Knowing any blood tests could result in being back at the Denton Hotel From Hell, I've been trying to treat my own symptoms and hope I don't fall over dead one day from what he's done to me."

Reese glanced from Nia to Simone. "That's why you wouldn't let them take Rachel to the hospital for blood tests. You're afraid she has the same anomalies you do and that Denton or one of his goons would find you."

Simone inclined her head. "Yes, or that the lab wouldn't know how to interpret her tests and would want to keep her in the hospital to run more. I can't risk anyone finding out and it getting back to him."

Dak interrupted Simone and turned to Nia. "Need that sample now."

She nodded, reluctant to leave Carrick's side, which was totally ridiculous. She was an independent, strong woman who didn't need anyone by her side.

Especially when she was relieving her bladder! But, just maybe, it wasn't about need. Maybe it was about this mysterious, inexorable link she now felt, and her desire to get him to herself.

Oh, she supposed it didn't hurt that she apparently had backup now; all three of these huge, protective guys. Especially if Denton was as much a threat as they seemed to think.

It just rankled that she wasn't able to defend herself, or Simone and Rachel. Wasn't strong enough anymore to go up against the threat Denton and his bullyboys posed.

No way was she going to end up back in that cell with his fucking needles, at his mercy. And definitely not at the mercy of whatever plans he had to impregnate her.

Nia clenched her hands together, remembering the IV treatments Denton had put her through, and shuddered at the thought of the other, more painful injections in her spine.

"Hey, baby." Carrick covered her clenched fists, his thumb caressing the back of one hand, calming her immediately. "I'm not gonna let that bastard at you again. You're safe with us. I'll make damned sure you get well and stay safe. You have my word, and my protection."

His vow slid through her like warm honey, chasing away the chill that had permeated her soul since her abduction and subsequent escape.

And although she'd never been one to be swayed by endearments, him calling her 'baby' just made their link seem even stronger. More than just a man protecting someone in need.

She sensed this big guy could be deadly. Not only deadly, but fierce in his determination and skill in thwarting his enemies. And in protecting those he loved.

Not that he loved her, but this connection they shared tied them together somehow. She quashed the brief flash of hope and desire that a man like Carrick could want her, love her. That her strength, independence, and intelligence wouldn't threaten his masculinity.

His eyes mirrored his verbal vow, along with— was that affection mixed with that swirling, passionate desire? Just crazy, but she was stellar at reading people; had to be in her previous life, and it was plain as day—this man was devoted to her. Even if they'd met only an hour ago.

Although, she reminded herself, the last man she'd trusted had betrayed her in the worst way, and she hadn't caught on until it was much too late. So, she would be cautiously optimistic.

She unclenched her hands, leaned into his side and pressed a kiss to his cheek, surprising the hell out of both of them. Covering her embarrassment, she jerked back with a wince, ignored the twinge of pain in her head, and pushed to her feet with his help.

Carrick immediately started to rise, but she pressed a hand to his impossibly broad shoulder. "I really am feeling better. Not dizzy anymore. Just a little headache still. I'll be fine, big guy."

With the small container clutched in one hand, she walked slowly and carefully down the hall to the bathroom, not wanting to face plant and give lie to her assertion she could make it on her own.

She entered and locked the door, hearing the murmur of Simone's soft voice in the background as she no doubt continued her story. She would ask Simone to repeat anything she'd missed.

As she washed her hands, she peered into the mirror above the sink and cringed. "Whoa, girl!"

Her pale visage stared back at her, her normally copper toned skin just this side of jaundice, despair warring with hope in her eyes, and sensual wonder for her protector who was currently, if she wasn't mistaken by the creak of that loose board on the floor in the hallway, making his way quietly down to the bathroom to ensure she hadn't lied through her teeth about being okay.

She placed a washcloth on the counter, opened the container and set it on the cloth, stepped to the toilet, pulled her leggings and panties down, then grabbed the plastic cup and peed in it to get the sample Dak asked for, too tired to care if Carrick heard her tinkle into it.

Finished, she reversed her actions, part of her annoyed at Carrick for ignoring her assertion she didn't need help and parking himself outside the door, no doubt listening to her do her business.

She'd told him she was okay, didn't she? The last thing she needed was an overprotective, bossy man in her life.

Then she reminded herself she'd been abducted, had barely escaped, then secured herself in this small fortress, and today thwarted a kidnapping, been punched in the head for her troubles, passed out when she made it home and needed rescuing.

Not to mention the mad scientist who'd taken her and Simone was the very guy who'd apparently been dogging Carrick and his buddies, the Garou who were mates to women like her and Simone.

Add to that mix the fact her new DNA and his Garoe genes linked them somehow—causing the bond he was describing? Out of all the people in the world, fate would have to be working overtime to ensure mate's paths crossed. So far, fate had fucked everything up. She wasn't about to believe in it now.

Put all this in a box, tie it up with a big purple bow—for lupus of course—and no wonder he was protective and ignoring her comment she could make it to the bathroom by herself. If she were he, she wouldn't have believed her either.

Well, dipshit, she scolded herself, what was there to do? Don't be the stupid, absurdly stubborn girl-who-goes-into-the-basement-to-die in the horror flick, that's what.

Go along with it, with him. Let them help her. Protect her, Simone and Rachel. The alternative? Land back in Club Denton. No fucking way.

Done with her business, and resigned to not be a stubborn twit, she left the container on the counter per Dak's instructions and opened the door to find Carrick leaning against the hall wall, muscular arms crossed over his massive chest, tree-trunk thighs encased in BDUs that didn't hide their musculature one iota, one combat-booted foot crossed over an ankle. A sexy six-foot plus package. She'd be afraid she was drooling if her mouth hadn't gone dry at the sight of him.

She looked her fill as they stood there staring at each other, their friends and family unable to see them. His stance showcased his massive quads, and she let her gaze travel up, lingering on the equally impressive bulge behind the zipper of his cargo pants—damn, girl—before burning a trail across the washboard abs clearly visible under the well-worn t-shirt tucked in his pants, before trekking up to muscular forearms crossed over those deliciously massive pecs, biceps to drool over, to his strong, corded neck that led to clenched jaws and finally, to be trapped by the fire in his molten silver eyes.

"Baby, you can't eat me up with your eyes and expect me to behave," he rumbled before pushing away from the wall, taking her face in his broad callused palms before pausing, clearly asking permission with those molten eyes.

At her small nod of acquiescence, he took her lips in a possessive, wholly sensuous kiss that blasted through every wall she'd ever erected. Heat swept through her body and set her pussy and clit to throbbing, as if he was teasing *it* with his talented lips instead of her mouth.

When his tongue invaded, she wrapped her arms around that strong neck, smashing her breasts against his pecs, his enormous cock pulsing against her tummy, then dueled her tongue with his, giving as good as she got, wondering how she'd made it through life never having a man wreak such delicious havoc to her senses.

How she'd not known kissing could bring her to the brink of orgasm. If his kiss set her on fire, what would happen to her when he got her naked and pressed that long, thick cock into her core? And why was she thinking that was a done deal?

When he gently pulled away, peppering kisses on her cheek, her eyelids, then the tip of her nose, she slumped against him, her trembling legs threatening to drop her on her ass.

She jolted when he scooped her up in those muscular arms she couldn't stop obsessing over, and strode down the hallway into the living room.

Resigned to giving herself into his care and trying to tamp down the fire he'd set to every erogenous zone she had, she stopped fighting it and let him do his alpha-protector thing.

She turned her face into his shoulder, confused, turned on, and still tired as hell. "I don't understand what's happening between us, but I do trust you."

"I'll explain. And thank you for your trust." He settled her back on the couch, touched a callused finger to her cheek, then turned and strode into the kitchen to retrieve her second energy drink, returned, uncapped it and handed it to her before sitting next to her again, fingers twining with hers as naturally as if they'd been together for years instead of less than an hour.

Max stayed alert but calm and gave a single wag of his tail when Carrick sat, and Simone stopped her recitation of events. Nia gave her a reassuring smile as she settled comfortably onto the cushions and leaned against his side.

No sooner had Carrick sat beside her, Dak disappeared down the hallway with his bag, no doubt to do that strip test he'd mentioned.

Carrick's rumbly voice caught her attention. "I get that you and Simone have been doing a good job of staying off the radar and hidden, but we don't know if Denton is behind Rachel's attempted abduction, or if it was random. Regardless, we need to keep you safe. I don't believe in coincidences, not after all you've both been through. And not after the disappearances from this area of the men we mentioned."

Nia turned and gazed up at him to see total protector-mode burning clearly in his otherworldly eyes. "I don't want to invade your house, not when I have more than adequate security here. Simone and Rachel can stay here with me until you get a handle on where Denton is."

Carrick was shaking his head before she finished speaking. "Having you isolated and alone out here won't work, especially when exertion leaves you and Simone both vulnerable. I don't mean to be an ass, but if Denton could abduct you when you were fit and working personal protection, then in your current condition you don't stand a chance against him and whoever's on his payroll. Simone, alone in her house with Rachel, even on a main road, much less here, isn't either. They've already proven they're willing to take risks, if in fact that was one of Denton's guys tonight who grabbed Rachel, attempting to reacquire Simone."

Nia wanted to argue, but everything he said was the absolute truth. She frowned at him but couldn't think of any intelligent counter to what he'd said. She was still trying to think of other solutions when Dak strode back down the hall and interrupted. "Positive results. We need to get you infused. Gotta go."

She was glad for the backup, frustrated by their bossiness, and struggling mightily to blithely agree to go with them, and be infused with a cocktail of stuff at their say so.

"I'd like a little more infor...."

She stopped mid-sentence and stiffened at Max's throaty bark of warning just before a robotic voice emitted from her phone, an echo of it in her office down the hall.

"West perimeter breach, three tangos. Exit the property. Repeat..."

Without bothering to check the app, she snatched her phone off the coffee table, tucked it into a pocket in her leggings and called out, "Max. Heel! Reese, grab my backpack?"

The voice played a constant stream of updates as Carrick leaped to his feet, scooped her into his arms and ran down the hall toward the back of the house, fierceness etched on his face and in the tension straining his huge frame. "What's the best way out the back?"

She'd never seen people move as fast as these men. Enhanced speed? Their movements went beyond merely athletic and spec-ops training.

Just before Carrick had pivoted and sprinted toward the back, she saw Dak sling his bag over a shoulder and in one long stride, tuck a big hand under Rachel to lift and secure her against his other broad shoulder, then wrap a big hand around Simone's bicep, pulling her along at a run behind them, her shorter legs struggling to keep up.

She looked over Carrick's shoulder to see Reese bringing up the rear, a wicked Mossberg in one hand and a ka-bar in his other, her backpack thankfully on one muscled shoulder, looking pissed and ready to take out anyone who breached the house before they made their escape.

The sound of an explosion ripping through her garage door made her jump. No doubt it would have blown in the connecting door and wall if not for the steel reinforcements she'd added when she moved in. Pays to be paranoid, she thought with satisfaction.

"Move it, people!" Carrick shouted.

Chapter Eight

CARRICK LEAPT into action before the voice in her phone spit out the last word of warning, scooped Nia into his arms as he stood, then pivoted to run toward the back of the house. "Time to go!"

No fucking way was Denton getting his hands on his mate, his family, or his friends. Of which he now considered Simone and her daughter.

Nia pointed to a door just before the room at the end and ordered breathlessly, "In there."

In a flash of insight, he knew this savvy woman had an egress bolthole in her office, and he trusted her to get them out of there.

He dodged into the room and kept going far enough to allow Max, Dak with Rachel, Simone and then Reese to clear the doorway and pull up behind them.

"Reese, where're you going?" His brother had turned and sprinted off toward the room at the end of the hall.

Nia twisted in Carrick's arms and called out to his brother. "I have a way out in here. Get back here!"

Carrick set Nia on her feet and she pivoted, then stepped forward to a tall, deep gun safe in the left corner of the room.

Reese ran back into the room and slammed the door, then one-handed shoved a huge, ancient metal desk across the room to block it. "I opened the window in your bedroom, so they'd think we left that way."

Carrick watched as Nia glanced behind her shoulder at the scrape against the floor, widening her eyes at his brother's ability to move a heavy-ass desk with one arm.

"Good thinking." Carrick gave him a nod before turning back to watch Nia.

As she twirled the combination, they gave a collective flinch when another explosion ripped through the air, followed by what was clearly a breaching tool working on the wall or door from the garage to the kitchen.

"Hurry, we're outta time!" Carrick warned.

"I know!" Nia wrenched open the safe door, reached in and pressed her thumb to a Glock decal on the wall next to the handle of a wicked, ancient looking ka-bar, almost a twin to the one currently in the sheath on his belt.

His mouth quirked to see the bottom of the safe slide out, then spread into a satisfied smile when she grabbed the knife and the backpack hanging next to it before stepping onto the first rung of a metal ladder leading into a deep basement.

Their eyes met and held, and he gave her a nod of approval and encouragement, pride for this brave, clever woman warming his soul. He waited until she was half-way down before following her, two rungs at a time before jumping to clear the last couple of feet, then checked to ensure she was still steady on her feet. It gladdened him to see her energy drinks were kicking in.

He held up his arms to Dak. "Hand me Rachel. Simone, you're next."

They flinched to hear the breaching tool clearly making headway into the kitchen, then a screech and the bastards were in, boots hitting the tile floor.

They'd just run out of time. Rachel was awake, crying softly as Dak dropped to a knee, leaned through the opening, and handed her down to Carrick, who immediately passed her off to Nia. The little girl calmed at the familiar sight of her new friend, patted her check playfully, then laid her head on Nia's shoulder, tucking a thumb into her mouth.

Carrick turned back to see Simone's petite form hustling down the ladder, Dak practically stepping on her fingers, with Max draped across his shoulders like a military dog being carried across the desert.

He reached up and plucked the small woman off the rungs when she was halfway down, ignoring her squeak of surprise, turned and set her on her feet next to Nia, who placed Rachel in her arms.

He turned back to see Dak jump to the floor and Reese step into the gun safe, then turned back to Nia at the sound of her hitting a button on the wall. He looked up to see the safe's door close with a soft thud. Reese skimmed down the ladder, boots clenched on the outside of the rails, both elbows hooked on the outer rim.

The second his head cleared the hole, Nia hit another button and the floor of the safe slid shut, the heavy steel effectively blocking the noise of the assholes rattling the office door, the heavy desk and solid wood door hopefully making them think it was just locked, since the sound of them continuing down the hall to the back bedroom echoed before the trap door fully closed.

Talk about cutting it close! Hopefully, they would see the open window in her bedroom and think they'd escaped that way, although he bet they'd be curious about the office door not budging.

He turned to Nia. "Damn, woman, that's hot as hell you're so clever and prepared."

She looked at him askance, a rosy blush blooming up her neck and across her cheeks before she turned and hurried to a door on the far wall.

"I drywalled the door in the kitchen leading to this basement. Unless they've seen the blueprints, which I highly doubt since the house is so old, they won't know there's a basement. Through here there's a tunnel going under Cinnabar Hills Road leading to an opening near a small caretaker's cottage I own half a mile away, between the road and the Hacienda Cemetery. It's titled under an assumed name, and I have weapons and clothing there, too. We can get my stuff and get gone. Pays to be paranoid."

Nia opened the door and stepped into the rock- and dirt-walled tunnel, reinforced with what looked to be sturdy railroad ties connected with four-by-four crossties. She stood next to the door and motioned them all through the opening, then closed and locked it before closing another steel door and securing it with an equally strong steel bar.

"This tunnel is apparently a holdover from when the cinnabar mines were first built in the early-1800s. Don't know why, though, since there aren't any mines in this area. I'm assuming there was a shack or original house where this one is now. I've checked it out, and it's still safe and sturdy."

This woman didn't fuck around with her safety, he thought admiringly. He wouldn't either, if he'd been abducted, experimented on, and escaped a madman intent on altering DNA and impregnating her to produce Garou offspring.

Denton must not know that only true mates can produce offspring together, or he wouldn't be pursuing this insanity. Unless he'd somehow circumvented that. Naw, Carrick couldn't believe the crazy bastard was smart enough to change the age-old mating bond being the only pairing to produce children.

Carrick's muscles loosened a bit to realize they had a good exit strategy. "That'll work in our favor, since I parked my FJ across Cinnabar Hills, just before the turnoff to your driveway, maybe even near the cottage, although we didn't see it when I hid the vehicle. I tucked it about a hundred feet into the trees and bushes, so hopefully the hit team didn't run across it, and concentrated on your place only. We should be clear, since Reese left the window open to fool them into thinking we exited the house that way, and if we're lucky, they'll be scouring the area behind your place."

Nia nodded and turned to Simone with an apologetic look on her face. "I'm guessing your Jeep and my Land Cruiser are toast, taken out in the blast, or at least compromised. No way can you go home after this, especially since we don't know if they picked up my trail and followed me from there, or if they had a bead on you and followed you here. If they found you, they'll have your license plate number, regardless. Don't worry, we'll get you and Rachel outfitted when we get to wherever we're going. I have plenty of money at the cottage, and access to a hidden account, courtesy of my sis—my sister."

She cleared her throat against the devastation that swept through her anytime she thought of Aleesha. "The cottage is way too small to stay in long-term, and security isn't as robust as here, so we'll have to find alternative lodging."

Carrick wondered at her hesitation when mentioning her sister. There was an unhappy story there, he'd bet his life. But the telling could wait for another time.

He pinned Nia with a look and said in a voice that brooked no arguments, "You're coming home with us. All three of you. We'll protect you, and there's plenty of room; the house is large, and I also have an empty cabin on the property. I'll call in reinforcements. Hell, I'll build more cabins if I have to. Denton won't stand a chance in hell of getting to any of us."

No way he could let innocents fend for themselves. He wasn't wired that way, especially against an evil like Denton and the heartless people working for him. Not to mention, no way in fucking hell was he letting his mate out of his sight until they'd neutralized the threat. He wasn't sure what he'd do if she argued and insisted on going off with Simone and Rachel by themselves.

"My place is pretty much rocket, bomb and fireproof. He'll have some nasty surprises if he tries this shit over there. Besides, we've stayed under the radar and just moved here a few months ago. I don't think he knows about us, specifically. We suspect he knows other Garou live around here and that he's behind the disappearances we mentioned earlier, but so far the three of us are invisible."

He knew by the look on her face she was going to demand he explain more about Denton and the Garou's history. He laid a hand on her shoulder before she got a word out. "Believe me, we'll tell you more about Denton, the Garou, and Cinnabar Twins, when we get to my home. The ranch is between here and Simone's place, near Black Mountain Road, back in the trees."

She huffed, but didn't press him on it. "Fine, I'll wait, but I want the full story; no holding back information."

Carrick nodded. "Absolutely. To give you a bit of info now, we were at Simone's last night in an official capacity. No reason for anyone to suspect we were anything but emergency personnel. We license our bikes, the motorcycles we arrived on last night, in a company's name in a different state, not in my name. We know he's in the area because our tech guru has tracked him. He has a history of scoping out the area around cinnabar mines, hoping to flush out Garou, but as I mentioned, so far the three of us have stayed under his radar in this area. I titled my ranch under my fitness equipment company, based out of Tennessee, purposely headquartered there because there are no cinnabar mines in that state. Add to that, he doesn't actually know what we look like. The three of us have kept our identities hidden, unlike some of the other, older Garou he's found out about."

Carrick held Nia's captivating eyes, willing her to agree without argument. He didn't want to be a controlling asshole about this, but it was non-negotiable as far as he was concerned.

The three ladies were coming home with him. If he had his way, it would be a permanent move for

Nia. He knew she had no concept what it meant to be a Garou's mate.

How alone, how fucking lonely he'd been for at least two-thirds of the little over one hundred-sixty years he'd been alive, craving his mate, sure he would never meet her.

Hell, she seemed to feel the mating pull, but it probably wasn't half as strong in her as it was in him. Only time would tell. Time, and anything and everything he could do to sway her over to his side.

He was still on a knife's-edge of sexual arousal; it was taking every ounce of self-control to will his cock to stay down where it belonged and keep his hands to himself. Not sexually, but the urge to just brush against her, to touch her face, her shoulder, her mahogany curls, to wrap an arm around that enticing curve of her waist was almost too much to resist. Her body beckoned him like a bee to nectar.

Inappropriate what with people trying to capture them, but he couldn't convince his body, or what seemed to be that other, primal part of him, that now wasn't the time to claim her. He wanted with every fiber of his being to make her his, to complete the mating bond. To know she would live longer, be stronger, and hopefully no longer be sick.

He didn't know what he would do if she didn't want him. He *did* know it would be so much fucking worse than having never met her to begin with.

They hustled through the tunnel, Carrick on Nia's heels in case she became dizzy or sick again, relieved when they reached the end, faced with a vertical wooden ladder attached to the wall, leading about twenty feet up to what looked like an ancient manhole cover with a long, slender lever to open it.

When she set a foot on the bottom rung, he placed a hand on her shoulder, braced this time for the zing that shot through him every time he touched her. He leaned down, his lips brushing the delicate shell of her ear, pushing aside the need to nip at the lobe when she shivered in response. "Let me get it, baby. Don't want you falling off the ladder if you get dizzy again."

He knew she was a capable woman. Hell, she'd escaped a madman and kept herself hidden and safe for almost a year. But she didn't need to do everything on her own anymore. She had him. For backup. For protection. For balls-to-the-wall sex and good lovin', if she'd only let him.

He relished the shiver and trust she showed when she leaned back subtly into his body. The stubbornness that flashed through her eyes morphed immediately into one of acceptance as she stepped down and brushed a hand down his triceps, causing his cock to jump and that invisible thread between them to strengthen even more.

He dipped and brushed a swift kiss over her plump lips, noting with satisfaction her expanded pupils and quick intake of breath before he took the rungs two at a time to the top. He stopped to listen, to get a feel for anyone in the exit's vicinity.

The Garou's enhanced senses had saved his ass on more than one occasion with the ability to sense humans and animals alike within a pretty good radius.

Relieved all was quiet, and sensing nothing more than the typical wildlife found in the area, he cranked the handle and pushed the cover up a couple of inches, then paused and concentrated again, just to be damned sure.

He glanced down at Reese and Dak, then at Max, getting a nod from the guys and a tail wag from the pup. All clear, according to the two- and four-legged protectors.

"After I get topside, Nia, you're next with Dak shadowing you and carrying Max again. Simone, then you with Reese bringing up the rear carrying Rachel. Nia, you take lead when we head out. We'll hustle to the cottage and grab whatever you want, then we need to get gone on the off chance they expand their search to this side of the road."

When Carrick hoisted himself out of the hole and onto land, he crouched at the small opening and took Nia's hand when she was half out of the hole and steadied her as she continued up and out. It heartened him when she didn't hesitate to reach for him.

He stood as she took to her feet, a steadying arm around the dip of her waist and watched as Dak and Max's heads popped out, Simone almost getting clipped in the chin by his boot-heel, she was so close.

He heard Reese crooning to Rachel, trying to keep her from wailing, and thanked all the gods and goddesses his brother had a way with kids.

When his brother's shoulders cleared the hole, Simone reached down and retrieved her daughter, who appeared to be happy as a clam and not traumatized by being held by a stranger. Reese leaped to his feet and landed in a crouch, turned and grabbed the lid to close it.

The cover was simplistic and effective, having some type of synthetic turf adhered to the top, with a dead tree stump and realistic debris and grasses glued to it, so there was no noticeable seam around the lid.

At Nia's command, they turned as one and started at a brisk clip, zigzagging around the brush and trees since there was no trail to follow. He transferred his arm from around her waist to a firm grip on her hand again, linking their fingers lest she stumble.

When he looked back to check on everyone, he gave Reese a chin lift, miming drinking from a bottle, silently asking for one of her energy drinks from the backpack still on his shoulder.

Without missing a step, Reese slid it down his arm, opened it and pulled out one of Nia's homemade drinks, passing it to him before closing the pack and hoisting it onto his shoulder again.

Carrick uncapped the bottle and handed it to Nia, garnering a look of surprise and a slow smile as she took it from him and gulped half before handing it back.

"Thank you," she said sweetly, clearly taken aback by his thoughtfulness.

Carrick dipped and brushed his lips across hers before taking her hand again and turning to Simone at the sound of a small branch breaking. "Try not to break twigs or branches as you pass through. A good tracker could follow us, but someone not used to tracking will have a harder time if we're careful not to leave an obvious trail."

At her look of fear and nod, he felt like an ass for scaring her. "I don't think they'll come across the road, especially this far back into the brush, but it pays to be careful."

At the sound of a loud explosion, Nia startled and would have fallen if not for Carrick's quick tug on her hand and arm wrapped snug around her middle to pull her back against him.

"Those motherfuckers are destroying my house, aren't they?"

She sounded equal parts pissed and devastated, and he wanted to kill the men responsible.

"I'm sorry, baby. I can't replace what you had, but we'll get you settled and set up at the ranch."

He leaned down and tugged on her chin so he could see her eyes brimming with tears. She was killing him with her sorrow. "Stay. As long as you want, baby. Stay with me."

She gave him a long, considering look, her eyes on his moving back and forth, and he counted it a win she didn't immediately shut him down. Had, in fact, given an imperceptible nod.

It was a step in the right direction.

Chapter Nine

NIA COULDN'T believe how her life had gone from sugar to shit in one night. She'd been so sure she was invisible and sufficiently hidden from that crazy asshole, but apparently something had changed. She was betting the attempted abduction last night had set off this terrible chain of events.

Somehow Denton had found Simone, sent someone in to grab Rachel to lure Simone back into his clutches, and when Nia happened on the scene and thwarted the snatch and grab, they'd followed her home. Or if not that scenario, then they'd followed Simone to her house tonight.

Probably so they could grab all three of them at once. Especially with Nia's home being isolated; the perfect scene for an abduction no one would be the wiser to.

Carrick was a miracle in the midst of this shitshow. As much as she tried to ignore and disbelieve her connection with him, not to mention the existence of Garou, she absolutely felt the irresistible sensual pull, heck, some invisible emotional, mental and physical link to the big guy. And it felt good—wonderful, even.

He gave off only positive vibes, nothing slimy or dangerous—well, nothing dangerous toward her. That was another side effect of the infusions; she could somehow sense evil intent or if someone had protective or positive intentions. She could even see through a hard, intense, seemingly violent outer layer to their good, solid heart.

Just in the short time she'd known him, he'd shown a core of fierce protectiveness to go with the gentleness he'd exhibited on more than one occasion. There was no evil slime or intent, like she'd sensed from Denton and almost all of his people. But she also knew Carrick would be fierce and kill without compunction to save innocent lives or himself.

Instead of being put off by his bossiness, and his familiarity in holding her hand, in brushing those sensuous lips against hers and wrapping that deliciously muscular arm around her, she reveled in knowing she had someone to watch her back.

Some sexy, uber-protective someone. And let's not forget the instant arousal the first time he'd touched her, and every single time since. Arousal mirrored in his eyes whenever they met hers.

She should be concentrating on where to go next to hide from Denton, on getting a new vehicle and accessing her money, of getting as far away from New Almaden as possible to lose herself in another state.

But instead, she was doing her best to ignore her throbbing clit, the warm rush of liquid wetting her panties, and how sensitive the hard nubs of her nipples were as they rubbed against her tank top with every step. A shiver ran up and down her spine at the thought of Carrick's mouth sucking her nipples and moving south to dance his tongue on her clit.

She startled when he gave a squeeze of his big hand and said in a low tone meant just for her ears, "What's wrong, baby. You need me to carry you?"

She glanced at him, her cheeks flushed and warm with her arousal, her irises probably obliterated by her pupils because of that arousal, too. His nostrils flared, and he missed a step before he strode forward again, holding her gaze.

The skin taught across his cheekbones, his own pupils becoming huge as he leaned close again, his rumbly voice a turn-on all by itself. "I can smell your arousal, Nia. As bad as I want you, and I'm tellin' you, I feel like I'll die if I can't have you soon, it's up to you, baby. Just say the word and I'm yours. I'll have you naked and under me in a heartbeat. But if you need more time, I'm a patient man. I've waited for you for what feels like forever; I can wait some more."

It was her turn to miss a step, and she gasped when he scooped her up as if she was as light as little Rachel, then moaned when he dipped his head to nuzzle the sensitive skin under her ear.

"I," she started, then had to clear her throat to start again. "I want you too, but I need time, Carrick. I've been betrayed…" She laid a finger over his oh-so-fine lips when he opened his mouth to reassure her. "I'm not saying you will, big guy. But I've been alone for so long, except for my sister, since my mama dropped my sis and me at the mall when I was twelve and she was eleven, and never returned. Then, the one time I placed my trust in someone as an adult, he sold me out to Denton for five measly grand. I'm just saying, I need time. Please."

He pressed a kiss against her finger before she pulled it away. "I'm sorry that happened to you, when you were a child and then betrayed to Denton. And I hear you, baby. Take whatever time you need. I'll be waiting. You don't need to beg or plead. I just ask one thing of you while you're thinkin' on it. Stay at my ranch, where I can protect you. I'll go fucking crazy not having you near."

The look in his eyes was pure heat, desire and alpha-protectiveness all rolled into one, and for the life of her, she couldn't think of one good reason to deny him. Being independent was one thing. Being stubborn for no good reason and denying herself this chance with him was just plain stupid.

She cupped his bristly cheek with her hand and said simply, "Okay."

His 'thank fuck' brought a small smile to her face before she turned and laid her head on his shoulder, suddenly weary to her bones and willing to let him be her packhorse to the cottage.

Some food and hydration, the rest of her energy drink, then to his ranch to rest would go a long way in getting her back to kick-ass readiness. She hated feeling dependent on others, even someone as devoted to her care and safety as Carrick seemed to be.

She directed him with gestures, and he stopped at the edge of the small clearing in front of the old, weathered cottage, setting her down at his side to lean against a skinny oak. Their small group gathered around her, and Reese took point, holding up a hand to indicate they wait for him to clear the area.

When Carrick leaned toward her, she reciprocated and tilted her head up as he said in a low tone, "I don't sense anyone in the area, but best to be safe and have Reese clear the area and then the cottage. We'll get in and out, and then to the ranch."

"Do you mean you can sense people because you're Garou?"

She had to lean closer to hear his reply.

"Yes, for a perimeter of about three hundred feet."

Carrick and Nia turned when Dak set Max on the ground, pulled his phone from a cargo pocket, unlocked it and pressed some buttons, then turned toward the northwest after examining a map on an app she didn't recognize. "The FJ is about one hundred yards northwest from here. Sensors show no one's disturbed it."

Nia glanced at Carrick. "You have sensors on your car?"

"Yes, can't be too careful. The same saved a cousin about a year ago when Denton's goons got too close. Activity, both visual and touch, turns on a couple cameras and logs video with sound into storage on our phones and a backup copy in Dropbox. Logged an explosive device they'd placed on his truck, and he called the local bomb squad and cops out. Had to fib and say he'd seen it happen, since we don't advertise what some may call paranoia. Don't want the cops asking too many questions about why we're so over the top in security, or about how and why we know who's after us but haven't reported it to authorities."

Nia nodded in complete agreement, since she was just as over the top as these guys were. If the blast hadn't taken out her Land Cruiser, which she was sure it had, then she'd have shared her toys with Carrick and compared tech security solutions.

She had all the code and schematics securely tucked away on a server in the cloud courtesy of her sister, but all her gadgets stored in the garage and her office were no doubt long gone. Besides, going back to get anything would be suicide, since Denton was probably monitoring the area. No material things were worth the risk.

She choked back a sob at the thought of her sister. The hole in her heart just wouldn't heal, and she missed her every damn day. Fucking Denton would pay for killing her. If it was the last thing she did, she'd take him down. In the most painful way possible.

She wasn't the least surprised when Carrick noticed her distress and leaned in again. "What's wrong? Dizzy again, or in pain?" He reached to scoop her up, and she laid a hand on his arm with a careful shake of her head.

"I'm okay, honest. I—can't talk about it right now, but will tell you the full story later. I'm too on edge and emotional right now, and I fricking hate crying. I'll tell you this much. Denton killed my sister when she tried to free me. She's the reason I had funds and a way to survive when I got away, but I couldn't save her. She gave her life for me."

Realizing she shouldn't have told him even that much, she choked on a sob and tucked her head into his shoulder, letting the tears fall. She knew in her heart she could count on him to hold her for as long as she needed and keep the others from questioning her.

She heard Simone asking what was wrong and couldn't raise her head to answer, grateful Carrick held her at bay. "She's okay. Overwhelmed and tired."

"Cottage is clear, let's move it. We need to get in and out." Reese had approached on silent feet and she jerked her head up, sniffing inelegantly as she pushed away from Carrick and wiped her face with both hands.

"Keys are in the small, zippered pocket on the front of my backpack."

Reese pulled the zipper open, grabbed the keys and strode to the door, unlocked it and motioned them through, then secured the door after they entered.

Dak held up a hand when Nia would have continued through the small main room to her bedroom. "Need to clear it first; wait here."

She was getting used to his bossiness and stinginess with words, and leaned against Carrick while Dak make quick work of clearing the small cottage. Besides the main room they were in, there were two bedrooms, with an ensuite off the larger one.

When he strode back into the room and gave a nod, Nia motioned to Simone. "Come into the bedroom to grab clothes and toiletries with me."

She turned to Carrick. "In the other bedroom, push the bed to the side and there's a trapdoor in the floor; electronic password is FuckThisShit. Caps start each word. Weapons and ammo are in there. Reese, there's a bag of dry food for Max in the pantry, and more of my energy drinks in the fridge. Grab those for me? Dak, spare laptop and electronics, and a medical kit, are in the closet in the corner."

Reese's face lit up. "Damn, woman, you're ready for anything. And love the password."

Carrick smacked him on the back of his head as he passed. "No flirting with my woman."

Even as she gave him a frown, pleasure speared through her at the thought of being his woman. She turned and strode into the bedroom with Simone following, Rachel asleep again on her shoulder.

Thank god it was the middle of the night, and the little one was worn out enough to sleep through most of this.

"What do you make of their story, Nia? I'd be skeptical if it weren't for the fact that hey, a mad scientist, who mentioned the Garou, and who wanted to breed us to them, kidnapped and experimented on us."

Nia nodded and opened the closet door, grabbing an empty duffle bag and a couple of full backpacks, dropping them onto the bed. She turned to Simone and motioned to a dresser against the wall. "I have clothing in there that will be a little big on you, but should work until we can shop. Grab as much as you can fit into this empty bag. The others I keep already packed."

She stepped into the large closet next to the bathroom, grabbed a couple jackets and tossed them on the bed, then pressed her thumb against the electronic lock on a tall safe attached to the back wall. Spring loaded, it popped open, and she grabbed a holster, slipped her arms through, then rotated her shoulders to settle it in place.

Plucking her Sig P320 off a shelf, she checked the magazine and chamber, slid it into the holster, then grabbed her Remington Model 870 12-gauge pump-action shotgun and a bag that contained ammo for both weapons.

She backed out of the closet to see Rachel snuggled in the middle of her bed, surrounded by pillows. Simone had emptied the dresser drawers onto the bed and was stuffing the previously empty bag as full as possible.

Nia set the pouch of ammo by the bedroom door. Then, still carrying the shotgun, stepped into the bathroom and grabbed a toiletry bag from under the sink, handing it to Simone.

"Will you put this in the blue backpack, please? I don't have locks for my shotgun or handgun, so won't be setting it down where Rachel can get to it, especially since she's walking, even if she's so young and not very strong. I'll order fingerprint trigger locks right away, but still plan to keep them out of her reach."

Simone turned grateful eyes to her, and Nia found herself the recipient of a hard, unexpected hug and was careful to keep the shotgun pointed down and away.

"Ooof! Hey, it'll be okay, Simone. Promise. Even if Carrick and the guys can't help us, I won't abandon you." Nia returned the hug with one arm, hanging on and trying to infuse some of her strength into Simone.

"I'm so scared." Simone shuddered and hung on even tighter. "I've tried to be strong, had to be strong for Rachel, but feel I'm going to fall apart ever since they tried to take her."

Nia clutched Simone's shoulder with her free hand and pushed her back a little to look her in the eyes. "I'm scared too, but I also think we couldn't be in safer hands than with these guys. I realize we don't actually know them, but they radiate protectiveness and a determination to keep us safe. There are no bad vibes at all."

Simone gave a nod and stepped back with a small grin and a sniff. "Oh, I think one of those guys feels something more than protectiveness for you. If instalove was a thing, I'd say Carrick has handed you his heart, and he's all yours. I'm betting if he could get you to himself, and you were willing, you'd be in for a wild ride."

"You're not wrong." Nia grinned and shook her head in wonder. "When I was in the bathroom before it all went to hell, I was thinking life had turned into one of those romances I like to read."

Simone clapped a hand to her mouth. "Holy shit, you're right! Complete with shifters, kind of. Do you think this means there's a Garou mate out there somewhere for me?"

They both turned to the door with a gasp when Reese spoke up. "That's a distinct possibility, Simone. There are Garou spread across the planet, living near cinnabar mines, and they travel frequently between the different communities. I'd say there's a good chance what Denton did to Nia he also did to you, so if you're in proximity to your mate, you and he will both know it."

Simone looked thoughtful, not fearful, and Nia wondered if they could actually stay safe and away from Denton long enough for her to connect with her mate. Wondered if being Carrick's mate was going to work out, if he really would stay devoted to her, protective of her, and if this out-of-control sexual desire would abate, finally burn itself out—or get even stronger, if that was possible.

Carrick and Dak appeared behind Reese, all three striding into the small bedroom. Nia's eyes widened in surprise when Carrick kept coming, wrapped one big hand around the back of her neck, and dropped a possessive kiss onto her lips, eliciting a moan from her.

He rested his forehead on hers. "Sorry, baby. I know you're unsure about us, but I'm finding it impossible not to touch you, to kiss you."

She rested a hand against his cheek. "You are kind of addictive, big guy, and I lo-, really like your lips on mine. I'm just not sure I fully believe in mates yet."

"Fair enough. I'll try to behave, but no guarantees on the kissing."

"I can handle that."

"Bro, we gotta get gone. Do your courting back home." Reese had the backpack with weapons across a shoulder, zipped the one Simone had quickly finished filling and picked it up too.

Carrick flipped his brother the middle finger over his shoulder, then glanced at Nia. "Got everything you need?" He eyed the shotgun still in her hand, pointed safely toward the floor, then the Sig in her shoulder holster. "I see you're prepared with firepower, too. Gotta love a woman with weapons."

Nia grinned. "I've always believed you can't have too many tools or weapons." She tipped her chin toward Rachel. "I want to order some trigger locks, since Rachel will be in the house with us. Not that I'll leave them lying around, but not going to take a chance with that little one. I'm assuming you have a safe I can stow them in?"

"I do, and I hear you; we'll take care of that tonight. We can order from Sons of Guns, an online store a Garou cousin in Austin, Texas owns."

They turned to see Simone scooping Rachel from the bed, Dak and Reese exiting the room with the rest of the bags.

A quick sweep of the main room confirmed they'd retrieved everything Nia wanted to take, and they waited by the door while Reese again cleared the area around the cottage before motioning them all to proceed.

Nia hoped they made it to Carrick's vehicle and then his house without incident. She didn't think she had the energy or ability to fight off a racoon, much less armed bad guys paid to take her back to Denton.

Chapter Ten

CARRICK ADMIRED the hell out of Nia. Fate couldn't have provided a better mate for him, one who was brave, strong, loyal, full of integrity and, holy shit, more beautiful than a perfect sunrise. The most beautiful, strong, sexy woman he'd ever seen.

He followed close behind her to ensure if she went down, he'd catch her before she hit the ground. He knew she was on her last reserves, the energy drinks she'd downed earlier no doubt worn off and the adrenaline dump giving her the shakes.

Not only that, the effects of being punched in the head, on top of the worry of Denton having her in his sights again—and her house being destroyed—must have her close to her last nerve. She thought she was homeless, but she was wrong. His home was now hers as well.

No fucking way was that bastard getting his hands on her. He and the guys would make sure not only Nia, but Simone and Rachel were safe. He'd sent a text to his buddies in Sonoma County, asking them to get to his ranch ASAP.

He'd also texted his mama and papa to let them know he'd found his mate, but there was danger surrounding them, and he would fill them in later. Not to come to New Almaden.

It had been a toss-up whether or not to let them know shit was going down, but he didn't want them showing up to meet her and land in the middle of a war, if it came to that, so he'd given them the bare bones in the text and told them to stay away. As expected, they were incredulous and ecstatic for him, and champing at the bit to meet her.

Hale and Bah were packing to drive down to the ranch, due to arrive in about three hours. Hale was their muscled geek, part of the research and security team the Garou's Wolven Council funded to provide protection as needed, as well as the ongoing research into the Garou history in an attempt to uncover what the virus had altered in the Cinnabar Twins so many years ago to make them invisible to their mates.

Bah was one of their council members and a doctor, and was also on call to travel and treat any injury or illness, since Garou didn't dare go to a mainstream hospital. They lived at the compound located near the Contact Mine in Sonoma County, funded by the Quicksilver Garou Society, in existence for over a thousand years, almost as long as the Knights Templar. Bah's clinic was also at the compound and serviced a good portion of the Garou in the San Francisco Bay Area.

Their small group made their way silently through the trees, Dak using the GPS on his phone to lead the way to Carrick's FJ. He couldn't wait to get Nia settled in his home, in what he hoped she would eventually consider *her* new home, if he succeeded in convincing her they belonged together.

Although thoughts of her bravery, courage, fortitude and rocking body filled his mind, and he wanted nothing more than to get her naked and under him, he was also fully aware of his surroundings, keeping his senses open to ensure no other humans, or dangerous four-legged creatures, were in the area.

When Nia stopped suddenly and held up her hand, then pulled her phone from her legging pocket, the group halted and circled her. "My security app alerted again. One of the outlying, back property sensors got a hit. I have a custom vibration pattern assigned to each sensor." With her phone in one hand, she swiped with her thumb to unlock the screen and pressed an icon to open what Carrick recognized from before as her security app.

She thumbed the volume down, then hit a red dot pulsing about a hundred feet behind her house, then held the phone out for everyone to hear.

"Fucking bitches couldn't have gone far," a nasally voice complained, "especially with a head injury and the other one carrying the kid. Didn't you say you'd popped the tall bitch in the head, Jimmy?"

"Yeah, got her good with a fist to her temple and collarbone," another low voice said, satisfaction and sick anticipation in his tone. "I'll pop her again for making me chase her. How'd they know we were here, anyway? That fucking reinforced wall took us too long to get through, and how'd they get that big-ass desk in front of the door?"

"Who the hell knows? All I know is Denton's gonna be pissed we let them get away. He's not happy with the women he's got locked down, or the Garou dude he wants to breed one of 'em with. I guess the curly-haired bitch who lives here is the one he thought would work the best, although he wants that shorter broad back, too."

At Nia's shudder, Carrick wrapped an arm around her waist and held on tight. They didn't have to wait long when an unknown voice chimed in, deeper and more authoritative than the others.

"Shut the hell up, you two. You want to be overheard by someone checking out the noise from the explosion, or let the bitches know we're on to them? Jesus, you're a couple of dumb fucks. Both of you, go another hundred feet up the hill, then we're outta here."

Carrick saw red, knowing they were talking about Nia being the one Denton thought would work and they were there to kidnap both women, and Rachel. It infuriated him Denton had a Garou and who knew how many other Cinnabar Twins captive. Were they all at the facility in the Umpqua Forest, where they held Nia and Simone?

He tucked Nia under one arm and turned toward the FJ again. "Motherfuckingsonofabitch! We need to hustle to the FJ and get the hell out of here before they get back down to their vehicle. One of us could go after them, put an end to them, but we don't know if they're the only ones here, and I don't want to risk an attack with only two of us left to protect Nia, Simone and Rachel. I wish to hell we had the other guys here. We'd get rid of the two idiots and question the third; he seems to be the guy in charge. We need to call your dad, Dak; fill him in. I know he'll want to get a team together right away to plan a rescue of the other captives and provide support here."

Nia muted her phone and tucked it back in her pocket. "The app records anything from the sensors on the property, and dumps it into cloud storage. We can review it again from your place to see if there's anything new."

Carrick acknowledged with a nod, taking her hand again and lacing their fingers together, setting off at a brisk pace. They all turned as one to follow and quickened their pace, Dak striding past to take the lead once again.

They arrived at the FJ a few minutes later, and Carrick thumbed the fob to unlock the doors. He walked to the front passenger door, opened it and cupped Nia's elbow as she climbed in, his eyes tracking the graceful, muscled curves of her legs.

Damn, the woman just did it for him. No matter what shit was going down, a part of him, that primal Garou part that recognized her as his mate, couldn't stop the heat from coursing through him at the sight or touch of her, couldn't stop the raging desire to get her naked and under him so he could claim her as his.

She must have felt the force of his desire, her eyes snapping to his, reciprocal silver and red flashing through the brilliant green before her pupils expanded to leave them rimmed in green fire.

It shocked him when she leaned forward and pressed a kiss to his lips before leaning back. "Let's go, big guy. Gotta get ahead of the bad guys."

He brushed a finger along her silky cheek. "I'm gonna want more of that, baby."

Her small grin gave him hope she was coming around.

He quietly closed the door, rounded the hood, and climbed into the driver's seat. A glance in the rearview mirror confirmed the guys, along with Simone and Rachel, had piled into the back seat while Nia's gaze had held him captive.

Reese cocked a brow at him as if to say, 'get your head in the game, bro', and he gave his brother a chin lift in acknowledgement as he fired up the engine.

He pulled around the trees and brush, rolling slowly toward Cinnabar Hills Road with lights out. He was fairly sure the hit team was still busy behind Nia's home and hoped those three guys were the only ones in New Almaden.

Well, aside from Denton, as they suspected. Carrick used his enhanced senses to feel out the area, not registering anyone outside the vehicle or anywhere near.

He turned left onto Cinnabar Hills and sped up slowly with the lights out until they were far enough away they wouldn't alert anyone of their presence.

Unable to keep his hands off his mate, he reached over and laid his palm across the clenched fists on her lap and was glad to feel her relax before she unclenched one hand and linked her fingers with his.

"We'll be at the ranch in just a few minutes. It's off Almaden to the left, as I mentioned, back into the trees. Has good security, although I'd like you to look at it and see if any modifications would help."

He glanced at her to see surprise in her eyes, as if she didn't expect him to respect her expertise or ask for her help. "Baby, you'll find I'm not some asshole who doesn't respect your brain and skills. When I mentioned mates, I meant a partnership, not some uneven hierarchy with me on top." He grinned at the flash of heat in her eyes and lowered his voice. "Although, by the look in your eyes, I gotta say being on top is really appealing right now."

The soft laugh that erupted from her plump lips made him feel good he could bring her some joy in the midst of this clusterfuck. He squeezed her hand and smiled back before concentrating on the road again, turning onto Bertram and then Almaden.

His gravel driveway came into view and he turned left, reluctantly letting go of her hand to reach forward and press another fob on his keychain to open the electronic gate barring entry to his property. It was fully open by the time he rolled up to it and he continued through, pressing the fob again to shut the gate behind them.

They were at the house within a minute after following the curving drive through trees and brush, and he pulled around back, a door rolling up to allow him entry to the wide, three-car garage attached to the sprawling ranch house.

He shut off the engine as the door closed behind them, cocooning them in safety for the first time in hours. He turned to see Nia slump against the passenger door, as if she'd been holding herself together by sheer will until she no longer had to be alert.

Her collapse didn't alarm Carrick, since he now knew she ran through energy like a leaky battery and just needed to replenish. He opened his door and stepped out, hurrying around the vehicle to her door. She looked like she was one blink away from passing out from exhaustion.

He lifted his hand to tap on her window so she would straighten up, thankful to see Dak lean forward to place a broad palm on her shoulder and one on her head to keep her from falling out when he opened the door.

Shooting Dak a chin lift in thanks, he eased open the door and stepped forward so her head could rest on his shoulder, his friend exiting the backseat, Max following, as soon as Carrick held her in his arms. He made quick work of unbuckling her seat belt, then scooped her into his arms, her sigh when she relaxed fully against his chest a boon to his soul.

He left Simone and Rachel in Reese's capable hands and strode toward the door leading into the mudroom and then kitchen, determined to get some food and another energy drink into her so she'd feel better. No way could she go straight to bed this depleted, she'd feel so much worse when she awakened, and recovery would be that much harder. The big recliner in his living room would do the trick, and he could get a fire going in the hearth to take the chill off.

"Hey man, let me get the door." Dak strode past, pressed his thumb to the biometric reader, then unlocked his phone to get the code from the authentication app, and entered that into the keypad. The door clicked as it unlocked and Dak pushed it open, Carrick preceding him into the mudroom, glad to hear Reese behind them ushering Simone and a now awake and babbling Rachel into the house.

His brother would get those two settled, and he could concentrate on Nia. He strode through the kitchen and down the wide hallway into the living room, gently settling Nia into the oversize recliner, her furry shadow at his heels. Her skin felt chilled, no doubt from the lower temperatures outside and her depleted system.

She was still out, so he pulled her forward and tugged her holster off, gun still snugged inside, and laid it on the end table so Reese or Dak could stow it in the safe.

He grabbed a throw depicting wolves running through a forest in the Czech Republic his mama had sent him for Christmas and tucked it around her, then cupped her face in his hands. She needed to be awake to take nourishment, and he knew Dak wanted to get an IV going with the supplements they'd discussed with her earlier.

She'd fight them on the IV, but he hoped she'd come around. It would make her feel better, and they couldn't give her the quantity she needed orally.

"Hey, baby. Wake up so you can get down some nourishment."

He turned to see Dak enter the room with his medical bag in one hand and her backpack on his shoulder. "How she doing?"

"Still out. She have any of her energy drinks left in there? I think she'll need one of those, and then the ElectRou BCAA protein shake I have in the fridge from the batch Bah sent us. The one that has electrolytes, protein, salt and fruit juices."

"You got it, man. Not sure she's going to agree to the IV, yeah?"

Carrick frowned and nodded. "Yeah, she's not a fan of needles, and can't say I blame her. We may need to wait on that."

Dak had retrieved an energy drink from her backpack and handed it to Carrick, then nodded at her holstered gun. "Put that in the safe?"

"Yeah, man, thanks."

"You got it. Be right back with the shake."

Carrick dropped to one knee next to the recliner, Max standing guard with his furry head resting on her feet. He was getting worried they wouldn't be able to wake her and didn't want to have to resort to an IV to replenish her system when she was out. That felt like a betrayal, and alienating her before he won her over was not the way to go.

He brushed her lips with his. "Come on, Nia, please wake up, baby."

Chapter Eleven

NIA FELT like crap and wanted nothing more than to keep her eyes closed and go back to oblivion where nothing hurt and she didn't feel like she was going to hurl, but that deep, rumbly voice was enticing and the lips against hers pulled her from the well of darkness.

Hmmm, kisses led to petting, which led to maybe getting that big, thick cock inside of her...

Her eyes popped opened as she remembered just whose cock she was thinking of, and whose lips had moved from hers to brush against the sensitive shell of her ear as that contrabass voice she was fast becoming addicted kept trying to wake her.

"Baby, you're worrying me. Come on, wake up and sip your energy drink, then I have a protein shake that'll help you feel better. How can I woo and court you if you don't wake up?"

That got her completely awake, the combination of soft lips against her skin and the promise of more.

Although her eyelids felt like they weighed a ton, she blinked, then dragged them open again to see

Carrick's silver eyes locked on hers, a look of relief and worry vying for dominance.

"There you are. You had me worried. Here, take a sip of your energy drink, and when you're done, you can start on the shake."

She attempted to raise her hand and realized she was a warm human burrito wrapped in a beautiful woven throw and snuggled into a plush chair with Carrick on one knee next to her and Max at her feet, keeping watch.

He chuckled when he realized she couldn't move her arms, and freed her, then handed her a bottle of her homemade elixir that would go a long way to making her feel human again. Well, human and Cinnabar Twin, apparently.

"Thank you. When I'm this depleted, it's just this side of coma or zombieland."

She was sorry to see his grin disappear and worry fill his eyes again.

"I'm hoping Bah, our doc, can figure out something so you won't get this depleted in the future. Here, let me help you so you don't spill."

Her girl-bits tingled at the feel of his big, callused hand cupping hers as she lifted the bottle to her lips, and she couldn't tear her eyes away from his as she drank it down.

"Thank you."

She released the bottle and watched as he leaned over her to set it on an end table, unable to quell the shiver as his muscular pecs brushed against her oversensitive nipples, the little hussies now standing at attention and begging for more.

Instead of retreating fully back to his side of the recliner, he stopped part way, hesitating as if the next move was hers. She was done fighting this wild attraction, this physical and psychical link they shared. Tired of feeling like shit, of being alone, and dammit, she wanted to feel something amazing for a change. And she knew, from the samples he'd provided, a fully involved kiss with this man would be beyond amazing.

Wrapping the fingers of one hand around the back of his neck, she pulled the other from her lap and splayed it across his massive lats, pulling till he was practically laying crosswise on her breasts. She then proceeded to kiss the daylights out of him, relishing in the masculine groan of approval and arousal.

Their lips opened and tongues played in a sensual dance, mimicking a more intimate act she planned to perform with this sexy man sometime soon. His agile tongue dipped into her mouth to tease hers, and she dueled with it, wanting to explore the heat of his mouth. She gasped in delight when he gently bit her tongue, then nibbled on her lower lip before pulling it into his mouth.

If he made love even half as well as he kissed, she was in for the ride of her life—if they ever made it to the privacy of a bedroom and got blessedly naked together. She couldn't wait to see him sans clothes, all those ridges and valleys of musculature laid out for her to explore.

"Ahem."

The deep voice had them jumping apart, and she suppressed a giggle at the disgruntled look on Carrick's face, as well as the surreptitious adjustment of his cock under the zipper of his BDUs.

He slanted her a look full of sensual retribution, and she realized she hadn't done a good job of keeping her giggle to herself.

Reese came fully into the room, protein shake in his hand and reached out to give it to her.

"This'll help get you back on your feet. A Garou company manufactures it specifically for our kind, and I think it'll benefit you, too. Has much of what's in your energy drink, along with some extra amino acids and minerals, without the caffeine. I know Dak still wants to get an IV going with the supplement mix he thinks you need, but until you're ready for that, this'll help. Tastes like a strawberry banana milkshake."

Nia reached out, glad to see her hand was a little steadier after consuming her energy elixir earlier, and downed half of the shake in one gulp.

"Whoa, that's delicious. I was afraid it would taste like so many other manufactured drinks, kind of chalky with a weird aftertaste, but it's more like an actual ice cream shake, just not as thick."

Reese grinned at her. "Yeah, the folks who make it worked a long time to get the balance of taste and ingredients that would appeal to the Garou. Glad you like it. There's plenty more, so don't be shy about drinking it."

Nia nodded and downed the rest, handing the empty bottle back to Reese, glad it settled nicely in her tummy. She could practically feel her body coming back to life.

"Thanks. Wow, I can actually feel it working already and my energy returning."

Carrick turned grateful eyes to his brother. "Thanks, bro. Simone and Rachel getting settled?"

"Yeah, Dak's in the kitchen feeding them. He's making enough for us all. Nia, if you're up to it, let's see if your app recorded anything after we listened to those asshats. Hale and Bah should be here in a couple of hours, give or take, and it'll be good if we can fill them in and let Bah look at your head injury and Rachel, too, if she's still awake."

Carrick turned to Nia, hoping she would eat a regular meal and not just consume the drinks. "Feel up to this? Dak's a great cook. He can feed us and we can relax in the kitchen and plan next steps, then I can show you and Simone to your rooms and you can decide if you want to nap or wait up for the guys to arrive."

Nia appreciated him asking and not telling her what she should do. She loved his alpha vibe but couldn't tolerate a controlling asshole, or alphahole, as she and her sis referred to them.

She'd encountered too many guys like that; guys who didn't know how to temper their protective alpha side with being aware women could make their own damn decisions just fine, thank you very much.

She pulled her phone from her pocket, unlocked it, and opened the security app. "Yeah, sounds great. Let's listen to the recording first in here though, so Rachel won't overhear, since she's in the kitchen."

"Good call. I'm gonna get Dak, though. Simone and Rachel can stay in there and finish eating. We'll share with her later."

Reese strode from the room and Nia's heart rate ramped up predictably when Carrick turned his beautiful eyes to her again. She'd never in her life had anyone really look at her, honestly give her their full attention, and his, coupled with the sensuous heat, was as unnerving as it was tantalizing.

"Baby, before the guys show, I want you to know you'll have your own room here, but anytime you want to share mine, you're welcome. No need to ask, just show up."

She blushed, actually blushed, at the thought of crawling into bed naked with this big man, her new mate of all the out-of-this-world things. Surprise filled her at the longing that thought evoked, along with a healthy dose of arousal and pure lust for this big guy. At the over-the-top desire she'd never felt for anyone before.

"I'd love to know what put that blush on your face." He leaned in and pressed a hard kiss to her lips.

"Jeez, man. Can't you keep your lips off hers for five minutes?"

His brother just couldn't keep from busting his balls. Carrick kept his eyes on hers as he murmured to her, but loud enough for all to hear. "I'm gonna kill him, okay? It'll only take a minute, and we can get back to what we were doing."

Nia laughed and shook her head at the silly man. "You know you love him and would never do that."

"I don't know, baby. He keeps interrupting us, I might be convinced he needs to go."

She watched with laughter in her eyes when Reese walked past Carrick and smacked him on the back of the head, then continued on to sit on the edge of the overstuffed couch across from the chair she was in.

Dak shook his head at their antics as he strode past, dragging an upholstered barrel chair next to her for Carrick to sit in, then joined Reese on the couch.

She'd yet to hear him joke around or even smile, so surprise tickled through her to see one side of his mouth quirk the slightest bit when he said, "Just say the word, Nia, I'll toss them both out so you can rest."

Wanting to keep that small smile on his face, she kept Dak's gaze, stroking Carrick's arm as he sat in the chair so he'd know she was joking. "I may take you up on your offer if these boys don't start behaving."

Her face heated again when Carrick leaned over to say for her ears only. "Oh, baby, you don't really want me to behave, do you? We'll have so much more fun if I don't."

The hand that had been stroking his arm smacked his hard shoulder, then gave it a squeeze before she raised her phone and pressed the button to pull up her app, backing up to the time stamp where they'd left off and pressed pause.

"Okay, here we go. It's voice activated and looks like the recording started up again about ten minutes after we last listened to them."

She leaned back and pressed play to hear what the app recorded after they'd left the cottage, then immediately tensed.

Chapter Twelve

CARRICK TENSED as the mic behind Nia's house picked up the assholes' voices again, the more authoritative guy speaking. "Denton's not going to be pleased. He wants to be at the facility, not down here wasting his time while we fail to reacquire his subjects. Did you see any sign of them at all?"

"We're not fucking subjects." Nia's voice was tight with anger and remembered pain.

Carrick clasped her hand and squeezed, knowing she wanted nothing more than to have a face-to-face with Denton when she was feeling strong, maybe with them as backup, so she could set the bastard straight and parse out some punishment. Then Carrick, along with Reese and their buddies, could make sure he never bothered her, or anyone else, again.

Whiney boy spoke up next. "She must have had cameras or something, letting her and the other bitch know we were here. Not our fault! Denton shouldn't have let her escape to begin with."

The sound of a fist meeting flesh preceded a cry of pain, and the third guy spoke up, whiney-boy's buddy. "I'm not carrying his ass to the SUV. How about you teach him a lesson when we get back to Denton's rental? Hey, who's left at the facility, with Denton here?"

"Why the fuck do you care? Got a crush on that leggy bitch in the cell Simone was in?"

"What? No, Jesus, she'd just as soon kill one of us as look at us. Just wondering how long we'd be down here trying to find the women."

"He's in no rush to go back. Said something about needing to give them time between infusions, and they'd be ready to breed with that big Garou dude in a week."

Their voices faded, and the mic stopped recording. Dak jumped from the couch and strode to the fireplace, only to pace back to the couch.

"They fucking have Garou there too?"

Carrick rose and clasped his shoulder. "Hey, keep it under control. Whoever they have locked up needs us to have clear heads right now."

He turned to his brother, noting the look of fury on his face as well. "Call Mateo, see who he can scramble so we can do a sweep on the facility while Denton is down here. Hopefully, there's limited staff left at the facility to monitor the women and Garou, what with his crew here with him."

They waited while Reese made the call, and Carrick turned to explain more about who they were calling for help. "Mateo is Dak's dad. He's one of the top guys in the Council—think of it like the FBI's HRT and SWAT teams rolled into one, only for Garou. He'll pull together a team, and they should be here by tomorrow morning at the latest. He lives in

Sonoma too, as do the other team members, so it shouldn't take him long to pack up and drive down here."

Carrick turned and strode over to Nia's side, holding out his hand. "Let's get you fed before Bah and Hale arrive, then it's to bed with you, unless you really want to stay up."

The second Carrick uttered the word bed, his cock rose to the occasion at the thought of her in his bed. It was worse than a Pavlovian response. The blush across her cheeks and huge pupils were just as telling in her reaction.

She placed her hand in his and murmured, "You're lethal, big guy. What am I going to do with you?"

He opened his mouth to give her as many options as he could come up with, closing it again when she scooted Max out of the way with a pat and soft word, lowered the recliner's footrest, stood and placed a slender finger across his lips.

"Shh, I have my own ideas. I'm just not strong enough yet to act on them."

Damn, he suppressed a shudder when his cock shot to full mast, and that primal voice growled in his mind, 'our mate, bed her, claim her!' He ignored it, along with his burgeoning cock, and tugged on her hand to lead her to the kitchen to feed her instead of all the other things he wanted to do with her delectable body.

"I'll behave. For now."

They entered the kitchen at the same time a tone went off on the monitor on the wall by the door to the mudroom; the screen showing a dark green Chevy Suburban sitting at the gate, two big guys in the front seat.

"How'd Bah and Hale get here so fast?" Reese asked. He peered at the screen, then turned to Carrick. "Looks like Bah and Ramil, instead. I wonder why Hale couldn't make it?"

Carrick shrugged. "No clue, but damn, I'm glad they're here. Nia, Ramil is another geek who also does protection, based out of Sonoma. Hale may be busy with another project and couldn't get away."

Carrick pulled a chair out from the table for Nia, Max a shadow sitting protectively next to her, then went to the system next to the monitor and pressed the speaker button.

"Am I glad to see you both. Come around the back to the garage and park inside."

He pressed another button, and the gate opened wide, allowing the SUV entry before closing again. Carrick headed to the door leading to the garage, swinging it open and pressing a button to open the big door, then watched as they pulled in, climbed from the vehicle, and strode toward him as it rolled closed again behind them.

"Glad you could make it!" Carrick held out a hand to Bah and tugged him into the kitchen and his arms for a hard hug.

Bah smacked him on the back, then held him at arm's length. "You being a trouble-magnet again, my man?"

"Hey, always wrongly accused!" Carrick smacked him on the shoulder as Bah walked past to greet Dak and Reese.

Ramil stepped into the kitchen, giving Carrick a one-armed hug. "Good to see you. We've got your back, and these disreputable dudes, too. Hale's run into some trouble with his current project and couldn't make it, so I volunteered." His first look at

Nia stopped him in his tracks. "Kamusta po, ate? Sino ka?"

At Nia's blank look, he grinned and translated. "How are you, sister? Who are you?" He gave her a wink. "You can take the guy out of the Philippines, but not the Filipino out of the guy. Even if it has been decades since I lived there."

When Nia gave Ramil a wan smile. "Better here than I would have been at home, that's for sure." She laid a hand on Max's head with a soft, "Friends, Max."

Carrick strode over to her and laid his hand on her arm, giving it a gentle squeeze, then turned to Reese. "Didn't you fill them in on the phone?"

"Hell, no. Didn't want to run the risk of anyone eavesdropping, even with our encrypted phones. Just told them we had a situation, and they needed to get their asses down here, stat."

Carrick turned to Bah and Ramil. "You are *not* going to believe it. This is Nia—my mate."

If the situation hadn't been so dire, Carrick would have taken great enjoyment in seeing both his friends' jaws drop as they took shaky steps to jerk out and land heavily into chairs at the table, then just stared at her, transfixed.

Bah recovered first. "How the hell? That hasn't happened in hundreds of years! Where? Why? How?"

Well, maybe recovered was too generous a term. He may have gained his voice, but his brain was way behind his vocal cords. And that was something for the cool-under-fire doctor and former council enforcer, now a Council Director.

Ramil had completely lost his ability to speak.

Reese stepped to the coffee urn and poured two cups, setting them in front of the newcomers. "It's going to be a long night, men, and have we got a story for you. You brought everything you need for blood tests, Bah?"

"Hell yes, said I would, didn't I?" He looked affronted they would even question his readiness and recovered enough to answer.

"Just asking. Nia here is the one in need, and you'll know why when we're done with the story."

Dak spoke up before they could get started. "Nia needs to eat and hydrate first. She's flagging again."

Bah's eyes shot to her and narrowed, and Carrick could see he'd switched to doctor mode, finally noticing her pallor and exhaustion. Bah rose and stepped around the table, approaching slowly, and stopped a foot away from her chair. "Mind if I do basic triage, Nia? Just blood pressure and the like. Nothing intrusive, I promise."

She looked warily at him, then at Carrick. It warmed his soul she trusted him and looked to him for her safety. He tipped his head in a reassuring nod, conveying with his eyes that nothing and no one would hurt her on his watch.

She turned back to Bah with a slight smile and incline of her head. "Sure, go ahead."

Bah sat next to her and turned in surprise when Ramil set his medic bag next to him. "Grabbed it from your vehicle, Dok."

"Thanks, buddy. Carrick, I think we need to wait on the story, get Nia checked out, fed and resting, then we can chat later. Unless there's something you need or want to tell us, Nia? Not trying to push you out of the conversation, just concerned."

She shook her head. "No, the guys know everything, and they can fill you in. I hate to say, but I need to lie down soon before I fall down."

Carrick went to the stove and dished chicken fried rice into a bowl, then turned back to Nia. "Didn't even think to ask. Do you eat meat? Anything you can't eat or are allergic to?"

Dak spoke up before she had a chance to answer. "Just so you know, I excluded from the menu anything people with lupus shouldn't eat. No nightshades, wheat or corn. It's fried brown rice with chicken, bamboo shoots, water chestnuts, eggs, garlic, pepper and Chinese five-spice seasoning."

Nia shot him a grateful smile. "That's about it for things I don't eat, and yes, I do eat meat. That sounds absolutely delicious. Thanks for cooking, Dak."

Dak inclined his head as Carrick set the bowl in front of her, along with another protein shake, and dropped a kiss on her cheek.

Bah sat back and nodded toward her plate. "Eat up, Nia, then I'll get your vitals afterwards. I'm pretty hungry myself. Let's all eat. I'll get Nia squared away and Carrick can get her to bed."

Carrick watched as Nia flushed appealingly again at the mention of him and a bed. It heartened him she was apparently as hot for him as he was for her. Whether she was actually ready to join him in bed, and when she did, she was ready to make love, was yet to be seen.

He'd be perfectly happy to do nothing more than hold her while she slept, to provide comfort and protection. His other-self grumbled a little at that thought, still pushing him to make love and claim her, then settled down as if it curled up in the back of his mind to keep watch.

They made short work of their meal, and Reese cleared the table while Bah pulled items from his cavernous bag.

Nia patted her tummy. "That was delicious. I feel a food coma coming, on top of the exhaustion. Better get your tests done, Bah."

"I'd really like to get some blood samples from you. Carrick has a basic lab set up here in the basement, and I brought additional equipment should we need it for the more advanced tests. We can expect to have the results in the next twenty-four hours, depending on the test."

At the fear that flashed in her eyes, Carrick pulled out the chair next to her and took one of her chilled hands in both of his. "I know you hate needles, baby. Bah has a reputation of being the best at taking blood, and you know how important it is we figure out what's going on with you."

He turned to Bah. "We'll fill you in on the full story later, but Nia was a prisoner of Denton's, and the bastard was experimenting on them with stem cell treatment, both IV and spinal—and they weren't gentle about it. Needless to say, needles aren't her fave things."

"That putanginang aso—that fucking dog!" Ramil shot a furious look at Bah, still frowning when he glanced at Nia, then over to Carrick again.

Carrick glanced at Bah to see his knuckles whiten around the handle of his bag, nearly crushing the material with the strength of his anger.

Tension mounted in Carrick as he waited for Nia's answer, holding her eyes, trying to convey his strength to her and confidence in Bah as a doctor. He knew she'd acquiesced when her eyes closed briefly before she laid her other arm, inner side up, on the table in front of his buddy.

His heart about broke when she turned back to him, her voice barely a whisper of sound. "Don't let go."

He leaned in for her ears only. "Never. I'll never let go, Nia."

He scooted his chair closer and wrapped one arm around her tense shoulders, resting his cheek on top of her head when she tucked it into his neck between his shoulder and jaw. He looked at Bah over her head and gave a slight nod, a look of profound compassion flashing through his friend's eyes.

"I'll explain everything I'm doing before I do it, Nia. I think first we'll get the blood draw out of the way so you're not stressing about it. I like to use a small-gauge needle, same as I use with kids, on a flexible tube that attaches to the test tube so when I change them out, you won't feel a thing. I'm fast and good, so it'll be over before you know it."

Ramil spoke up at that statement. "Yeah, the ladies are always complaining about that, too."

Nia huffed a short laugh and snuggled her face further into his shoulder. Carrick shot a grateful look at Ramil, who gave him a chin lift in response, his eyes also full of compassion for his woman.

Bah turned to Carrick as he pulled items from his bag. "I know you're going to give us the scoop after Nia heads to bed, but I need a little more information, so I know what tests to run and how much blood to draw. Do we know what else they did to her besides stem cells?"

He felt Nia tense a little at Bah's words, and Carrick took his hand from her shoulder to slide it around her waist and tug her closer to him. He gave Bah the basic rundown on her symptoms and the experiments Denton was running, shaking his head at

Ramil and Bah to curb any outburst when anger again crossed their faces and they looked like they were going to fire questions at him.

They both subsided, practically vibrating with pent-up curiosity and fury, and the desire in their eyes to kill everyone involved in hurting his mate flashed hot through his soul.

"Okay, Nia, I have everything ready." Bah spoke again in his calm, deep voice. "Let's get this wrist blood pressure cuff on and let it do its thing. Then a tourniquet onto your bicep to draw blood from this beautiful, fat vein that's introducing herself to me. Is your vein flirting with me?"

Carrick grinned at his buddy when Nia giggled at him, glad to see his bedside manner was just as good now as it had always been.

"Yes, Bah, I think my vein is flirting with you. Better get at it before she changes her mind."

"Gotcha! Okay, tourniquet on, cool alcohol pad and inserting the needle in three, two, one."

Carrick winced when Nia flinched and spoke up to distract her while Bah switched out several tubes as they filled. "It'll be over before you know it. Do you think your vein will flirt with me too? We need to chat about your veins flirting with other men. I mean, come on, I'm your mate, not this guy sitting on the other side of you."

Nia giggled again, then sighed. "You're so bad, Carrick. Yes, I do believe my vein, and other parts of me just might deign to flirt with you a little later. When I'm feeling better."

"Just say the word, baby, and I'll be ready."

With a flick of his fingers, Bah loosened the tourniquet band and let it fall away. "Okay, Nia. All done. Needle coming out, cotton ball and elastic bandage going on. Just need to keep the bandage there for about ten minutes. Sit up and look over here at my finger."

Carrick loosened his tight hold on Nia as she straightened and turned her head to face Bah, staring at his finger as he moved the pen light back and forth with his other hand. "Eyes look good. Let's take a look at your blood pressure. Hmm, just a little high, to be expected after what you've gone through, but nothing to be concerned with."

He brushed her curls away to look at the lump on her temple. "Took a good hit there, eh? Any blurry vision, dizziness? Did you lose consciousness? Swelling doesn't look too bad."

"I was dizzy right afterwards, and then again once I got home, but I'd attribute that to the exhaustion that hits when I expend energy. No dizziness since I've downed the energy drinks and protein shake. Carrick can fill you in. Started after the damned infusions."

"Ah, okay. I'll get the scoop from Carrick. I'd say it's time for you to hit the sack. You're clearly running on fumes and sleep will go a long way in letting your body and mind cope with the injuries and rebuild your strength."

"God, yes, I think I could sleep for a month. Thanks, Bah."

"My pleasure, Nia. We'll figure this out and get you well."

Carrick sent a look of gratitude Bah's way. "Thanks, man. Back soon."

She turned to Carrick, rose from the chair and staggered, Carrick catching her before she could fall. He slipped one arm under her muscled legs, the other under her back and lifted her sweet weight into his arms before striding out of the room and down the long hall, taking a right when it split into a T at the end of the hallway leading to the bedrooms.

"Your room's down here right next to mine. You can see the hallway branches off in two directions, making this part of the house into a long T-shape. One large guest suite with two bedrooms is straight ahead, my room and another single guest room is in this wing to the right, and two more singles at the end of the other branch. Simone and Rachel are in the end room, and Dak will stay in the room next to it in case they need anything. Reese, Bah and Ramil will take turns staying in the suite in the middle, since they'll be rotating, monitoring the property and house; it's more like a hotel suite with a small sitting room in the middle and two bedrooms on either side with a shared bathroom. Someone will be up and keeping watch at all times, on rotation. Reese and Dak actually have their own cottages on the property, back behind the house, and there's an empty guest cottage, too, but we'll all be staying in the house while we're dealing with the threat from Denton and his men."

He strode into her room, glad to see someone had pulled back the bedding and placed her backpack and the other bags from the cottage, except Simone's duffle, on the big chair in the corner. He laid her gently on the bed, knowing she was too wiped out to undress herself but not wanting to make her nervous or take liberties by undressing her without asking.

"I know I mentioned it before and want you to know I was dead serious. If you need or want me, you're welcome to come to my room. Just call out when you first enter so I know it's you, although I think I'll wake just having you enter."

He got a small nod from his mate and knew he had to be patient. It was different for her. She'd just learned about the Garou and Cinnabar Twins—and mates. Arousal, and their link, had blindsided her. It would take her a while to get used to it.

He leaned over and saw she was still awake, barely, and watching him intently. He smoothed a hand down her arm and gave a gentle squeeze to her hand. "Okay if I help you undress and under the covers? By the way, Dak put your Sig and shotgun in the safe."

When she didn't answer him, but kept looking at him through half-closed eyes, he leaned the rest of the way and pressed a chaste kiss to her lips. "It's okay, baby. Sweet dreams. I'll be in the kitchen for a while, then in my room if you need me." As he turned to leave the room, a hand on his forearm stopped him in his tracks.

"Do you have a t-shirt I can sleep in? I do need your help. My brain is just slow to catch up and answer you." She gave him a wry grin as her eyes slid closed.

"Of course, be right back."

Carrick double-timed it to his bedroom, grabbed the softest, biggest t-shirt he owned from his dresser, and was back in her room before she could drift to sleep.

"Okay, arms up and off with the tank top." She was wearing a bra, so he knew she wouldn't feel totally exposed to him. He'd love nothing more than to see those beauties bared to him, but he wanted her aware he was looking, and a full participant. He pulled her tank off and tried, but failed, to keep his eyes on her face.

The lush mounds practically spilling out of her bra captivated him, and just that glance had him hardening in his pants again. He started to tug the t-shirt over her head but stopped when she spoke up.

"I'm too tired to be embarrassed, and might just be tomorrow, but will you also take off my bra? It'll be way too uncomfortable to sleep in if I leave it on."

"Of course, sweetheart. No need to be embarrassed." He swallowed hard and, with a flip of his wrist, unhooked the front clasp, and then, hard as he tried, couldn't pull his gaze away as the full mounds burst free. He was dying to tease the turgid peaks of her nipples with his tongue.

He extricated her arms and pulled the bra from under her, tossing it onto the chair. He jerked his eyes back to hers and noted an answering arousal swimming in her beautiful, exhausted eyes.

"I wish undressing you was under other circumstances." He dropped a kiss on her lips, keeping his eyes on hers, before reversing the process and pulling his shirt over her head, holding it while she threaded her arms into the sleeves.

"Me too." Her voice slurred, and he knew she was close to succumbing to exhaustion.

His shirt swamped her, and that primal, possessive part of him loved seeing her wearing his clothes. He hoped it was as comfortable to her as a soft nightgown would be. "Leggings next, Nia?" At her nod, he slipped his hands under the shirt and tugged both her yoga pants and a tiny slip of lace that barely passed as panties down and off, tossing them to the floor next to the chair, wincing at the sound of her phone hitting the rug.

He reached for the phone, swiped down and muted it, then set it on the nightstand. When he turned back, she'd rolled to her side facing him, hands tucked under her cheek, sound asleep. Her muscular legs seemed to go on for miles and were as much a turn on as her breasts. Damn, this woman just did it for him.

As much as it pained him to leave, he needed to get back to the kitchen and read the guys fully in on the situation, then come up with a plan for keeping Nia, Simone and Rachel safe while they stormed the Umpqua facility.

He pulled the covers up to her waist and leaned down to press another kiss to her temple. "Sleep tight, love. I'm so glad I found you."

When he turned, she shocked him by muttering, "Glad too, Carrick. Mate." And then she was out.

He'd been sure she was sound asleep and couldn't hear him, but apparently some part of her was aware enough to respond. His heart filled with affection and love. Yes, love for this woman, even if he'd known her less than twenty-four hours. That's apparently what happened when you found your mate. Having her say what she did when her defenses were down, when what she thought she should feel wasn't coloring what she actually felt deep inside, made his heart sing.

He just hoped she still felt that way when she woke.

Chapter Thirteen

NIA WOKE disoriented and afraid in a dark room; she always left a nightlight in her bedroom on. Why wasn't she in her bed? Did Denton grab her again? She bolted upright, thankful there was no lingering dizziness, and swung her legs over the side of the bed in panic before realizing the bed was plush, not the hard, musty smelling cot she'd grown to hate in that small cell.

She saw, by the dim light from the hallway filtering through the cracked-open door, this room was large and well furnished. The soft canine whine behind her had her swiveling her head to see Max stretched out on his belly, crawling toward her, no doubt to provide comfort.

"No, boy, it's okay. Lay back down. I'm fine." Her brain finally kicked in and she realized if she was back in Denton's clutches, she would be in a five-by-five concrete cell on an army surplus cot and scratchy wool blanket with a porta potty in the corner behind an almost transparent screen.

And the creepy guard would be watching her through the rectangular window in the steel door. She shuddered at the memory of the constant fear he would sneak into her cell when she was asleep and take what he so evidently fantasized about doing to her. Sometimes she could tell he was jacking off while he watched her from the hallway, just by the look on his evil face through the little window.

As she sat and caught her breath while the rush of adrenaline abated, memories came back of meeting Bah and Ramil, of Carrick carrying her to bed, of him undressing her and how aroused he was by the sight of her when he'd freed her breasts to his gaze.

And how much a part of her had wanted to invite him into her bed to feel his lips and callused hands on her bare skin. She also remembered his parting words before he left, when he'd thought her asleep. 'Sleep tight, love. I'm so glad I found you.'

As crazy as it was, if she concentrated just a little, she could feel the link with him. She also felt that enticing buzz of arousal still burning through her body since the second he'd touched her. Just remembering upped the zing, her nipples tightening to hard buds, craving the sweet torment of his lips.

Her clit pulsed, wanting his big, blunt-tipped fingers to brush against it. Her pussy wanted those same fingers, or better yet, that thick cock of his to slide into her, buried to the hilt, then pumping away until he was just as ready to blow as she was.

Screw the rules of dating—he was her mate. He was Garou, and she was apparently a Cinnabar Twin, and they truly were just like a couple in one of her paranormal romances.

And didn't she always think the heroines in those books were stupid twits if they waited to cement the deal and get busy with the hot dude because they'd 'just met'?

Conventional rules went out the window, she thought, when it came to situations like this. Even though she wasn't Garou, apparently being a Cinnabar Twin meant she felt the rightness, the tightness of their bond. Could feel that link, the out-of-this-world attraction—sexual, emotional and psychical.

A full-body flush of arousal swept through her. *Time to pull up, or pull off, my big girl panties and embrace my man. Time to go find my man.*

She stood, turned once more to give Max a pat on his big head and the signal to stay, then walked out of her room, so conveniently located right next door to Carrick's, glad to see the door ajar enough she could peek in. The nightlight from the hallway cast soft light into his room, and she could just make out his large form sprawled across his bed.

She lifted her foot to step across the threshold, but hesitated, wondering if he really wanted to be disturbed. What if he'd just gotten to bed and was as tired as she had been?

When was the last time he'd slept? Was she being selfish? Should she wait until tomorrow, and they could actually plan a tryst? Damn it, where did her courage go?

"Baby, don't make me get out of bed to carry you to mine. I can practically feel that smart, busy brain of yours overthinking whether you should come in. Get in here, woman, and make both of us happy."

Nia gasped at the sound of his deep, rumbly voice, a rush of liquid flooding her core. She walked through the door, nudged it shut, crossed the room with hips swaying and pulled off her sleep shirt, baring herself fully to him for the first time.

She'd always been confident in her sexuality, but wondered if he found her as appealing or sexy as she found him. She craved this man and wanted her hands and mouth all over the enticing ridges and valleys of that sexy, hard, sculpted body.

She reveled in the growl that rose from his throat as he erupted from the bed, wrapped her in his muscular arms and kissed the daylights out of her. Well, she thought dazedly; she had her answer. And that was the last coherent thought that crossed her mind.

She wrapped her arms around his lats and clutched his ripped back, silently acknowledging being a 'muscle hussy', where porn for her were huge pecs, lats, delts, biceps and triceps. Oh, and let's not forget quads and calves, and a tight muscular bubble butt. Not that she didn't appreciate a sexy package, too, she thought in a daze as his thick cock nudged her belly.

His soft but masculine lips on hers were ambrosia, and his tongue dueling with hers sent joy to her nipples that rippled all the way down her center to her clit. She reveled in his shirtless chest, sporting a thick mat of curls that teased and abraded her nipples, making her a hair away from climaxing on the rioting sensations alone.

She groaned into his mouth and the wicked man upped his game by slipping a hand between their bodies to tweak a nipple between thumb and forefinger, then brush it with the backs of his fingers.

"Oh, Carrick! Your mouth, please, suck my nipples." If he wasn't as evidently as turned on as she was, her groaned plea would have been embarrassing.

"Yeah, baby, tell me what you need. I've been dying to get those beauties in my mouth and cupped in my hands. You have the prettiest brown nipples just begging for my tongue."

He gave a last suck on her tongue and nibble to her lower lip, then ducked his head to take a tight nipple in his mouth.

She would have collapsed if he hadn't wrapped a muscular forearm under her butt and lifted so her breasts were right where he could do the most good—even with that talented mouth of his. She squirmed, trying to get relief for her clit but not wanting him to stop the action on her breasts.

"Gotta get you in bed, baby, where I can feast on you."

"Oh, yeah." A gasp escaped when he lipped and tongued her nipple, then moved to nibble the lush fullness around her areola, teasing her to the brink of insanity. She could barely remember her own name, and grabbed a handful of his hair, glad it was long enough to clutch the strands with her fingers and tugged him back where she wanted him.

He laughed in delight. "Oh, that's the way it is, huh?"

When he latched on the other nipple to give it the same sensuous treatment, Nia lost the ability to form complete sentences. "Need to touch you. Need to see you." Thankfully, Carrick seemed to have no problem understanding her.

He backed toward the bed and dropped, taking her down gently with him to lie atop all that masculine perfection, then started devouring her mouth again.

When he slipped a hard hairy quad between her legs and ducked his head again to switch his mouth back to her breast to again torment her pebbled nipple, she rode his massive thigh as if her life depended on it.

"Ohhhh, Carrick! Ahhhhhh!" Her climax came out of nowhere and swamped her. It wasn't a slow buildup, like she usually needed before getting off. It was a tsunami wave crashing to the shore. An earthquake toppling mountains. An avalanche of sensations that overwhelmed her and tumbled her into ecstasy.

He was in perfect tune with her, somehow knowing the enormity of her climax was unfamiliar to her, that she needed gentling and to calm down before he revved her up again. She wondered if it was their intrinsic link that allowed him to know he should slow her movement on his thigh, to press gentle kisses on her breast, her cheek, her lips.

To brush his big hand down the back of her head and continue down her spine to the curve of her ass, finally cupping one butt cheek with his wide palm to just relax with her in his arms.

His cock was a pulsing rod on her belly, but Carrick simply lay and gentled her, letting her know without words he would always put her first, that her feelings and comfort were foremost in his mind.

She could love this man, she thought dreamily.

Her strength roared back at the thought, along with the fantasy of sucking that sexy appendage still nudging her tummy into her mouth, to drive him crazy before she took him into her body to give him the ride of his life.

She pushed up, swept her hair from her face, rested her forearms on his pecs and dropped a kiss on his lips, her curls again avalanching forward to cocoon them.

"I've gotta confess, not that I want to bolster your ego, but normally my orgasms are more on the mildly pleasant side, and only when using a small personal appliance. That was practically an out-of-body experience. Was…"

She hesitated, not wanting him to think she was insecure, but her curiosity had always gotten the best of her if not satisfied, and would linger and fester. "Will it be…"

"Spit it out, baby. You can ask me anything. I won't lie to you. Ever. I also won't ever look at or want another woman, now that I've met you. Touched you."

Nia looked him in the eyes and blurted out, "Will it be like this all the time with you, for you too, or is it more intense and better because we're, well, because we're mates?" Twenty-four hours ago, if anyone had told her she would utter a sentence with the word mates in it, she'd have blown them off and headed in the other direction.

He let his hands roam across the sensitive curve of her butt, up her back, up, up, enticing her all over again until he cupped her face, then used his magnificent six pack to lift her effortlessly and brush his lips against hers.

"It has never been this intense for me, Nia. I've never craved a woman the way I do you. I've never felt my heart would beat right out of my chest if I couldn't touch you. My cock has never felt it would explode if we didn't make love. I've never felt I could come just from thinking about a woman, looking at a woman, touching a woman, much less filling your fine pussy. And we haven't actually done that last one, yet. Can you imagine what it'll be like when we do? Damn, baby, will we even survive? It's all you, Nia. It's our link, that you're my mate—it's the fact you're an amazing, smart, independent, beautiful and sexy-as-hell woman. And that you're mine, and only mine."

She couldn't stop the tears from falling. Happy tears, but they must have scared the hell out of her man, if his reaction was any indication.

"Hey, hey! What did I say? What's wrong?"

"Nothing, silly man. I'm just..." She sniffed inelegantly. "I'm just so happy! That's exactly how I feel about you, and why I'm in your bed less than one full day after meeting you, after learning about Cinnabar Twins and Garou and mates. I've never felt this way, never believed I would have someone devoted to me. Someone loyal. Someone as smart and protective and sexy and strong and handsome as you—just for me."

She gave him what she hoped was a sultry look. "Now, how about I give you a sample of how I feel about you and your fine-ass body?"

With that she slid down his rippling abs before he could stop her, knelt between his massive quads, wrapped her hand around the base of his thick cock, cupped and gently rolled his balls, and licked from base to mushroom head, then wrapped her lips around that hard length as far as she could go and sucked.

When he clutched a handful of her hair in his fist, tight enough to pull but not hurt, her arousal ramped up, knowing she was driving him crazy with her actions.

"Baby! Dayammn! I'm not gonna last if you do that. Holy shit, yes, just like that."

She slipped her mouth off with a pop and asked saucily, "So, how long does it take a Garou to recover and be ready again?"

His low growl when she took him in her mouth again, then pulled up and off, slow as molasses, shot satisfaction through her, and she glanced up to see his eyes molten and locked on her lips before pinning her with his heated gaze.

"Not…" Another growl when she gave a second, slow swipe of her tongue, his hand clenching in her hair before releasing again, always oh so careful not to hurt her. "Not long. With you, baby, maybe one to five minutes, although I'd bank on the lower number."

"Well, big guy. How about you lie back and let me enjoy myself, and just say 'challenge accepted'? I'm lovin' having you at my mercy and in my mouth."

The look he gave her was pure fire and desire. "Oh, baby. Go for it, and then it's my turn to slide this bad boy home and send us both to heaven."

She about melted onto the covers at his words. She knew, after that mind-blowing orgasm he'd graced her with, he wasn't bragging and would more than deliver on his promise.

"You've got yourself a deal." She slid her lips down again to engulf his rock-hard cock and fondled his balls, then drove him crazy.

His groans, growls, and fists clenching the covers told their own story. He lasted maybe two minutes before he arched his back and erupted into her mouth with a roar.

"Nia! Fuuuck!"

She took him all and swallowed, pulling her mouth off carefully, knowing how oversensitive his cock would be, then peppered kisses along his amazing Adonis belt before sliding back up his body to lie full length, twining her legs with his, the crisp hair covering hard muscles tickling her smooth legs.

THIS WOMAN, HIS MATE, and the chemistry they shared blew Carrick away. He'd never received a blow job that practically blew the top of his head off. The one on his shoulders.

He'd clenched the covers to keep from reaching down and burying his fists in her curls, for fear of hurting her with his strength.

He wondered if he'd be able to move, to fulfill his promise. Hell, his brag, of only needing a few minutes to recover. Until she started sliding that perfect body up his, that is.

Damn, every erogenous zone he had and some he'd never been aware of woke and howled their pleasure, along with that unfamiliar voice in his head, growling and commanding, 'claim mate, make her ours!'

It was going to take some getting used to, having that other-self, demanding, growling, ordering him around in the back of his mind. He'd heard his dad and other older Garou mention it in passing, but thought it was a euphemism for listening to their sixth sense.

He'd never imagined that meeting his mate would actually bring to life the animal part of him that, before now, had been silent, hidden, apparently waiting for their mate to show.

He'd heard long ago the claiming involved biting the woman at the moment of ejaculation. That the

Garou had extra prostaglandins in their blood and semen, and combined with the serum injected from the fangs into the Cinnabar Twin when the Garou bit their mate at the time of ejaculation—along with the small amount of blood the Garou consumed from the bite—was what cemented the bond.

Made it permanent. So much stronger. Provided the same longevity for the Cinnabar Twin as for the male Garou, along with improved health and increased strength.

As much as he wanted that bond with Nia, craved it, wanted her to be stronger, to live longer, he couldn't, wouldn't do it without her permission.

When Nia spoke up, insecurity in her voice, he realized he'd been lost in thought for much too long. "Change your mind, big guy?"

He rolled her over till he covered her with his body and caught her gasp in his mouth as he kissed her senseless.

"Never, baby. I'm sorry I made you think so. I want nothing more than to slip inside you and drive you as crazy as you did me. To make you mine."

At her moan, he slipped his tongue in her mouth to duel with hers, then nibbled gently on her lush lower lip before pulling back to cup her beautiful face in his hands.

"But for a Garou, that means more than for regular humans. I want you to know I would never take that decision away from you. I was hesitating because I was thinking of the stories I've heard through the years, told by my parents, my aunts and uncles, about how when a Garou meets his mate, a primal 'other' part makes itself known. We can't actually shift, like werewolves in fairytales or anything—although rumor has it at one time we could—but apparently this other-self talks to us. I'd never actually paid much attention, hadn't really believed it was real, after all this time."

At her skeptical look, he continued earnestly. "I'm not talking shit, here, Nia. My other side wants me to make love to you, to protect you. It also wants me to claim you as ours. But claiming you means that, when we do make love—when we fuck, to put it crudely because my other-self can be crude when it's trying to order me around—in order to claim you, my incisors will elongate to become sharp fangs, and I'll bite you where your neck meets your traps. I'll receive some of your blood and the fangs will share with you, inject if you will, a serum unique to the Garou males. That serum, combined with you receiving my semen containing prostaglandin unique to Garou, will cause an unbreakable bond and link between us, even stronger than what we feel now. We'll be able to sense each other easier. You'll be stronger and will live longer. Be healthier. Did I mention I'm a little over one hundred sixty years old? My parents are over four hundred and counting. I've actually lost count."

Her gasp of surprise and jolt cause him to tighten his hands on her face, staring into her eyes, wanting desperately for her to believe him. To believe in them.

"Carrick. I'm…" She swallowed hard, looked away, then back. "You know I'm drawn to you; can feel the connection linking me to you. But… I'm not ready yet to make a commitment like that. Please don't think I'm rejecting you. God! I'm not, okay? I just need more time to understand; to really believe."

He understood this was all new to her, that she'd have to be crazy to agree blithely to mating the same day they'd met, but his primal-self sure wasn't on board with her waiting. It howled and encouraged him to seduce her, to bite her, to make her theirs. Right. Fucking. Now!

Finally getting used to that second growly voice in his head, he quashed those thoughts and sent back a stern 'be patient', then opened his mouth to reassure her he understood, wouldn't pressure her, but he didn't get one word out before she spoke again.

"I'm sorry, Carrick. I'm not saying no. I'm just saying I need more time."

He thought he'd put on a good poker face, but apparently he was crap at hiding his emotions from his mate. When she raised her arms and mimicked him by cupping his face in her hands, he closed his eyes, dropped his forehead to hers, and tried to reassure her.

"I know, baby. It's that primal part of me who thinks we need to be mated in order to provide you total protection, to strengthen you so you can face whatever fucked up shit Denton throws our way. It's hounding the hell out of me to convince you to say yes. Don't worry, sweetheart. I'm in total control and won't push. I'm still dying to make love to you, but I promise I won't betray your trust and will wait until you give the go. I gotta admit I want nothing more than for you to want me as much as I want you, to want to complete the mating bond and bind us together, but I will not pressure you. Okay, that's not absolutely true. I want you safe, and well, first and foremost."

He leaned in and brushed his lips against hers, gladdened when she opened for him to explore the warmth of her mouth, and further heartened when she reached a hand down, slipped it between their bodies and stroked his already hardening cock, then pushed gently against his chest till he released her lips.

Her soft smile and glistening eyes conveyed how much his words meant to her. "Thank you, Carrick. Just give me time, yeah?"

He watched in awe of his mate when she rallied and shot him a sexy look beneath her lashes, clearly trying to lighten the mood. "Were you just bragging, big guy? You have to know I'm soaking wet and feeling pretty empty down there right now." She shot him a slightly panicked, questioning look. "We can do this without completing the mating, can't we? I don't have to wait, do I?"

"On, absolutely we can, sweetheart." He grinned at her, then frowned. "Well, dammit."

Nia frowned back and stiffened. "What do you mean, 'Well dammit?' Second thoughts, or we really can't?"

He hastened to reassure her, feeling terrible she misunderstood the reason for his cursing. "Baby, I want more than anything to slide into you and savor your beautiful, lush body. But, I don't have condoms. It's been years since I've been with anyone. There didn't seem to be a point, anymore, if a woman wasn't my mate. I'll totally understand if you want to wait, but also want to reassure you that the Garou are impervious to human diseases, so you don't have to worry about that aspect."

Carrick barely breathed waiting to see what she would say, what her response would be. She had no reason to fully trust him, but a guy could wish.

"You know I trust you, right? Or I wouldn't be here naked in your bed." She started stroking him again, pumping her hand up and down, swiping precum over the bulbous head on every up sweep and driving him batshit crazy.

"Yeah." His raspy voice betrayed his arousal, and he wondered where she was going with this question.

"If you're disease free, and actual mating involves biting—and if you can keep your teeth to yourself—then I'm onboard. I have a contraceptive implant and am disease free. I've always used protection in the past, the few times I, well, had sex. So, we can forgo the condoms."

"Yeah. Damn, baby, no issues here. Bareback just might do me in, though. Just the thought has me almost shooting off."

Almost frantic to feel his uncloaked cock slip into her hot, wet sheath, Carrick supported his weight with his forearms and slipped his hands under her shoulders.

He was hard enough he lined up without a helping hand and slid halfway home, then had to stop to savor the feeling of being inside his mate for the first time.

He rocked back and forth—she was oh-so tight and he was thick—until he'd fully embedded in the heat of her channel, gritting his teeth and closing his eyes tight against the need to shoot off. No way was he going to be a two-second wonder and not bring his mate to climax again, this time around his cock.

His other-self growled in satisfaction and for once wasn't ordering him to claim her. Must have been as shellshocked as he was at the feel of her tight, warm channel squeezing him. At the soul-deep feeling he was finally home, where he belonged.

The feel of her strong, slender hands on his back, her short nails scraping along his spine, her other hand sliding down to cup his butt, sent him into action.

He pulled out until only the mushroom head was sheathed inside and pumped back in, the tug and pull of her tight core against his oh-so-sensitive cock causing his balls to pull tight and the zing of an impending orgasm already shooting up and down his spine.

Gritting his teeth, he buried his face against her cheek, shocked to feel his canines elongate and sharpen, and had to force himself not to sink them into her trap muscle. Fuck!

He jerked his head up and stared down at his mate; her face breathtaking with the mahogany cloud of curls spread across the pillow, her gem green eyes flashing sparks of red and silver and her copper-toned skin aglow with arousal. He saw shock, awe, and a little trepidation in her eyes, and he realized his fangs were protruding enough to be visible over his lower lip.

He pinned her with his gaze and repeated his vow. "Nia, I won't force you. You have my word."

At her nod, affection and arousal shining once again from her beautiful, multicolored eyes, he pumped his cock into his woman, gaining speed until her command to 'fuck me hard' sent him over the edge.

His hips pistoned, his tight balls slapping the globes of her perfect ass, and he reveled in her expulsion of breath every time his groin hit her clit.

"Uh, uh, ohhhhh! I'm. Almost. There! Damn!" The frustration in her voice sent one of his hands searching for that small bud hiding between the soft lips above her pussy to brush the knuckle of his forefinger against the swollen, protruding nub.

He exerted a bit more pressure, and she went off like a rocket, her core tightening around his cock to where he lost his rhythm and jerked erratically, close to losing himself in her.

"Yes, Carrick! Oh, yes!! Ohhhhh!"

Her cry as she arched into orgasm sent him right over the edge with her as he buried himself hard and roared out his release. "Fuck! Nia, baby, yessss. Mine!"

He barely remembered to roll as he collapsed so he didn't suffocate her under his bulk, wrapped her in his arms and reveled in the sensation as her full lips pressed into his neck with a soft, lingering kiss and sigh of completion.

He'd worn his mate out and pleasured her to boot.

Chapter Fourteen

NIA STRETCHED herself awake, slight twinges of discomfort bringing a slow smile to her lips in remembrance of the night before. Wowza, who knew? No sexual fantasies she'd ever come up with came close to what she'd shared last night with Carrick.

And she had a pretty darned good imagination. They'd slept a bit and made love once more before she'd been down for the count, exhaustion overriding her desire to make love to her man all night long.

Good thing they'd stopped, since she was shaky again this morning after expending so much energy. She grinned at the memory of just how they'd expended that energy, a shiver of arousal zinging to her core and outward like a starburst from head to breasts to toes before centering once again on her clit.

She rolled over, craving her man's lips, disappointed to see only an indentation where he'd lain with her the night before. Usually she was a light sleeper, but the big guy had worn her out last night and she'd apparently slept through him getting up, dressing and leaving the room.

A quick glance at the door ensured it was closed, so she rolled over and slipped her legs off the bed, clenching her toes in the plush shag of the royal blue throw rug under her feet. She felt bad for leaving Max alone in the guest room overnight, but with his canine hearing, she was sure he'd known she was okay and just next door.

She still felt bad for abandoning her buddy, but couldn't regret her time with Carrick. One of the guys had no doubt let Max out to do his business, and he was probably in the kitchen begging for treats and getting spoiled by one, or all, of the men.

As she glanced around, she spied a note propped against an ElectRou protein shake sitting in an ice-filled bucket, along with a bottle of ibuprofen. A sigh of delight slipped through her lips to realize her man was as thoughtful this morning as he'd been since the moment she'd met him.

She picked up the note and read, '*Baby, I didn't have the heart to wake you, although it took all my strength not to roll on top of you and slide in while taking those lush lips of yours and fondling those beautiful breasts. Yeah, yeah, I'll behave. You'll find us in the kitchen. Mateo and the guys got in early, so it's a houseful. Yours, Carrick*'.

Well, darn the man for being just shy of perfect. Not that she'd found any flaws yet. No one was perfect, though, so there must be something. Maybe he snored?

She popped the cap off the ibuprofen and shook two out, then pulled the shake from the bucket and uncapped it. Dropping the pills in her mouth, she took a long drink and hoped it kicked in quickly.

She rose and slipped on the t-shirt she'd worn for a brief time last night, and walked to the closed door, listening to ensure no one was in the hallway.

Opening it a crack, she poked her head outside, confirmed the hallway was empty, then exited and hurried next door to her room.

She was glad to see someone had put her backpack and bags from the cottage in her room, then realized if anyone but Carrick put them there, they were aware she'd slept with him last night. Unless they were already there when he'd carried her to bed and she'd just not noticed.

Surely, with all the guys being Garou, they knew mates wouldn't wait to get it on? Well, she wasn't going to worry about that. She was a grown-ass woman and would decide when it was time to get busy with her man.

She grinned at that thought, then frowned as she remembered the flash of disappointment in Carrick's eyes last night when she'd told him she wasn't ready to be claimed.

She knew he understood, but also knew he must be more than ready for them to do the deed, so she'd be his mate in every way. How would it feel to wait over a hundred years, thinking you would never find your mate, only to stumble across her but not know when, or if, she'd agree to cement the bond?

Well, she hadn't meant she was going to reject him when she'd told him she wasn't ready. And if things continued as they were, it wouldn't take long at all for her to cave.

Like maybe within a week. This was the real deal, in her opinion. Regular humans could date for months or years and then have it fall apart, anyway.

Being a Garou mate seemed like more of a sure thing, without being bound by some artificial, human-constructed period of waiting or nebulous connection.

She stopped and concentrated for a second, realizing she could tell he was close by. And now that she'd identified and acknowledged it, this invisible thread that linked them together, she wanted—no, needed—to be close to him, to kiss him good morning and touch him.

She wrapped her hair in a towel, made quick work of showering, rummaged in her bags and threw on comfortable, well-worn jeans, a sexy demi bra that celebrated her cleavage and a tank top.

She'd worry about shoes later. She leaned upside town and ruffled her hair, glad the curls let her get away with just shaking them out and fluffing a bit. The curly-girl's way of brushing without a brush, since getting bristles through curls like hers was pretty much impossible. Besides, she loved her wild hair.

Nervous about meeting a large group of Garou, but trusting Carrick, Reese and Dak, not to mention Bah and Ramil, she stiffened her spine, opened the door and plowed right into the unmovable block of muscle that was Carrick. "Ooof!"

He grabbed her biceps to keep her from bouncing backwards to the floor, and the first touch of his big, callused hands to her bare skin made her girl-bits rise up and practically whimper for more of the action from the night before. Her eyes shot to his, the heat and beauty of his molten silver eyes captivating her.

"Whoa, handsome. How'd you know I was on my way out?"

When he dipped his head to brush his lips across hers, she rose on her toes, slanted her head and upped the heat level of the kiss.

"Damn, woman. Keep that up and we'll compare beds to see if yours is better than mine."

She about turned into a puddle of romantic goo when he pulled back, cupped her cheeks in his big, callused palms, and snared her eyes. "You just get prettier every time I see you. And more irresistible."

She tiptoed again to plant another smacking kiss on those masculine lips. "Thank you. But sweet talking me will not get me naked and under you, especially with a bunch of guys in the kitchen who can probably hear us, am I right?"

She rolled her eyes and blushed when no less than four deep voices shouted, "You're right!" Another voice yelled out at Carrick. "Get your ass back here, man, and bring your woman with you so we can meet her!"

Nia knew she was bright red from the men's words and ducked her faced against his chest with a groan.

"Jeez, you sure it isn't bat genes you guys have in your DNA, instead of some wolf-hybrid, with hearing like that?"

At the answering '*Awoooooo*' from the kitchen, several human and the one canine she recognized immediately, Carrick chuckled and swept a hand over her curls and down her spine to just above the curve of her ass. "Shut it, West! Ignore them, they're just jealous I've found you."

Nia loved how affectionate he was and graced him with a smile. When he dropped another kiss on her lips, then dropped his hand to caress her ass, she felt a flood of moisture prep her for penetration.

Maybe they could just head back to bed?

When she felt the prod of his cock on her stomach, and saw his nostrils flare and his pupils take over his irises to leave a ring of deep silver, she realized his Garou senses had picked up the scent of her arousal. When he opened his mouth, no doubt to comment or entice her back to bed, she pressed her forefinger against those marvelous lips with a, "Shhhh! Don't you dare!"

He pressed a kiss to her finger, took her hand in his, then turned toward the kitchen. "Come on, baby. I'll introduce you to the degenerates hanging out, drinking up all the coffee, and you can put them in their place."

She shared a grin with him at the smack-talk coming from his friends and entered the kitchen, stopping just inside the doorway, a little overwhelmed by the wall of testosterone in the form of intimidating, muscular men lining the kitchen counter.

The sheer presence of these guys, the determination coming off them in waves, almost made the air thick in the kitchen. Reese looked to be cooking at the stove, Ramil sitting at the end of the table next to an older man, and everyone else lined the counter, butts propped, arms crossed.

Ramil lifted a hand her way and grinned. "Kamusta ka na, ate? How are you, sister?"

She turned a grateful smile his way. "Better than last night, Ramil. Thank you."

Carrick turned to her in concern when she just stood there and opened his mouth as if to speak, but the older guy next to Ramil interrupted him.

He looked to be in his mid-fifties, but she was assuming since he was Garou, he must be much older. She suppressed a grin and wondered if it was

something like dog years—seven for one human—
and made a mental note to ask Carrick when she got
him alone, if for no other reason than to tease him.

The older guy shot the men lining the counter a
stern look. "Sit down, men. Nia doesn't need a wall
of muscle standing over her while we chat."

She glanced at him when he spoke, and he shot her
a wink as he stood and strode to the end of the table
near her and Carrick, while the men who'd been
standing obeyed him, each pulling out a chair and
sitting with a nod in her direction.

He dipped his head at her and pulled out the chair
nearest to where she was standing. "Have a seat, Nia,
while this unruly group sits their asses down like I
asked them to. Can I get you a coffee while we get
the introductions going?"

Nia grinned at him, gratitude filling her eyes at his
thoughtfulness in putting her at ease and for the offer
of coffee. "I'd love coffee. Oh, and another one of
those ElectRou shakes from the fridge, too, if you
don't mind."

"Darlin', I'm happy to get you whatever you
need."

He held out one of his huge hands—all the Garou
must be massive, if not in height than in width and
muscle, based on who'd she'd met so far—and she
placed hers in it expecting to shake, but he had other
ideas.

He dropped to a knee next to her, wrapped both
his hands around hers and spoke in a low, deep voice
while Carrick stood behind her, one big palm on her
shoulder.

"I want you to know you can trust every man in
this room to help you, to help Simone and Rachel.
She's putting the little one back to bed and will be

right back. We'll stand in front of, next to, or behind you—whatever you need, Nia. From what Carrick and Simone have said, you're a kick-ass lady, so we're here to aid, protect, defend, or kill if necessary, to keep you safe and alive. We're going to erase the people threatening you, and release the people being held at that facility."

A chorus of 'damn straight', 'roger that' and 'fuck yeah' filled the room as the other men agreed with the older man. Nia wasn't a crier, but damned if his vow and support, and the support of the other guys, didn't turn on the faucet.

She also wasn't a pretty crier, like some women pulled off, and it always embarrassed her. Her face turned red and blotchy, her nose ran, and she looked like a drowned rat.

She dropped her face into her free hand as the tears broke free, surprised and comforted to feel the older guy wrap an arm around her back and tug her onto his shoulder, then murmur in her ear.

"I'm Mateo, Dak's dad, and am always looking to adopt more adult kids. Don't cry, honey, it'll be okay." She registered Carrick smoothing a hand over her head and down her back, acknowledging her moment and Mateo's fatherly hug and vow.

She choked back her tears and straightened, uncovering her face, a napkin thankfully placed in her hand. She swiped the wetness away and surreptitiously wiped her nose, then looked at Mateo, still on one knee in front of her.

"I'm so happy to meet you, Mateo. And I can't tell you how much what you said means to me." She gave him a watery smile and sniffed. "You sure you want to take on more adult kids, especially ones in a shitstorm like we are, what with already having to wrangle this motley crew behind me?"

She grinned at the mock-complaints from the guys at her words, and Mateo grinned back at her. "Well, Nia, seeing how I don't have any daughters, and I could use a kick-ass one who can occasionally help me keep them in line, I'd say you're a shoo-in."

She heard Carrick's deep belly-laugh, reached up to pat his hand on her shoulder, then leaned forward to put an affectionate kiss on Mateo's sandpapery cheek.

"You've got yourself a deal, then. I've never actually had a dad, so this'll be a learning experience for me, too."

She regretted having said that when a look of sadness flashed through Mateo's eyes, and she hastened to reassure him. "Hey, no feeling sorry for me. Looks like I'll be able to make up for that, and who knows? You may tire of me asking to borrow the car."

She knew she'd successfully lightened the mood when Mateo stood, threw his head back and laughed uproariously, then turned to Dak. "You been sharing car-borrowing stories with her, son?"

Dak gave that quirk of his lips Nia now recognized as a full-on smile for him. "Nope. Apparently she has your number even without stories, pops."

When Mateo returned to his seat, Nia turned to the table and realized her coffee and protein shake had been delivered by one of the guys during her mini-meltdown.

She called out a general thanks to whoever delivered it, picked up the shake, twisted the cap off and downed half at once, then set it on the table and grabbed her coffee for a sip.

"Aww, that hits the spot. Now my brain can wake up, too."

Hopefully, between getting good sleep the night before, endorphins from getting it on with Carrick and downing a couple of these this morning, she'd have most of her energy back; until the next adrenaline rush or activity that depleted her again.

She needed to take part in the rescue. No way did she want to be sidelined when these men risked their lives while she stayed safe and hidden at Carrick's ranch.

Deciding it was time to take the bull by the horns, horse by the reins, or Garou by his... Well, she wasn't going to go there. She turned to the group, gladdened to feel comfortable with the guys she'd met so far, and wanting to meet the new ones. "So, introductions? You said Simone already met ya'll?"

"I did." Simone entered the room a little timidly, voice soft and visibly uncomfortable with the newcomers.

Nia didn't know her well enough to figure out if she was naturally timid around strangers and introverted, or just overwhelmed by the sheer number of unfamiliar faces—not to mention the disaster that was yesterday—all tossed on top of the attempted abduction.

She also had no clue what Simone had suffered through during her captivity. No wonder the poor woman looked wan and ready to bolt.

Nia held out her hand and Simone grabbed it like a lifeline. "Come sit down and we'll answer their questions, fill in any gaps in information, and then get a plan of attack going. Between the two of us I hope we can give a fairly accurate map of the facility, at least the area we were in, and the lowdown on Denton's guards and medical personnel."

Simone took a seat, sending Nia a grateful look, and Reese delivered a cup of steaming tea to her, garnering another soft look of gratitude and surprise. Nia turned back to the men while Mateo took over the introductions from his seat at the end of the table.

"Nia, the new guys are West Ramsay, Flynne Mahigan, and Etienne Beauchamp. We're all members of the QSC—the Quicksilver Garou Council—an organization tasked with keeping Garou across the globe safe, helping to relocate them when necessary, and also the unfortunate need to take into custody any Garou breaking the law. We aren't all law-abiding, unfortunately. Each member of the council brings a unique skill set to the table. West and Flynne are retrieval experts. They can find folks others have given up on and are ace at breaking and entering, as well as hand-to-hand combat. Etienne is our marksman and martial arts expert, as well as a geek like Ramil. He'll take care of any alarm system. I'm council director for the Southwest United States, formerly based in Monte Amiata, Italy. Long, long time ago."

Nia met each man's eyes as Mateo introduced them, to convey respect and gratitude. "I can't thank you enough for dropping everything to help the women and men being held in that place. Thank you also for helping keep Simone, Rachel, and me safe."

"Yes, thank you." Simone's soft voice echoed her gratitude.

"Those motherfuckers will not get their hands on you again, ma'am, you can bank on that." Nia turned at Etienne's low vow to see the muscles jump in his jaw and pain swirl in his eyes before he banked it.

There was a story there, and she made a mental note to ask Carrick when they were alone. She gave him a solemn nod in acknowledgment and was glad she'd never be on his bad side.

Feeling her energy drain like mercury out of an old, broken thermometer, she uncapped her shake and drained the rest, then practically gulped her coffee.

It surprised her to see Flynne rise, take two steps to the fridge, open it and grab two more shakes, along with the carafe of coffee on the counter next to it.

When he delivered the drinks and carafe, she gave him a grateful smile. "Thanks. Since the infusions, my energy depletes like I've hiked a mountain while fasting. I'll need to take a couple of cases of these with me when we hit Denton's facility."

Carrick's growl, sounding just like a four-legged, fang-bearing wolf, had her swiveling to see his eyes molten, only not in desire this time, and a muscle ticking in his jaw.

Even Max, who'd never reacted aggressively to any of these guys, raised his head and zeroed in on Carrick, answering with a warning growl of his own.

"I know I'm not the boss of you, but there's no way in hell you're going with us to Denton's facility when you can barely make it an hour of mild activity without getting shaky."

She was ridiculously turned on at the sound of his voice, and the possessive, heated look in his eyes— until she registered what he was saying. Her own eyes narrowed when the turned-on part of her switched right over to pissed-the-hell-off.

"If you think I'm staying behind and letting you all go without me, you're off your rocker. I was in that hellhole for six fucking months and was actually lucid for a good part of it. They injected me with who knows what, I was under threat of rape or worse every damn day, and lost the most precious person in my life in that place. I'll be vital to the mission of finding the captives once we're inside and keeping them calm. Do you think the women are going to just trust a bunch of armed warrior-types drenched in pissed-off testosterone? You think I'm actually going to agree to stay here? You're nuts!"

Carrick stiffened as her voice rose and she couldn't keep it from turning frosty as the first snow. He looked like he was on a roll to ramp up his edicts and arguments when Simone clasped her forearm and piped up in her soft voice. "Are you sure you're strong enough? Wait, don't be mad. I'm just worried about you, and I can't go along. I don't know how to fight, and need to think of Rachel. To stay here with her."

Nia patted Simone's hand, realizing she wasn't mad at Simone for voicing the same concern Carrick had, but she was furious at him for trying to hold her back. The difference was he was trying to control her, whereas Simone worried about her and wanted to talk it out.

He'd previously acknowledged her ability to kick ass and take care of herself. Granted, she did better when not exhausted, but she'd stayed alive all by herself these past months, thank you very much, with no one having her back. "I'm not mad at you, Simone. But I need to do this."

She turned back to see myriad emotions swirling through Carrick's captivating silver eyes. She felt bad for her verbal attack, but dammit, the man knew how important this was to her. Denton and his ilk had killed her sister! He was crazy as a loon if he thought she was staying behind.

Taking a deep breath, she let it out slowly and measured her words as she spoke. "I know you're worried, probably even more so since I'm your—mate." She still had a hard time uttering that word. "But Carrick, you have to know how important this is to me, how much I can help when we're in the facility. I won't be able to live with myself if any of you get injured, or god forbid, killed because I stay safe and sound, hiding in your house. I need to make it right. He killed my sister."

The stubborn look on his face didn't bode well for their first fight, and Nia feared if they couldn't get past this altercation, they wouldn't be able to mesh as a couple—as mates. If he couldn't respect her decisions, respect her knowing her own limits, and not try to impose his will on her on this important mission, then would he try to control her in other aspects of their life together?

When he stood abruptly and shoved his chair back, Mateo also stood and stalked around the table to stand next to Nia, Max mirroring his actions, jumping to his paws and padding to her other side to pin Carrick with a menacing look, hackles raised on his back.

Carrick ignored the dog and looked at Mateo in disbelief. "What the hell, Mateo? I would never hurt her! You all must know how absurd it would be to let her go. She can barely stand after fighting or running, and even adrenaline spikes deplete her reserves. We'd end up carrying her out, along with any incapacitated captives. No fucking way is she going."

Nia couldn't believe her ears. She jabbed a finger in his chest and barely refrained from shouting. "Oh, I'm going alright. If not with you all, then on my own with Max. Since you don't want me dead, I'd suggest you let me go with you!"

She was a hairbreadth away from bursting into tears and no way was she going to humiliate and embarrass herself in front of these men. As a woman, Simone would understand the tears were mostly from anger, some from hurt feelings, from what she considered his betrayal. But she didn't want any of these men to think her weak.

It was bad enough she'd already cried in front of Carrick more than once. No way would she go there again. She turned on her heels, cursing silently when dizziness caused her to stagger, and was thankful Max pressed against her to offer his furry head for her hand to lean on as she stalked carefully from the kitchen to her guest room.

To hell with going back to Carrick's bedroom; she would damn well stay in her own room and plan her own damn mission.

Chapter Fifteen

CARRICK STOOD there, Mateo by his side and wondered how the hell they'd gone from having wild, passionate sex—no, not just sex, making love—just the night before to her storming away after telling him off.

Didn't she understand he was only looking out for her wellbeing? She'd been living with debilitating exhaustion for ten months, according to what she'd told them. Why on earth would she think it was the least bit smart to go on a recovery mission where guaranteed there'd be fighting?

He sat heavily back onto his chair and scrubbed his hands down his face before turning to scan the men sitting around the table. "Do any of you think it's a good idea for her to join the mission? She'd be a liability to the team and a danger to herself and whoever had to help her."

All but one of them shook their head, agreeing with his assessment. When he saw Etienne lean forward, elbows on the table and hands clasped, the man's gaze drilling him, Carrick waited, knowing he was carefully formulating what he was going to say.

Etienne was the most intense and serious of the group, next to Dak, and Carrick was one of the few who knew he also had something key in common with Nia. They'd both lost siblings to murder, Etienne's several years back, and they suspected Denton was behind it. He didn't have to wait long for him to speak up.

"When they murdered Darley, vengeance and retribution was a living thing in me. He was all that remained of my family. He kept me centered when I stayed inside my head too much. All I could think of, all I could focus on, day and night, was finding Denton and killing him—slowly and painfully. Making him suffer. The fact I wasn't able to has eaten away at me all these years. That we weren't able to find where they'd held my brother, or save anyone still captive—to put an end to Denton—still haunts me. Think hard about this, Carrick. You don't want this to be the one thing that splits you apart before you're even mated."

Carrick heard and understood what he was saying, but if she went with them, chances were she would die. Or he would, trying to save her.

Because no way in fucking hell would he let anyone harm one hair on her head, or any other part of her beautiful, precious body. He would rather have her alive, and not with him—as fucking painful as that thought was—than have her dead and buried like her sister.

"I hear you, man. I do. But the thought of her dying, of Denton or one of his goons killing her; or capturing her when we're busy fighting and hiding her away again? That's like a knife to my heart. To my soul."

Etienne gave him a long, somber look before shooting him a chin lift, silently letting him know he supported whatever decision he made. When Mateo laid a hand on his shoulder, Carrick turned and gave him a humorless smile.

"I'm gonna think on this while Simone shares her info, then we'll see about getting Nia to come back in so she can fill in any gaps."

He paused and concentrated, his enhanced hearing picking up Nia's weeping and Max's low whine in commiseration. Fuck! It took every ounce of willpower not to stalk from the kitchen into her room and attempt to comfort her.

The only thing holding him back was knowing she'd either refuse him entry, or she'd let him in and their fight would escalate, resulting in her leaving him and the safety of his ranch, exposing herself to Denton and his crew, with no backup.

He turned to Simone, hating to see her huddled in her chair as if trying to make herself invisible, and bit back the urge to delay their fact-finding meeting until he could concentrate and not worry about Nia, so Simone could relax and not be on pins and needles.

They didn't have time to wait, though. Who knew what was happening to the Garou and women still being held at Denton's facility? They needed to get this shit planned, gather weapons and supplies, then hit the road by no later than midnight that night, so they'd arrive before sunrise.

He turned back to Mateo, still standing at his side, and gave a head tilt toward Simone. Nia had reacted to his fatherly approach, and he thought it would be best if Mateo led the questioning instead of having all nine of them interrogating her. And he definitely wasn't in the mindset needed to put her at ease and lead the dialogue.

Mateo was quick on the uptake, turning to sit in the chair Nia had occupied and leaning his elbows on the table, no doubt to appear less threatening, not looming over the petite woman. "That little girl of yours—lei è una torta cutiesure—she is a cutie-pie, Simone."

Carrick relaxed a little, realizing Mateo had used the best icebreaker there was in getting Simone to open up—talking about her daughter.

"Thank you. What language is that?"

"Ah, Italiano, Simone. It still slips out, after these many years."

Simone perked up a little at his answer, her shy, huddled demeanor lessening a bit. Carrick rose and stepped toward the other end of the table, addressing the guys in a low tone. "I'll grab my laptop from the office to take notes. I also have floor-planner software we can use to diagram the facility if needed. I'll send a link to the information to your tablets when we're done."

They all glanced at Etienne when he suddenly stood and strode from the room. Carrick glanced down the hallway to see him turn toward Simone and Rachel's room, realizing he must have heard the little girl wakening, and hoped Rachel didn't cry down the house at the sight of a big, badass stranger.

Etienne's hearing was many times stronger than the average Garou. He'd probably heard Rachel roll over or whimper. Knowing him, she could have taken a deep breath, and he'd have checked on her.

Etienne stepped back into the room as Carrick was heading to his office, Rachel propped on one broad shoulder, her little thumb in her mouth. Carrick heard him ask Simone in a low voice, "If you need to step out to feed her, we can wait."

"Oh! I'm, uh, I'm not... She drinks from a bottle, or when she's more awake, a sippy cup. There's a bottle ready in the fridge. Maybe Reese can heat it up? He helped me last night."

Carrick strode back into the room with his laptop, detecting stress in Simone's voice, along with—surprise they would think she was still breastfeeding? Or embarrassment? He wondered idly why that would surprise her? And there was no reason to feel embarrassed, although sometimes she seemed on the shy-side.

She must know this room of badasses would not think twice about whether she used a bottle instead of what nature provided. He tabled that thought for another time and sat next to Mateo again, laptop at the ready to take notes as she provided what he hoped would be valuable information.

As Reese heated the bottle for Rachel, Simone turned back to Mateo. "What do you need to know?"

Mateo lead her through recounting her time in the facility while Rachel sucked down her warm milk like it was the last bottle on Earth. As Carrick took notes, he realized there were parts of her experience she stumbled over.

It was as if she was reciting something she'd read or been told, or memorized to retell, instead of something she'd actually experienced, and he realized they were all about when Rachel was born and her first couple of months of life.

She said she'd escaped captivity ten months ago, and Rachel was a little over a year old, which meant Simone had given birth while held captive, but she didn't mention being pregnant when captured, and also didn't mention difficulties being pregnant during captivity.

He glanced at Simone, then looked more carefully at Rachel, then Simone again, trying to find similarities in features. Granted, Rachel was still young, but now that he was concentrating on the two together, he could see the little girl looked nothing like her mama. Nothing at all. Not that children didn't sometimes favor one parent over the other, but maybe he was on to something.

Could it be she wasn't actually Simone's daughter? As that thunderbolt of a thought hit him, he shot a glance at his brother, who was also looking at Simone and her daughter thoughtfully.

He wouldn't bring it up here, but would get Reese, Dak and Bah aside later and broach the subject, then decide whether to ask Simone. He didn't want her to feel she had to hide something like that from them. This was a no judgement zone, and they just wanted to protect and support her and Rachel.

IT HAD TAKEN almost two hours to finish interviewing Simone. He'd hated to see her tension climb the longer Mateo had questioned her, and she'd all but curled in on herself if one of the other guys piped up, but the information she shared was crucial to their success.

At Reese's encouragement, she'd even managed to eat a moderate breakfast and down several cups of Lemony Lady Grey tea as she was talking.

It was apparent reciting her ordeal exhausted her, and Rachel started fussing and needed a diaper change, so Reese had encouraged her to put the little girl down for a nap and take one herself.

Thankfully, the diapers and other supplies Reese had ordered from Simone's shopping list had arrived early that morning. With a grateful smile, Simone had hurried from the room like the fires from hell were at her heels.

They still needed to finish their interview with Nia, but Carrick being in the same room when they talked would be counterproductive. He'd saved the notes and facility layout from Simone's interview to his private server in the house, as well as their encrypted cloud server, then distributed the shared link via their homegrown message system, similar to Slack but locked down tighter than the Pentagon.

Ramil was a genius when it came to tech, and he'd set everything up here when they'd first moved to New Almaden, duplicating what he'd installed in their facility in Sonoma.

He slid his computer across the table to Reese for notetaking, then rose, stretched and strode to the refrigerator to grab two ElectRou shakes and a sport bottle of cold water.

He set the shakes on the table, kept hold of the water and strode to the door leading to the garage, then turned to his friends. "I'm not going to stick around when you chat with Nia." He noted the concerned looks and held up a hand to forestall any arguments. "You know she's pissed at me, and you need her concentrating on sharing information, not how she'd like to skewer me. I'm gonna check out the perimeter, then the property and cabins. One of you text me when you're done and I'll come back in."

With that, he stepped into the garage, shut the door behind him, and strode to the tall, broad gun safe in the corner. He spun the combo lock back and forth till it clicked, then tugged the heavy door open and pulled out his spare holster, shrugging it over his shoulders, then grabbed his Smith & Wesson M&P nine mil, checked the slide and chamber and snugged it into the holster, and finally pulled out his BK7 combat knife and shoved it into the sheath on his belt.

He patted his pocket to confirm his phone was there, hit exit mode on the alarm system and the button to open the smaller garage door off to the side.

As he swung a leg over his Ducati and fired it up, he couldn't help the premonition that skated across his spine at the thought he was going to lose his mate before he claimed her.

Carrick glanced around and opened his senses to confirm no intruders were present, save a coyote he could sense in the south corner. He closed his eyes, took a deep breath of the cool autumn air, and concentrated on his link to Nia, gladdened to feel their bond. It terrified him to think that if she left, this amazing sensation would be a shadow of what he now felt. And if she died? He couldn't even go there.

His breath stuttered at the thought of her sneaking off to Denton's on her own and getting killed, or deciding she didn't want to be with an overbearing Garou mate and disappearing on him.

If she left, and was far enough away, their bond would feel like a ghost of a sensation, not like it did now. He didn't think he'd be able to deal with that. How could he, after finally knowing what it felt like to have his mate linked to his soul? To his heart? After finally knowing her body intimately, craving the feel of sliding into her slick heat.

No! He felt an echoing howl from his primal self, and the sensation of that other being stalking back and forth in his mind, ears back and fangs bared, set him off balance. It was bad enough he was coping with his own emotions; now he had to cope with a pissed off, worried—what? A fucking wolf in his head?

He would just have to convince Nia how foolish it would be for her to go. That she could—and should—rely on him and the guys to handle the job without her. To handle avenging her sister's death and ensure the bastards responsible hurt no one else—Garou, Cinnabar Twin or human.

Chapter Sixteen

NIA HAD exhausted herself weeping, and then alternated between being angry as hell at Carrick, missing him like crazy and back to pissed off again. It terrified her they wouldn't get past his stubborn desire to wrap her in cotton batting and protect her.

What happened to him realizing she was competent and could take care of herself? Could fight and prove to be an asset on the mission, not a liability? When they'd been at her house, he seemed to admire her independence and ability to kick-ass. Now he wanted to stifle her and all but put her in a padded cell.

If she stayed on top of ingesting the ElectRou shakes and her energy drinks, and as much as it panicked her to think about, if she gave in and let Dak or Bah infuse her with the IV solution they'd proposed, she knew she'd be able to kick ass and not be a liability. Couldn't she? Fuck it! She would not start second-guessing herself just because Carrick didn't believe in her.

She'd get her shit together and follow if they refused to let her accompany them. Nia jolted at the sound of a motorcycle gunning past her room and she wondered who was leaving and where they were going.

She pulled the curtain back, but it was already around the house and out of sight. Could it be Carrick, or one of the other guys checking out the property? Or was there a development elsewhere, and they were leaving to check it out? Even though she'd just met the other guys, she hated to think of them being in danger.

Max gave a soft woof just before a knock sounded on her door, and her heart took off racing as she wondered if Carrick was coming to apologize and change his mind about her accompanying them.

When she opened the door, she had to quell her disappointment at seeing Mateo filling the doorway, not the man who was making his way into her heart. When she saw his eyes fill with compassion, she realized she hadn't been successful in keeping a bland expression on her face, her pain still written there for all to see. Or maybe he was just good at reading emotions?

He leaned against the doorjamb, arms crossed over his massive chest. "I bet you haven't had more than the cliff-notes version of what and who the Garou are?"

Nia shook her head and then nodded. "No, I mean you're right. Carrick, Dak and Reese gave Simone and me a brief rundown, but that was when we were escaping and just after we arrived here. They didn't have time to give many details before I passed out for a few hours." She felt the blush heating her face at the thought of what she and Carrick had done after she'd woken from her nap and hoped Mateo couldn't read minds.

"Well, after you share your info with us, we'll give you a more complete history on the Garou and Cinnabar Twins. I think the look on your face just now was you wondering how I knew you were disappointed to see me and not Carrick. I can't read minds, you'll be happy to know, and you did a pretty good job of keeping your expression neutral, but part of my enhanced Garou senses involves being able to feel or read emotions. So, even if someone doesn't outwardly show what they're feeling, if I'm not actively blocking, I'll feel their emotions. The only time it doesn't work is when I meet a sociopath. Their emotions are so neutral and narcissistic, they rarely emit any, unless they're in a rage."

"Holy shit. Isn't that exhausting, and, well, intrusive?" Nia didn't want to offend Mateo, but she wasn't sure how she felt about her feelings being so transparent to him.

"It was when I was younger, until I was in my late teens and finally learned how to put up, I guess you could call it a psychic-wall, to ward off most emotions. That's what I meant about actively blocking. There are times my walls aren't powerful enough, when folks around me are feeling heightened emotions. When that happens, I really have to work hard to get it erected again. I'd lowered it when talking to Simone, so I would know when to take it easy on her, when it was getting to be too much, and then didn't even think of raising it again when I came to talk to you. I apologize if I've offended you."

Nia touched his hand briefly and shook her head. "No, you didn't. I'm not sure why, since I just met you and don't trust easily, but I do trust that you wouldn't do anything to hurt or betray me." She shot him a grin and tried to lighten the atmosphere. "Is now a good time to ask to borrow the car, dad?"

Mateo threw back his head and laughed, then surprised her by wrapping her up in a fatherly hug. "Nia, if I could have wished for a daughter, I'd have wanted someone just like you." He let her go, grabbed her hand and tugged as he led her toward the kitchen. "And no, you can't borrow the car."

She appreciated this man, who'd come to feel like she'd known him for years, and already felt like a surrogate dad. As they entered the kitchen, she glanced around the room to see all eyes on her and immediately felt self-conscious considering her earlier outburst.

Wanting to break the ice, she shot a glance at Dak, then sat and looked up at Mateo. "Well, dad, if I can't borrow the car, then Dak shouldn't be able to either." She glanced back at Dak to see the edge of his mouth quirk and knew they'd all heard Mateo and her conversation outside her bedroom.

Mateo laughed again and sat next to her, pushing the two ElectRou protein shakes Carrick had left on the table toward her. "Drink up and we'll get down to business. Simone gave us more information on other captives, doctors, technicians and guards she saw, as well as helping map out the part of the facility she was in. The lab and about four cells down the right-hand corridor as you exit the lab. She said she was never in the back part of the building, which I think Carrick said was where you exited when you escaped. We'll want to get an info dump from you on anything and everything you remember, the people and even the areas she described, since you may have had different perceptions or experiences."

Nia uncapped one shake and downed half, grabbed a napkin to wipe her mouth, then canted her chair to face Mateo and the rest of the men. "How is Simone?"

Reese spoke up from across the table. "Exhausted, but she was a trooper. She ate and had tea while we talked, fed Rachel, and they're both back in their room for a nap. While you share info, I'll be taking notes and using floor planning software to add to what Simone provided."

As hard as she tried not to worry about where Carrick was, she couldn't hold back her question and attempted to be casual about it. "Where's, uh, where'd Carrick get off to?" She gave herself an internal smack. What was this, middle school and she was lusting after the quarterback?

Mateo patted her hand, as if he knew she was embarrassed to have asked and worried about the damned man. Well, of course he knew, if she was still projecting her emotions like they were being shot from a cannon.

"He's checking out the property and cabins. He'll be back later on."

Probably after she was back in her room, since he was no doubt still angry with her for arguing with him. That was one fight she wasn't backing down from, though.

She'd been told what to do, her every action controlled, for six long, excruciating months in Denton's facility. No one got to tell her what to do or where to go anymore. Not even the man claiming to be her mate.

Time to get her head back in the game and get this show on the road. "Since I've already shared with the guys how they grabbed me, and about the infusions—

I'm sure Dak, Reese or Carrick have shared with you—I'll describe the facility and who I saw and interacted with."

She took another long swig of the shake and a deep breath, dreading revisiting her captivity, and stared at the table in front of her while gathering her thoughts.

"There were only four guards that I saw, working two, twelve-hour shifts, but I killed one when I escaped. Max, and I, objected to him wanting to take advantage of my inability to fight him off. My body had burned through the last sedative they'd injected me with, much quicker than usual, and I had no energy at all. Isabella had slipped me a scalpel during my infusion just a few hours before, because she'd heard the guard joking about getting it on with me that night. The fucker. He came into my cell while I was napping and dropped on top of me. When he slapped a hand over my mouth and started tearing at my clothing, Max attacked and bit his shoulder, which distracted him enough I could use the scalpel."

She gave a shudder, closed her eyes at the memory, thinking of what fate would have dealt her had she and Max not been able to subdue that bastard, and the horrible spurt of blood when she'd cut his throat. Bile rose in her throat and she swallowed convulsively, trying to hold back the nausea. "I, uh…"

It startled her when Mateo placed his big hand over her clenched fists. "We don't need the details, honey. Have more of your shake and just skip ahead to anyone else you interacted with and how you got out of the facility."

Her eyes shot to Mateo's as he untangled her fingers and took one icy hand to chafe between his.

She gave the older man a grateful smile, took a slow, deep breath, and continued.

"There was only one doctor, and two nurses. They sure didn't wear an RN name tag like in a hospital, but they seemed to have adequate knowledge and deferred to the doctors. The two doctors—one had the night and one the day shift—and the male nurse were assholes and didn't care whether they hurt us during infusions. They were rough, and it always bruised me at the needle site. The female nurse, she typically worked nights, was always kind, looked like she was about forty or so, and always made it as painless as possible. She whispered her name to me one time, Isabella."

Nia stopped and mulled for a moment, trying to remember in more detail the different visits to the laboratory when Isabella was there.

"Now that I think about it, I don't think she was there voluntarily. Mind you, I was pretty doped up whenever they brought me to the lab, but she showed up once with a black eye, and another time I saw fingerprint bruises on her arms. She was always very professional, almost stilted in her demeanor, when the doctor and anyone else were around. I think they'd told her not to talk to me, which would make perfect sense if she was a captive too but being forced to work in the lab."

She glanced around the table, horrified to think that sweet lady was one of Denton's captives, being forced to work for him and possibly suffering the infusions, too. "We have to help her! If she's a captive too, we need to free and take care of her."

Each in their own way, the men all looked pissed at the thought of the nurse being forced to do Denton's bidding and being mistreated. It no doubt meant she was a Cinnabar Twin, too, and possibly a Garou's mate. Possibly one of theirs.

West gave her a nod, mirrored by the other men. "No worries, Nia. We'll scope it out and take care of her if she's not willingly part of Denton's crew."

"Thank you. I can't stand the thought that I abandoned her and others there, that they've continued to suffer since I left." Feeling her energy flag, dammit, she uncapped the second shake and took a long drink before continuing.

"Other than Denton, those are the only people I saw there." She felt her heart stutter before she spoke in a hoarse whisper. "Other than my sister, that is." When it looked like Mateo was going to call a break, she tightened her grip on his hand and shook her head. "No, let me get this out while I can. About three days before I escaped, Denton stopped by my cell, threw open the door and walked in. His biggest, meanest guard stepped through the door, my sister held in front of him. They'd beaten her, and she could barely stand, but had her trademark defiant look in her eyes. She holds—held—a red and black belt in Brazilian Jiu-Jitsu, and I could tell by the damage to the guard's face she'd given him a good beat-down before he'd subdued her. Denton bragged about how he'd caught her trying to break into the facility, and that he'd known she was my sister. How the hell he knew that, I have no idea. We had only been together a few years again, and were having so much fun reconnecting."

Realizing they didn't know what she was talking about, she explained, "When our mother abandoned us, they placed her and me in different foster homes—I was twelve and Aleesha eleven—until we aged out, a year apart, and moved in together, becoming as close as we'd been as kids."

She steeled herself for the next part of the story. "He told me since she was my sister, he bet she had the lupus anomalies too, and he was going to enjoy infusing her and breeding her. The guard shoved her at me, told me to say goodbye because we wouldn't see each other for a long time, and we fell to the floor together. When we were tangled up on the floor, she tucked a thumb drive under my waistband, hugged me tight, and whispered if anything happened to her, the drive had everything I needed to hide and start over."

She gave them all a wry look. "Aleesha was a genius at security, and also at picking pockets. In one of her foster homes, it came in handy when they didn't feed the kids enough. She'd pick the wallets of the foster dad and mom, then buy food for her and the other kids."

Nia couldn't look at Mateo or the other guys, knowing if they showed an ounce of sympathy, she'd be a waterfall of tears. "The guard dragged her away, and I heard the cell door, one or two down from me, clang open. She must have lit into the guard again because all I heard were feet and fists hitting flesh, and the guard cursing her before there was silence. Denton rushed out and locked my door. Then he was the one cursing the guard, and I heard him shout, 'She doesn't do me any fucking good dead, you asshole'. I was screaming and yelling at them, and when I looked out my cell window I saw the guard walking past with Aleesha tossed over one shoulder, blood flowing from her scalp, Denton trailing behind." She looked up then, drilling each man with her eyes, so sad and fucking mad she could barely sit still.

"He'd killed her, and I'm going with you all, and I'm going to kill them. We're going to rain vengeance down on each and every one of them. We're going to free that nurse and every captive he still has there. Then we're going to torch the place and burn it to the ground. If you think to leave me here, I'll follow you and you'll have to tie me up to keep me out."

Nia couldn't sit there any longer. She didn't care about giving them information on the layout right then. She'd ask Reese for the laptop later and fiddle with the room planner herself to ensure they had correct info.

She knew the latest they would head up there was midnight that night, so they'd arrive just before dawn, when it was still dark and well before shift change. She released Mateo's hand and leaned in to brush a kiss across his whiskered cheek. "I'm going to my room. Reese? I'll work on the layout later." She grabbed her shake, turned and hustled to her room with Max, the ever-present shadow at her heels, his soft whine letting her know he sensed her pain and wanted to snuggle and make her feel better.

CARRICK STAYED gone for two long hours, tempted many times to say fuck it and return to check on Nia. To ensure she was even still at the house, although he could still feel their connection, and he knew the guys would watch over her for him.

Would have called him immediately if she'd tried to leave. Everything around the house, property, and cabins looked undisturbed, and he'd been cooling his heels for thirty minutes under the gnarled old oak tree about fifty yards from the back of the house.

He concentrated again on his link with Nia, torturing himself by imagining how painful it would be to go back to how it was before he'd met her. Before that magical, invisible thread had strengthened and seduced him at their first touch. Before he'd realized a part of his soul, his heart, had been missing before he met her.

His phone buzzed in his pocket, thank god, interrupting his depressing thoughts and he pulled it out to see a text from his brother.

> *Reese: Nia's back in her room. Told us about her sister and got fired up all over again. Get your ass back here. Need to talk.*

Fucking hell. He'd been hoping she'd cooled off some, but it seemed just the opposite. He texted he was on his way, flipped the red switch up and hit the black button to start the bike, twisting the handle to race to the garage, the sensor on the bike activating the automatic opener for the small garage door.

He rolled in and shut the bike down, put it to sleep, nudged the kickstand down with the toe of his boot, then dismounted and looked up to see the door to the house opening to a grim-looking Reese. He strode to and through the door, knowing shit was bad when his brother clapped him on the shoulder and gave it a squeeze.

With a nod of thanks, he headed into the kitchen and leaned against the counter, one ankle over the other and arms crossed. He knew his posture was defensive, but that's how he felt. Like a boulder was about to drop on his car when he rounded the bend. Inevitable and nowhere to swerve.

Time to pull off the bandage, even if it took skin. "Okay, lay it on me. Reese says you talked to Nia, and she's still bound and determined to go."

As one, the guys turned to Mateo, who shook his head at them and muttered, "Bunch of kids, the lot of you. He's not gonna kill the messenger, you know."

Carrick rolled his eyes, held out a hand and curled his fingers in a gimme gesture, then crossed his arms again and waited for the boom to lower.

Thank fuck Mateo didn't make him wait or beat around the bush. "From what she said, I don't think you got the full story about her sister. Is that true?"

Carrick nodded, wondering where this was going, and afraid to find out. "Correct. She gave us a synopsis and pretty much all we got was that her sister died while trying to rescue her."

Mateo nodded, and Carrick lowered his arms to grip the counter, hard, as his friend shared what Nia had told them. Motherfuckingsonofabitch! His muscles bunched, and his blood burned through his veins to realize what Nia, and her poor sister, had suffered.

When Mateo got to the end of his recitation, Etienne rose and strode around the table to stand in front of Carrick, hands on hips. "You remember what I told you before, about my brother."

It wasn't so much a question as a statement to get Carrick out of his own head, to focus on Etienne and what he was about to say. He gave a nod, holding the man's intense gaze, his own tension not lessening a bit, and waited for him to continue.

"I get you're worried about her, man. I'm also the first to admit I have no fucking clue how you're feeling, her being your mate, since we're all waiting to find ours. But I gotta remind you, Carrick. You make the wrong decision here, and you're gonna lose her. Either because she doesn't trust you to trust her, to have her back, and leaves you to go rogue, getting herself killed; or by some miracle, lives through the raid and then disappears on you. Think hard, buddy, before you go in there and talk to her."

Carrick dropped his head and stared at the floor for a moment, then looked up to meet Etienne's eyes again. "I hear you." He glanced around to see Mateo watching them, compassion in his eyes, Reese's filled with pain for him, Dak and the rest of the guys giving them as much privacy as they could by feigning interest in their android tablets, considering they were in the same room and had hearing like a bat.

Etienne gave him a single nod, a clap on his shoulder, and walked back to his chair to take a seat.

"Okay, fill me in on the other information Nia shared and let's get this operation nailed down so we're ready to head out by midnight at the latest." He looked at his G-Shock watch, noting it was currently twelve-hundred, which meant they'd have time to plan, organize their weapons, rations and ElectRou shakes, grab their go-bags and pack the vehicles, then get some shuteye before time to head out at twenty-four hundred. Leaving at the dot of midnight would get them there just before sunrise at seven am.

He sat next to Dak, who pulled up the floor plan of the facility they'd cobbled together from Simone's information. They told him Nia would share her facility layout info later and then got down to business. He tried, but failed, to quell the distraction of knowing he needed to decide how to cope with Nia's decision to go with them, or go rogue.

To decide whether he should be a controlling asshole and lock Nia down at home when they left, risking her hating him and leaving after their return, or accepting her as part of their team, knowing she could die in the takedown and rescue.

Chapter Seventeen

NIA WAS rearranging her backpack to prepare for the drive to Umpqua National Forest in Oregon, where the facility sat on what used to be a sprawling ranch, when she heard Carrick's motorcycle rev up to the garage before quieting to a loping idle and then silence as he shut it down.

She strained to hear him enter the house, but the garage door into the kitchen was far enough away she couldn't hear it open or close and could only hear an inaudible murmur from that direction. Their connection vibrated the closer he got, and she tried to ignore the desire to be with him, touch him. Get naked and busy with him again.

If her hearing was as good as the Garou, she could eavesdrop on their conversation. She wasn't foolish enough to head to the facility by herself. She didn't even have a vehicle anymore! But she would damn well climb into one of their vehicles before they left, if she had to camp out and sleep in one to ensure they didn't leave without her.

Knowing she needed to keep up her strength, but not wanting to head into the wolf's den to get food and more ElectRou shakes, she texted Simone in the hope she was awake and could get them for her.

> *Nia: Hey, can I trouble you to grab me something to eat and a few shakes?*

She'd texted her earlier to ask how she and Rachel were, but they must have still been asleep. She didn't have long to wait for Simone to text back.

> *Simone: Are you sick? What's wrong?*

Nia was reluctant to fill her in via text about her argument with Carrick, so kept her answer brief.

> *Nia: Not sick, don't worry. If you're able to, I'll tell you when you bring the stuff to my room.*

She looked at her phone, waiting for Simone to respond, but nothing appeared. She should have known Simone wouldn't badger her, was too sweet and kind to insist she be told right away.

Waiting by the door with her ear pressed to the wood, Nia felt like a kid again scoping out a new foster home, hoping the people in the house would be kind, but not holding her breath.

She sighed, knowing that wasn't the right analogy, since every single person in this house treated her with nothing but respect and kindness, unlike many of the homes they'd placed her in.

Even though she and Carrick were at odds, even though she wasn't sure they were going to make it off second base and to home plate, as far as a relationship went, she knew he respected her. That his insistence she hid like a coward at his ranch was because of his fear she could die if she went with them. Because he cared for her. Because they were mates.

Although they'd just met, he had to know she wasn't the type of person to sit back and let others do the hard and dangerous shit. Surely he could tell she was a fighter and had to see this through. As much as it pained her, she didn't see a way to convince him to stop fighting her on this.

The light knock on the door had her jumping back, even though she knew Simone was on her way. She stepped up to the door again and opened it to see her friend carrying a tray with two plates of meatloaf and mashed potatoes, four shakes, two glasses of water and two brownies. What a sweetheart!

She grabbed Simone gently by her elbow and pulled her into the room, not wanting to talk to Carrick or any of the other uber-alpha men in the kitchen if they ventured into the hall, then closed the door quickly.

Nia relieved Simone of the tray, then turned and walked to the small table under the window to set it down. "You're a lifesaver and an angel. Where's Rachel? You're going to eat with me, yes? You have two of everything. I hope that means you're staying to have dinner with me, although it is a bit early for it."

As she grabbed her plate and one water, turned to sit on the bed cross-legged and then looked up, she realized Simone was just standing there with a grin on her face before the petite woman reached for her own plate and water. "I had no idea, when I met you, that you were such a jabbermouth."

"Ha! Only when I'm annoyed or have been with my own company for too long. I haven't had a woman to talk to since my captivity, much less someone who's become a friend to me; I didn't dare make friends after I escaped. I bet you were the same."

Simone nodded fervently. "God, yes. It's been just Rachel and me since I got away, and the only girl-talk I've had is when Rachel blows bubbles or babbles baby-speak to me. Not that I understand her, mind you. I didn't dare make friends or talk to anyone for fear I'd wind up on someone's social media page and back in that place."

"Exactly. Same here." Nia looked up when the silence stretched out to see Simone eyeing her as if she was dying to ask a question but was afraid to broach the subject. She sighed and gave her a go-ahead gesture, then set her plate down, jumped off the bed and pulled her phone from her pocket. "Wait a sec."

She didn't want the guys to listen in to their conversation and wondered if turning on the sound machine app in her phone and setting it in front of the door on the floor would work in muting their conversation.

Unlocking her phone, she thumbed the app on her home screen, then hit play, causing myriad water sounds to emit. She turned the volume up, set the phone on the floor, then walked back to the bed and climbed back on to sit again.

"We'll keep our voices down, too."

Simone looked at her with a glint in her eyes and grinned, then said in a low voice, "Hopefully that foils the bat-ears those guys seem to have, although I understand Etienne has super-charged hearing, way better than the others. Now tell me why you're in here, while the guys are in the kitchen planning. I thought you'd cool off by now and be right back there in the middle of it. I gotta tell you, Carrick looked like crap while I was in the kitchen just now."

Nia swallowed a bite of meatloaf and took a long swig of water, then nodded. "You were there when he basically shut me down and told me in no uncertain terms I wasn't going; that I was going to stay here. That's one button of mine no one should push. No one tells me what to do, especially after being controlled, abused and infused while in Denton's lab. Carrick knows how important it is for me to go."

Simone leaned over and gave Nia a quick hug, then sat back. "I know, I guess I was hoping one of you would come up with a compromise that would satisfy both your needs."

Nia felt her eyes burn with tears again, remembering their argument. "Nope. He's been scoping out the perimeter and just came back inside a while ago. Haven't talked to him. I'm going with them if I have to sleep in the SUV tonight."

Simone gave Nia a considering look, scooted closer and leaned forward to whisper. "I have an idea, of how you can become strong enough to go, but I don't know if you'll go for it. And I also don't know if it will work fast enough. Just hear me out before you say anything. Promise?"

Nia eyed Simone warily, wondering what the heck kind of idea she could have, and what did she mean by it not working fast enough? Willing to try almost anything, Nia nodded slowly and waited for her to start.

"Remember when Dak and Carrick were telling us about the Garou, and how after the mating, the

Cinnabar Twin is stronger, they live longer, and their bodies heal faster. That they're harder to kill?"

Nia's eyes widened at her words, thinking Simone crazy to suggest she mate with Carrick just so she could go with them, but on the heels of that thought, she knew in her heart she would do almost anything to avenge her sister. To save Isabella and the other captives, and to keep Simone and her little girl safe.

She opened her mouth to respond but didn't get a word out before Simone spoke up again.

"Shhh! You promised you'd listen. I know mating is for life. But I've seen you and Carrick together, and also how he treats you. If what the guys say is true, not one of those men, especially Carrick, would mistreat or betray you. Just think. Those guys have been waiting over a hundred years for their mates; have thought it was hopeless, and they'd never find them. Think, too, how Carrick has treated you. Except for when you argued, and he got all bossy. And that argument was because he's terrified he'll lose you, that you'll get killed. Wouldn't you feel the same, if you were in his shoes and you'd finally, miraculously found your mate? I've also seen how you look at him, how you're drawn to him. And, I, uh, got up last night to get a snack and, well, it sounded like you were getting along *really* well. I honestly don't think you can go wrong, Nia."

Nia flopped back on the bed and stared at the ceiling, embarrassed her new friend had apparently heard her getting busy in Carrick's room the night before.

She wondered why she hadn't shot Simone down immediately, wasn't immediately retorting with an emphatic no! Oh, who was she kidding, she knew exactly why. She was halfway in love with the big guy, even if she'd known him less than forty-eight hours.

Probably most of it was the pull of this mate thing the Garou's had going, but she had to admit, from everything she'd observed, he was an honorable man who respected her, and honestly wanted the best for her. And wanted her for himself.

He wasn't an asshole who mansplained and thought women should be meek and two-steps behind. And he was her ideal man, physically. All those muscles, that hard-angled face, and those mesmerizing silver eyes that went molten when he looked at her.

He'd told her the connection they both felt was much stronger for him because he was Garou. She couldn't imagine feeling more than she did right now, as she once again concentrated on that link and felt an almost irresistible tug to go to him. To be with him intimately, but also just to be near the man.

She appreciated the fact Simone stayed quiet and didn't rush her into a decision. Her friend knew it was a monumental choice, and one Nia wouldn't take lightly.

But really, what choice did she have? She couldn't remain weak and needy. Besides, the more she was around Carrick, the more she wanted him, and she couldn't imagine not being with him. Especially after giving herself to him in the most intimate way a woman could. Although it sounded like actually mating was even more intimate.

She sat suddenly on the edge of the bed, refusing to be indecisive, and grabbed Simone's hand between both of hers. "I'm scared shitless, but you're a genius. Thank you for being my friend and having my back. I'm going to do it. Well, if Carrick will agree. Will you please ask him to come see me? I don't want to be underhanded about it, so I'll tell him exactly why I'm agreeing to the mating. But there's no guarantee he'll agree. I may be back to square one, where I'm blackmailing him into letting me go."

She leaned closer and gave Simone a hard hug, then climbed off the bed and helped her friend down.

"Yes, I'll go talk to him right now." Simone grabbed their empty plates and gave Nia an earnest look full of compassion. "Good luck. I'm going to take Rachel back to our room. Text me later, before you leave, if I don't see you before then? I heard them say they were leaving at twenty-four hundred, which according to West is midnight in military-speak."

"Yes, I'll text you. You be safe here. Don't go anywhere, better yet, don't even leave the house, and listen to whoever they leave here to guard you and Rachel, and the ranch."

Nia walked with her to the door, scooped her phone off the floor, then turned off the sound machine app and turned the knob.

"I will. You be safe, too. I don't want to lose you now that I've found a friend. I'll tell Carrick you need to see him right away."

After Simone left the room, Nia wiped her suddenly sweaty palms on her leggings and paced, afraid to go through with this crazy plan, but knowing the only way she'd be able to have the strength to make a difference during the raid on the facility was if they completed the mating.

She'd talked a good game to Carrick, but in her heart, she also knew it would be hard as hell to make it in and out unscathed if she wasn't stronger, and became incapacitated from pretty much any outlay of energy.

If she felt she had any other choice, she would wait, wouldn't agree to cementing their mating until after enough time had passed to convince her they could make a go of it together as a couple. As mates.

She knew she could choose not to go with them, but also knew she wouldn't be able to live with herself if she took what she considered the easy, cowardly way out. Especially if any of them were injured, or god forbid killed, during the raid. The thought of Carrick dead about froze her heart.

She needed to reclaim the chunk of her soul taken from her when they'd killed her sister, not to mention keeping her in that fucking small cell at their mercy. Always under the threat of rape or death. Or to become their damned breeding stock, when they forced a mating between a Garou and a woman presenting the anomalies in their blood—namely her, Simone, and the other captives. She shuddered at the thought.

Could she convince Carrick, though, to go through with the mating? She knew from his actions and all he'd said, it was possibly the most important thing in the world to him. The thing he craved most in life, like an addictive drug.

She paced back near the door and jumped, hand to chest, at the light knock even though she knew Simone was going to send Carrick to her.

She took a deep breath, gave another swipe of her sweaty palms down her leggings, stiffened her spine, hardened her heart a little, and opened the door.

Carrick's height and bulk took up the entire doorway, and her eyes involuntarily trailed from his unusual silver eyes down his corded neck, across those impossibly wide shoulders, the ridges and valleys of his huge chest and washboard abs discernible underneath the tight, gray t-shirt, the interesting bulge behind the buttons of his jeans, and kept going down his amazing quads to his—bare feet. Even his feet were sexy.

She'd noticed his size before, of course she had, but it really hit her what an amazing example of an extremely fit, large—no, make that huge—male he was. Realizing she'd all but undressed him with her eyes, she jerked her gaze back up to his and saw they'd gone molten with heat.

Even worried and angry at each other, she couldn't deny the incendiary fire and desire they felt for each other. Now she just had to convince him he needed to seal their mating, so she'd be strong and healthy enough to accompany them on their mission.

Chapter Eighteen

CARRICK WANTED to pounce on Nia when she opened her bedroom door, carry her to his bedroom and make love to her all night long. His inner wolf howled at the injustice of their being apart and was giving him shit again for not claiming her.

He'd been surprised when Simone told him Nia wanted to see him. It still scared him to death she was planning to leave, to head up to Denton's lab on her own. In his head, he knew she was smarter than that, but his heart hadn't gotten the memo.

She knew her limitations, that she wasn't strong enough to try it on her own, which no doubt was why she hadn't gone up there in the time since she'd escaped.

"Simone said you wanted to talk." He left it at that, afraid if he said anything else, their conversation would devolve into another argument, with her giving him the boot from her room and then stowing away in one of their vehicles. Or following them up there and inserting herself in the mission, knowing it would be too late and too dangerous for them to oust her. He could totally see her borrowing his Ducati or one of their other vehicles to do just that.

"Yes, I want to ask you something. Please come in and shut the door." Her voice was soft, and he could practically feel the nervous tension rolling off her. She hadn't exhibited nerves since he'd met her and wondered what was going on.

He strode into the room, pushed the door shut, then turned and stood at parade rest, hands clasped behind his back, and gave her a nod to go ahead.

She sat on the edge of the bed, then jumped to her feet as if poked with a stick and started pacing back and forth in front of him. She was going to drive him crazy if she didn't settle down and tell him why she'd asked to see him.

On one of her passes back to the other side of the room, Carrick reached out and gently grabbed her elbow, then dragged her toward him until her luscious body was barely a hairsbreadth away.

He trailed his hand down her arm to link their hand together, then settled the other at her hip. It took every bit of his strength not to tug her the rest of the way into his arms.

The startled look on her face morphed into one of desire and longing as she stood gazing up at him, her gem green eyes flecked with silver and red, along with a curious mix of passionate heat, and what looked a lot like trepidation.

What was making her so nervous? Afraid? Brushing an unruly curl from her cheek, he dropped a soft kiss where it had lain, letting his lips linger before straightening again. "Sweetheart, just ask me your question."

The deep breath she took brushed her breasts against his diaphragm, causing his cock to salute and beg for attention. His eyes shot down involuntarily to see her nipples pebble against the soft shirt she wore, and he forced them back to her face to catch mirrored desire flash in her eyes. This was not the time to be distracted by human hormones, or his wolven-self howling in his mind.

"Will you hear me out and not interrupt?"

Now he was more than curious and knew from her question he would not like what she was going to say or ask him to do. What was going on with this woman?

He couldn't promise he wouldn't interrupt, so he promised the next best thing. "I promise I'll try not to interrupt. I'll never lie to you, Nia. You need to just spit it out—you have to know you're tying me up in knots here."

She glanced down as if to gather her thoughts, her eyes widening when they landed on the prominent bulge at his groin, and she jerked them back up to stare at the middle of his chest for a few seconds before again meeting his eyes.

"When you told me about Garou, after we made, had se…—gah! In your bed, last night, you said when a Garou and Cinnabar Twin goes through the mating—I don't know what to call it—ritual? That when mates have sex, and the male bites his woman and climaxes, those extra Garou-only prostaglandins in the semen and the serum in their fangs cause the woman to become stronger and healthier. She'll live longer, and depending on the mate being converted, it will enhance some of her senses too."

He realized she was waiting for confirmation from him, so he nodded and added one piece of clarification, just for full disclosure. "That's all true, if the mating is between male to female, or Cinnabar Twin. We have male to male matings too between Garou, and in that case, the mutual sharing of blood and serum from the fangs simply strengthens and cements the bond."

She reached up and clenched the side of his t-shirt in her fist, apparently completely unaware of this telling gesture.

"If... If you were to bite me and, well, climax of course when we're making love, er, having sex, then I'll become stronger, get healthier, and it will enhance one or more of my senses, although we don't know which ones. I'll live longer and be harder to kill. You and Dak hypothesized that if we mate, and I also get infused with that special cocktail of ingredients he has, I probably wouldn't have this debilitating exhaustion."

Carrick stared at her, afraid he knew exactly where she was going with this, and his human-self wanted to howl in pain for the reason she wanted to complete the mating, while his wolven-side wanted nothing more than for Carrick to pick her up, toss her on her bed, strip her of her clothing and sink his cock and fangs into her.

His wolven-side was totally on board and apparently didn't give a fuck what her reasons were, just as long as she was theirs.

If he wasn't totally off his rocker, she was going to suggest they mate so she could go with them on the raid of Denton's facility. Not because of their connection or because she was falling even a little in love with him. Fuck!

As much as he wanted this mating, to bind them together permanently, he fucking wanted her to want it because she'd decided she couldn't be without him. That she felt the same amazing bond he did.

That she was, just maybe, falling a little in love with him, regardless they'd only known each other just under forty-eight hours. But no, instead his mate just wanted to reap the physical benefits so she could wreak vengeance on Denton and help rescue anyone still in that fucking facility.

His heart hurt and his wolf kept pushing him to make her theirs, insisting they'd have plenty of time to convince her after the raid that she belonged with them permanently. And then she'd fall in love with both of them.

He opened his mouth, closed it, leaned his head back to stare at the ceiling, amazed to feel choked up for the first time in his entire life, then looked down at her beautiful face, into her turbulent eyes, afraid she'd see the sheen of tears currently burning his.

His jaw ached from holding back what he really wanted to say, to tell her fuck no, he wouldn't mate with her for those reasons, but he finally went with what wouldn't piss her off and possibly alienate her.

"Yes, all of that is true. Remember we're guessing, though, since there hasn't been a mating in hundreds of years. We have no idea how much Denton's infusions have altered your genes or DNA."

She ignored his warning, steamrolling along with her plan. "Dak mentioned it happens pretty quickly. That I would feel the benefits almost immediately, maybe a few hours at most, and the only side effects might be some muscle aches, like having a mild flu. It's just a little after noon right now. I could be well and ready before midnight when you're planning to leave."

Although she'd made it a statement, Carrick knew she wanted confirmation of what she'd said, so he bit it out and tried to shut down his emotions. Good fucking luck with that. "Yes, also true." His voice sounded pissed and like he'd eaten ground glass for breakfast.

He could see a flash of hurt on her face at his curtness, but with his emotions all over the board, he couldn't help the brevity of his answers. He was afraid if he didn't just spit them out in as few words as possible, he'd spit out something that would get him in trouble again. That the emotional pain she was causing him would be apparent, which was the last thing he wanted.

He didn't want to cause her pain, but he didn't have it in him to make this easy for her. He fucking well wouldn't make her beg, but she needed to spell it out. If she wanted to go through with their mating just so she could go on the mission, she could damn well ask him straight out. He stood there, stoically waiting for her to speak again, pinning her with his gaze and refusing to look away.

Her hand opened and clenched again on his shirt, catching some skin that time, the tiny pinprick of her short nails causing his traitorous cock to jump again, making him wish she was clenching a fist around its thick length. The fingers of one hand, still laced with hers, tightened involuntarily and she swayed toward him before seeming to catch herself before jerking away.

He released her hand, stepped back to lean against the wall, crossed one ankle over the other and his arms across his chest, prepared to wait her out, no matter how long it took.

He watched as she paced back to the bed and sat on the edge again, her expression impossible to decipher. He wanted to believe it was yearning and affection, but what the fuck did he know?

She dove right in, her words almost tripping over each other. "I'm going to the facility when you all do, either with you or I'll follow. You want to protect me. We're attracted, mates, according to you. And I feel our bond. I can sense you. I…" She glanced away and back. "I—yearn for you when you're not around."

That sentence at the end encouraged him to think she cared, beyond her desire for revenge. He wasn't getting his hopes up yet, though.

"I want you to finish the mating bond. I want to be a powerful partner when we go, not a liability, but believe me when I say I'm not staying here. I don't mean to hurt you by doing this, although I can tell by the look on your face I am. I know it's for the wrong reason, not the reason you want. But, Carrick, I *do* want you. If you believe nothing else, believe that— and we can grow to care for each other."

Carrick was going to throw in the towel and give in. His defenses crumbled under her look of entreaty. The fear became even stronger that he was going to lose her if he didn't agree. Either to death or she would ditch him. But first, he was going to make damn sure she understood the consequences. What she didn't understand was that he already cared for her, was already more than halfway in love with her.

"I want you to understand what you'll be agreeing to, what we'll be doing and the consequences in the future." Man, the thought of completing the mating had his cock weeping as it pulsed and throbbed to the beat of his heart. He stood plastered to the door, afraid if he sat next to her his wolven-self would pressure him to get it done. Right there on her bed.

She shot him a look of annoyance and impatience. "You already told me last night."

"I told you the basics, Nia. I listened to you, how about you show me the same courtesy?"

He saw it was her turn to clench her jaw in annoyance. Well, too damn bad. If they were going to do this, and he had no doubt in his mind they were, she could wait until he laid out all the facts.

No way did he want her surprised and regretting her actions after they mated—were permanently linked—physically, mentally and emotionally. When she gave a small nod, he unglued himself from the wall and strode to the overstuffed chair near the bed. He sat and leaned forward to prop his forearms on his quads, hands clasped, eyes on hers.

"Dak and I told you the basics, exactly what you recited earlier. I didn't go into depth, didn't have all the knowledge until Reese and Bah shared it with me earlier today. How what you've referred to as an invisible thread connecting us becomes so strong we'll be able to feel each other, regardless of where the other is. When we aren't together, we'll feel anxious, like a part of us is missing. You'll feel another—self, for want of anything better to call it— in your head and body. For Garou, the males, it's like having a wolf-half, a primal being harping at us, telling us what to do when we hesitate to act." He cocked his head and let the heat he felt for her shine through his eyes. "For instance, my wolven-self wants me to strip you naked, slip my cock in your hot, tight sheath and sink my fangs into you so you'll be ours forever. Right. Now."

Her eyes widened in what he thought was fear, until he saw her nipples pebble again, her pulse flutter wildly in her neck and her pupils expand in arousal, almost obliterating her gem-green irises, flecked again with red and silver.

It took everything in him to control his wolven-half and not take her, then and there. He must have broadcasted his deep desire, if her small gasp and squirm of her thighs were any indication.

He put the skids on his arousal and continued. "We'll constantly crave each other, especially for the first few weeks after the mating. We'll both want to fuck every chance we get, and if we can't, then we'll at least need to be in contact as often as possible. As time goes on, that lessens a bit, but we'll always have a craving for each other, for being near, for touching and making love. We'll also crave the touching of our minds. Oh, we won't be able to read each other's minds, but if we concentrate on the link, we'll be able to feel a psychical connection, a melding that satisfies and comforts. I've heard that we'll feel each other's emotions; arousal, fear, compassion—love."

He kept her pinned with his eyes, wanting, needing to drive this point home. "If you or I lose that, Nia. If you think you can mate with me, have me bind us permanently together—avenge your sister and rescue the others, do away with Denton and his cronies—and then leave me, you have another fucking think coming. It would devastate both of us. I wouldn't try to stop you. You wouldn't be a prisoner like you were with Denton. But you'd feel you were dying inside. We would both feel like that, if we don't have the physical and psychical connection of living together, being together, making love—of eventually falling in love."

He stood, stalked to the door and grabbed the handle before swiveling his head to look at her over his shoulder, his heart about breaking in two. "Think hard about it, Nia. You have about thirty minutes to decide before we cut it too close to do this and give you time to recover, before we have to leave. There's also no guarantee you won't have a more dramatic, negative response to the mating since we don't know what Denton's infusions altered in you. You may end up sick enough to need to stay here, anyway." He turned to face the door, unable to hold her eyes and have her see the pain in his. "And then you'll no doubt regret having mated with me."

He scrubbed a hand down his face in frustration, his calluses scraping against the stubble, and yanked open the door. "You'll find me in my room when you decide. Do me a favor and let me know, one way or another."

With that, he jerked the door open and stalked out, barely in control of either his human or wolven sides. He needed to get to his room and calm the fuck down, so whatever Nia's decision was, he reacted with the love he was coming to feel for the stubborn, beautiful, frustrating, amazing woman.

So if she wanted to go through with it, they would both remember the mating act with affection, or at least without a boatload of regret.

Fucking hell.

Chapter Nineteen

NIA SAT, her bloodless fingers clutching the edge of the bed, and stared at the door Carrick just exited. The look on his face, in his eyes, while he'd explained in blunt terms what being fully mated to a Garou meant, hit a bullseye to her heart with the knowledge she'd deeply hurt this man.

Not that she'd thought he was without feelings; she just hadn't realized the depth of his desire or burgeoning affection for her. Clearly not just physically, but emotionally and mentally, too.

Shit! She'd been so damned lost in her anguish over her sister's death. In the guilt that ate at her for being the reason Denton had captured and murdered her sister.

Pile that on top of her anger at Denton and his army of assholes for what they'd done to her, to the others. Add on the betrayal of the man who'd sold her out to Denton for a mere pittance, and she was a mess.

What she'd felt for that ass, what she'd felt for any other man in her past, paled so much compared to what she felt for Carrick after only a couple of days, as to be almost transparent.

What he didn't understand was that she had feelings for him, but dammit, he needed to wait for her to catch up to his intensity. Her feelings were growing by the hour. Hell, maybe even by the minute—in leaps and bounds—but all this crap with Denton and her illness and her sister's death was muddying up what could have been a whirlwind romance and subsequent mating.

She fully understood what he described, about the link or thread or whatever the hell people wanted to call it. Theirs was already there, and she had trouble imagining it even stronger, as intense as he described.

Yes, she was nervous about tying herself to a man she'd known less than two days, but from what she'd seen, and could feel, he was a man of integrity who would stand beside her and not try to control her. Who would treat her as a partner, and who already seemed to feel affection for her.

She knew his controlling behavior in the kitchen stemmed from his emotions roaring to the front, his fear of her dying, of losing her. If not for those heady emotions, she was sure he wouldn't have been such an ass.

But she knew she was strong enough not to put up with that shit, so that one instance wouldn't be a deterrent to her going through with the mating. She could hold her own with him; she just didn't want to have to do it all the time.

Was there really anything to stop her? Any red flags? Hell, any orange or pink flags? She honestly didn't think so. It boiled down to one question; did she think her feelings would grow enough that she wouldn't chafe at being with him for the rest of her life?

Since she didn't plan to put herself in danger regularly, she felt he could and would curb that uber-protective, you'll-do-what-I-say behavior.

Decision made, insides quaking, she dashed into the bathroom to brush her teeth and shake out her curls so she at least tasted and looked good.

She'd planned to ask Dak for his IV cocktail before going to Carrick, but they were running out of time, and no way was she going to rush the big guy after almost blackmailing him into finalizing their mating bond.

Her lady-parts pulsed and flooded with wetness at the thought of him touching her intimately again. At the thought of his big, thick cock slipping home in her sheath. Taking a deep breath, she exited her room and padded down to Carrick's door, only to freeze literally on his doorstep.

Her heart started beating triple-time, and she was lightheaded from a spike of anxiety and adrenaline. She hated this, her inability to turn tail and rush back to her room, or get a grip and knock on the door and enter. She propped her shaking hands on the door and rested her forehead against them.

When the door suddenly opened, she fell right into muscular arms that wrapped around her like they'd never let her go, and the anxiety that had consumed her turned into a burning desire to be one with this man.

"God, Carrick, take me to bed. Can you forget what I said and just be with me, mate me, and don't hate me?"

"Oh, baby, I don't hate you."

His basso profundo voice, coupled with those muscles that went on for days, always made her want to crawl all over the man. She gave a sigh of relief when he scooped her up in his strong arms, kicked the door shut and strode quickly to his bed, laying her gently in the middle before following her down to cover her completely with that masculine, muscled body she couldn't get enough of.

Her legs naturally opened to cradle his groin, that delicious prominent package pressed intimately against her core, especially her throbbing clit, eliciting a moan from deep in her throat.

His answering groan caused an involuntary shudder to sweep through her body, her hips pumping to press her clit even harder against his iron-hard cock.

Emotion swamped her when, instead of tearing off her clothes and getting right to the act, he cupped her face with his callused palms and pressed gentle kisses to her closed eyelids before trailing his lips down her cheek to capture hers in a sensuous kiss full of promises.

His sudden stillness and forehead pressing against hers caused panic to take hold. Had he changed his mind? Did he no longer want her because he was remembering why she'd agreed to this? God, she hoped not!

She pushed against his chest, to ask him if he'd decided he didn't want her, but halted at the plea in his gravelly voice. "Nia, baby. Please be sure. I want this so badly, I crave you. Can't imagine my life without you now. You must be sure."

She pushed harder, and he rose a little so she could see his starkly masculine face, and hold his molten silver gaze. "I *am* sure, Carrick. Even if you think it's for the wrong reasons, I'm sure. I crave you too. I'm sorry I'm not at the same place you are in wanting this. That was never my intention, to cause you pain. I hate that I've hurt you."

When he shook his head and levered himself off her, she clutched his sinewy forearm. He was leaving! He'd decided against the mating. Oh, god! What would she do? She had to be stronger; she had to go with them!

She clutched her chest with her other arm, her heart suddenly pained at the thought he wouldn't mate her. It wasn't only about being stronger, she suddenly realized, but she didn't have the time to explore any possibility of deepening feelings.

She snatched her hand from her chest and brushed angrily at her tears. "Don't go! Please!"

He was back on top of her before she could go on, and she gasped at his speed and power. "Nia, I'm not leaving, sweetheart. We *will* fully be mates tonight." His eyes roamed her face, and he brushed the wetness away from her face. "Tears, Nia?"

She could tell he bit back what else he was going to say, rolled his lips inward, then gave a puff of breath. "Let me be clear. I'm going to get undressed, then I'm going to peal your clothes off to reveal the most beautiful body I've ever seen. And then I'm going to worship it, and you, before I slide my cock home in your welcoming heat, where it fucking belongs, and sink my fangs into your trap, where your neck meets your shoulder. You'll feel a slight sting, and if the stories prove true, since god knows no one my age has ever experienced it, we will both feel euphoria and have the best damn orgasm we've ever had or ever will. And then our link will be even more amazing than it already is."

Her eyes widened the more he spoke, another rush of liquid flooding her pussy and trickling down her thighs while her clit pulsed wildly. His nostrils flared and his pupils dilated till only an enthralling dark silver ring rimmed the black.

"I can smell your arousal, sweetheart, and your eyes are flashing silver and red again in the green band around your pupils, like they do whenever you're deeply aroused, as when we made love last night. And mark my words, Nia, we made love last night. That wasn't just sex or fucking. Still onboard with this?"

The paralysis caused by his words, and erotic pictures flooding her mind the more he talked, finally snapped when he asked that question.

She reached up, wrapped her arms around his neck and pulled him down to lay a kiss on him she hoped he would never forget; one that conveyed she was not only on board, she was desperate for him to take her and make her his.

She hadn't been able to dismiss the panic she'd felt at being left behind, the real reason she'd agreed to this mating, until just this moment; until his words eclipsed those troublesome thoughts and she was nothing but pure, passionate desire and affection.

All she now felt, all she wanted—needed—was a mutual taking, a sensual ravaging, and yes, his fangs sinking into her, linking them forever.

His groan when their mouths melded, tongues dueled and bodies writhed against each other was the best aphrodisiac she'd ever known. She let go of his neck, her fingers digging into his massive shoulders to hold on tight, frustrated desire coiling inside her. He needed to be naked—now. She let go of his thick shoulders to grab fistfuls of his t-shirt and pulled.

"Off, clothes off! Now, Carrick. I need to see you, touch you, taste you."

Again astounded at his preternatural speed, he fairly leapt from the bed to land on his feet, reached one hand behind his neck to fist his shirt and tugged it over his head. He flung it backwards to send it sailing across the room, baring those massive pecs, shoulders that rivaled the longest broadsword, boulder size biceps and washboard abs.

Her eyes drank in his gloriously naked body, and she was breathless to see the rest of that beautiful, masculine perfection.

"You need to be naked in about four seconds, Nia."

His growling voice sent sensual vibrations up and down her spine, and it tempted her to tease the wolf and ask him what he'd do if she didn't comply. One look at his eyes showed a wildness she'd never seen before, and when he spoke, she saw the hint of fang touch his full lower lip.

Maybe she'd poke the wolf some other time and just get these clothes off. Using both hands, because she'd never mastered that sexy one-armed tug to remove her shirt, she pulled her tank top over her head, her cloud of curls cascading over her shoulders, breasts and back.

His eyes feasted on her bare breasts and her nipples became even more turgid at the desire burning in that silver gaze. When his eyes jumped to her face, she saw emotion flash through them she couldn't decipher before he banked it and gave a nod at her leggings.

"Off." More growl than word showed his wolven-side was bursting forth, and instead of frightening her, she found it sexy as hell.

She shoved her leggings off, leaving a scrap of lace behind, as he unbuttoned his jeans and pushed them down, taking his boxer briefs with them to fully reveal the part of a man that frequently made women stupid—the Adonis belt.

Those defined muscles along the side of the abs that seemed to guide the eyes right down to that impressive cock, currently standing at attention and throbbing to the beat of his heart. Holy shit, how had that fit inside her last night?

She arched toward him when he took one big hand, wrapped his thick fingers around his pulsing length, then stroked, once, twice, the action catapulting her from his bed to fall to her knees in front of him and take him in her mouth before he could utter a word.

"Fuck! Nia! Damn, baby." He gently pulled her off, swept her in his arms and took them to the bed, falling on her like a man lost in the desert coming across an oasis.

CARRICK WAS on the brink of losing control to his wolven-side, his human and primal selves wrestling to take over. No way was he going to cede full control to that wildness for something this important. This special.

He would allow that other wild part of him to bask in her becoming theirs, the fangs to come forth to complete the mating, but his human side would be in control, would call the shots. Would revel in the emotions consuming him.

When his woman dropped to her knees in front of him, breasts bobbing and swaying, and locked her mouth around his cock, he about shot off at the first touch of her those plump lips and hot tongue.

Holy. Fuck! She surprised the hell out of him with her actions. No way was he coming in her mouth, though. No, he would make love to his woman before sinking his teeth into her, even if it killed him to pull her mouth from his cock.

He would definitely not rut and finish the mating as if she wasn't the most precious thing in his world. She'd become his everything, and the sooner she realized that, the better.

He scooped her up and dropped onto the bed, coming down on top of her, his cock homing in like a heat-seeker missile. He stopped just shy of pressing against her core, rose to his knees and hooked his fingers into the waistband of that bit of lace trying to pass as panties, tugging them down her shapely legs and off.

He sat back on his heels, transfixed by the sight before him. He was still astounded at her lush curves and sinewy muscles—and that she was his. His mate. Holy hell, he was the luckiest bastard on the planet.

He let his eyes roam from that enticing triangle of curls at the juncture of her thighs wet with her excitement, up her tucked in waist and over her belly to her breasts, jiggling slightly with her rapid breaths, up even farther to her beautiful face framed by those amazing curls. Oh, yeah, his lady was just as excited as he was.

His hands followed the path his eyes had taken, while keeping his gaze on hers, tracing a path around the thatch hiding her pussy, taking in the blown pupils, rimmed by her brilliant gem-green irises flecked with red and silver, an amazing contrast to her copper-toned skin.

Her breath hitched in anticipation, but he skirted the hidden goods and trailed fingertips across her taught belly to tease the underside of her glorious breasts.

"Carrick! Tease me later. You're driving me crazy." Her voice was breathless with desire, but he wanted her right on the edge like he was.

"I'm not teasing, Nia. I'm sampling, I'm learning what you enjoy. I'm in heaven touching your body, glorying in the fact you're mine to savor."

He watched as her eyes softened and filled with—hell; he hoped with affection. Leaning forward, he braced one forearm next to her shoulder, cupped a breast in his hand and brushed a knuckle across one nipple, while lowering his head to tongue the tight bud of the other, causing her to almost catapult off the bed.

"Yes!! Oh, yes, just like that!"

Yeah, his woman was sensual and responsive as hell, and he had to tighten his abs and quads to keep from shooting off all over her stomach. His fangs slid out even farther, which was freaky as hell and something he still wasn't used to. Maybe he didn't have as much control as he thought.

He took care not to nick her breast with a fang when he wrapped his lips around a turgid nipple, sucking and flicking the puckered bud with the tip of his tongue, while continuing to gently pinch and roll the other. She was now a wild thing under him, her hips pumping as if reaching for his cock, her hands wrapped as far around his triceps as she could reach, her short nails pricking his skin.

Reveling in the feel of her, he lost even more ground to his wolven-side while his human-side fought for control, when she wrapped a small fist in his hair and gave a mighty pull.

"I love, ohhhh, I love what you're doing. But I'm so empty, Carrick. I've been so empty all my life and feel like I've been waiting for this. For you. Fill me. Make me yours!"

Carrick completely lost it at her words and actions. Part of him, the part hurt and damaged by her desire to mate only to be stronger, to wreak vengeance, was still there, but another part of him wanted to believe what she was saying.

That she wanted this as much as he did because she cared for him. Needed him—almost—as much as he needed her.

With a growl, he nudged her legs farther open with one of his thighs, stretched out over her, tucked his forearms under her shoulders, lined his cock up and slid partway in.

She was so fucking tight, and he was so thick and long, he had to rock back and forth to fully slide his cock inside her. He buried his head against her neck, the urge to also bury his fangs a living thing in him. Fuck!

"Ohh, wait, wait. I forgot how big you are." Nia moaned, sliding her hands around and clutching his biceps even tighter. Not pushing him away, but not relaxed, either.

He stopped, shaking with the effort to keep still and not pump for all he was worth, afraid he was hurting her. Although drenched and ready for him, he still eased his way in, since he was big all over. "Are you…" His larynx tight from the stress of controlling himself, he cleared his throat and tried again. "Are you okay?"

"Oh, yesssss. I just, just needed a moment—to relax—my muscles."

"You're strangling my cock in the best way, Nia, but I don't want you in pain."

She cuffed him on his shoulder, then grabbed hold again as if she'd never let go. "I'm not in pain, Carrick. Or at least, it was the oh-so-good kind of pain, and a bit of a surprise. I love how thick you are in me."

Her voice had softened to a purr, her words and tone setting a fire in his soul and groin. He was barely in control, but enough so he felt he had to ask for her consent to the mating one more time, before they both lost themselves in each other.

"Be mine, Nia. Tell me, honey, are we still okay? If you want me to stop, god please don't want me to stop, you gotta tell me now. My wolven-side is right on the edge, and you have to know I'd never hurt you, but it's going to get to the point I'll have trouble pulling him back."

He felt slender, strong hands cup his cheeks, pushing him back enough for them to look each other in the eyes. She gave him a little shake, raised up to pepper kisses on his lips before her head dropped back to the bed.

Her voice was fervent and heartfelt when she gave her permission. "Carrick, I will not change my mind. You need to move or I'm going to go crazy. Take me, sink your fangs into me and make me yours, honey." She dropped her hands from his face and circled his neck to pull him back down, then wrapped her lithe, muscular legs around his hips.

Taking that as full consent, and more turned on than he knew how to deal with, Carrick pulled out and pumped back in, realizing on that inward slide into her heat he was only a moment, two at the most, away from coming. "Baby, not going to last long this time. You're slaying me with your body and words. I'll make it up to you. Next time—I'll—go longer. Oh, hell. Nia!"

He lost it, hips pumping faster, the friction of her tight sheath against his cock driving him nuts. His pace picked up as she lifted her hips in time with his downstrokes.

Feeling his balls tighten even more, lightning streaking down his spine and into his cock, he gritted his teeth and held back his orgasm by sheer willpower. When she sank her own blunt teeth into his shoulder, though, his soul howled in pleasure and he threw his head back, roaring his release.

His wolven side took control as he dropped his mouth to her trap and sank his fangs into her muscle while he came in long, hard spurts, drenching them both.

Nia gasped when his teeth pierced her skin, then raked her fingernails across his lats, threw her head back and moaned. Pure ecstasy filled her voice as her words tumbled out. "Yessss! Carrick, ohhhhh, yesss!! Feels sooo good."

Elation rolled through him and he groaned long and loud as he pumped through their orgasm, the sensation of the serum ejecting from his fangs into his mate painfully exquisite.

His heart felt close to bursting, his soul finally complete, and the streaked lightning coursing through his entire body, like one fucking tremendous orgasm, had him close to passing out.

His fangs receded, and he lapped at the blood dotting her shoulder, cleaning the small wound. He realized that part of the mating was complete, but the need to keep slowly pumping as her sheath pulsed around his cock wouldn't stop.

He realized Nia was still coming, panting and moaning, tears leaking from her tightly closed eyes. "Carrick, oh Carrick. How could it be this good? This—ohhhh, a-mazinggg…"

He slowed the motion of his hips, his cock finally softening as the pulsing of her core also slowed until they were both still, marveling in what they'd just shared.

Bone deep exhaustion suddenly swept through him, and he lurched to the side so as not to crush her as his arms gave out. He wrapped an arm around her and tugged her to his side, settling her head on his shoulder. "Gotta rest, sweetheart."

She nodded and settled next to him, half on him, mumbling and already half-asleep. "So tired, Carrick. Gotta sleep for a while—love…"

Her voice was an echo in his head as he felt her body relax bonelessly against him, and he jerked at her last word, wondering if he'd heard wrong.

Was she saying she loved him, or calling him love as an endearment? On that thought, sleep took him down and he succumbed to the darkness.

CARRICK WOKE to shivering and moaning, briefly confused until the intense heat of a body curled against him brought memories of their mating flashing back.

He'd experienced nothing like it before, and his cock rose for round two as he remembered their mutually monstrous orgasm when he'd bitten her.

He wiped one hand down his face in an attempt to clear the cobwebs from his mind, then tucked it under her head to roll on top of her and waken her to slide his cock into her heat again.

He jolted in alarm when Nia gave another violent shiver along with chattering teeth, and he realized her face was like a furnace on his shoulder. She was burning up!

He quickly but gently rolled her off his shoulder, sat and clicked on the bedside light, then turned to get a good look at his woman. His heart lurched and raced at the sight of her drenched in sweat, cheeks flushed red, shivering as if she was naked in the snow.

She rolled to her side and curled into a ball, fists clenched, a grimace contorting her beautiful face. Fuck! Had to be from the claiming. Dammit, he'd hoped any reaction would be mild, as Reese had explained.

"Nia, sweetheart, wake up. Show me those beautiful green eyes."

When he got no response, he jumped from the bed, stalked to the door, and wrenched it open. "Bah, Dak! Need you! Grab your kit."

Leaving the door open, he grabbed his boxer briefs, jerked them on, then draped the sheet over Nia to preserve some modesty. His friends were well aware he'd completed the mating with her last night;

what with their exceptional hearing, how could they not be? They could have heard them getting it on from the far reaches of the property, much less elsewhere in the house.

He instinctively focused on his link with Nia, reassured to find it immeasurably stronger than before they mated, and sent every bit of love and affection he felt for her along that thread.

He had no clue if she could sense what he projected, but his wolven-side was insistent he do so. His fanged-self also wanted him to curl up around her and share their warmth and protection, like their furry four-legged brethren did when their mate was ill or injured.

She suddenly quieted a little and rolled back toward where he'd been laying, her voice a mere remnant of her usual husky, sexy tone. "Carrick. Need you."

Her plea about broke his heart, and he concentrated even harder on their link. Could it be she was actually feeling the love and care he was broadcasting? She'd responded, so maybe so.

He sat quickly on the bed, piled pillows against the headboard and eased back, gently pulling her up and next to him, tugging her closer until she was slightly reclining against his torso, wrapped securely in his arms.

He pulled the sheet up till it covered her breasts and tucked it under her arms so Bah would have access for whatever tests or procedures he needed to do, and she'd not be embarrassed if she woke when Bah and Dak were in the room.

Bah ran into the room, taking the situation in with a glance, and hurried to the other side of the bed, his medical backpack on one shoulder, with Dak on his heels. Simone appeared in the doorway, a worried frown etched on her face, Rachel cradled on one shoulder. "What's wrong?"

Carrick sent Dak a look of gratitude when the big man reversed course and strode to Simone, wrapped an arm around her shoulders and ushered her back down the hallway, reassuring her they would come get her if need be.

As Carrick caressed Nia's arm and sent more reassuring waves of love through their link, she settled, still shivering and much too warm, but not as restless. When she fumbled and then grasped one of his hands tightly, clutching it to her breasts, his heart cracked open even wider for this amazing woman.

"You're going to be fine, sweetheart. Bah and Dak will fix you up in no time." Carrick squeezed her hand gently and glanced up at his friend when he spoke, wanting Bah to confirm his vow. He got questions instead.

"Any other symptoms? Did they just start? Has she been conscious since you woke?"

"I just woke. Her shivering awakened me, and no, she hasn't. Don't know how long she's been like this. I'm sure you know I claimed her last night. We both passed out afterwards. Literally passed out within a minute or two."

He glanced at the dial on his watch. "That was about two hours ago. She's not been conscious that I know of, just the mumbling you've heard. No other symptoms I'm aware of other than the fever, shivering, and not waking."

Bah grabbed an extra pillow and set it on her lap, propping one of her arms outstretched on it, inner arm up, then quickly and efficiently wrapped a blood pressure cuff around her bicep and pressed a button to activate it. He slipped a pulse oximeter on the forefinger of her right hand and kept one hand on her forearm in case she startled or jerked.

"Nia, Bah here. I have a blood pressure cuff on your arm. It'll turn on and off every few minutes so I can monitor you. The sensation on your finger is a pulse oximeter, so I can monitor your pulse and oxygen levels. I'll use a temporal thermal thermometer to check your temp. I'm not doing anything intrusive, and if we need to hook up an IV, I'll let you know first. Carrick is right here with you, and Dak will be right back."

"Thanks, man." Carrick appreciated Bah's bedside manner on the off chance she could hear and understand him, especially in light of Nia's previous experiences with doctors, technicians and needles at Denton's facility. He hoped to hell she didn't need an IV, afraid she would panic in her unconscious state and hurt herself.

They both looked to the door when Dak strode back in. "I let Simone know what's going on. West, Mateo, and Etienne are outside monitoring the perimeter, and I updated them via text. Ramil and Flynne are catching combat naps. We'll postpone the mission if need be until Nia's okay, then evaluate and decide if she goes or not. Yeah?"

Carrick nodded at Dak. "Yeah. It's only fifteen-hundred, so we still have nine hours before go-time." He turned to Bah, anxious to know what was wrong with Nia, and saw him taking her temp at her forehead with the thermal reader. "How's she doing, Doc?"

Bah turned to check her blood pressure and the oximeter, then faced Carrick and Dak, concern in his eyes. "Her blood pressure is elevated at 145 over 90, though not dangerously so. Her pulse is high at ninety, oxygen is great at 99, but her temp is too high at 104. We need to get that down. I hate to say, but we need to get an IV going and Dak's cocktail hooked up. She's probably already dehydrated, depleted and exhausted from, well, your antics last night, being upset earlier and the claiming just a while ago."

Nia's arm jerked under Bah's hand, and they collectively held their breaths to see if she'd settle or panic. When she did nothing more than moan, Carrick breathed a sigh of relief.

Bah checked the oximeter again, then turned back to Carrick. "I tested her potassium level when I took her blood yesterday, and it was low, so I'll add that to the IV and hopefully it'll help make a difference in her blood pressure. Dak, you have glutathione and vitamin C bags, yes? We'll add those."

Dak turned and strode from the room to prepare the solutions, and Bah pulled the IV cannula, needle, and attached tubing out of his pack. "You think she's out of it enough it won't trigger her fear of needles and IVs?"

Carrick shook his head. "Not sure, man. Better to explain it to her like you said earlier. I'll be ready to hold her down if necessary." The thought of restraining her while Bah inserted the IV felt like a betrayal, but he would do anything at this point to ensure she survived the mating and was stronger and healthy again.

"You have any idea how long her symptoms will last? Have you read about severe reactions in historical records?"

Bah looked thoughtful before replying. "I've read of accounts where there were adverse reactions, but they typically weren't this severe, and the women were actually back to normal and feeling fine in just a couple of hours, with no memory of being in pain or having suffered afterwards. With Nia getting those damned infusions in the lab, no telling what DNA or RNA changes occurred, or if it means this will take longer or not. Her reaction is definitely more over the top than any I've read or heard about. They're typically what Dak explained yesterday, slight muscle aches, as if the person has a mild flu and some tiredness that lasts just a few hours."

Carrick leaned down to press his lips against her feverish forehead. "Nia, Bah needs to insert an IV." No reaction. He turned to Bah. "Where will you be putting it?"

"In the antecubital region—the inside of her arm, just below the crook of the elbow."

Dak strode back into the room, wheeling an IV pole with one hand and holding several solution bags in the other. He placed the pole near the head of the bed on Bah's side, laid the bags on the bed, then started hanging them one at a time and arranging the tubing.

"Thanks, man." Bah pulled the cap from the cannula and gave Carrick a nod, then swiveled his head to Dak. "Stay here in case I need you to immobilize her arm."

Carrick tensed, fully expecting the worst, but always hoping for the best with his woman. "Nia, he's going to need to insert the IV just under the crook of your inner arm. I understand he's a champ at this, and you'll barely feel anything. You need to remember you're safe, and I will let no one do anything to harm you. If you can hear me, trust that

Bah, Dak and I have your best interests at heart. Okay, here we go, sweetheart."

He gave his buddy a nod, and Bah deftly rubbed an alcohol-soaked cotton ball across the area, tossed it on a tray he'd set on the bed, and deftly inserted the IV needle with cannula.

Carrick was never more thankful for their enhanced speed than right then, when Nia jerked back, gave a small cry and tried to wrench her arm away from Bah, while popping him in the eye with her other fist.

"Fuck, that hurt."

Bah's head bounced back, and Carrick had to give him credit for holding tight and barely reacting, although he could tell it hurt like a son-of-a-bitch, and they realized right then she was indeed stronger than before they mated. The man kept her arm in a gentle iron grip and Carrick wrapped his arms around her torso, under her breasts, to keep her still.

"Dak!" His friend was already kneeling on the bed next to Bah, holding down her thrashing legs while Carrick murmured softly to her. "Nia, baby, it's Carrick. Bah had to insert an IV. You're having an adverse reaction to the mating. It's just the cannula right now, not hooked up to anything yet. Come on, sweetheart, please relax. No one's gonna hurt you here. You're in my house, in my bed, remember?"

It heartened Carrick when she stopped struggling. Although still strung tight as a bowstring, she'd at least stopped fighting them. "Bah's going to hook up the solution Dak described earlier, along with a bag of glutathione and one of Vitamin C. It'll be okay, baby. That's it, feel my arms holding you, my lips on your forehead—concentrate on our link."

He glanced at Bah and then Dak to see deep concern in their eyes, and if he wasn't mistaken, affection for his mate. She was working her way into everyone's hearts by being brave and kind, by surviving a terrible ordeal. Then not only surviving after her escape, alone, lonely and afraid, but putting herself at risk to save Rachel and Simone. They knew the shit she'd gone through and it triggered their alpha-protectiveness. Especially because she was a Cinnabar Twin and ever so rare to the Garou.

She relaxed a little more and Dak leaned forward. "Nia. Gonna let go of your legs, yeah? We're here to help and protect you, girl. Not gonna let anything happen to you. Relax, okay?"

Bah spoke up to offer his reassurances. "Hey, Nia, opening the flow in the tube now, from the solution bags to the IV. You'll feel a coolness in your vein near the IV site. Nothing to worry about. I'll be monitoring the flow, along with your temp, blood pressure, pulse, and oxygen. I won't let anything go wrong. By the way, congratulations on that superb left-hook. Gonna have a shiner, for sure."

Carrick eyes burned with unshed tears, watching his buddies being so gentle and caring to his woman. Knowing even though unrelated, they were like a band of brothers and had each other's backs.

They'd added Nia as a sister to that band. He knew if either of these men, or the others in their group, found their mates, he would do everything in his power to ensure their safety and wellbeing.

He gave both men a chin lift. "Thanks, man. Means the world to me." He knew they understand what he meant, even with the brevity of his words.

When she relaxed further, he cautiously unwrapped one arm and brushed away the curls sticking to her face, then stroked his fingers up and down her other arm to distract her from the feel of the IV solution entering her vein.

If she survived this, he would thank every deity out there and never take this woman for granted.

Chapter Twenty

NIA GROANED, wondering what brick wall had collapsed on her during the night. Every muscle, tendon and ligament felt like someone had beaten them with a ball peen hammer. Gah!

Did she have the flu? She had no idea what time it was, or even what day it was. A headache pulsed behind one eye and it wouldn't surprise her a bit to find out even her hair hurt if she touched it.

When she tried to roll to her back, she realized she was wrapped securely in Carrick's powerful arms, spooned by his muscled front to her back, his knees tucked in behind hers, his cock soft but still impressive against her ass.

She pried her gritty eyes open, one at a time, to see Bah sound asleep in a chair by the bed, his head resting on his big bicep and one of his broad hands clutching her outstretched arm, which sported a cotton ball in the crook with stretchy green tape holding it tight.

What the fuck? A quick glance confirmed the sheet covered all the important bits, and with Carrick at her back, she wasn't flashing anything she shouldn't. She flinched when that sudden movement caused a spike of pain behind her eye. "Ahh, that hurts."

It was as if someone had poked both men with a stun baton as soon as the groaned comment passed her lips. Bah jumped to his feet, his hand pressing down to hold her arm to the bed, the other grabbing her shoulder, and Carrick's arms tightened around her, holding her tight to his chest.

A squeak escaped when Dak practically leap across the room from wherever he'd been to grab her ankles. What the actual hell?

She kept perfectly still, squinting against the headache still throbbing in her left eye, and cautiously looked back at Bah, who stared at her like she was going to lead with a right hook. Come to think of it, he kinda looked like someone already did.

She gasped, wondering if she caused the rainbow bruise circling one eye. "Um, guys. I'm guessing I slept through something not so good? I kinda feel I should apologize for your eye, Bah, even without knowing what went down."

His look of relief was almost comical. To think a woman her size was any match for a man of his bulk, especially a Garou, was ridiculous. She had to quell a giggle to see Dak and Bah stand and back slowly away from her, then turn and move toward the door.

"I'd say she's almost good as new, Carrick. Nia, your man will fill you in. Take two ibuprofen for that headache, okay? It'll help with any lingering inflammation and muscle pain, too, but I think you can expect that to disappear pretty quickly now that you're awake." He stroked a finger under his eye, across the red and purple bruise. "Also, I can attest that completing the mating did indeed strengthen you." With that parting shot, a salute and a grin tossed over his wide shoulder, he and Dak turned and exited the room, pulling the door shut behind them with a click.

When Carrick clasped her shoulder and tugged, she rolled carefully to her back to find him looming over her, one hand cupping her face, the other still grasping her shoulder. "You scared the hell out of me." His voice was raspy, as if he'd been yelling or gargling glass. "But you're okay now."

He closed his eyes and shook his head. "Damn, baby, you had a terrible reaction to our mating."

He bowed his head and nestled it between her breasts, one ear firmly planted over her heart, as if ensuring it was still beating. His muscular body was as tense as a cat cornered by a dog. She had to strain to hear his low voice rumbling through her chest, his words a direct arrow to her heart.

"I thought I was going to lose you, just when I've come to lo…, to care for you so very much. About broke my heart, Nia."

Had she heard him right? He'd almost told her he loved her. Didn't he? His words, muffled against her breast and so low, were hard to understand.

Feeling enormous tenderness for this man, she raised her hand and swept it over his head and down the ridge of muscle along the deep indentation of his spine, repeating the motion when she felt him relax with each stroke.

"I feel fine now, Carrick. Better than fine. Well, except for a headache in one eye and some muscle aches. Will you tell me what happened? What time is it?"

She shifted when he raised to his elbows and caught her eyes, seemingly unwilling to move away from his position over her. When his gaze lowered to her lips and he dipped his head, she met him halfway.

The kiss burned like the fiercest fire, full of promise, heat, and affection. They simultaneously angled their heads to take it deeper, then Carrick jerked back, and she whimpered a protest.

"No. You need to rest a little more."

She felt her lips moue into a pout, something totally out of character for her. The pain behind her eye gave a vicious throb, and she conceded she probably wasn't up for round two with the big guy's thick cock. Hmmm, but those fangs. Damn, that was ah-mazing!

"Hey, you okay? Still with me? It's about twenty hundred—eight pm. We both literally passed out after the mating, and I woke to you burning up with a high temp and shaking like a leaf."

As Carrick informed her what had transpired while she was unconscious and struggling with her reaction to the mating, she cringed inwardly at the thought she'd fought them and had no memory of it.

"Poor Bah. His eye looks painful."

"He's had worse, don't worry about him. I was going out of my mind until you turned the corner about an hour ago and your symptoms disappeared. You woke enough to answer a few questions and then fell asleep, and I guess we all dosed off too."

She stroked the sexy scruff on his cheek. "I hate I worried you." It suddenly dawned on her they were only four hours away from the time to leave for Denton's facility. "Is midnight still the target?" When she saw a muscle tick in his jaw, she hurried on. "We have four hours to monitor how I'm feeling.

Like I said, the only symptoms I have now are some muscle aches and a headache behind one eye. I'll take the ibuprofen Bah left for it, and even if it's not totally gone, it wouldn't hinder me on the mission. If I'm strong enough to pop Bah in the eye, I bet I'm powerful enough to endure the strike on the lab."

She held his eyes, praying he wouldn't go caveman on her again and force her hand. When he did nothing more than close his eyes, take a deep breath, and lean in for a soft kiss, she let herself hope he'd learned his lesson in trying to keep her off the team.

"As much as I'll worry, you were right, about it not being my choice what you decide to do. Where you decide to go. I'm sorry I tried to strong-arm you, but can't honestly say if you still weren't strong enough after the mating, I wouldn't at least try to come up with a plan to keep you off the front line during the raid, with as debilitated as you got. I'm counting on you not tiring like before now that we've mated. I'm not embarrassed to say you being injured—or killed—would crush me. I don't know if I would survive it, Nia."

He dropped another quick kiss on her lips before climbing from the bed. "I'll get you the pain reliever, a protein shake, and water. If I stay in here, the musky smell of your arousal is going to drive me crazy and we'll never get out of this bed. Damn, woman, you were enticing as hell before we clinched the deal. Now I'm gonna have to use every bit of my control to keep my hands off you."

Her pheromones must have been broadcasting like a bass speaker if the hard ridge outlined under his tight boxer briefs was any indication, not to mention the rapid pulse beating in his neck and hint of fang on his full lower lip.

She shamelessly watched him pull up a pair of sweats that hung low on his lean hips and hugged his muscular ass, prominently displaying his wicked Adonis belt, and she had to concentrate on the game plan, not all the things she wanted to do to that magnificent body.

She shot him a look and debated dropping to her knees in front of him, dragging his sweats and briefs down, and indulging in a quickie. "You weren't kidding about that, were you? The desire ramping up after mating. I want you back in this bed, and it's a toss-up whether I want to drive you crazy with my mouth or ride you like a stallion."

Her eyes widened when he cupped his cock with one big hand and took a long step toward the bed. She threw up a hand like a stop sign. "Whoa, big guy. Pain reliever first, gather everything we need for the mission, then if we have time, we'll see about getting lucky again."

"Damnnnn, baby, you're killing me. But you're right. Midnight is still the target, and I bet we'll have time for at least one, if not two tumbles before we have to leave. *If* your headache is better."

As much as she wanted to tumble him into bed right then, she conceded and shot him a look of sultry promise. "I'll take a quick shower to wash off this stickiness—you know, for our tumble later—while you get the stuff, then pack. You have my shotgun and Sig in your gun safe?"

"Yeah, we can get them on the way out, along with my weapons and more ammunition. I have some additional ordnance I think you'll appreciate, too."

"Sounds good. Now get going before I lose all good sense and invite you into the shower with me. Besides, my bladder is suddenly screaming at me."

At his considering look, she threw him a get-going look and shooed him along with a wave of her hand, marveling at the difference between now and when they were at odds just a few hours ago. Mating seemed to have mellowed both of them and tightened the bond they'd already been feeling.

Oh, she wasn't naïve enough to think he didn't still have hurt feelings, or that he didn't wish she'd agreed to the mating for reasons of love or passion, but at least they weren't sniping at each other, and some of the previous ease seemed to have returned.

As he strode out of the room, pulling the door closed behind him, she rose carefully but quickly from the bed and headed into the bathroom, now totally getting the phrase 'I need to pee like a racehorse'. She was glad to realize, other than the now-mild muscle aches and slight pain in one eye, she was feeling pretty darned good.

Nia made it to the toilet with seconds to spare and peed for what seemed like forever. She wondered just how many bags of IV solution they'd given her. After rising, she pivoted and looked in the mirror, shocked at her visage. "Holy shit, I look like death warmed twice over."

She leaned toward the mirror and took in the obvious differences, other than looking rode hard and put away wet. Her eyes now had silver and reddish flakes permanently sprinkled amidst the even deeper green of her irises.

When her gaze landed on the two small, already healing puncture marks on her trap, she jerked upright. The fact she was now—what—part Garou?

She had no fucking clue, but the fact she was different really hit home. That she would be stronger, as evidenced by Bah's bruised eye, live longer to match Carrick's life span, and have enhanced senses.

What senses mating would enhance was yet to be determined. Carrick said it was different for each person, and she wouldn't know until something happened and it, or they, kicked in.

It would be interesting to find out, and she hoped the enhanced sense or senses were something useful. Maybe, after the raid, she could help Carrick keep watch here in New Almaden? Provide security installations, and private security, to the other Garou in the area?

She didn't want to hide and sit on the sidelines of life anymore. If they got rid of Denton, she'd be able to move freely about New Almaden, and probably San Jose, too. Who knows, maybe she'd even be able to travel with Carrick to other Garou communities, if needed.

She had skills that were getting rusty, and the Garou in this area had need of those skills. Even when they dispensed with Denton, folks will need security and protection.

He wasn't the only evil asshole out there. Putting aside thoughts of the future, she turned on the shower faucet and concentrated on her link to Carrick, waiting for the water to warm.

With just a thought, the link almost vibrated with life, at least a hundred times stronger than before the mating. And that got her remembering the feel of his thick cock pumping inside her, the moment his fangs sank in, causing the most explosive orgasm she'd never imagined, just the memory bringing her to the brink of another one. Shew!

She doubted she'd ever experience anything like that again; and she remembered Carrick saying the mating would be amazing. It was that and more.

But what would it feel like now? Would it be just like the first time, pre-mating? Intense and wonderful, but not earth-shattering? Heat flooded her core, and she felt a trickle of moisture run down her inner thigh.

Damn, just thinking of him made her hot and bothered enough to consider taking herself in hand in the shower to take the edge off, in case they didn't have time to get it on before they left.

She gave an uncharacteristic squeak when the bathroom door opened and Carrick strode in clad only in his form-fitting boxer briefs, every ridge and vein of his currently hard cock showcased behind the tight material. He shot her a look filled with heated promise and peeled the briefs down his tree-trunk quads, then kicked them into the corner.

He stood there, his warrior-magnificent body just begging for her lips and hands, and she felt an answering rush of liquid between her legs.

"Baby, you're broadcasting some pretty horny vibes through our link. No way can I concentrate on weapons when I'm enticed by remembering the feel of your soft skin under my hands, my body. My mouth on those tight, sweet brown nipples and engorged clit. We'll make time this morning, or neither of us will be able to concentrate beyond our desperation for each other."

"Oh, yeah, I'm onboard with that, big guy." She held out her hand, quickly engulfed in his big palm, and tugged till he was flush against her oh-so-sensitive skin. She wondered if it was possible to have an all-over orgasm just from being plastered to his massive pecs, with those biceps worthy of their own porn show wrapped around her.

She grabbed fistfuls of his short hair and tugged hard to pull his lips to hers, then devoured his mouth, tongues dueling, lips enticing and teeth nibbling. She jerked to feel the point of a fang and pulled back in fascination to see them jutting over his full lower lip before lifting her eyes to meet his gaze.

His eyes were feral as he held hers, his breath gusting as if he'd sprinted a mile, and his fangs elongated until they protruded well past his lower lip.

"When we make l…, uh, have sex, are there times you'll want to bite me again, or do they just extend because you're aroused?"

"No fucking clue, since this is all new to me, too. I didn't get that far in the history Reese shared with me. But I will not take the chance you'll have another reaction, so I'll keep them to myself today." The look he gave her was scorching. "Let's find out another time, sweetheart. Right now, I just want to savor and worship your body."

"Oh, yeah." Was that breathy, sexy voice hers? She'd never in her life been all sex-kitten breathless with a man. But then again, she'd never been a fraction as turned on with past lovers as she was with Carrick. "I'm so on board with that, Carrick."

He looked momentarily confused when she placed her hands squarely over his pecs, unable to resist tweaking his flat, male nipples and causing him to groan, before she pushed him back a step, turned and leaned over the wide bathroom counter, bracing herself with her forearms, ass out and legs open to his incursion.

With a bold look in the mirror at his molten silver eyes, she jutted her ass out even more and raised to tiptoes, giving a shimmy and making her desire even more evident with the trickle of wetness on her inner thighs.

"Damn, baby, you slay me."

Holding her gaze, he griped her left hip with one big hand, took his throbbing cock in the other, and teased her opening, sliding down and under to tease her clit with the bulbous head, his jaw clenching all the while.

"Carrick! Not the time to tease. Come inside me. Please. Now!"

He obeyed by notching the swollen tip to her slit and pumping his hips, causing the head to breech and slip in, his hand reaching around to fondle her breast and tweak a nipple.

"Ohhhh, yesss! More!"

Another pump had what must have been half his long, thick member slide in, then he pulled out slowly and pumped again, burying him to the hilt. "Ohh, you're so thick! Almost... almost too big."

When he stopped moving and pulled back, she reached for his lean hip and held on tight. "I didn't mean you should stop! Take what you want, Carrick, and give me what I need, what I crave." She'd glanced in the mirror to look between her legs, then raised her eyes again to meet his, letting down her guard and allowing emotion to shine through.

"I know what we have is more than fucking, Carrick, but right now, right here, please fuck me. Hard."

She'd never seen his eyes darken the way they did at her words, nor had she ever seen him slip his control quite like this—except for when he'd bitten her during the mating. It thrilled her and caused her heart to crack open a little more for this complex man.

He took her at her words, and she reveled in their wild coupling. One of her hands slapped against the mirror to hold herself in place, while his broad palms gripped both of her hips as he hammered into her, his groin pounding her ass cheeks.

"Nia! Mine, baby. MINE!"

"Yesss! Ahhh!"

It took mere seconds for their eruption of pleasure, his growling shout and her gasp and groaned words of satisfaction no doubt heard across the property.

She slumped against the counter, boneless and sated beyond belief, while he leaned over her, cuddling her breast in one hand and cupping her head with the other, peppering small kisses against her hair and shoulder.

"You okay, sweetheart?"

This man. Always taking care of her. Her heart swelled, and she turned to drop a kiss on his bristly cheek, a soft smile curving her mouth. "I'm more than okay. I don't always need gentle, especially now that I'm stronger and not going to collapse after some sweaty, energetic sex."

A hard knock at the bedroom door had her jumping, and Carrick raised to stand, pulling out with a groan, his arm banded under her breasts to bring her up with him. She almost purred when he stroked a finger down her cheek.

Bah's voice sounded from the hallway. "Hey! Let's head out in a couple hours. No more quickies."

Nia turned and buried her face in Carrick's chest, her nose tickled by the crinkly thatch of chest hair, her voice muffled when she spoke. "You need to soundproof your bedroom."

Carrick chuckled. "*Our* bedroom. That might work for everyone, except Etienne. His enhanced sense is his hearing, you know."

"Well, we'll just have to send him to the movies, like parents do with their teenagers."

"Mommm, Daadd, let's go!"

Another shout from the kitchen, this time from Etienne if she wasn't mistaken, had her laughing along with Carrick, albeit in equal parts embarrassment and humor, especially knowing Etienne was the most intense of the group, and he'd resorted to humor to get them out and ready to get on the road.

Carrick dropped a kiss on her sweaty forehead and pulled away, swatting her ass as he strode back into the bedroom. "Better get your shower done and get packed. No way can I be in there with you without taking you again."

Likely taunting the wolf, she threw out her own rejoinder. "Or I'd be taking you, big guy. In my mouth." As she stepped under the hot spray, she grinned at the growl emanating from the bedroom, and then she sobered.

They had no clue what they would find when they arrived at Denton's facility. Had others died at his hands or behest since she'd left? After all this time, had he been successful in impregnating any of the female captives? Was that location still viable and running with the same staff?

Time to wash off the sweat, hit the road and find out. To wreak havoc, sow vengeance and free those suffering the same fate she and Simone—and her poor sister—had.

Chapter Twenty-One

CARRICK HELD his hands loosely on the steering wheel of his FJ Cruiser as he drove the lead vehicle, Nia riding shotgun in the passenger seat, with Etienne sprawled in the seat behind them.

Mateo was driving his Chevy Suburban, with Bah keeping him company, and West was driving Reese's older Chevy Tahoe that sported three rows of seats, with Flynne as his passenger.

They'd brought the third SUV, since they had no clue how many people they'd be liberating today.

They'd been on the road about six hours and had just turned off I-5 onto a two-lane rural road that led to a couple turnoffs and would finally take them to another two-lane road leading to the property the facility was on, which they'd confirmed through Ramil's research was indeed a converted ranch in the middle of the Umpqua National Forest in Oregon.

He hoped they didn't encounter anyone on the skinny road, and that the animal trail a half-mile or so before the edge of the property they'd seen via the satellite imagery would accommodate their vehicles and provide adequate cover.

They planned to stop well before the ranch property, which looked to be around eight-hundred acres, based on public property records. Not that the property was in Dentons's name, but it was the only property in the area with buildings on it seen via satellite imagery that matched Nia and Simone's descriptions and general location.

For navigation, they were using a map tool Ramil had created a couple of years ago. It had great security, which was vital considering it also had a hidden nav item that identified Garou council member locations, and piggybacked off a government satellite that was never down.

It also had an emergency button that, when pressed as a call for help, would ping other council members and send their current location. He hoped they wouldn't need it today.

The small clearing they'd found to tuck their vehicles in would get them close enough they'd only have to make their way across about half a mile of forest, then another quarter-mile across ranch property, which looked to be a meadow sparsely populated with a mix of conifers and oak trees.

Satellite imagery also showed they wouldn't have much cover when they were making their way across the meadow, but at least there wouldn't be any security surprises in the outlying areas. Unless Denton had made changes, Nia's information showed the only security was in the actual facility that contained the captives and the lab.

She'd overheard they'd abandoned additional perimeter security because of the wildlife forever setting it off, and the idiot guards also constantly tripping it when they moved from their cabins to the building holding the lab and prisoners, resulting in it being ripped out and the idea abandoned.

She'd also said Denton was arrogant and narcissistic enough to think no one would ever find him or discover what he was doing, so the only security needed was to keep his prisoners in, not to keep anyone out.

He felt that familiar hum of anticipation and battle-readiness for anything they encountered, but this was the first time going into battle he also felt an edgy fear for one of his teammates.

Of course, he'd always cared how his other teammates fared in previous skirmishes, emotion especially heightened for his brother on the occasions he'd been part of a dangerous raid or mission, but this was the first time he'd been in love with a teammate.

Since he didn't have the luxury of having seen Nia in action, defending herself or anyone else, he had to rely solely on her word she was proficient, and on his gut, which was telling him now that they'd mated, she could handle anything thrown her way.

His gut wasn't quelling the genuine fear that a Garou, or Cinnabar Twin, when shot or stabbed in just the right place—say, the heart, spine or head— was just as fragile as regular humans.

He glanced at her in the passenger seat, and a wave of love and inconvenient lust washed through him. Boy, Reese and Bah hadn't been kidding when they said his libido would be on the edge of control for several days after culminating the mating ritual.

His skin went prickly and his cock stiffened uncomfortably behind his fly at just the thought of Nia under him while he pumped into her, over him with her head thrown back while she rode him, or on her knees, sucking him into her mouth. He reached down to adjust and heard Nia's quick inhalation, then scented her arousal.

He shot a glance her way and connected with her now-hazel mix of gem-green with red and silver flecked eyes currently filled with desire. In his peripheral vision he saw her rub her thighs together, no doubt to quell the throbbing of her delicious, swollen clit.

Damned inconvenient hormones and vivid recall.

Wanting to sidetrack their mutual desire to strip and fuck like there was no tomorrow, but unable to quell the need to touch her, he reached for her hand, linked their fingers and asked, "Nia, can you run through the layout again of the facility, and then the outbuildings on the ranch? Sometimes, with repetition, new information will occur to you. We'll need whatever you can give us, since the asshats we're here to do away with have the home-court advantage."

"Of course." She gave his hand a squeeze and angled her body toward him, in profile to Etienne.

She recounted again the details of her abduction, when she first woke in her cramped cell, and realized someone had kidnapped her. The infusions, subsequent illnesses, pain and terror.

She relayed the memory of when Denton first mentioned Garou, although he didn't go into detail, and when she'd first realized the nurse, Isabella, was an ally and not there of her own free will.

"Oh! I can't believe I'd forgotten this, although I was pretty out of it the day Isabella told me." Tension filled the vehicle as she shared additional details. "They'd doubled up on the sedatives since I seemed to have some resistance to its affects. I told you

Isabella was a nurse assisting the night-shift doctor. One night, after I'd been there a couple of months, they left both of us alone in the lab, which they'd never done before. Apparently one of the male prisoners—which I now figure was Garou—was acting up, and they needed the doctor to sedate him."

She turned stricken eyes to Carrick. "Isabella was being coerced into helping them because they had her sister locked up in a cell. I only saw her once and hadn't realized they were related. Isabella told me that's the only reason she was helping them—they'd threatened to kill her sister. How could I have forgotten that? Especially with what they did to Aleesha?"

Carrick's heart turned over at the pain evident in his mate's voice and gently squeezed her hand again. It heartened him when she immediately squeezed back and held tight, like he was her lifeline.

"When the doctor and Denton had left the lab, she pretended she had to adjust the IV drip for the infusion and while she did that, she kept her mouth hidden and whispered that if she could, she'd help me escape, and explained why she was helping them, and that they were experimenting on her too. That's when she slipped me the scalpel I used on the guard to escape. I hope she and her sister are still there and we can free them! Or better yet, I hope they escaped too."

His mate was fierce in her convictions, and his pride and love for her grew with each passing hour. "If they are, we'll bring them and the other captives back with us to the ranch and get them settled in the area or provide the means for them to settle elsewhere."

She gave a decisive nod. "And Simone and I will help them recover and reintegrate."

WITH SOME FANCY maneuvering, they'd been able to tuck all three vehicles off the deer trail they'd targeted, in a small glade surrounded by old-growth trees, invisible from the air or the road.

West had jogged along the trail back to the road with a bucket of debris from the forest floor to sprinkle over any tire tracks they'd made driving in, then wove his way parallel to the trail through the trees back to their location.

They donned their covert tactical earpieces to communicate without being right next to each other. Another one of Ramil's inventions, a year out of prototype and proven effective in other missions.

They were using their initials to shorten their names in order to keep talking to a minimum and speed up communication, except for Carrick, Nia and Mateo, since N and M sounded too much alike, along with C and E. When you were whispering or talking in low tones it was frequently impossible to discern male from female. Since her name was already short enough, they'd use Nia for her and Mat for Mateo.

He'd gone over protocol with her so she'd know what to do and expect during the mission, and they did an equipment check before setting out. "Coms check."

Carrick turned to each person as they replied. Etienne gave him a nod. "E." Flynne saluted. "F". West tipped an imaginary hat. "Dub-ya."

They all gave him the side-eye, knowing he'd purposely reverted to his Tennessee dialect to lighten things up, instead of just saying the West Coast hard 'W'. Come to think of it, dubya was actually faster to say than double-u.

Mateo cuffed him on the shoulder, always the Dad of the group. "Mat." Nia blew Carrick a kiss. "Nia." He grabbed Nia's hand, the recent mating driving the need to at least touch her, if they couldn't get busy and naked. They started into the forest, his voice low when he said, "Car. Hey, West? Your name is actually shorter than your initial. Just go with that."

Carrick led the way through the dense forest, about a quarter of a mile from Denton's property line, and half a mile from where they would cross over. Everyone spaced out a bit, except him and Nia. They opened their senses, so they'd know in plenty of time if humans, or aggressive four-legged predators, were in the vicinity.

He'd explained to Nia how to open her senses and could tell she was experimenting as they weaved their way through the old growth, around fallen logs and over moss, needles and cones littering the forest floor.

They still didn't know what her enhanced sense or senses would be, but she should have the basic Garou senses, enhanced smell, eyesight, strength and the ability to sense if human or animal was in the vicinity.

They traversed further into the forest along the west-side of the property, bringing them closer to the facility and farther away from the cabins that housed the guards and medical personnel. Less chance of them running into anyone, since according to Nia, the guards were strictly indoor and didn't walk the outside perimeter.

They stayed near the tree line, bisecting the meadow on this side of the property and the forest. As it approached oh six hundred, the sun was at the horizon, and between the lightening sky, the full moon shining through scattered clouds, and their enhanced vision, they could see without flashlights.

They had another couple of hours before sunrise, the perfect time to infiltrate, under cover of darkness, when the night shift folks had nothing but getting to bed on their minds, and the day shift was still sound asleep and unsuspecting.

They'd left Max back at the ranch, although he'd whined and pitched a fit until Nia sat down, looked him in the eyes and explained things. After she'd finished, it was as if he'd understood and agreed with her. He'd swiped his tongue across her face and trotted next to her to the garage door, then sat next to Ramil without fuss.

She'd been afraid he would get killed or injured trying to protect her, and knew from experience the guards wouldn't hesitate to shoot her furry protector, or them.

Nia halted suddenly and held up a fist, everyone stopping dead in their tracks. She cocked her head, eyes unfocused, then held up three fingers and pointed ahead, toward the meadow. Etienne looked impressed, not having heard or sensed anyone, even with his abilities.

"Three people, one okay, one injured and the third, hmm, maybe unconscious? About four-hundred yards ahead near the tree line." She waited a few seconds, eyes unfocused again. "They're not moving, and they aren't the guards. I think the injured and unconscious are Garou. I realized earlier today you all feel a little different from Simone and Rachel."

Carrick pointed at West, then Flynne, wanting them to flank whoever it was, with Mateo and Etienne taking a direct route toward them. Keeping his voice low so it wouldn't carry, he explained to Nia what would go down, then followed silently in Mateo's wake to provide backup.

"They'll get eyes on whoever it is. If they are guards, although you don't think so, they'll subdue and restrain. If not, they'll wait for us so you can get eyes on them and see if you recognize them, and if so, keep them calm when we move in."

Careful to stay off the noisy cones and stray twigs, Carrick and Nia silently made their way to just behind Mateo and Etienne, who motioned her to move in between them so she'd have a bird's-eye view of the middle-aged woman and thirty-something man huddled over another man prone on a soft bed of moss, sheltered in front and to one side by waist-high shrubs still holding their leaves.

Nia's gasp was almost inaudible. Before they'd left the vehicles, he'd shared some hand signals with her he and the men used in previous missions. The first one she flashed was for friend, another for Garou, and a third for captives.

Not knowing if West or Flynne had seen her signals, Carrick intoned, "Nia says they're friendlies, captives she thinks, and confirms the guys are Garou. Move in on three, two, one."

West and Flynne appeared like wraiths from the trees on both sides of the small group, guns still holstered but ready to quell any attack or escape attempt.

Mateo and Etienne, with Nia between them, walked silently toward the small group, the moss muffling their steps, while Carrick watched their six. The older woman stood abruptly at their arrival and placed herself between them and both the men with her.

She frowned and stared at West and Flynne first, then Mateo, but when she laid eyes on Nia, she gasped. "Nia! ¡Madre de Dios! We did not know if you were dead or if they'd caught you and put you in one of his other facilities!"

Before anyone could respond, she leaped toward Nia.

Chapter Twenty-Two

NIA STEPPED back in alarm when the woman leaped toward her, a surprised oomph escaping when she was wrapped in a hard hug, tears streaming down the woman's face as she rocked Nia as if she was her long-lost daughter.

Just as suddenly, she grasped her shoulders and leaned back to look her up and down and started talking a mile a minute. "You look well! Who are these men? What's happening? Oh! You may not remember me. I'm Renata, Isabella's sister. She was one of your nurses and always tried to make things easier for you. She was being infused, too, as was I. We need to get out of here. They'll soon realize we are gone!"

Before Nia could get a word out, Mateo stepped forward, grasped Renata's arm and gently pulled her away from Nia. She saw a flash of what looked like disappointment in his eyes as he guided Renata back. She would mull on that later.

"We'll help you, but we need a sitrep." At her blank look, he explained. "We need a status, a situation report. Tell us what's going on, who's in the facility, when the shift change is. How did you escape? Are there any other—you must know about Garou? Are there any others still being held prisoner, besides these two men? Any other women? Don't worry, as soon as you give us info, we'll get you tucked away in a safe place and finish what we came here for."

The woman nodded, a look of profound relief on her face, and turned to walk back to the men. Taking a closer look, Nia could see injuries on both men; the one still on his feet was swaying and appeared ready to join the other on the ground.

Bah strode forward, took the young man's arm and eased him to the ground. "Sit here and relax while I check on this guy." He dropped to a knee beside the prone man, laying two fingers on his neck for a pulse. He turned and gave them a nod, then unzipped his backpack and started pulling out items he would need.

"Pulse is strong. I'll check his other vitals, see if I can get him awake. Renata, what happened to him? We may need to pack him back to the vehicles if he doesn't regain consciousness."

Recovering from her shock, Nia strode to Renata and touched her shoulder. "I do remember you, vaguely. I saw you once when they were taking me back to my cell, but I didn't realize at the time you were Isabella's sister. Were you in a cell down the corridor, nearer the lab?"

She nodded. "Yes, but they also had me cleaning the lab and drawing blood, although I didn't see you there; I was a phlebotomist in Tacoma before being captured. Isabella and I were having dinner one evening, and they abducted us from the parking lot and brought us here."

Renata turned to Mateo, gesturing to the extremely fit man, perhaps fifty years old, laying on his side facing them, with one leg cocked. His chocolate toned skin seemed ashen, and he sported salt and pepper hair cropped close to his scalp, and a short goatee sprinkled with gray. He hadn't so much as twitched since they'd arrived.

"The man on the ground is Mark Seaver. They beat him earlier today for defying Denton's doctor and guards, and he sustained another head injury during the escape. He made it this far and collapsed a few minutes ago."

Renata then gestured to the thirty-something also extremely fit man, now sitting on the ground with dazed silver eyes similar to Carrick's. He looked to be about five-ten with a swimmer's lean, muscular build, light-chocolate skin and straight black hair brushing his broad shoulders.

"We don't know his name, but I've asked him if I can call him Milagro, because it's a miracle he didn't die when they first brought him in, he'd been in such terrible shape. He joined us about three weeks ago, had a severe concussion, and hasn't been able to remember anything about his past but two words— almaden and quicksilver."

Etienne moved closer and pinned the woman with an intense look. "Are the guards after you? Do they know which direction to look for you?"

Renata shook her head. "No, but they'll know soon. I've been messing with the cameras in the lab and attached corridors for a couple of weeks, so they'd get used to images flickering and snow appearing, then pictures returning. As I'd hoped, they've become complacent about checking it out. They're mean, but lazy, thank God. Mark and I knocked out the night-shift doctor and locked him in my cell." She hesitated, a fierce look crossing her face. "And the night guard, he won't be torturing or molesting prisoners anymore."

Carrick tipped his head in acknowledgement and turned to the men. "E, West and F, head toward the facility just to the property line and monitor things until we decide a course of action. Mat, watch our six?"

Nia watched as the men slipped soundlessly into the trees and disappeared as if they'd never been there. Mateo strode through the shrubbery to the side of their group and circled his finger in the air to show he would walk the perimeter.

She stepped forward and laid her hand on the woman's arm. "Where's Isabella? She wasn't..." Nia swallowed hard, afraid to ask the hard question, and opted for something neutral. "Is she safe? Is she still being held in the facility? We'll get her out, I promise!"

Renata's eyes shimmered with tears and her chest heaved before she burst into quiet tears, dropping her head onto Nia's shoulder and sobbing. Nia hugged her tight and whispered, "Oh, no. What happened? How did she—die?"

Renata leaned back suddenly and grasped Nia's biceps. "She's not dead. ¡Gracias a Dios! But she's out there, on her own, and injured too. She escaped thirty minutes before we did. I fear she may have a broken arm, and other injuries, too."

Carrick touched Renata's shoulder to get her attention. "I'm sorry, but we have to get going if we're going to be successful. I promise, we'll find and help Isabella, too, but our more pressing concern is getting you, Mark and Milagro to the vehicles or tucked away where they can't find you while we raid the lab and cells."

Renata took a shuddering breath and straightened her shoulders. "Of course, you are right. Yes, I will give you information quickly, then we can hide until you return."

"Good, let me ask some questions, and if you think of anything you feel will be helpful, let us know. How many guards are in the facility, and when is shift change?"

"There were two guards on duty, one I—killed, and one is still alive and unconscious. I locked the doctor and guard in Mark's cell." She glanced down at the analog watch on her wrist. "Shift change is in two hours. There is one more guard in his cabin who is due to change places with the pendejos there now."

Carrick nodded, then murmured quietly, "Did you get that, E?" He turned back to Renata. "You said you locked the doctor in Mark's cell. Is there anyone else in the facility who will give us trouble? How many other captives are there?"

Her brown eyes gleamed with satisfaction when she replied. "You need not worry about the doctor in Mark's cell. He is taking a long, long nap. I stabbed him with a needle attached to a syringe full of the sedative he uses on us. I'm feeling bloodthirsty and hope he had a reaction to it."

She glanced at Nia with a smile. "Your sister told us over and over to be strong, that perhaps you would come back for us, although she knows Denton told you she was dead." Her smile dimmed. "But it's been so long, we were afraid he'd killed you, or captured you and was holding you in one of his other places."

Nia stumbled back into Carrick, his massive body and the muscled arm he wrapped around her the only thing keeping her upright. She clutched her tight throat and barely croaked out her response.

"What? What do you mean—my... my sister? I heard them kill her! I watched when they carried her lifeless body past my door, and Dr. Adam took great pleasure in describing to me later how they'd disposed of her body!"

Renata gasped, then clutched Nia's hand. "El es malvado—he is evil!"

Nia's legs wouldn't hold her, her eyesight went dim and a loud buzzing sounded in her ears. If Carrick hadn't wrapped her in his powerful arms, she would have fallen to the ground.

She was vaguely aware of Renata stroking her hair, Carrick murmuring in her ear, and Mateo's strong fingers taking her pulse. Bah's voice seemed to come from far away.

"That son-of-a-bitch. You got her, Mat?"

"Yeah, it's all good. She'll be fine, won't you Nia-girl? Just rest a moment."

A staccato of sound came from their earpieces, Etienne, West and Flynne furious on her behalf. "What the fuck? Fucking asshole. I'll kill that motherfucker."

"Baby, come back, come on, let's go find your sister and reunite you. We'll take care of these fuckers and make sure they never get their hands on another Cinnabar Twin or Garou."

Carrick's words finally registered, her brain kicking in again after the shocking news. She knew, when they'd discussed the mission, they'd planned to kill the people responsible for the murder of Garou men, and the torture of the women who had the Cinnabar Twin DNA anomaly.

She'd been okay with the thought of killing, having suffered terribly at their hands and thinking her sister dead. Had wanted to end them for that alone. Was more than okay with it now, knowing Denton lied to her, and because of that lie, she'd abandoned her sister to a terrible fate for ten long fucking months.

"She probably thinks I was never coming back; that I'd died or something terrible had happened to me." She barely got the words past her tight throat, her voice growing stronger with each utterance, until she was almost shouting in her conviction. "Because you can believe, and she knows, I would have set the world on fire to rescue her if I'd known!"

She turned to Carrick. "We have to go—go now to save her and anyone else."

She held on tight when his hand took hers. "We will, sweetheart. We'll put a stop to this, right fucking now."

He turned again to Renata, who was now clasping Nia's shoulder in support. "How many others are captive?"

"Just her sister. She planned to sabotage the facility and told me to get Mark and Milagro out, that she would leave right after us, but I'm worried about her. We've been here about twenty minutes already. There is one other terrible man you must stop, who I'm afraid may have been able to detain her, but you must be very careful."

Nia wanted nothing more than to run straight to the facility and get her sister the hell out of there, but knew they needed all the information they could get in order to be successful. She clenched her fists and waited impatiently when Carrick motioned for Renata to continue.

"He is—I think he is like you. You are Garou, yes?"

At Carrick's nod, she continued. "I found some of Denton's files about the Garou on a computer the doctor left unattended. This wicked man, he is Garou, but is a traitor! I've only heard his first name, Bowen. He is Denton's right hand, and the reason Isabella ran away, and we fought to escape today. They finished the course of infusions on Isabella and tonight he planned to force her—to rape her and try to impregnate her. She and I planned the escape, to get her away before this could happen, and that is why she is not with us. He is usually locked in a cell, but he is very strong and I don't know if it will hold him for long—perhaps he got free and has Aleesha. You must be very careful, he is muy malvado, very evil."

Carrick's hand tightened almost painfully on Nia's as he turned to her. "That motherfucker! Bowen is one of the men who went missing from Almaden. We thought Denton had abducted or killed him. I bet anything he's the reason Milagro is here, why he's injured, and why Mark is here."

His anger at the betrayal by another Garou pulsed off him, and Nia squeezed back in commiseration and solidarity as he reassured Renata. "We'll be very careful. He won't be harming anyone again. Not Isabella or Nia's sister, or anyone else. Let's get you and the men tucked away until we're done, and we'll pick you up on the way back. Do you know how to fire a gun, Renata?"

"I do, yes. My father was a police officer in Corpus Christi, Texas and taught both Isabella and I how to handle guns."

Carrick opened his backpack and retrieved his extra S&W MP9 Shield pistol, held it by the slide, barrel pointed down, and transferred it to Renata in the same position, watching closely no doubt to ensure she was telling the truth and wouldn't accidentally shoot one of them.

She nodded as if in approval. "My father favored the Shield, so I am familiar with it."

Her finger stayed off the trigger as she pointed the gun away from them and down toward the ground, then checked that the safety was on before ejecting the magazine. She checked it was full, then inserted it again and, although this model Shield had a loaded chamber indicator, pulled the slide back till it locked to ensure there was no bullet in the chamber before sliding it back. "I am ready."

Nia was anxiety-ridden, wanting, *needing* to get to the facility and free her sister. She strode over to Bah to see if she could get them moving.

"Bah? How's Mark? Can we move him without causing more injury? If so, I saw a couple of fairly secluded spots on the way here; bushes loosely clumped together, and there looked to be space in the middle for these three. It'll be tight, but they shouldn't stay out in the open while we're gone. That'll work, yes?"

"Yeah, let's get them moved. Carrick, can you carry Mark? I'll carry the packs and help Milagro, since he's still unsteady."

Carrick nodded and strode over to where Mark was laying. "Mat, we need you. The rest, hold position until we get there. We'll get these people stashed and meet you to take care of business."

Nia watched as Carrick dropped to a knee next to Bah, helped him sit Mark up, then stand him supported between them. Carrick positioned him for a fireman's carry, stooped and lifted effortlessly.

Even with her emotions careening all over the place, Nia still took a few seconds to appreciate her man's extreme musculature and fitness.

She wondered how much stronger she was now that they'd completed the mating. Would it be enough to make a difference if she had to fight any assholes they ran into while freeing her sister and putting an end to Denton's crew?

CARRICK WAS CAREFUL to keep Mark's head away from tree trunks and brush. That he was still unconscious was worrisome, and he knew it didn't bode well for his recovery.

Especially since he was Garou. He should be able to shrug off injuries easier than a typical human, unless they'd dosed him with something that was keeping him under. Maybe Renata knew.

"Hey, Renata? Any chance they drugged Mark, and he's not just injured? Garou can usually handle some hard knocks without being affected this much."

"Oh, I hadn't thought of that, since he hadn't been in the lab when we escaped, but it is possible they'd recently finished with some procedure or infusion and had sedated him, since he always gave them a fight. I bet that is what's wrong. The head injury on top of being drugged would certainly cause him to be unconscious, especially if the doctor hit him with a tranquilizer dart, although I saw nothing on him when he caught up with us. Perhaps the dart hit him, and he pulled it out or it fell out."

Bah looked back from his point-position. "That would be a better outcome than him being out this long from a head injury, although I'm concerned about what drugs they've been using on Milagro and Mark. Do you know what they gave them, Renata?"

"I don't, I'm sorry. Although they had me clean the lab after infusions, they didn't let me near any of the medication or drugs, and none of the injection vials I saw had labels. I imagine they are fairly potent, though, since the doctor was out like a light just seconds after me stabbing him with the syringe. I gave him a full ten cc's, when they normally give Garou just four."

Carrick enjoyed the note of satisfaction in Renata's voice. "Good for you. I hope he feels like shit when he wakes up—if he wakes up." He planned to take everyone in that facility down. People reached a level of evil where he had zero compassion for them; knew that if someone didn't put a stop to them, they would continue to torture, rape, and kill. These fuckers had far surpassed it. There was no redemption for them. The military had methods of taking care of this type of evil, with snipers and C4.

Well, they were fighting a war, all right. The Garou and women with the lupus anomaly were being hunted down, abused and held prisoner. Not only that, but who knew what Denton's plans were for any children he was successful in creating through his intrusive, horrific methods?

Carrick remembered the clump of several bushes they were approaching which, at first glance, looked to be a dense, circular wall of leaves until he rounded the south side. Sure enough, there looked to be a point of ingress, and hopefully enough space to get into the middle and tuck them in.

"Nia, see if you can hold back some of these branches without breaking them. Mat see if there's room in the middle for Renata and the guys."

Nia hurried to his side, brushed her fingers down his arm in a soft caress, then slid in front of him and grabbed several of the pencil-sized branches and pulled. Sure enough, there was a space big enough for Mat to sidle into the gap, allowing him to mimic her actions to see, and get to, the small middle clearing.

"Yeah, just enough room. Bring Mark on in, Milagro and Renata can follow. Then we need to get moving."

Carrick carried Mark through the skinny space and gently laid him on his side in the small clearing, then waited for Renata and Milagro to enter. "Okay, Renata, you have the pistol and these bushes will conceal you all. No talking or moving around and be patient. It'll seem like we're gone forever, but that's just because being the one left behind is hard as hell to deal with. We *will* be back for you."

"Thank you, Carrick. Yes, we will wait for your return. Do not worry about us. Stay safe."

He gave her a nod and let Mateo precede him, then sidled through the opening. The second he saw Nia's beautiful face, he tucked a hand behind her neck and tugged her into his chest for a heated kiss. "You're not allowed to get hurt when we kick ass, got it?"

He loved how breathless she became whenever they locked lips, and that it took her a few seconds to open her eyes and recover. With a nod and her own peck on his lips, she shot back her own command. "You either, big guy. Got it?"

He stroked a finger down her cheek and wrapped her in his arms. "Let's hoof it to the guys and get Aleesha out of that hellhole, then make it so Denton has nothing to come back to."

Carrick's head shot up as the sharp report of a gun echoed all around them, but there was no confusion where it came from. It wasn't hunting season for any animal, except humans or Garou, apparently.

"Motherfucker, why the hell would someone from the facility be in the woods where our guys are? Renata, you all stay put. Let's go! E, report." He didn't wait for a response and took off at a jog toward the other men, weaving through the trees and around shrubbery.

"We're good. Dude came out of one cabin with a big boxer dog and started toward the facility. He reached out and tapped the dog with what looked like a stick, but I think it was a stun baton or something, and it went apeshit. Dog turned on the guy and attacked, ripped into his forearm. He let go of the leash and shot at it, but the dog had already booked it around the facility and is in the wind. Another guy stuck his head out the door of the cabin next door. The guard called him doc, told him not to worry. The doc went back inside. We're gonna have trouble, though. Dude's on his way to the lab and cells. Looks like the dog got his dominant arm, though, so that's in our favor. Holster is on his right hip and he was super awkward with the gun in his left hand."

Carrick huffed a sigh of relief. "No time to wait for us. Head in and subdue him. We'll question him. Should be there in five."

Nia hoped the dog hit a vein and severed nerves. "I'm not surprised the dog attacked him. I remember that poor boxer. The guard was sadistic. Used a stun baton on it, and us, when we didn't react fast enough to his orders. I'm guessing E's right. He zapped the dog with it and poor thing finally had enough. I hope the dog made him bleed."

Carrick turned livid eyes toward her. "That sonofabitch. He used it on you? He's gonna regret every touch."

"The guards were just as evil as Denton, and I remember Bowen. Did not know he was Garou, though."

Carrick turned to see Nia's shudder when she uttered the Garou's name. "What did he do?"

"It wasn't so much that he abused us—the guards were the primary culprits there, and they did it on the sly so Denton wouldn't know. Bowen took great pleasure in describing how he was going to enjoy impregnating us after we finished our course of infusions."

At the sound of Flynne murmuring his progress as he worked on the lock on the facility door, they stopped talking. "Idiots used a mediocre knob lock, and the guard didn't secure the deadbolt when he went in. Aaand, there we go." An almost inaudible snick sounded through their earpieces.

"We're going in." At Flynne's announcement, Carrick picked up speed, gladdened to see Nia keep up effortlessly. He hadn't even given her previous, pre-mating state of constant exhaustion any thought since they'd arrived; probably because she had exhibited no symptoms and seemed to have the same endurance as them.

He indulged in a quick glance and jolted when her intense eyes met his, the mix of red and silver amidst the brilliant green signifying her as his mate settled into his heart and soul. He gave her a thumbs up and quick 'ok?' hand signal, glad to see her immediately respond in kind with the same, along with a be-safe gesture.

They halted at the meadow, still under tree line cover, and swept the area with their eyes, opening their senses. He turned to Nia, curious to see if she could discern where everyone was, like she did with the small group they'd left behind. She didn't disappoint.

With her eyes unfocused, she gave them a quick rundown. "Situation static. Doctor is still in his cabin. I think the guys have the guard situated?"

Her eyes went from unfocused to sheened with tears. "I can sense Aleesha, but she's radiating anger and tension, and there's a Garou near her. I'm assuming it's Bowen." She grabbed his forearm in a tight grip. "I'll kill him if he's hurt her."

Carrick clasped her hand and squeezed. "I'll help you. Let's go."

West's voice came over the com with a sitrep. "I neutralized the guard; we're in the lab. E is checking out the cells on the left corridor and has the keys. F is watching the corridor leading to the front door. You're cleared for entry."

As one, they sprinted the hundred feet from the tree line to the door, going for speed, not stealth, and reached the building in about fourteen seconds.

Mateo took point, standing to the left of the door near the knob and indicating he'd go in high, gesturing for Bah to take the right and go in low. Carrick and Nia would cover their backs on entry.

They wouldn't take chances, even with West's go ahead. Take nothing for granted. Missions could go from sugar to shit in a heartbeat.

As Bah counted down, Carrick tensed, knowing they were almost at the pinnacle of their mission. He hoped to hell Bowen hadn't hurt Aleesha, or god forbid killed her before they reached her, and they all got out of here unscathed. He didn't think Nia could take losing her sister for a second and final time.

"Three, two, one."

They entered the door, Carrick breaking into a sprint when Flynne gave the sign for 'safe'. Since they'd all studied the layout based on Nia and Simone's memories, they could disperse to their predetermined tasks.

Mateo gave a chin lift toward the hall straight ahead. "E headed that way." He turned down the hall to the right. "I'll see if I can get eyes on Aleesha down this way."

Nia turned to follow Mateo, first grasping Carrick's forearm.

"Carrick—I've got to…"

She hesitated, no doubt wondering if he'd give her shit for wanting to head off with Mateo instead of staying where he could watch over her. Carrick held her eyes and covered her hand with his before letting go and giving her a gentle nudge.

He knew there was no way in hell he could, or should, keep her with him and away from her sister, no matter how worried he was not being by her side. As hard as it was for him to do, he gave her what she needed.

"Go, baby. Get your sister safe and meet us in the lab." Her look of surprise, then gratitude and affection, filled him with love for this amazing woman. He needed to keep his head on the mission, and not how much he wanted and craved his mate.

At his nod, she pivoted and sprinted after Mateo, while he and Bah headed toward the lab where West had the guard situated.

"Well, fuck me." The blond guard, securely strapped prone to a stainless-steel surgical table, was muttering and turned a shade of pale just this side of milk when he saw Carrick and Etienne enter lab. Having worked for Denton on his Garou and mate project, the guy must know how strong they were. And how pissed off they'd be.

Carrick stalked up to the man and loomed over him, then turned his head to West. "He share anything yet?"

"Nope. Being a bit stubborn, our guard is. Maybe Doc can convince him to share?"

Carrick didn't think it possible, but the guard blanched even more. "Yeah, I'd say that's a go. This the only one left?" He motioned to the guard, then to Bah to get started and tried to keep his focus in the lab, not down the corridor with Mateo and Nia.

West shot him a look, then returned his attention to the guard. "Yup. Their doctor didn't make it."

They'd muted their mics so as not to distract each other, but he wasn't worried about that. A great feature of Ramil's covert earpiece was that when voices reached a certain decibel, the mic unmuted automatically.

If Nia or Mateo were in trouble, he'd know about it at the first shout—or scream. One or the other of them could easily sound the alarm. He was more worried Bowen would harm her sister before they freed her.

Bah gave Carrick a nudge with his shoulder, bringing him out of his momentary lapse of concentration. This wasn't a done deal yet, and he needed to keep his head in the fucking game. His focus back where it belonged, he gave the guard a grin filled with promise as Bah told him what was going down.

"How fucking convenient Denton has arm and hand straps on these tables, isn't it, Car? Although it boils my blood to think of the women tied down like this. Hope he has a good vein for me to stick the IV, but then again, I'm not really worried how many times I have to poke him, or how much pain it causes. My version of truth serum will have him singing in a hot minute. Side effects are a bitch, though."

"You can't do that! I have rights!"

The guard blustered and fought his restraints, and it was almost comical how he thought they were cops and had to adhere to any version of rights, especially considering Nia's stories about how he'd abused the captives and his dog. Carrick set him straight.

"Well, dude, considering we aren't cops, that we're in fact all Garou, and the one woman who got away—you remember—one of the female captives you got off on hurting and tormenting? She's my woman, which means you have no fucking rights. Shut the fuck up or I'll tape your lips until they're needed to spew out all Denton's secrets."

Waiting no further, Bah slipped the IV into the bulging vein in the guy's inner arm and adjusted the IV flow regulator to administer the serum.

"I'm not gonna tell you bastards anything!" Spittle flew from his lips as he struggled and cursed them.

"How long till he talks?" Carrick ignored the man, eager to get any info this guy had tucked in his pea-brain and get to Nia. He didn't want to engage her mic and possibly distract her at a crucial moment.

"Bout twenty seconds." Bah reached out and gave the guard's cheek a not so gentle slap. "Ready to sing for us, fucker?"

"That motherfucker!" Everyone stilled when Nia's voice rang out over their mics. "E, I need those keys!"

Chapter Twenty-Three

NIA MET her sister's gaze in the small window embedded in the steel cell door, shock and pure love mirrored in their eyes.

Her sister's right arm was bleeding sluggishly from a long cut on her left bicep, her right eye was swollen to a mere slit and her lip split, a trail of blood dripping down the front of her torn gray tank top.

Bowen was unconscious, prone at her feet. They were handcuffed together—her left wrist to his right—the skin abraded where it chafed. It terrified Nia he would wake before they got her uncuffed and out of that fucking cell.

Mateo's deep voice rang out next to her. "We'll get her out, Nia. She's subdued him, but we need to get in there before he comes to."

Pounding feet coming up the corridor from the direction of the lab had them both turning and dropping into defensive positions, relief coursing through her to see Etienne and Carrick sprint around the corner.

Etienne shouted, "Here! Get her loose!" and lobbed a ring of keys to Mateo, who snatched them midair. Nia's muscles ached from tension as she waited breathlessly for him to fit the key in the lock, turn and push the heavy door inward.

She heard a note of anxiety in Etienne's voice she'd never noticed before, and it came to her in a flash that he, and all the Garou helping her, must wonder if Aleesha was their mate. Holy hell, that had her wondering the same thing.

She brushed past him and flew to her sister, carefully enfolding her in a hug. The feel of Aleesha's unshackled arm circling her back caused tears to run down her face. "Aleesha, oh sweetie, I thought you were dead. They told me you were dead. I saw your body; I never would have left you."

The feel of her sister's head dropping wearily to her shoulder about did her in, her soft familiar voice a balm to her soul. "Sis, I know. Shhh, I know you'd never leave me. Denton took great pleasure in telling me you thought I was dead, and that he would hunt you down and bring you to a different facility so we couldn't be together."

"That son-of-a... oooph!"

"Look out!"

Carrick's shout was the only warning Nia got as Bowen leaped to his feet and shoved her to the side with a hard hand on her shoulder, throwing her off balance. He jerked Aleesha across the room away from them, his roar echoing in the small cell. "Bitch is mine, get the hell back!"

Nia caught her balance before she fell and brought her arms up to defend herself, Carrick, Etienne and Mateo appearing next to her as if in magic. They all stopped moving when Bowen's burly arm wrapped around Aleesha's slender neck.

This asshole didn't know she and Aleesha used to spar together and that Nia had mated a badass Garou, which meant she was now strong in her own right— maybe even as strong as Bowen.

She shot Aleesha a hand signal that had her tilting her head to one side and launched herself at them, putting her entire body behind a throat-punch, while Aleesha grabbed a handful of his junk, squeezed and twisted.

He went down with a howl and gurgle, releasing Aleesha to clutch at his throat and crotch as he dropped to his knees.

Her sister dropped to one knee and drove her fist into his groin a second time, her body powering into the punch, while Nia executed a roundhouse kick to his temple, driving him fully to the floor. He groaned as he collapsed, his body sprawled on the ground their reward. She turned and wriggled her sore fingers for the keyring, knowing a handcuff key would be among them.

"Damn, baby, I'd say strength is another of your enhanced senses." She let the pride and awe in Carrick's voice sink in and take root in her heart, turning to shoot him a look of affection before concentrating on her sister again.

Carrick and Mateo were at her side in a heartbeat, Mat's big hand reaching for the handcuff and making quick work of getting her sister unhitched from the asshole on the floor.

While he introduced himself and pulled a bandage from his backpack to wrap around the slice on her arm to quell the bleeding, Etienne crouched at Bowen's head, ready to take action if he woke, and

Carrick dropped a big hand on Nia's shoulder, giving her a squeeze.

"Hey, Aleesha. I'm Mateo. Got a bunch of us here today to free you and the others, and do cleanup. We tucked Renata, Milagro and Mark away in the forest and we'll pick them up on the way back to our vehicles. Isabella got away and is in the wind, but we'll find her. Got a couple more men in the lab, encouraging the guard to share."

Aleesha scooped her mass of coffee-colored, shoulder-length corkscrew curls off her banged-up face and swept them all with dark chocolate eyes that glittered with tears. "Can't tell you how happy I am to hear that and see you all."

Nia cradled her sister's head when she turned and leaned into her shoulder again, a sob breaking free. "Especially you, sis. Dammit, I'm not a crier."

Nia wrapped her other arm around Aleesha's back and rocked her gently. "Shh, I know, your badass status is intact, never fear." She knew how much her sister hated to exhibit any weakness in front of strangers and tried to lighten the moment until she could get control of her emotions again.

She got the choked laugh she was going for, thrilled when her sister raised her head and graced her with a small grin, followed by a grimace. "Ow, that hurts. Note to self, no laughing for the foreseeable future."

Aleesha peered closer at her sister's eyes and asked, "Am I imagining things, or are there silver and red flakes in your eyes? Are you wearing contacts?"

Nia grinned and shot a glance at Carrick. "Not contacts, but part of a story I have that you won't believe."

"Hey, everything okay?" Bah's voice interrupted in their earpieces focused them again.

"Yeah," Carrick responded. "Nia and Aleesha solved the issue and we're gonna head your way in a minute." He turned to Etienne. "Secure this guy and we'll lock him in the cell again."

Etienne shook his head. "No need. He's not going anywhere." Etienne's tone of satisfaction and respect had them all turning to see he had two fingers pressed to the guy's carotid. "Can't question him even if we wanted. These badass ladies took care of this problem for us. He won't be hurting anyone again."

Nia and Aleesha looked at Etienne and then Bowen in shock, Nia not realizing she packed enough of a punch to do that much damage, and it sank in she'd taken a life.

She waited for remorse to roll in, and realized amazingly enough that knowledge didn't bother her a bit, considering who it was. "Well. I'm—actually okay with that."

"Damn straight." Carrick eyes narrowed and his voice filled with loathing when he spoke. "He was pure evil, just like Denton and the others here. No quarter given, no remorse if we need to end them. If we don't? We'll be the ones six feet under."

Deep voices filled the room and earpieces as every one of their party agreed with his statement. Etienne strode toward the door and Nia detected a small crack in his demeanor, a flash of emotion crossing his face as he glanced at her sister and then away. Hope, and then disappointment to realize she was in fact not his mate.

Etienne took point while Mateo took position at Aleesha's other side. "Mind if I help you out?"

Nia turned his way, grateful to see Mateo had donned his 'dad' hat when interacting with her sister.

Aleesha turned a sweet smile his way. "Not at all. Oh, wait! Isabella hid a thumb drive in her cell but wasn't able to retrieve it before she had to run. She downloaded info from the lab's computer and Denton's laptop. It's two cells down, further along the corridor. Look under the sheet and pull the middle button off her mattress; you'll find it buried in the ticking."

Etienne nodded and took off at a jog out the door, hooking a left in the opposite direction of the lab. While they waited for his return, Nia touched her sister's shoulder, careful of the gash on her arm.

"Aleesha, I'd like you to meet Carrick. You know all the crap Denton told us about trying to rekindle our dormant DNA so we can mate with Garou?"

At her sister's nod, she grinned and continued. "Well, sis, I'm here to tell you it wasn't crap. The part Denton had wrong is that it's a one-to-one mating; that not just any Garou is or can mate with women who have our altered DNA. Mates can tell when they're near their one-and-only, or when they're in an area where their mate recently gave off a bunch of pheromones, like during a high adrenaline situation. It's a weird, wonderful sensation, and if you don't know what's going on, you'll think you're sick. I'll tell you all about it later, but my point is, Carrick is my mate. And when you actually go through the mating, I guess you can call it process, then the woman is stronger and will live longer. Minor injuries and illnesses heal quickly, and it can also result in enhanced senses, which are supposedly different for each person. And, the irises of their eyes are flaked with silver and red, like cinnabar ore. I still have lupus, and am pretty sure I'll still need to be careful to stay outta the sun and watch what I eat, but the debilitating side effects from the infusions aren't an issue any longer. That's also what Carrick meant by my strength being one of my enhanced senses. Apparently, I pack a heavier punch than I used to."

Aleesha turned incredulous eyes toward Nia, then turned narrowed eyes to Carrick, threat heating her gaze when she asked Nia. "Were you forced? Like Bowen was going to do to Isabella, and then me because she got away? That's why the asshole handcuffed me."

A chorus of 'motherfucker, that fucking asshole, dude better be dead' echoed in their earpieces.

Nia was glad to see Carrick calmly hold her sister's eyes while he waited patiently for her to answer. The fact he didn't defend himself or get all bristly spoke volumes about his integrity and temperament.

"No, sis, not at all." She turned to Carrick, his attention going from Aleesha to her, causing her sister to turn toward Nia, too. "He's gentle, supportive, protective, courageous, chock-full of integrity—and loving."

The last came out in a whisper, and she watched as his eyes turned molten. This time not in lust or passion, but—could it be? God! She hoped it was—love? *Don't get your hopes up yet, girl*.

She shot him a grin. "Although, he can get a little bossy sometimes."

"Ha! For your own good, woman!" An answering quirk of his mouth accompanied his retort.

Her sister interrupted their moment, turning to Carrick to give her blessing—in a totally *I'll hunt you down and kill you if you don't behave* way typical of Aleesha. "Oh, well, in that case, I'll let you live."

Nia huffed out a laugh and chuckles echoed through the earpieces; she'd even garnered one from uber-intense Etienne, who'd just reentered the cell, thumb drive in hand.

It shocked Nia when he turned to glance at her sister, a flash of envy or longing briefly lighting up his typically intense eyes. "Damn, her mate's gonna be one lucky son of a bitch."

Aleesha raised a brow and turned questioning eyes to Nia.

"Tell you later."

CARRICK FELT FOR Aleesha and all she'd gone through. He was so damned relieved they'd reached the cell before Bowen could go through with his plan to rape her. To impregnate her by force. The fucker.

Although, after seeing her in action, he wasn't sure the big Garou would have been successful.

As they made their way down the corridor, he strove to fill her in on the other men here with them and what to expect at the ranch. "We'll get you and the others settled at the ranch, it's about a seven-hour drive from here, in a small community in south San Jose, California. My brother Reese, and another buddy Ramil are keeping watch on Simone and Rachel. She escaped…"

Aleesha gasped and broke in. "Simone! She's there too? She's okay? And Rachel's with her?"

Carrick turned to see Nia pat her arm, a confused look on her beautiful face. "She's fine, and so's Rachel. I didn't know she was from here until she helped me when I collapsed—I'll tell you the full story later. I hadn't seen her when I was here. How do you know about her when you came after she'd escaped?"

Aleesha stopped walking and tucked her arm around Nia's waist, leaning into her before responding. Carrick could see she was clearly coming to the end of her endurance.

"I hacked Denton's laptop a few nights ago; that's when Isabella downloaded data onto that thumb drive. Simone and Ginger were the first two brought here and became friends, then Isabella and Renata, then you, and finally me. Isabella was with Ginger when she died after one of her infusions."

"Motherfucker. Was that before or after Simone escaped?" Mateo glanced back at Nia, then at Carrick. "Simone hasn't mentioned Ginger to you?"

Nia and Carrick both shook their heads and turned back to her sister.

Aleesha glanced at Mateo and continued. "Yes, before Simone escaped. It's why she left. A few days before Ginger died, she begged Simone to take her daughter if something happened to her. To find a way out so they didn't subject Rachel to the same infusions, or god forbid, kill or sell her if they decided a baby was too much trouble. I think she escaped during the chaos when Ginger died."

Carrick swiped a hand across his face and shot a glance at Nia to see her mouth drop open. "I was wondering if maybe Rachel wasn't her daughter, but with everything that was happening before we headed up here, I forgot to mention it to you. When we were questioning Simone, she tripped up answering some questions about when Rachel was a baby, and the more you compare their features, the more they look nothing alike. I'm assuming Ginger was a redhead, like Rachel?"

Aleesha nodded. "Yes, total redhead, freckles and all, green eyes, Irish all the way, she was fond of saying before she got so sick. Both her parents were from Ireland. The poor girl was about seven months pregnant when they abducted her, and they infused her when she was pregnant. I wonder if she had such a terrible reaction because of the heightened estrogen and progesterone hormones from her pregnancy. And Denton wouldn't stop them, even when her reactions worsened, until during the last one—she'd given birth just a couple weeks before—she had an anaphylactic reaction and they couldn't revive her."

Aleesha turned to Carrick. "And the mating, or matching of Garou to their—mate—it's one to one? I mean, Nia is the only woman you match as a mate with, and I would only match with one specific person?"

Carrick nodded. "Yes, we can explain more once we get in the car if you want or wait till we're back at the ranch and you're feeling better. Up to you."

Nia chimed in. "And I can fill you in on where I've been since I escaped and where we're going." She turned anxious eyes to her sister. "We can't go home, you know. They probably foreclosed on our home by now as abandoned. Denton is out there searching for me, and he'll be looking for you, too, when he learns what happened here, although he won't know who did this. I have—had a home in New Almaden, near where Carrick's ranch is, but a couple of days ago Denton's guys attacked and we're pretty sure blew it up. We haven't actually checked, yet, what with everything that's happened. We barely escaped. Oh, that's another story to tell you, about Garou needing to live near cinnabar ore. His ranch is huge, a big main house with three cabins on the property and setup with outstanding security. It will even impress you."

She turned a sly, teasing look to Carrick before turning back to her sister. "Although, I'm sure you can improve it. Wait until you meet Ramil. He's a geek like you."

Nia laughed when Aleesha mock-punched her arm and said, "I'm not a geek! I'm a badass."

Laughter rang out in the earpieces, and West chimed in. "Yeah, that's what Ramil says, too, cause he can kick ass with the best of them. But the dude's a geek, no doubt about it. Walks like a duck, Leesha, talks like a duck."

Aleesha broke out in laughter and gave it right back. "Yeah, I'll show you a duck, whoever you are."

"West, ma'am. Pleased to meetcha."

Flynne's voice interrupted over the coms. "Hey, hate to break it up, but we need to get gone before the other doctor shows up. Who's setting the charges in the cells and here?"

"Already did. Just need to add a couple to the lab and we're gone." Etienne jogged away from them into the lab, pulling his backpack off his shoulder.

Carrick spoke up. "Mateo and I are going to get Aleesha and Nia to the treeline and we'll wait for you there. Hustle it, guys."

West responded and they could hear bustling activity in the lab, along with a chorus of, "roger that" and "you got it".

When Carrick turned to follow Nia, Mateo, and her sister to the front door, Aleesha stumbled and would have gone down if not for Mateo bracing her while Nia did the same on the other side.

Mateo patted her shoulder. "Got just the thing for you. Hey, Bah. Need you here. Bring the backpack with the ElectRou shakes. I think Aleesha's on her last legs."

"Call me Leesha, and I can walk. I'll be fine."

He watched as Nia shook her head fondly at her sister. "Yeah, you sound just like me when I first met Carrick. I was suffering acute exhaustion from any little exertion, much less an adrenaline rush and dump. I'd just gotten home from rescuing Rachel—that's another story I owe you—and was on my ass in the garage when Simone, Reese, Carrick and Dak showed up. I was a little argumentative, I guess you could say. This protein shake will help replenish some energy, and then Bah can help if you need more support."

"Fine." The grumbled tone did indeed make Carrick think of Nia when he annoyed her. He bit back a grin, not wanting Leesha to think he was laughing at her.

As they passed the lab door, Bah joined them, and Nia noted the same look of hope warring with anxiety on his face, then the flash of disappointment before he shut it down and handed an open protein shake bottle to her sister. No doubt he, too, had been wondering if Leesha was his mate.

Carrick wondered about the men back at the ranch. Were any of them her mate? What were the odds, with Garou spread across the globe, that one of Carrick's friends would turn out to be Aleesha's mate?

Less than slim to none, probably, although who'd a thought he would run across his mate in New Almaden, of all places?

"Gulp that down, it'll do you wonders. Created by a couple Garou explicitly to boost energy and strength during skirmishes or illnesses, although Garou don't get sick very often. Aren't susceptible to human viruses. Injuries are another thing, but thankfully we heal quickly. Name's Bah. Bahadur actually, but call me Bah or Doc. Happy to see you alive and kicking. You mind if I take Mateo's place helping you out? It pains me to admit he and Carrick are better fighters and can sense intrusions before I can. But I'm better at patching folks up."

His wink let her know he was talking smack, and at her nod slipped under her arm when Mateo vacated his position.

Leesha took a few seconds to down the drink, finishing it in two long swallows, then handed the empty back with a smile. "Thanks, and nice to meet you."

They made it outside and a quarter way across the meadow before Leesha's legs gave way and she crumpled. "I gotcha, Leesha." Bah scooped her up in his arms without breaking stride and took the rest of the field at a ground eating pace.

"Sorry, totally out of steam now." Leesha dropped her head on his shoulder.

"We all need a hand sometimes. Don't you worry about it. We have your back."

Carrick acknowledged the rest of the men as they jogged up behind them, some moving forward to provide protection should any unforeseen enemy appear, the others watching their six.

About halfway back to Renata and the others, the boom of multiple explosions rent the air, and Carrick gave a grim smile of satisfaction. He gave zero fucks that the guard died in the blast, considering letting him live meant even more danger for Nia, the two Garou, Renata, and Aleesha. Damn, and Isabella, wherever she was.

If they'd allowed them to live, the bastards would continue working for Denton, sweeping up potential Cinnabar Twins to infuse, torture, rape and kill. Not to mention whatever fucked up reason they were snatching Garou, too.

He swiped a hand over his bristly face, so fucking glad the mission was over, with no one in their group injured badly. He hated that Aleesha, Mark and Milagro were suffering, and Isabella out on her own worried him, but he was thankful Renata seem well.

He wondered if he should have West stay here to look for Isabella? He'd ask Renata where her sister would head off to, and if she thought it was worth someone hanging back, or if it would be better to not call attention to her in this area by actively searching for her.

Besides, depending on how resourceful she was, she may not be in the area anymore. It might make more sense to launch an investigation and search once they got back to New Almaden.

He'd get everyone they'd rescued today squared away on his ranch and on the road to physical and mental recovery.

He wanted to book it back home, knowing the remaining doctor tucked in his cabin across the meadow would be on the horn reporting to Denton, who was no doubt still in New Almaden trying to sniff out Simone and Nia. Maybe this would distract the asshole enough he'd head back here and give them some breathing room.

He'd wanted to level Denton's house, and the other cabins, too, but they'd decided it had too many layers of complexity and possible FUBAR— 'Fucked Up Beyond All Recognition'—of their mission.

Not that Denton could do anything while in New Almaden, but he didn't want the man to double-down on his search for Nia and Simone, not when there was only a skeleton crew protecting the ranch.

They made it to the shrubbery with Renata, Mark and Milagro tucked away, but halted in their tracks at a low, menacing growl.

They took position in a semi-circle at the opening of the bushes and pulled their guns to confront whatever had joined Renata and the men. Bah set Aleesha on her feet, tucking her behind his back, and positioned himself to defend her if necessary.

Carrick knew there were a handful of wolves in the forest, but didn't think there were any in this area. "What the hell? Renata, you okay?"

"Yes, Carrick. Did you find Aleesha? Is she okay? You're all well?"

Before Carrick could respond, Aleesha reassured the woman. "I'm okay, Renni."

When growls turned into yips and whining, accompanied by a scrambling sound in the bushes, he motioned everyone back, stood at an angle and leveled his pistol at the opening of the tangled tunnel leading to the center, but pointed away from the small group.

"Renata, you all stay where you are!"

Carrick shot a questioning look at Nia and got a shrug, then looked back at the small opening. What was in there with them? Renata didn't sound distressed, but she wasn't getting any answers until he evaluated the possible threat.

A large brindle dog, if he wasn't mistaken, the boxer Etienne described as attacking and running from the guard, erupted from the brush and bounded straight toward Bah. Before anyone could react, Leesha stepped around him and gave a small cry, dropping awkwardly to her knees before falling on her butt.

Nia cried out, "Don't shoot!"

Carrick had already jerked his gun up, muzzle pointed in the air, not daring to track the animal now amidst their group. Bah lunged toward the dog, attempting to grab his collar, but the agile animal dodged him and planted itself in Leesha's lap, like it wasn't a seventy-plus pound pooch.

Everyone stared in astonishment when she burst into tears for the second time that day, wrapped her arms around the dog and buried her face in its muscular neck.

Nia dropped to her knees next to her sister and got a canine tongue swipe across her cheek before the dog placed both forelegs up on Leesha's shoulders, then laid his blocky head on one.

She sniffed and swiped a hand under her nose, then repeatedly ran a hand down the dog's back. She glanced up when Renata, Milagro and a now conscious, slightly unsteady Mark Seavers squeezed through the skinny opening and into the clearing.

"I—I thought Oso was dead." Aleesha turned eyes bright with tears toward her sister. "The guard in charge of him, he brought me back from the lab one evening, they'd given me too much sedative and I was really out of it." She turned to drop a kiss on the big dog's head and got a tongue across her face.

"Instead of shoving me in the cell like usual, he must have realized I couldn't fight back and started tearing at my clothes, describing all the horrible things he was going to do to me. I couldn't defend myself; I was so weak. Oso attacked him, drove him back, and wouldn't leave the cell. The asshole didn't have his shock baton on him, and Oso forced him to back out the door. He didn't return that night, and this brave pooch guarded me all night long. When the guard returned the next day, he'd brought the shock baton and used it on this poor girl. He never tried to rape me again, but he always carried that damn baton and would laugh when he used it on me or Oso. That's what these small scars on her back are from."

"That motherfucking bastard." Mateo kneeled next to her and held his fist out for Oso to sniff, similarly rewarded with a wet tongue, before the dog attempted to curl up in Aleesha's lap like it was a Chihuahua.

Carrick wished he'd heard this story before they'd blown the place up. He'd have shown the guy what a shock baton could do when used strategically. "Looks like you have a new furry buddy, Leesha."

He turned to see Bah standing with Mark, taking his pulse and chatting quietly, and Renata hovering like a mother hen near Aleesha, tears running down her cheeks while she watched the sisters together on the forest floor, with Milagro looking a little lost, over to one side.

It didn't feel right, leaving with Isabella still out there. "Renata? Did your sister have a plan for getting out and away from the forest? Should someone stay here to look for her, or do you think she'll be long-gone already?"

"She is very resourceful, Carrick, and will be far away by now. There is a small forestry station with a lookout tower about twenty miles from here that has a shed where they keep extra equipment and a motorcycle. We heard the guards discussing it one day, although I don't know why they'd been snooping around. Her plan was to get there and hot-wire the motorcycle, then head out. She got online one night and set up a Slack account for us to communicate, and I'm to check it daily."

"Okay, we'll trust that she's executed her plan successfully and we'll all head home. We'll get you a computer and download Slack; get the channel set up for you. Everyone, let's head out. We've got a long drive ahead of us." He turned and strode over to Mark, hand outstretched. "Glad to see you awake, man. Did Renata fill you in on who we are?" At his nod, he continued. "You have a place at my ranch while you recuperate, and we can get you back home whenever you're ready, if that's what you want. No rush though, hang with us as long as you need to. We can even get you settled in New Almaden if you like."

Mark took his offered hand, a look of profound gratitude on his face. "Can't thank you enough. I'll take you up on that offer until I get back on my feet."

Carrick turned to face the group, motioning as he directed. "Etienne, take point. Mateo? You're with Aleesha—if that's okay, Leesha?" At her nod, he continued. "West and Flynne, watch our six; Bah and Renata, hang with Mark and Milagro, and Nia, you're with me."

Before he took a step, his phone vibrated with an incoming text message. "Hang on, got a text." He pulled his phone from a pocket in his cargo pants, tapped the message notification on the home screen, and swiped the security pattern to unlock, a message from Dak waiting.

> *Dak: On my way to Sonoma. Doc there attacked. Needed a Garou medic ASAP to run the clinic. Reese & Ramil have it handled here. You all okay?*

> *Carrick: Heading back in 10, be there in about 7 hrs. Went well, will fill you in later. Tell Reese & Ramil to watch their asses; don't let Simone or Rachel out of their sight.*

> *Carrick: How's the doctor?*

> *Dak: Banged up, broken leg and arm, okay otherwise. On it. Out.*

"Shit." Carrick looked up at Nia, then Bah, knowing how pissed and worried about his friend he'd be. "I'm gonna lead with the good news; the doc in Sonoma is going to be okay. Some fucker attacked her, and she has a broken leg and arm. Dak is on his way there now to lend a hand and run the clinic until you can make other arrangements. Reese and Ramil are on heightened alert at the ranch; they have Simone and Rachel on lockdown."

Bah stiffened, shoulders and fists bunched, then closed his eyes and took a deep breath, letting it out slowly. "Okay, thanks for that. The doc is a friend of your mother's, Carrick, around the same age. She's mate to a Garou originally from Spain; he runs security up there. Dak will take care of things just fine. Let's get gone, okay?"

"Yeah, with Denton and his head guy in New Almaden, we need to get back ASAP."

Aleesha looked up from her position on the ground. "He may have more than just his head asshole with him." She looked around gravely. "Isabella's snooping and my research showed he has at least two more facilities like this, in other parts of the US, so he has others at his disposal whenever he needs to increase his ranks at one place or another. We need to find Isabella, and beef up security at your place, Carrick."

"Damn that motherfucker to hell and back." Mateo paced back and forth. "We need to find her and get her to the ranch. She can't be out there on her own!"

Carrick knew Mateo always felt the weight of responsibility, even more than he or the rest of the guys did.

"I hear you, Mat. I promise we'll find her and get her home with us. Then figure out how to raid the other facilities."

Chapter Twenty-Four

NIA BREATHED a sigh of relief as they rolled down the gravel drive on Carrick's property. It had taken them thirty minutes less to get home than their drive to the facility, still a long six and a half hours, and she couldn't wait to get her sister and the others settled.

She felt torn between desperately wanting to drag Carrick into his room and demand he make love to her, and her desire to connect with her sister and get her settled. The new mating bond still rode her hard, every erotic zone on fire for Carrick.

The sister she'd believed all these months to be dead. The guilt thinking she'd caused that death had flown away like doves out of a bell tower when she'd finally laid eyes on her, although she still harbored guilt at the thought of her sister imprisoned all these months.

As happy as she was to have her sister back, and to have rescued the others, the drive had still been fraught with tension. Everyone had worried Denton would somehow discover Simone and Rachel at the ranch with only Reese and Ramil to protect them.

Who knew if there were other traitors in the Garou community, either in New Almaden or any of the other enclaves around the world? If so, depending on who the traitors were, Denton could conceivably get hold of locations and addresses of other Garou and target them strategically.

Her sister had finally fallen into a fitful sleep about two hours away from the ranch and was lying on her side on the back seat, Oso tucked in a furry ball behind her bent knees, both snoring softly.

Nia was going to be sure her sister's four-legged protector had bones from the butcher for the rest of her doggy life.

Bah had cleaned and bandaged the cut on her bicep and abrasion on her wrist, and she'd thankfully not needed stitches, just butterfly bandages. For part of the drive, they'd been on a group call that included Reese, Ramil and Simone, so the debriefing wouldn't need to be repeated once they got home.

Etienne had ridden with Mateo and Bah, with Mark, Renata and Milagro riding in the larger Chevy Tahoe with West and Flynne. Everyone was ready to get home and get some sleep so they'd be ready for Denton if he found out where Simone and Nia, and now his freed captives, were being hidden.

Dak wasn't available, having arrived in Sonoma by private plane and busy getting things squared away there. They would give him a synopsis when he came up for air. Before they'd left the forest, Carrick had sent him a text telling him about the Garou traitor, Bowen, and warning him Denton may have found other Garou to recruit. Maybe that's what had happened in Sonoma.

Nia climbed from the FJ with a sigh, stretched, then glanced around. She caught Carrick's smoldering eyes locked on her breasts, his nostrils flaring before he raised his gaze to hers, his desire sparking across the thread of their link and setting her feminine core on fire. Boy, this post-mating constant arousal was inconvenient and had her on edge. Whew!

She quickly glanced around to ensure no one was watching, then pointed at him and mouthed, "Stop it," before paying him back by looking at the hard ridge behind the placket of his cargo pants and slicking her tongue across her bottom lip, then meeting his eyes again, clear sultry promise in hers.

A grin lit her face at his look of retribution when he stepped back up to the FJ to hide his rising need for her, palmed his cock and pointed back at her before grabbing his jacket to hold in front of his groin when he turned to watch everyone climb from their vehicles.

Nia noticed, as everyone was exiting the vehicles, that the men still looked pretty fresh and ready for action, should the need arise. Even Mark and Milagro looked worlds better than when they'd departed the forest.

"Is it your Garou DNA that gives you so much stamina? I mean, I feel like I could sleep for a week, but you guys look like you just returned from the range after firing off a few rounds."

When her eyes landed on Carrick, he raised one brow and mouthed, "Stamina?" She could feel the heat of her blush and immediately felt an answering tingle between her legs, her body perking up even more.

West was helping Renata from his SUV, and turned to answer, oblivious to Carrick's teasing. "Yeah, it's saved our asses in the past, too. We do reach a point where we need to sleep and recharge, but I'd say we can probably go at least twice as long, maybe longer, than a typical human. True, Bah?"

"Yes, I'd say that's accurate."

"That's amazing. At least I made it through today with energy to spare, even if I'm not as ready for action still as ya'll are." She stepped to the rear passenger door of the FJ and pulled it open, then laid a hand on her sister's calf to wake her.

She realized her mistake at once when her sister kicked out, flailing and shouting. "Don't touch me, you bastard! Back the fuck off!" Oso jumped to her feet on the seat and planted herself between Leesha and Nia, barking her head off.

Oh hell, she'd triggered a memory and fight reflex, more than familiar with what her sister was feeling. She and the pooch barely dodged the next kick, and Nia backed away to give her sister space and a chance to figure out where she was, murmuring to her all along. "Leesha, it's Nia. Oso, stop it, lay down, girl. Sis, you're safe. We're at Carrick's. We're home. You're not at the lab."

Oso realized no danger was coming from outside the truck, and obeying Nia's command, turned and lay down full length on Leesha, whining and nudging her cheek with her nose.

Carrick had sprinted around and stepped behind her, wrapping a muscular arm around her waist to tug her further away from getting a foot to the face.

From the corner of her eye, she saw Mateo rush around and open the door near Leesha's head, careful not to alarm the dog further, and murmured reassurances in his deep voice. "Leesha, you're safe. I promise, you're safe and those fuckers are dead. Won't ever touch you again. Wake up so Nia doesn't worry. You know how sisters are. Oso's watching out for you, too. Come on, open those eyes and you'll see you're at your new home, at Carrick's ranch, safe and sound."

The sound of his calm voice, or maybe it was his words penetrating her tortured memories and flashback, along with Oso nudging and whining, had Aleesha stop her struggling and open her eyes, one still swollen almost shut.

She'd clenched her fists, her muscles tense and ready to fight, but when her gaze landed on Mateo's kind face, then on Oso as she crawled up and planted her big blocky face right next to hers, and finally across the vehicle to Nia's shimmering gaze, she expelled a long breath and slumped bonelessly onto the seat. She wrapped her arms around Oso and held on tight.

"Damn, I'm sorry. Did I hurt anyone? Nia, you okay? What about you, Oso-girl, huh? I didn't hurt you, did I?"

Nia approached, careful not to touch her again. "No, it's all good, Leesha. I'm sorry, I touched your leg when you were asleep. I should have known better, should have remembered."

Aleesha dropped an arm over her eyes, the other one still wrapped around the pooch. "Yeah, that would do it. The guard who had Oso? He used to sneak into our cells—Isabella's, Renata's and mine—supposedly to wake us for the day, but his way of waking us involved a lot of groping, until I woke enough to kick his ass into next week. Isabella and Renata weren't strong enough to fend him off, but Oso put a stop to it for them before it could ever get out of control."

West and Flynne echoed each other. "That motherfucker!" Rage etched Etienne's face. "Had I known that when we had him in the lab, his interrogation would have gone much differently."

Nia turned to Carrick. "Can we get everyone into the house while I sit with Leesha for a few minutes before we come in?"

He dropped a kiss on her lips, then lingered for a second, deeper one before leaning back. "Of course, baby. You'll call me if you need anything?"

She turned to whisper in his ear. "I will. I just want to give her a minute. If I know her, she's embarrassed to have woken up like that."

His gaze turned fierce, and he responded in a low voice. "You tell her she has nothing to be embarrassed about in this house. No one will judge her or think less of her if she has moments like this. Hell, she could have a total meltdown and we'd understand."

Nia may not have been in love with this man yet, had been falling but not yet there, she willingly fell all the way just then. His actions today, his unwavering support—even considering why she agreed to the mating—his words just now to support her sister, cracked her heart wide open and welcomed this big, wonderful, sexy man to move right on in.

She cupped his face in her hands, her eyes moving back and forth on his, and decided she wouldn't waste any more time being unsure or distrustful. She would tell him tonight, and hope she'd not ruined everything by how she'd approached their mating, by turning it into something to be used, and not something to be cherished, as it should have been.

"What is it, sweetheart? What's wrong?" Carrick looked confused and concerned.

She shook her head and smiled. "Not a thing, Carrick. Go on in now. We'll be there in a few."

He looked like he was going to push for a better answer, to wait her out, but instead gave her a nod, dropped a kiss on her forehead, then turned and ushered everyone into the house.

He would need to figure out sleeping arrangements, maybe having Mark and Milagro share a room, since they knew each other. He'd check with Renata to ensure that would work.

Mateo hadn't left his post near her sister's head yet, still talking gently to her while she hid behind her forearm. "Okay if I unbuckle the strap holding your torso?"

Leesha's quiet voice sounded calmer when she answered. "Yes. And Mateo?" Her arm finally lowered to her waist, and she opened her eyes to glance up at him. "Thank you so much."

"Il mio piacere, tesoro." At Leesha's bemused look, Mateo translated. "My pleasure, sweetheart. You'll find I mix Italian and English when I speak. I was born in Stazzema, Italy where I lived for many years before venturing out into the world."

Nia watched with tears in her eyes as Leesha tugged Mateo down and pressed a kiss to his bristly cheek. "I'll see you in the house in a few minutes. I think Nia and I are going to sit out here for a bit."

"Just shout if you need anything." With that, he turned and entered the open door to the house, pulling it almost closed behind him.

"Scoot Oso onto the seat and let me help you sit up." Nia unbuckled the strap around Leesha's legs while her sister scooted toward the front edge of the seat, patting behind her and waiting for Oso to climb off her to the seat, then gave the big pooch a face rub.

Nia reached an arm across and clasped Leesha's uninjured forearm, giving her a tug. As soon as her sister was upright, Nia hoisted herself up and onto the seat next to her, Oso curling up on the other side, head in Leesha's lap. Nia clasped her sister's hand like they used to as little girls, when they held hands and wandered around whichever neighborhood they happened to be living in at the time, sharing secrets.

"Oh, your poor eye and lip. How are you really, Leesha? Anything you need or want, you just tell me. Oh, I'll also give you the logins to our bank accounts and my Amazon account, so you can order whatever you need. We'll have it delivered to an Amazon locker and one of the guys will pick it up."

Her sister took so long to respond, Nia thought she wasn't going to. When she finally started, it took everything in her to stay calm and not leave the ranch to track down Denton, and kill him slowly and painfully.

"The only thing that kept me going was a bone deep belief that you'd escaped. After Denton taunted me with how he'd told you they'd killed me, I knew you wouldn't be back; you'd have no reason to. But I vowed then and there to escape and find you. To make sure you were alright, and then we could hide from the bastard and come up with a plan to ruin him."

Nia squeezed Leesha's hand, her throat so tight she had trouble getting the words out. "If I had known, Leesha..."

"Shhh, sis," Leesha said. "Don't you think I know you would have moved heaven and earth to help me? You've been the one constant in my life, the one person I trust explicitly, that I know loves me unconditionally. The one I knew I could count on no matter what. I know you would have charged through flames for me. So just hush about that. No guilt. He played us like a proverbial fiddle, only he's going to fucking regret it now that we're free and back together. He'll be playing banjo with the devil before too long."

"Damn fucking straight he is, and he will. You'll discover Carrick and his friends will be our greatest allies in this, Leesha. And you don't have to worry about where to live. There's plenty of room here in the house. Dak and Reese have their own cabins on the back property, and there's a guest cabin there, too. We can work together, maybe with Ramil, to figure out where Denton's other facilities are so we can free whoever he has prisoner there."

"Can't tell you how much that means that I can stay here with you. And yes, we will free any others, and get them set up and safe." Leesha gave her a sly look. "When I'm feeling better, and more awake, you'll give me all the sexy deets on your guy?"

She covered her mouth on a wide yawn, her suddenly sleepy eyes drifting shut as she laid her head back. "I think I could sleep for a week. How about a couple more of those delicious protein shakes and a bed? Don't think I'm up to talking to anyone or staying awake any longer." Leesha waved a hand at the damage to her face. "And don't worry about this. It will heal. Really, as you know, this is the least thing to worry about, and the pain is absolutely worth it know Bowen is dead and can't hurt anyone ever again."

"Of course. Let's get you settled and you can sleep into next week if you want. Oh! How could I forget to tell you about Max!" At Leesha's confused look, she laughed. "When you were snooping around the facility, did you see a Belgian Malinois accompanying one of the guards?"

At her sister's nod, she continued. "That's Max. He's the reason I escaped, and he's been with me ever since. I was afraid he would attack the guards and get himself killed, so we left him here. I'm surprised he isn't out here checking things out."

Leesha's crooked grin was amazing to see. "That's so fitting, that two of their guard dogs protected us and turned against the assholes. So perfect. Can't wait to meet your furry buddy."

Nia grinned back, climbed out of the FJ and turned to help her clamber out. They both turned and Leesha patted the floorboard, then snapped her fingers at the garage floor, instructing Oso to climb down and jump out before closing the door. When Nia pushed open the door to the mudroom, a streak of tan and black fur hurtled toward her.

Carrick chuckled as he followed behind Max, reaching out to trail his fingertips down her arm. "He was so patient when I told him he had to wait until you came in the house. I swear, that dog understands English as well as most toddlers."

Nia had a moment of concern when Oso stiffened and gave a low growl, before both dogs seemed to recognize each other and turned into butt wiggling puppies as they circled and sniffed, Oso running true to the boxer personality by standing on her hind legs and boxing at Max with her front paws.

"I'd say they're glad to see each other!" Nia grinned at her sister.

Leesha gingerly gave a quirk of her injured lips and followed Nia into the kitchen. "I'm just glad they know and like each other, so we don't have any territorial crap to worry about. Looks like we won't have to introduce them and hope they get along."

"So true. This is great!"

Nia looked up to see Reese and Ramil watching from the table, that same look of anticipation morphing into disappointment when they realized Aleesha wasn't their mate. Damn, she felt for these guys.

The other men were at the counter where someone had set out sandwich fixings, water, energy drinks and soda. They turned, gave Nia and Leesha chin lifts and went back to creating Dagwood sandwiches to replenish from the mission.

Reese rose from the table but stayed near his chair. "I'm Reese, Carrick's brother, and this tech-head is Ramil, normally out of Sonoma but down here giving us a hand. I can't tell you how happy we are you're here and safe. Simone is putting Rachel down for a nap, and wanted me to tell you how happy she is for you and that she can't wait to meet you. I've readied the room Dak had been staying in, next to Simone's, since he's out of town, and when he gets back, he'll stay in his cabin on the property. Ramil is ordering some clothing for you to get by until you're up to doing the ordering yourself. Nia texted us a while ago and shared sizes and preferences. Packages should arrive tomorrow morning at the latest."

He motioned to the muscular tech geek at the end of the table tapping madly away on his laptop. Ramil stopped long enough to look up, shoot her a grin and sketch a salute. Nia mouthed thank you to him and got a nod and her own grin.

Reese sat again, popped Ramil on the shoulder good-naturedly and Carrick spoke up. "You'll find water, protein shakes and snacks next to your bed so you'll have something if you wake hungry and don't want to run the gamut of this unruly bunch, and there's food and water in bowls for your pooch."

Nia laughed when the guys gave Carrick a bunch of shit about his comments.

"You're the only unruly one."

"And after the nice things I said about you!"

"What the fuck, dude?"

He grinned at her sister. "See what I have to put up with? I'll totally understand if you sleep for, oh, twelve to forty-eight hours just so you don't have to deal with them. Although I bet Nia will be in there checking on you if you're out for more than ten."

Nia was proud as hell of her sister when she smiled at the guys, then turned and patted Carrick's arm. "Thank you so much for opening your home to me, and the others."

She turned back to Reese and Ramil. "And thank you for readying things for me." She waved at the room in general. "I have no adequate words to give any of you, but you have my undying gratitude."

She included Carrick and Mateo, standing next to her. "But I will tell you this—all joking aside. I will walk through the fires of hell for each and every one of you, if need be. Any of you need anything, and I mean anything—you ask, and if I can pull it off, it's yours."

As one, each gave her what looked to be their version of a courtly bow. Reese and Ramil stood and also inclined their heads, which made Nia remember these men were hundreds of years old. Back in the day, some type of bow or physical gesture was typical in greetings or as a show of respect. Tears burned her eyes when each one verbally expressed their own vow to her sister, starting with Etienne and rounding the room, ending with West and Flynne.

"And we for you, Leesha."

"You call, we're here. No matter where we are."

Her sister looked astounded, and tears trailed down her cheeks. "I'm not a crier, dammit! Thank you. Thank you all. Including those of you who were here, making sure Simone and Rachel were safe. And please, thank Dak, too."

Mateo walked over to where they were standing when everyone sat again, going back to their business, providing Leesha time to recover from her crying jag. "As I told Nia when she first arrived, and as you may have surmised by my hovering during the mission, I'm the unofficial dad of the group. You haven't met my son Dakarai yet. If you remember, he's the one had to head to Sonoma to pinch-hit for Bah and the injured doc. You need anything, even if it's just a sounding board or a big dad-shoulder to cry on, I'm your man."

When he turned and grinned at Nia, she grinned back, knowing exactly what he was going to say next.

"Your sister says she and Dak will have to haggle over borrowing my car." He chuckled, as if the thought of her going up against Dak was hilarious. "I'm guessing now I'll have another daughter asking for my keys. Hell, I may need to buy a couple more vehicles just so you three aren't arguing all the time."

Nia loved hearing Leesha's laughter and her heart opened even more to allow Mateo entrance. It would be aces to have a dad who actually cared about his albeit grown kids, and who she and Leesha could count on. They'd never had that. Looks like they'd finally scored in that department.

Leesha patted Mateo's shoulder and grinned up at the big man. "Well, dad, I won't be borrowing the car for a few days, but look out Dak. I can be sneaky, so he may not get the car as often as he used to."

Mateo threw back his head and guffawed, looking delighted by her rejoinder, and having a new kid to add to his crew.

"I look forward to seeing that, Leesha. I think you can give him a run for his money. Who knows, between you and Nia, maybe you can finally get my son to loosen up a little. Now, let Nia get you settled and we'll see you when you're ready to come out of your cave."

Nia turned to Carrick and murmured, "I'll be back in a bit." Then she leaned forward and pressed a kiss to his lips, lingering for a second, feeling their bond become even stronger, if possible, along with the mating lust revving up again.

She flushed and opened her eyes to see his turn molten, the only sign he was as affected as she was but was holding it in check until he got her alone again.

He squeezed her bicep before stepping back and nodding to her sister. "Sleep well, Leesha. See you in a bit, Nia."

Holding Leesha's hand again, Nia led her to the bedroom Dak had slept in when she and Simone had first come to the ranch. She pushed the door open, releasing her hand before gesturing for her to enter.

"Do you need anything, sis? I feel like I need to sit by your bed to keep watch over you. I'm afraid I'm dreaming right now and when I wake, you won't be here."

Leesha turned and wrapped her in a hard hug. "I'm going to be fine, honest, Nia. I'm so damned glad to be free, and to see you, and I feel perfectly safe with so many men—scratch that, Garou—in the house who're willing and able to kick ass for us."

Nia walked further into the room to fold back the covers, inviting Leesha to sit with a pat on the mattress. "Okay, okay, I'll not hover. Um, I'm not sure any of the guys thought to change the bedding, but I'm pretty sure Dak just laid on top of the covers when he napped and really only used the pillow."

Leesha waved her hand. "That's the last thing I'm going to worry about, sis. Go on, be with your man. And don't think either of you were being sly with those heated looks." She laughed and sat down with a grin. "Besides, I really am going to sleep for about twelve hours before I show my face again. I'm so exhausted I can barely think."

Nia felt that damnable blush creeping up again. "Shew! This mating thing is new, and one side-affect is the desire to jump each other's bones for about seventy-two hours after actually, well, mating." Nia laughed and gave her a wry look. "And we, uh, consummated the mating a few hours before we left for the facility."

Leesha shot her an incredulous look and then laughed again. "I'm surprised either of you could concentrate! I truly am okay, and between you and me? I'm really looking forward to snuggling in this enormous bed with Oso and not coming out for hours."

Nia squeezed her arm. "I hear you. When I first escaped, all I wanted to do was sleep, knowing no one was going to barge in or hurt me. It was heaven. Okay, the basics. Attached bathroom is through the door in the corner. Closet over there, although I'm not sure what's in it, but feel free to snoop and use anything you find. You need me, turn left when you exit the room and Carrick's, uh, and my door is second on the left."

Leesha smirked at Nia as she stumbled over her words. "Okay, off with you. I'm going to lie here for a minute, then shower and sleep. Maybe just toss one of your tanks and shorts in here for me to sleep in. Don't worry about making noise. Oh, leave the door open a crack, so when Oso and Max finish hanging out, she can come in?"

"Sure thing. I'll let her out to do her business, then usher her in when she's done."

She watched fondly as her sister sat on the bed and dropped sideways on the cushy pillow with a sigh, only to have her face go suddenly pale, a gasp escaping her lips.

Nia leaped toward the bed. "What? What's wrong?"

Leesha rolled onto her back. "I don't—I don't know. I got really dizzy suddenly and feel kinda shaky. Adrenaline crash? I haven't eaten in forever."

Nia's alarm had her dashing to the door. "Bah? Come here for a sec!"

She heard heavy footsteps jog across the hardwood floors, and not only Bah but Mateo and Carrick ran into the room, Bah hurrying to Leesha's side.

"What happened?"

"She laid down and went pale. She suddenly doesn't feel well."

Nia watched as Bah pressed two fingers to Leesha's wrist while looking at his watch, then laid his hand across her forehead. "Hmmm, elevated pulse and you feel feverish. When was the last time you ate? Do you have any injuries we don't know about?"

"God, I don't remember. Sometime yesterday. Oh, but I had that shake when we were hiking to the vehicles and then the one you gave me when we arrived here."

Bah turned to Nia. "Open a shake for her and let's get her sipping it."

He turned back to Leesha. "Did they sedate you last night or yesterday?"

Leesha's forehead wrinkled. "Uh, maybe? I don't remember."

He nodded. "Okay, when was your last infusion?"

Her face cleared. "Two days ago. The doctor said it was literally my last infusion. That's why Bowen dragged me to his cell, because Isabella had gotten away. She'd been their first choice for him to mate with."

Bah's face tightened and turned fierce. "Well, that motherfucker will not bother you anymore. I think you're just exhausted, dehydrated and hungry, and probably having symptoms similar to what Nia was experiencing. We can get an IV going tomorrow to replenish nutrients and electrolytes, with a big dose of magnesium and glutathione. I'm hesitant to do anything tonight. Drink plenty of fluids through the night to help flush out anything in your system, and see if you can down a shake whenever you wake."

Nia relaxed at his words, and Mateo spoke up from the doorway.

"Leesha, do you mind if I wake you a few times tonight, just to make sure you're okay and to keep you hydrated? I know you feel you could sleep a week, but I think we need to ensure you're doing alright throughout the night. I'll just open the door and call out to you; I won't enter the room."

"Oh, I'll wake her, Mateo. You don't need to stay up to do that." Nia felt a bone-deep responsibility to watch over her sister, now that she had her back in the fold.

Mateo shook his head at her. "You and Carrick, well, you know, yesterday morning, and you had that reaction. I think some rest will do you good, too."

Nia kept her eyes averted from Carrick's and hoped her blush stayed down on her chest where no one could see it. He'd pretty much just announced to everyone that she and Carrick had mated yesterday morning.

Although she knew with their enhanced hearing and senses that every last one of them must have been aware what she and Carrick had been up to, it was still embarrassing to have it out in the open. And she knew, the second she was in Carrick's room and the door was closed and locked, they'd be naked and at it as many times as possible through the night. One look at her sister's face said she knew it, too.

Leesha shook her head at Nia, her mouth quirking, then glanced over to Mateo. "Yes, that's fine, Mateo. Thank you."

Bah rose and headed toward the door. "Okay, let's give her some privacy and quiet."

Mateo strode forward and laid a smartphone on the nightstand, with a green post-it stuck on the screen. "Ramil set this up for you, has security and encryption, and your new number's on the post-it. All of our numbers are in the contacts, along with Nia's and Simone's. We'll all be here at least a few more days, and a few of us will stay on after that. Promise you'll call one of us if you don't feel well tonight."

Nia felt love swell for this older man, that familiar spark of regret flaring for not having a dad like him when she and her sister were growing up. She grinned at her sister's next words, although she could see the older man's words and the fact she had people watching out for her touched her deeply.

"Yes, dad."

Mateo chuckled as they all filed out of the room and back into the kitchen. Nia walked over to lean against the counter and asked Reese, "How's the doctor in Sonoma? Dak doing okay?"

"Yeah, the doctor will be out of commission for about six to eight weeks, although in a week or two she'll be able to do research or consult on cases."

"And Dak?"

"Oh, he's texted a few times and has taken charge at the clinic. I'm sure you could tell by being around him for only a couple of days, that man uses as few words as possible, and will text so he doesn't have to talk."

Carrick shook his head. "Isn't that the truth? He say anything about how the investigation is going on the attack?"

"Nah. Said they're still looking into it. Conveniently, the attack happened in a slice of the parking lot at the medical supply store where the cameras don't reach. They'll track it down, though."

Nia looked around the kitchen and spied Max and Oso under the table, tongues lolling as they kept vigil for a fallen piece of meat or bread. "Don't you guys be feeding those goofballs any table scraps." One look at Ramil's face and she'd found the guilty one.

"Don't try that innocent face on me, Ramil. Leesha used to give it a go and wasn't any more successful than you."

He laughed and confessed. "Okay, okay, you got me. But Oso looked so pitiful! And I can't show favoritism, can I? Max had to have a bite too. How can you resist those faces?"

She shook her head at the forlorn look he shot her. "I resist by knowing it messes with their stomachs and turns them into table goblins, who will eventually annoy you with their begging." Snapping her fingers, she motioned for Max and Oso to come out. They obeyed, but grudgingly, looking pitiful with their heads bowed. She hooked a finger in Max's collar and had him sit beside her, then pointed down the hall while looking at the boxer. "Oso, go to Leesha. Go on."

With a woof, she trotted obediently down the hallway and Nia heard Leesha murmuring to the pooch a moment later. Carrick came up behind her, hands holding two plates with scrumptious looking sandwiches and a pile of chips on each. "Grab some drinks for us? These guys can decompress, and we can eat in our room and get some rest."

She shot him an incredulous look, not daring to look around the room, since every one of these guys knew exactly why Carrick wanted to get her alone and was using the guise of eating to get her into his— their bedroom. Gah! She'd have a permanent blush by the time the mating fever settled down in the next couple of days.

Striving for nonchalance, she headed to the fridge and pulled it open, welcoming the coolness on her hot face. "Sure, be right there."

CARRICK STRODE DOWN the hall and into his bedroom, setting the plates on the small table near the window. He was so damned glad her sister was alive—he'd *never* forget that look on Nia's face when she'd found out—and they'd been able to retrieve almost everyone, relatively unharmed.

Isabella was a worry, though, since no telling how well outfitted she was, and or whether she actually made it to the look-out tower to requisition the motorcycle and get to safety.

They'd left no one behind to look for her, since her sister seemed confident she'd been successful in reaching her goal and getting away, but it troubled him not knowing where she was. He knew Flynne had worked his magic on his tablet on the way back to the ranch, trying to track her down by hacking into traffic cams on the highway she'd end up on after escaping the forest on a motorcycle. So far, no luck in finding her. It's entirely possible she stayed off road for as long as she could.

Renata had shared a ton of information about her sister that would help in his search for her, and Ramil was providing Renata with a secure laptop with Slack downloaded so they could monitor the channel Isabella had set up for her.

Now, if he could just get his mate in this room and strip her bare and inspect every delectable inch for injuries, he'd be feeling a whole lot better.

And then he was going to nibble, lick and caress every inch of that luscious body before he slipped his cock home in her hot, wet sheath and show her how much he loved her.

Because he realized he *did* love her. He'd been sliding toward it since connecting with her, but her bravery during the mission, her compassion toward the captives, her love for her sister, and even her caring for another four-legged fur baby had him doing the big slide into home base.

He heard her walking down the hallway and turned to drink in the sight of her as she entered the room, sexy hips swaying. He strode to her and plucked the drinks from her hands. "Close the door, sweetheart."

She pivoted and pushed it shut with a click, then turned, hands on hips. "You know everyone's aware just why you want us to eat in your room, right?" She mesmerized him when she reached both hands down and slowly peeled her tank top up and off, flinging it toward the overstuffed chair in the corner.

"Damn, baby. You keep that up, and we'll bypass dinner and go straight to dessert."

"Nope, big guy. We're going to have a picnic on the bed. Clothing optional. Off with your shirt."

No way was he going to argue about getting naked with his lady. He reached one hand back, grabbed a handful of his t-shirt and tugged it off over his head, flinging it to lie across hers. He chuckled at her smirk and spread his hands as if to say, next?

"Now we're going to see how much dinner we can get down before one of us caves, and thus loses. Or wins, depending on your definition."

The smirk on her face was full of mischief, and he couldn't wait to see what she had planned. More than willing to play along, he turned and grabbed the plates, setting them in the center of the bed, then took a long step and scooped her up in his arms.

"Hey, no fair! You're cheating!"

"Nope, just expediting activities." He deposited her gently at the end of the bed before heading into the bathroom for washcloths to use as makeshift napkins.

On the way back, he grabbed their water bottles, put a knee on the bed and crawled to the head of the mattress to sit cross-legged opposite her.

His movement jostled the mattress, and his eyes automatically locked on her lush, bouncing breasts, barely encased in satin, his already hard cock becoming a steel rod in his pants. His eyes roamed up her slender throat to her unusual cinnabar eyes, and since she had said nothing about not touching *themselves*, he held her gaze and leisurely brought one hand up to rub across the mat of hair on his chest, then followed the trail of it down his abdomen to the button on his cargos.

"You don't mind if I undo this, just to be comfortable, do you?"

Her eyes had predictably followed his hand, and at his question, snapped back up to his. "What? Oh, no, go ahead."

He held back his grin when her eyes immediately lowered again to his busy hand when he slid the zipper down and, with one flick, undid the button. His cock, conveniently already pointed straight up, didn't need adjusting, but a stroke or two would feel amazing, especially while watching her expressive face and imagining those luscious lips of hers circling his stiff appendage and sucking it like an all-day lollipop.

He felt a telltale zing up his spine and had to tighten every muscle in his body to keep from shooting off. Not cool, and he definitely didn't want to waste an orgasm on his imagination alone. No, he wanted to be buried balls deep for their first time tonight, then enjoy her lips and her hot, slick channel all night long.

Her pupils almost obliterated her irises, leaving a bright green ring flecked with silver and red. He cupped his balls through his pants, wrapped his hand around his cock and pumped once, twice, watching her lean toward him, her pink tongue slicking across that full bottom lip.

When he realized his ruse was going to backfire, and he was going to either jump her or come by his own hand, he gave one more stroke, then reached for a sandwich and handed it to her. She didn't react, seemingly still mesmerized by his cock now pulsing against his stomach to the beat of his heart.

"Want to take a bite, sweetheart?"

Her eyes snapped up to his, and she was nodding and moving her hand toward his rod before she registered he was handing her a sandwich, not inviting her to nibble on his cock. Her eyes narrowed when she realized she'd been played.

"If you knew me better, you'd know how invested I am in getting even."

He smirked, reached for her hand, and plopped her sandwich in it. "You're gonna need your strength tonight, Nia. Better work on that dinner."

His smirk turned into burning desire again when she stared him in the eyes, lifted her hoagie, widened those full lips and wrapped them around the end with a moan. Holy shit, he'd released a clever seductress, and was no longer confident he'd win this round.

Unable to avert his eyes, he missed his sandwich on the first grab, succeeding on the second, and took a healthy bite of his own.

Time to get dinner done and move onto dessert. Namely, his mate. When they'd both finished half of their hoagies and downed some water, she set the remaining sandwich on her plate, lifted it and leaned over to place it on the floor, along with her water, her beautiful breasts swaying even encased in lace.

He was curious as hell to see what she was up to now, and figured he better get his food out the of way too, mimicking her actions and setting his on the nightstand, unable to look away from those luscious mounds.

When she lay back on the bed, then unsnapped her cargo pants and shimmied out of them, he about swallowed his tongue. His eyes didn't know where to land, since every part of her muscular, curvy body was a feast on its own.

One of the miniscule thong panties she favored barely covered the neatly trimmed thatch of curls at the juncture of her thighs, his blood heating to boiling when she trailed a fingertip up her quad, scooted the silk out of the way to bare her clit and toggled it with her finger. He again had to tighten every muscle, and then some, to keep from surging into orgasm.

"Fuck, baby, yeah. Play with that little pearl and make yourself come."

She shot him a coy look and pouted. "It looks like I'll have to, since you're more interested in that ole sandwich than what's sandwiched between my thighs."

And with that proclamation, she played and pinched her clit until her torso, neck and face suffused with an enticing blush, the light sheen of sweat on her tantalizing curves giving off that enticing cinnamon and nutmeg scent uniquely hers.

He no longer cared who won this competition. All that mattered was that he got his hands, his mouth and his tongue on her as a prelude to sliding his cock in her tight, wet heat.

He jumped from the bed, hooked his thumbs in the waistband of his pants, then dragged them down his legs to the floor, startling her, but not enough to make her stop working herself with that finger he'd grown envious of.

A knee on the bed gave him the perfect position to move over her body and clasp her hand, pulling it away from the jewel she was playing. "Mine, Nia. I will make you come, not your finger."

Her voice was breathless when she taunted him. "I'd say you lost the bet, Carrick."

"No, baby, I won the prize. I still can't believe you're mine." And with that, he cupped her face in his hands and ravished her mouth, gentle nibbles on that lush lower lip, tongue darting in to tease hers, only to retreat and force her to follow. Her mouth was a thing of wonder, and he could spend hours doing nothing but kissing her.

And her beautiful body, that wonderful mix of muscular and soft, those curves that went on for days! One hand trailed down her neck, between her glorious breasts, to lie flat and revel in the steady beat of her heart.

His own heart skipped a beat at the thought he could have lost her during the mission if anything had gone sideways. He forced that thought aside and again concentrated on her soft skin, smoothing his hand over to cup the lush fullness of a breast, frustrated by the barrier of her bra keeping him from the turgid nipple.

"Still too many clothes." With a deft twist of his fingers, and blessing front-clasp bras, he flicked it open and nudged the cups to either side. Reluctantly abandoning the pleasure of her mouth, he sat back on his haunches and stared at the twin peaks, just begging for attention. His cock begged for its own attention, saluting the ceiling and pulsing, pre-come glistening on the head.

"Damn, baby, every time I see you, I'm amazed all over again at how fucking sexy and absolutely perfect for me you are."

Her cinnabar eyes flared with even more heat, the silver and red flecks almost glowing amidst that gem green. When she reached for his cock, he gently grasped her hand, knowing a single touch from those long fingers would have him spurting all over her abdomen.

And while that was an enticing picture in his head, he wanted to come inside her this time; a union of affection—and love on his part—not just the act of sex and appeasing the mating fever still raging through his body and soul.

He moved down her delectable body until his mouth aligned with her breasts, leaned forward and dove in. There was nothing tentative about his taking. He pulled an engorged nipple into his mouth and sucked, thrumming the strawberry peak with his tongue.

If he'd been a smaller man, one with less strength, she would have launched him right off the bed when she arched, pushing that breast against his mouth and clenching her strong fists in his hair. The sting was affirmation she loved what he was doing and silently begging for more—right now!

"Ohhhhh, Car... Car... Carrick!"

It was now a constant battle between his willpower and his unruly cock, a full-time endeavor to keep that electric zing up his spine from shooting straight through his balls to his cock and painting her stomach with his come. His wolven-self was growling and insisting he bury balls deep in her heat and make her theirs all over again.

Knowing he was on a short timer, his cock on a short fuse, and the wolf inside him vying for control, he switched his mouth to her other breast, eliciting another moan, then scooped his hand down to strip off the silken barrier of her panties. His finger unerringly found her wet center and slid in, curling to find that spot sure to drive her crazy, and he thanked any and all gods that she was more than ready to take his cock. He leaned on an elbow and forearm while his other hand was busy making her even wetter.

"Nia, can't wait to have you. I'll make it up to you. Take more time later. Got to have you."

Far from getting a complaint, his woman presented her own demands. "God yes! Take me, make me yours again."

At her words, Carrick inserted his thighs between her legs and spread them wide, reveling when she instinctively wrapped those mile-long legs around his hips, heels pressing deep on his ass.

He circled a fist around his cock and teased them both by rubbing the mushroom head up and down her slit before placing it at her center and pressing, pressing, until it slid in an inch. He tucked one hand behind her head, still balancing on his forearm, and clutched a curvy hip with his other palm.

He stopped, dropping his head between her breasts, amazed to feel his fangs slide out as if they were mating for the first time. He raised his head, lips parted, their eyes meeting, their link thrumming and stronger than ever.

Her eyes widened when they dropped to where she saw the sharp tips of his fangs denting his lower lip, and he jolted when her core clamped down on his cock.

"Fuck, Nia. I'm about twenty seconds away from shooting off in you. I want you to come on my cock; my wolven self wants me to share a bite with you when I do, as if we're just now mating. I don't want to hurt you."

The trust shining in her eyes was almost his undoing. Especially knowing her trust issues were valid and real and hard to put aside. Her next breathless words made him love her even more.

"Carrick... Yes, take me. I'm yours, you're mine. We're meant to be. Bite me, come inside me. Do it!"

He pumped hard, sliding all the way home, his balls slapping her ass, but he refused to take his pleasure before knowing she'd found hers. Removing his hand from her hip, he levered up enough to slide a knuckle back and forth over her swollen clit, pressing and rubbing while she went wild beneath him.

A lightning bolt of pleasure speared into his cock when she tightened all her muscles, trembled and came apart in his arms. When her pussy rippled and pulsed with her orgasm and she gasped his name, he pulled his hand from her clit and slid it under her shoulder to cup it tightly, pulled his cock out and pumped in hard strokes.

He knew she needed it rougher, not painfully so, but she was a powerful woman, and she wanted to feel it. To fully experience their passion. Demanded he not treat her like spun glass.

"Yes, harder, like that. Love those long strokes."

Fuck! He pistoned his hips as commanded, sweat pouring off his face to bathe her already glistening breasts and neck, and when she tilted her head, baring her trapezoid muscle for his fangs, he swept her curls aside and sank them home at the instant his cock sank home, strong spurts filling her channel.

She cried out again and came with him, her sheath clamping down on his cock, and as the Garou serum spurted from his fangs, the sweet taste of her blood and his name on her lips was ecstasy to his heart and soul.

They lay there boneless, and it took another act of sheer will on his part not to fall and crush her under his heavy weight. His shaking arms heralded impending collapse, and at the last minute he shoved sideways, taking her with him wrapped tightly in his arms.

She nestled her head on his shoulder, breath coming in harsh pants, mirroring his. He stroked a hand down her back at the same time she lifted her slender palm to stroke his bristly cheek, his neck, before burrowing her fingers into the thatch of hair on his chest.

"Carrick."

Her soft voice saying his name was a gift he would never take for granted, but he couldn't stop from tensing as he waited for her to continue, still afraid she could never love him, or would decide the sex was good, but not worth sticking around for the long run.

He loved her independence and strength, but the betrayal she'd suffered as a child and as an adult colored her world in murky shadows.

He forced himself to relax. "Yeah, baby?"

When she leaned up on an elbow and cupped his face, he was hesitant to meet her eyes, afraid of what he would see in their depths, but taking the coward's way was never an option for him in anything.

He opened his eyes and held her gaze steadily, unable to read or translate what he was seeing—the absence of former shadows? Affection?

She climbed onto his lap, half sitting, now cupping his face with both hands, and leaned down to place soft kisses on his lips, her full breasts pillowed on his pecs.

With her bewitching eyes on his, she softly murmured, "I love you, Carrick."

He lay there paralyzed, not sure he'd heard her correctly. "You—you love me."

He repeated it as a statement, afraid if he worded it as a question, she would snatch it away from him.

Her soft smile said she understood, and she repeated herself, firmly and with solid conviction this time. "Carrick. I. Love. You."

"Oh baby, I love you too. Gods, I was afraid you wouldn't take a chance on us."

His wolven-self took over at that point, wanting to reinforce their bond to match her words, as he clutched her full hips and lifted her enough to bury his suddenly hard cock in her sheath.

He stiffened, shocked when he saw tiny fangs protrude from her mouth, the tips just overlapping her full bottom lip, and his cock swelled to even greater proportions. "Holy hell, baby, can you feel that? You have fangs."

"You didn't say this could happen!" Her voice incredulous, she opened her mouth and touched the tip of her tongue to one sharp point. Her eyes flashed sensuous fire, along with sexy curiosity.

He gave her verbal and physical permission as he tipped his head to one side, offering himself up for her pleasure as he gripped her hips, his cock pumping in and out of her sheath.

Her hissed, "Yessss," was sexy as fuck just before she dropped her head and latched onto his trap, small fangs penetrating his skin, causing both of them to shoot into orgasm—immediately, simultaneously, more forcefully than ever before.

"Nia, baby, damn!" He'd no idea Cinnabar Twins grew fangs, could, or would want to bite their Garou mates, but holy shit, he'd just had the best full body orgasm, the best everything, at the moment she penetrated his skin with her teeth.

He could feel her fangs retract and she sat up shakily on his abdomen, shocked eyes wide. "That was as intense as when you bit me. Holy shit. Is that a thing? You said nothing about the female mates being able to do that!"

"Sweetheart, I had no idea, but holy hell, that was... you know what? I have no words. That was so fucking amazing, I have no words to describe it."

She smirked a little at that. "You don't need words, Carrick. If it was anything like how I feel when you bite me, I know how amazing it feels, how nothing compares."

He pulled her down next to him, reveling in the fact his smart, strong, brave, beautiful mate loved him, as he loved her. His last thought before they both drifted off to sleep was he'd never imagined he could ever have this. And no way in hell was he going to lose it, or her, to Denton or anyone else. He'd kill anyone who tried.

Epilogue

NIA WATCHED her mate circle the kitchen table like a wolf protecting its mate or young. A week had passed since they'd come back from the mission, and she'd told Carrick she loved him.

And that love grew every day, if possible. She couldn't imagine life without him and looked forward to the—possibly—hundreds of years ahead together. If they could get rid of Denton.

"Carrick, come sit down, you're making us dizzy." He'd been pacing for a good five minutes and if he didn't sit down, she'd have to take him down, and it wouldn't be in bed. "Don't make me get tough with you."

He stopped and turned, hands on lean hips, a scowl on his beloved face. "I just don't like the idea of Mateo going out on his own to look for Isabella. We should work in pairs, since Denton has proven himself good at gathering Garou traitors and taking down fit, strong, intelligent men like Mark. And Milagro."

Mateo flashed him an impatient look. "You can't afford to send anyone else with me, Carrick. We're a little short on folks who can get here in time, and we can't leave Isabella out on her own and hope for the fucking best. She hasn't left a message for Renata yet in their Slack channel, and I'm worried something has happened to her."

Currently, Renata and Simone were in the back bedroom packing to move to their new cabin. Reese, West and Aleesha were outfitting four new cabins the guys had built on the property just this week, to accommodate the ever-growing Garou and Cinnabar Twin population who would live at the ranch for an indefinite period of time.

There was a prefab company they're ordered readymade cabin parts from, and it took only a day to put each three-room home together—living room/kitchen combo, bedroom and bathroom.

He planned to add a small, attached garage to each one at a later date for parking their vehicles, so they could lessen the danger in exiting and entering their domains.

Aleesha was wiring the new cabins, along with adding security, and Reese was finishing the plumbing and securing the structures to foundations they'd poured.

She and Nia were also working to bolster security around the ranch and looking into setting up martial arts training for local Garou.

When Carrick had offered to let Aleesha stay in the house permanently, she'd insisted she wanted to live in one of the cabins, saying she felt like a third wheel in the house, and after the loss of privacy in the facility, she really needed her own place now.

Aleesha had been afraid of hurting Nia's feelings, considering they'd just reunited after thinking her dead, but Nia reassured her she totally understood her sister's desire for her own place.

Besides, Leesha's cabin was the extra one nestled between Dak's and Reese's, so all three of them could watch out for each other, although Dak wouldn't be returning for about another week.

Simone, Rachel and Renata would share a larger cabin they'd ordered, since Simone felt she was intruding, living in the house, but was afraid to be by herself with the little girl. They'd sat down with Simone and confessed they knew Rachel wasn't her daughter by birth, but fully supported her raising the little girl as her own.

Ramil had created a fake birth certificate showing Simone as the mother, with no name for the father. And Mateo's and Ramil's cabins would bookend Renata and Simone's cabin to provide security and support should need be.

Etienne and Flynne were out sniffing around New Almaden, trying to get a lead on Denton, Dak was still in Sonoma working in the clinic, and Ramil had escorted Mark Seavers to Sonoma, since Mark was from the San Francisco Bay Area and wanted to try to settling in that area again.

Ramil would return within the week to stay on for a while, providing dedicated tech and research services, and extra muscle, in their mission to find and do away with Denton once and for all.

The Wolven Council was setting Mark up in a new condo, bankrolling his first few months until he was back on his feet and decided what he wanted to do. He'd been a fitness coach in San Francisco, to the Garou population in that area, and was thinking of setting up in Sonoma in the same occupation, which the council was fully in favor of.

Milagro was asleep in his bedroom, the concussion and resulting amnesia causing severe depression he was struggling to get out from under. Carrick had reassured him he had a home here until he was ready to head out on his own, regardless of how long that took.

Ramil was researching and trying to discover who Milagro really was, but no luck yet. Although Milagro had mentioned Almaden, he didn't match the description of the second missing Garou. It troubled them all they had no clue where the second guy missing from New Almaden was, or where Milagro was from.

Carrick paced across the kitchen again. "I don't think we should ignore the danger and have Mateo out there without someone watching his six. After what we've seen and heard, I'd think you'd all agree with me. Don't get me wrong, I'm worried about Isabella too, but what good will it do if Mateo gets ambushed and taken? Then we're looking for both of them!"

"For fuck's sake." Mateo's voice was a growl, and Nia looked at him in shock, never having heard him curse or sound pissed off. Wanting to stop a fight before it started, she fell back on humor. "Uh, dad, no fighting in the house. Your rules."

Her eyes widened at the fierce look he shot her, and she saw the minute he realized he was being aggressive with her. He wiped a weary hand down his face, then looked up sheepishly, if a Garou could actually pull that look off.

"Okay, sorry daughter." The quirk of his lips said he knew exactly what her game was. "How about we do this. We'll split our time running searches for Denton and Isabella, and we concentrate on Isabella first. Flynne, Etienne and I can team up, with one staying here providing tech support and research, and the other two out in the field actively looking. We'll switch around on who stays here and who pairs up out there. It's apparent Denton has gone to ground, whether here or back in Oregon, and Isabella is in peril, both from him and any unknown dangers she may run across trying to meet up with Renata."

Nia perked up at that, looked at Carrick, then back at Mateo. "Perfect solution, yes Carrick?"

She breathed a sigh of relief when Carrick's face relaxed and he finally sat next to her, picking her up as if she weighed nothing, and plopped her in his lap.

"What are you doing?" She laughed as he nuzzled her neck and nipped at her ear. Her token complaint lost its sting when she gave him a smacking kiss on his lips. That now familiar frisson of excitement zinged through her body at the brush of his full, firm lips against hers. It amazed her their zest for each other hadn't waned after a few days like they'd thought it would. Not that she was complaining.

"Just want you to be comfortable, mate of mine. That chair must be hard on your sexy bum."

Mateo raised an eyebrow, slanted them a look, and walked toward the door leading to the mudroom and out to the garage. "Think I'll go see if your sister, West, and Reese need any help."

The second the door closed behind him, Carrick rose from the chair, Nia cradled in his muscular arms. "Hey!"

His mobile mouth cut off her words, his tongue and teeth on her lips cut off her ability to think. He lifted his head, and she saw his eyes had gone molten silver with arousal. "What were you going to say, baby?"

"What?" She could barely remember her own name, much less what she was going to say.

His mouth quirked before dipping again in a ravenous taking, his tongue dueling with hers before taking her lower lip between his teeth and pulling gently, eliciting a low moan deep from her throat. She felt the prick of a fang and had no clue if it was his or hers. Didn't matter. What mattered was they both got naked in their big bed.

Nia had moved into Carrick's room—now their room—the day after they'd returned from the mission. She couldn't imagine sleeping apart from her big guy.

She dove into the kiss, both of them careful not to do damage with their fangs, and were both breathless by the time he tumbled them backwards on the bed, her on top so as not to be crushed under his considerable weight.

"I crave you every minute of every day, Carrick." Her desire and love for this remarkable man was enormous and growing every day, every hour—every minute.

"No more than I you, Nia. I'd thought I would never have this. This closeness, companionship, this bond I can feel strengthening that lets me know you're near and safe. This passion and love."

"Oh, sweetheart. I'm sorry I ever doubted you, that I…"

"Shh, no recriminations." He swept her curls from her face and cupped her heated cheeks between his hands. "We're right where we belong, and if we got there on a crooked route—well, that just doesn't matter. We have a long, long journey ahead of us; a wonderful, amazing life to live and experience—together. Thank you for being mine—my mate, my everything."

She lowered till their lips met, not in a passionate kiss; no, this slow, sensuous kiss promised love and laughter, an unbreakable bond of affection, trust and respect.

"I love you so much, Carrick. Never did I think I would find anything close to what we have. You're my miracle, my heart, and I'm never letting you go, or letting anything happen to you."

Their lips met again, going from soft to ravenous, and with their bodies they danced the dance of love, one showing the other what was in their hearts, their souls.

Forevermore.

Stay in Touch!

Sign up for my VIP newsletter, and be rewarded with an adult coloring & puzzle book! I send one to two newsletters a month with information about new releases, contests, and all things paranormal romance.

Go here to sign up:
https://BookHip.com/NTFASXP

Find Fiola in these virtual worlds:

Website: https://www.fiolafaelan.com/
Facebook: @fiolafaelan
Facebook group: @shiftintoromance
Pinterest: @fiolafaelan
Instagram: fiolafaelan
Twitter: @fiolafaelan

FIOLA HAS always loved to read and write, with her first mini-story crafted at age five. She's come a long way from chubby fingers wrapped around crayons putting words, albeit misspelled, to paper.

Nowadays, Fiola loves to dream of romance, and has exchanged crayons for a laptop so she can bring *Shift into Romance* to life. She lets her characters go crazy so they can indulge in paranormal sexy-times between the pages, where alpha men embrace their wild side and strong, independent women learn that muscles and fangs not only help them survive, but also find sensuous satisfaction while doing so.

She grew up a devout tomboy, tackling every tree on the block when Silicon Valley wasn't even a gleam in San Jose's eyes. Back in the day, she hit life full-tilt, from barrel-racing her Appaloosa as a teen, to running parkour across the Morro Bay breakwater, to surf-fishing in Hawaii in her twenties, and walking barefoot on the beach dreaming of romance.

Her travels these days are via the interweb's virtual worlds, where she's always on the lookout for that next story, that next place to bury the body. Or lock lips with an uber-alpha, muscular man who knows his way around a woman's body and embraces feminine strength and all that entails.

Every experience garners even more fantasies for her characters, whether she's crafting men with a wolven-self, or there's a bear roaring to burst forth and claim his mate. Who knows, maybe one day, IRL (in real life), she'll find her own man with a wild-side whose abilities include kissing her 'til she forgets her name.

She kicks-ass, takes names and crafts characters in the beautiful Portland Metro area of Oregon, where she cohabitates with her amazingly talented son and equally talented daughter-in-law, and their most affectionate cat Nudge.

Visit Fiola from time to time in her virtual corners of the world, where sexy men and women misbehave while she weaves them into stories, and if you have time, pop over to visit her alter-ego, Gemma Blake. See what she's been up to, maybe drop her a line!

Trademark Acknowledgements

The author acknowledges the following trademarks of products mentioned in the book:

- ➢ 4Runner (Toyota SUV)
- ➢ BK7 (Becker, knife)
- ➢ Chevy Tahoe (vehicle)
- ➢ Chevy Suburban (vehicle)
- ➢ Dagwood (cartoon aka sandwich)
- ➢ Ducati Multistrada 950/950 (motorcycle)
- ➢ KA-BAR aka Kabar (knife)
- ➢ FJ Cruiser
- ➢ Google
- ➢ Jeep (vehicle)
- ➢ Remington Model 870 (firearm)
- ➢ Sea Wolf (the song)
- ➢ S&W MP9 Shield (firearm)
- ➢ Sig Sauer (firearm)
- ➢ Sig P320 (firearm)
- ➢ Slack (messaging app)
- ➢ Smith & Wesson M&P (firearm)
- ➢ Wolf at the Door (the song)

CPSIA information can be obtained
at www.ICGtesting.com
Printed in the USA
LVHW010347201021
700870LV00003B/20

9 780986 327346